DEATH IN DISGUISE

A BETH GETTY MYSTERY

Karen Neary Smithson

Relax Read.Repeat.

DEATH IN DISGUISE (A Beth Getty Mystery, Book 1)
By Karen Neary Smithson
Published by TouchPoint Press
Brookland, AR 72417
www.touchpointpress.com

ISBN-10: 1-946920-40-1
ISBN-13: 978-1-946920-40-9

Editor: Kimberly Coghlan
Cover Design: ColbieMyles, ColbieMyles.com
Cover Photo Credit: Karen Neary
Author Photo Credit: Pierre Parker

First Edition

Printed in the United States of America.

In memory of my parents, Roy and Shirley Neary,
who always believed in me and for my husband, Chuck Smithson,
who showed me how to believe in myself

ACKNOWLEDGEMENTS

The course of writing *Death in Disguise* has included several versions, all marked with the intention of creating an intriguing and entertaining mystery. This process was enriched by the encouragement of those who read and offered suggestions on various drafts. Therefore, I offer my deepest thanks to Karen Esibill, Shirley Pratt, Tynese Daniels Cunningham, Lois Anderson, Carol Hutchinson, Lydia Sanfilippo, and Clair Ferguson. Your generosity of time and willingness to point me in the right direction is truly cherished.

A million thanks to Jennifer Haskin, a jewel of an agent, who championed Beth Getty et al. and found them a home at TouchPoint Press. Unending gratitude to Sheri Williams, publisher/editor at TouchPoint Press, and to my editors Kimberly Carlisle Coghlan and Jessica de Bruyn.

A special thank you to my critique group, *Dreamweavers INK Writers*: P.J. O'Dwyer, R. Lanier Clemons, Lisa Trovillion, Clint Jullens, Mike and Regina Sage, and particularly Missy Burke and Kim Hamilton. All of you possess talent that inspires me—your support, brilliant comments, and suggestions aided me tremendously.

For their unfailing support I'd especially like to thank my siblings: Roy, Patricia, and Thomas. Thanks also to Pegi Taylor, Pierre Parker, Dee Papania, Tom Duckhorn, Amy Harke Moore, and above all to my husband extraordinaire, Chuck Smithson.

PROLOGUE

Tucked into a fetal position, Eliana winced as convulsions racked her thin body against the bedroom's scarred floorboards. *I'm supposed to be going home.* Her mind raced, confused by the force that caused her muscles to contract and quiver. One thing was certain—it was the priest's handiwork.

"This isn't what it seems." His usual jovial voice sounded different. The singsong lilt had vanished, leaving a sharp, hard cadence. He grabbed her white-knuckled fist and stopped it from hammering against her chest. With a firm grasp, he straightened out her fingers and kissed her palm. "I'm actually doing you a favor." The priest released her arm. She couldn't stop it from banging against the floor like a dead weight.

He slid closer and stroked her cheek. She wanted to slap his hand away, but the tingling in her arm, a new sensation, scared her. His fingertips swept across her cheek, brushed her lips, and then stopped at her dimpled chin—and lingered there.

"You're so delicate and beautiful." He sighed. "Perfect, in fact."

"Padre Clancy," she managed a husky whisper. She closed her eyelids as the twinges rippling down her arm stopped. Except for a stinging pain in the small of her back, she felt almost normal. She slipped her hand beneath her thick, dark hair and touched what seemed like a fish hook stuck into her flesh.

"Why?" Her question hung in the air.

He snatched the Taser, an arm's reach away, and pressed the electroshock weapon into her shoulder. She screamed as the explosive jolt of electricity coursed down her spine, causing her muscles to contort and twitch like an epileptic in the throes of a fit.

To her surprise, the instant he removed the device, her muscles relaxed. No tingling.

No spasms—only exhaustion as if a deep wave of fatigue had washed over her—and a weird sense of peacefulness. She flashed her eyes open. He hovered above stroking his graying beard with one hand and gripping the Taser with the other.

"Just as I imagined. The drive-stun is as effective as the cartridge."

"I no understand—"

"Of course you don't." He placed the weapon on the floor, reached in her direction, but stopped short of touching her, and stood.

Eliana imagined a trace of sadness clouding his eyes. It lasted only a second.

He thrust his hand into the pocket of his black suit coat. "Here." He pulled out a rosary and dangled it in front of her before releasing the string of beads. It hit the floor with a clatter.

She grasped the ebony beads and brought the small crucifix to her lips not daring to pull her eyes away from him as he headed toward the bed. As he lingered there, she wondered how many minutes had passed since she'd raced into her bedroom to gather her belongings. The prospect of being reunited with her family in Ecuador now seemed like an illusion: a blinding act of trickery that drew her into this nightmare. The dresser drawer hung half-open, and its meager contents never made it to her satchel but lay strewn across the floor. She fingered a couple of the wooden beads with silent prayer then lifted the rosary over her head and placed it around her neck.

The click of his briefcase locks startled her. She jolted onto her knees, but the quick movement seemed to cause the room to whirl as if she were a rider on a carousel speeding out of control. She wanted to cry, to scream, to squelch the ache for her mother's comforting arms, but most of all, she wanted to escape. She grit her teeth and crawled to the room's far wall and the window she'd opened when the rays of the morning sun filtered through the glass panes.

It'll be easy enough to slip out...if only...

She banished the negative thought before it fully developed. Dizziness and fear blurred her sight as she patted the cracked plaster wall until she smacked her hand against the rough-hewn, wooden sill.

"Eliana." The priest's voice sounded like thunder.

She curled her fingers around the molding and pulled upward. A gentle breeze touched her face as she rose on wobbly legs. She sensed his closeness and fumbled a sneaker-clad foot over the sill. Viselike grips squeezed her forearms and sent her flying backward. A sharp beat of pain shot through her lower back as she landed on the floor.

"I admire your spunk. But you're no match against me."

Nausea gripped her. She grasped her stomach and forced down the bile choking her throat. "You promise I go home," she whispered.

"I didn't lie. I always keep my promises."

She grasped the rosary's silver crucifix and enfolded it in her hand. "Take me to the airport."

"No need for a plane. This will do the trick." He grabbed something from inside the opened briefcase.

She squinted trying to make sense of the object in his hand. A syringe with a long slender needle.

"I have no other choice. The stakes are too high."

"Let me go. Please, *Señor cura*. Please."

He stepped closer, fell to his knees, and grabbed her hand. "You're only making things harder. Trust me."

His movement had been so quick she barely realized the needle had penetrated her skin.

"Why you do this?"

"It's the only way to send you home." He pressed the plunger and emptied the barrel. "For all eternity."

CHAPTER ONE

"More tea, Father Clancy?" Sibeal 'Beth' Getty asked the stout priest seated in a cushy wing chair. She gestured toward the Belleek teapot.

He raised his cup. "There's nothing better on God's green Earth than a good cuppa Irish tea."

Without a touch of makeup and dressed in a pink t-shirt and a pair of faded jeans, Beth looked younger than her twenty-six years. She prepared the tea as he requested: a third of a cup of cream, two teaspoons of sugar, and a sprinkling of ground cinnamon. She lifted the pot and filled the priest's cup to the brim. After a quick stir, she handed it to him.

He took a long swallow then smacked his lips. "Just the ticket to soothe these old, achy bones."

"Biscuit?" She offered him a platter of cookies.

He selected a vanilla cream and placed it on the edge of his saucer. His eyes flicked around the room as he dragged a tapered finger through his thick auburn beard laced with streaks of gray, which rested against his Roman collar. "Your parlor is like a picture taken straight out of an Irish country cottage. Truly cozy."

"Most of it was sent over from Ireland." She swept her hand through the air. "And speaking of our homeland, where do you hail from Father?" Beth returned the platter, and it clinked against the serving tray nestled on an oversized hassock. She reclaimed her spot on the couch opposite him.

"Armagh."

"In primary school, Sister Anne told us about the grand cathedral. She called Armagh the city of saints and scholars. For some reason, I've never forgotten that."

"Ah... Éire, I miss her sorely, I do. Even though years have passed since the Agreement, it seems as if the Troubles persist, dear girl. Just look at the loyalist protests in North Belfast last summer. It's enough to break one's spirit, 'tis." A slow shake of his head caused a lock of russet hair to fall over and brush shaggy eyebrows. "Perhaps we should be grateful. Years back, bombings, turbulence in the streets, and the unending military presence took quite a toll. Such shameful atrocities as the romperings—"

"Father..."

"Are you alright? You're white as a ghost."

She reached for her teacup but then let her hand drop.

"Surely, dear girl, such trauma wouldn't have touched you growing up in the Republic. Your accent strikes me as belonging to a Dubliner."

"My father's family is from Derry. I don't know the whole story, but *me Da* had to escape the North a couple of years before I was born."

"No matter. 'Tis a distressing topic for sure." He took a quick sip of tea. "By the by, I'm not here to talk politics, but the burgeoning of my mission. And of course, to solicit your assistance."

She leaned back against the sofa. "I'll be more than glad to help, and the timing is perfect." She tucked a stray lock of auburn hair behind her ear. "I've been searching for a worthwhile project. Just ask my husband, Shane. Oh, did I tell you he's a detective with the Los Angeles Sheriff Department?" Not waiting for a reply she continued. "I've always wanted to help impoverished kids. This project is like a dream come true."

"Truly, I'm pleased."

"How could I refuse? Even the Archbishop has given you the green light." She lifted the letter next to the serving tray, unfolded it, and glanced at the prelate's signature. "With his blessing, our project is definitely off to a grand start." She handed the paper to the priest. "Shane will be thrilled. Between you, me, and the gatepost, I think he's been a wee bit worried. Since I've retired from modeling, I've been struggling, trying to find a purpose, a new direction to concentrate my energies on. This project will do the trick, so."

"As the good book says, the harvest is plentiful, but the workers are few. I can't thank you enough that you've agreed to be one of those workers, Sibeal."

"Call me Beth. I've dropped the Irish."

"But why?"

"Sibeal is my public name. Since that chapter is closed, I'm happy with just being Beth Getty."

Instead of commenting, he lifted the cookie, popped it into his mouth, and chewed, causing a trail of crumbs to settle on his lapel.

"I'm a bit preoccupied, Father. Can't seem to get the heartbreaking news of those murdered teenage girls out of my mind. I was reading about the latest victim right before you arrived." She nodded in the direction of the tablet on top the leather face of an antique desk. "A young Latina barely fourteen. Eliana...I've forgotten her last name."

"Mendoza. Eliana Mendoza. A lovely girl. So full of life and talent. She had the lilting voice of a songbird, she did."

"You knew her?" Beth shook her head. "I don't get it. Why do such awful things happen?"

"If I had the answer to that one..." He raised the tea cup. "I'd been able to scrape up enough money to buy Eliana a ticket back to Ecuador. Sex traffickers had smuggled her into East LA. Being a pure, Christian girl, she was horrified to be forced into a life of prostitution. Luckily, I was able to rescue her from that hellish existence. If only me old car hadn't broken down, maybe I could've saved her from such a heartless, cruel death. It still causes chills to run down me spine when I think the poor girl was murdered in her room, inside what I considered a safe house. My volunteer who was looking after her is devastated. Eliana used to call him *abuelo*—grandfather—they were very close. Tragic." He brushed the errant crumbs off his black suit coat.

"These murders reinforce the fact that a shelter for street kids is crucial. Te sooner the better. I'm going to start right away scouting buildings for a potential facility. Mark my words; before long, your dream will become a reality." The doorbell sounded. "Excuse me. Help yourself to another biscuit." She rose and visibly shook.

"You alright, lass?" He reached for the armrests as if to stand but then dropped his hands and rested them against his rounded stomach.

"It comes out of nowhere." She rubbed her temples in a circular fashion. "My granny called it *fey*."

"*Fey?*"

"Oh, you know, the sixth sense."

"Of course. Where is me old mind these days?" The words skipped off the tip of the priest's tongue. "I take it's not good news."

"Never is."

The bell chimed again. Two quick rings.

She gulped a deep breath then hurried out of the den. Her sixth sense had issued a warning. As she crossed the expansive foyer, her sandals slapped against the marble floor, causing a dissonant beat that shattered the stillness surrounding her but not the vexing confusion offered by her *fey*. Something to do with the priest? She paused a second then shook her head as she yanked the door open.

Skye Andrews faced her with a scowl as she clutched her seven-year-old daughter's hand. "I can't believe it. Zach's done it this time. He's filled the nanny's head with sheer drivel. He's told Lexi she has what it takes to be the next Meryl Streep. He even set up a meeting with our agent, and now I'm stuck with..." She glanced at the child. "I was wondering—"

"Now don't be telling me all your woes on the doorstep. Come in. I have a guest. Father Clancy from Northern Ireland."

She ignored the tightening of Skye's lips and the narrowing of her large, cerulean blue eyes. Her body language read like an open book. Skye wasn't interested in meeting the priest.

"He's planning to set up a shelter for runaways. It'll offer much more than food and a bed. There'll be health screenings, job training, and educational opportunities like tutoring to help earn their GEDs. The cool thing is, he wants my help." Along with her rising exuberance, Beth's brogue became more pronounced. "It's going to take a lot of man hours and a substantial amount of start-up money. He's decided to keep the government out of it, so it's going to be a one hundred percent publicly funded agency. Come on; you have to meet him. I'm sure you'll be impressed." As the words escaped her lips, a wisp of doubt about Father Clancy's sincerity crossed her mind. *Is that what my fey was warning me about? Ah, don't be thick,* she chided herself. *After all, he's a man of God—a man with a mission.*

"Really, Beth." Skye shook her head. "I'm in a hurry."

"Nonsense. No one's ever too busy for a nice cup of tea. It's sure to help soothe the effects of your latest crisis." Beth's sight fell to the little girl, and she offered her a wink. The child's face brightened.

Skye exhaled an audible sigh and tugged her daughter as she obediently followed Beth into the den.

"Father Clancy, I'd like you to meet Skye Andrews and her precious little girl, Emma," Beth said as she moved toward a corner cabinet in search of a cup and saucer for Skye.

The priest rose and extended a hand. "Oh my. 'Tis quite an honor. I'm afraid I'm quite overwhelmed. When one of the ladies from the Sodality suggested I contact Sibeal, I mean Beth, to aid in me mission, I was bowled over. But I knew deep in me heart, she's a good Irish girl brought up in the Church." The words tumbled over each other so fast that with a sudden pause, the priest sucked in a deep breath of air. "I enjoyed your role immensely in *The Imposter* years ago in a Belfast theater. Since then, I've been an ardent admirer." He lifted a cookie from the plate and offered it to Emma. The child reached for it, but then looked at her mother.

"Take it." Skye shifted her attention back to the priest. "That was my first film. Years before I met Zach. Zach Greyson."

"Your *fear céile*?"

Skye widened her eyes.

"I have a habit of slipping into Gaelic at the oddest times. I meant your husband. Is the actor, Zach Greyson, your husband?"

"At the moment."

His eyebrows drew close, and frown lines marred his smooth forehead. A second later, any sign of distress had vacated the priest's ruddy face.

"I would've never thought. A priest aware of my work. And a foreign one at that." A smile broke across Skye's face, lighting her eyes with wonder. "I'm not Catholic. I thought priests spend all their time in drafty old churches, on their knees endlessly counting those beads or whatever."

"Skye." Beth raised her voice holding the teapot in midair.

Father Clancy chuckled. "We're allowed the odd evening off."

"Skye and I met when I was still modeling." Beth handed her friend a porcelain cup filled with Lyons tea.

"We kinda hit it off right away." Skye sat on the sofa's edge. "And now that she's out of the limelight, spending her time clicking pictures and volunteering at of all places, a cat rescue, she's become a bona fide lady of leisure. In fact, she's offered to mind Emma for a couple of hours since her nanny apparently is missing in action."

The silver tray shook as Beth nearly dropped the pot on it. "Watch Emma?"

"It's an emergency. Michele is doing me a great favor dropping by his salon in Malibu."

"Michele?" Father Clancy's forehead wrinkled once again. "I'm afraid, I'm lost." He reclaimed his seat after reaching for another cookie.

"Michele Vinazie. He's the most wonderful colorist. Known as the stylist to the stars. And for good reason too."

"But your hair looks lovely. Shiny. Like spun gold with flecks of rose amber."

Skye waved her hand as if dismissing the priest's compliment. "I have a big night planned." She paused a moment. "Anyway, I wouldn't expect a man like you to understand, but Beth, you know how important image is. I can't be seen in public with dull, dingy hair. I'll pick Emma up around five." She focused on the priest. "Beth's already told me about your project to set up a shelter. And that you need funds." She placed the cup of untouched tea on the tray then reached into her Gucci python tote and pulled out a checkbook.

An open smile filled the priest's face, revealing stained teeth and a prominent overbite.

"Should I make it out to Father Clancy?"

"Hope's Refuge, Inc. would do nicely. All throughout me ministry, whenever I've suffered doubts, I've met caring people like you, and my faith in humanity is amply restored. Dearest Skye, you and Sibeal are truly a godsend for me struggling mission. A godsend."

Skye ripped out the check, handed it to him, and glanced at her watch. "I have to be at the salon by one." She retied the blue velvet ribbon around her daughter's ponytail. "You be a good girl, Emma." With a tiny wave, she hurried out of the room.

Beth squatted and became eye-level with the little girl. "How 'bout we go to the lake and feed the ducks?"

Emma's dark eyes grew big as her lips turned upwards.

"I see you have your hands full. I'll just be on me way then." Father Clancy hoisted free of the comfortable chair.

Beth stepped toward the door.

"No need. I know the way out."

"I'll give you a ring." She patted her jeans pocket where earlier she'd slipped his business card.

"God's peace be with you." Father Clancy took a couple of steps then stopped and faced them. Without a word, he extended a hand and touched Emma's head as if bestowing a blessing. Then, with a display of reverential silence, he lifted his arm and sliced the air in the sign of the cross.

Once out of the room, Father Clancy heard Emma questioning his actions but didn't pause to hear Beth's explanation. A moment later, quick steps carried the priest down the flagstone walkway toward the ancient two-toned '77 El Camino. Reaching the rust-spotted driver's door, the priest looked at the rambling Holmby Hills house with a slow curl of the lip that formed into a wide smile.

CHAPTER TWO

Mike Alder sat at the diner's lunch counter clenching his cell phone. Telephoning Lexi had been the right thing to do—even if it had taken all his inner strength to dial her number. He wasn't used to being dumped. Regardless, he was determined to win her back. He placed the phone on top of the Formica countertop, swept back a lock of sun-streaked blond hair that had fallen over his eyes, then lifted the BLT, and took a bite.

Still holding the sandwich, he tried to compose a strategy to salvage his relationship with Lexi. He hadn't gotten far when his phone pinged.

He dropped the sandwich on the plate, grabbed the phone, and checked the text. Not Lexi. He balled his fist and banged it against his thigh. Right after lunch, he decided, I'll contact Sofia. He didn't know a whole lot about Zach Greyson's maid. The foreign accent was obvious, but he'd never been interested enough to find out where her homeland was, her future plans, or even her age. The only thing he knew for sure was that Sofia Fedoruck had a major crush on him. It hadn't been difficult to persuade the young woman to become his eyes and ears inside the Greyson mansion. In exchange for a dinner or a movie, Sofia supplied him with tidbits of information she'd gleaned from Lexi: mundane everyday stuff to the all-important facts regarding her feelings about him. He'd also instructed her to keep a log of Lexi's comings and goings, which he checked every couple of days.

After a month of being his informant, Sofia rebelled. The past week had been touch and go. It had come to a head yesterday. After listening to a fervent harangue about Sofia's dislike of spying on her co-worker, he pulled her close and kissed her with a passion he felt only for Lexi. His performance dispelled her qualms. She spilled the news that Lexi had developed a budding interest in acting.

The waitress leaned against the counter. "You don't like your sandwich?"

"Huh?" He blinked a couple of times and refocused. "It's fine." He took a bite and washed it down with a gulp of coffee.

"Seems like something's bothering you." She faced him with her chin nestled in her cupped hands.

"My girlfriend broke up with me." As soon as the words escaped his lips, he wanted to take them back.

"Really?" She offered him a napkin. "It's her loss, if you ask me. Anyway, her dumping you doesn't seem so terrible. I bet girls are pushing each other out of line, hoping for a chance to date you."

He attempted a smile as he glanced at her nameplate. Tiffany. "It wouldn't be so bad if she hadn't left me for a freakin' artist. Some tree-hugging, nerdy guy, like that frizzy-haired painter on TV. You ever seen him?"

She squinted. "On the internet, I've seen the dude with all the happy little trees and clouds and stuff. He's like really good."

"He's the one."

"His voice is kinda soothing, you know what I mean? But he's no hottie like you. So, the new boyfriend is a bona fide dork." She offered him a timid smile. "I bet you're a surfer."

"I surf, but my main interest is bodybuilding."

"That's like pretty obvious." She reached across the counter and touched his rock-hard bicep. "Hmmm."

"You'd think Lexi would appreciate a guy like me." He flexed his fingers a couple of times as he looked into the rather plump, but pretty face. He noticed her eyes were Windex blue and her best feature. For a split second, he wondered if she was eighteen. He decided she wasn't. Sixteen tops.

"I think I could appreciate you. Big time."

"I bet." He wondered how a waitress he'd just met had been able to free him from the depressing grip of the blues. The fact that he'd shared his relationship troubles with her surprised him even more since he made it a practice to always keep personal business to himself. He definitely hadn't told Sofia the real reason he wanted her to spy on Lexi. He'd offered a flimsy story about how he was like Lexi's big brother and didn't want the Greysons—Skye especially—to take advantage of her.

Tiffany walked toward the coffeepot. He followed her movement and enjoyed the way her hips shifted from side to side. She returned and topped off his cup.

"Anyway, Lexi works for Skye Andrews. She's a nanny."

"Cool. Does she like it?" She glanced over her shoulder as she dropped the pot onto the burner.

"Seems like now she's interested in acting."

"Oh God." She rolled her eyes. "Well, then, good luck to her. She has like what...one in ten million chances of that ever happening?"

"Zach Greyson may help her. He thinks she's got talent."

"Oh." The waitress paused a moment then shrugged. "If that happens, it's a good thing she did break up with you. She'll forget all about that artist guy, too. She'll become so damn full of herself, she won't give the likes of us the time of day." She ran her tongue across her lower lip. "My shift ends in twenty minutes. Why don't we hook up for the afternoon?"

She flashed him a bright, wide smile. It wasn't until then he noticed the braces on her teeth.

"You're kinda bold, Tiffany. I like that. Too bad you're still in high school."

"I am not. I dropped out. But that doesn't matter. I always date older guys."

"Is that so?"

"God's honest truth."

"Talking to you has cleared out some of the cobwebs." He tapped his temple. "I am the kinda guy most girls would give their eyeteeth to date. You made that crystal clear. So, I'm not gonna let Lexi walk out of my life without a fight. And I know exactly how to win her back."

Tiffany crossed her arms.

"She's crazy about poetry. I'll write her a damn poem. Let her see my sensitive, creative side."

"Dude, you lift weights."

"Why didn't I didn't think of this sooner?" Mike dropped a twenty-dollar bill next to his plate and offered the now pouting waitress a wink. He grabbed his phone, lifted his six-foot-two frame from behind the counter, and swaggered out the door.

CHAPTER THREE

Maiah Weston arrived home frazzled but filled with a measure of satisfaction and even a sliver of pride. Charity work, she thought with a bemused shake of her head. Being her mother's daughter truly laid the groundwork for her education in soliciting on behalf of many a worthwhile cause. Though, today had been more exhausting than usual. She dragged herself upstairs to the master suite. The only thing she wanted was a nap—a long, dreamless one. That wouldn't be feasible so she set the alarm for twenty minutes.

The piercing buzzer jostled her awake. She moaned in protest but bolted out of bed and headed for the shower. The cold water, like little spikes of ice, revived her. After quickly drying off, she wrapped herself inside a peshtemal towel. Even if she wanted to, she couldn't squelch the rising anticipation of her guest's imminent arrival. Nearly two years had passed since she'd seen her old companion. She hummed as she applied fresh makeup and dressed.

Within the ensuing hour, her enthusiasm dampened. The snack she'd ordered the cook to prepare—a plate of spicy ground turkey lettuce wraps—had to be boxed and placed in the refrigerator. She tapped her foot against the thick carpet and peeked out the window of her study as she strained to spot the overdue cab. The expansive, picturesque countryside offered no clues. She freed the cell phone from the pocket of her midnight silk crepe trousers and checked her messages. Nothing. It finally dawned that she'd been an idiot for not calling the airport to check if the flight had been delayed.

She glanced at the phone's illuminated clock display and realized Harry would be home soon. His afterschool art program ended at half past four and the school bus dropped him at their front door promptly at five. It was already nearing three thirty. She had an important favor to ask of her friend, and once Harry arrived, it'd be hard to get a word in edgewise.

She placed the phone on top a marble pedestal and looked outside again. At that moment, a taxi pulled through the opened gate into their long driveway. Relief pumped through her as she fled the office and headed toward the main staircase. She raced down the steps, crossed the wide foyer, and pulled open the front door. A touch of nervousness caused her to smooth her creamy satin blouse and rearranged the paisley print scarf stylishly coiled around her neck. She stepped outside and waited on the veranda.

The moments dragged until she caught a glimpse of the woman who had been the strongest force in her life. Johannah Everhart. Her childhood governess. To keep her emotions under control, she focused on the cabbie who tugged an oversized, leather suitcase.

"Place it there." Maiah pointed inside the house toward the wide staircase.

With a dour expression, the man hoisted the luggage into the foyer. Not until he'd retreated down the walk and out of earshot did she allow her feelings to surface. She beamed as she grasped Johannah's sturdy hands.

"*Mein liebster schatz*," Johannah whispered. "I've missed you."

Johannah's slight German accent didn't even register since Maiah had become accustomed to the guttural trill of her words growing up under the woman's diligent care.

"You must be exhausted." She led the older woman into the house. "It won't take the housekeeper but a few minutes to unpack your things. I'll call Hap and have him take your suitcases upstairs."

"Hap? Who is this Hap?"

"That's his nickname. And really, I hardly ever address him that way. Roman—Roman Dorian—my stable boy." She noticed a flicker of disapproval in the tightening of Johannah's lips so she hurried out her words. "Roman does all sorts of odd jobs. He's completely trustworthy. In fact, a model employee. Not like some of those deadbeats at father's estate." With a shake of her head, she linked her arm with Johannah and steered her into the formal living room. "How was the flight? Good, I hope."

"Nothing but one delay after another. Incompetence."

"Traveling can be quite arduous," Maiah said. "Rest here." She stopped in front of a seating arrangement composed of authentic Queen Anne furniture. A walnut tea table with cabriole legs separated the two chairs.

Johannah dropped heavily onto the crimson and cream cut-velvet wing chair.

"Now that I'm finally here, I feel one hundred percent better." She let out a sigh.

Maiah searched the face she'd known so well. She grieved a bit noticing that Johannah had aged over the past couple of years. Her once chestnut hair, now steely gray, was arranged in a tight chignon, and new lines creased her mouth and etched her face. But her milky white skin, rosy cheeks, and clear blue eyes were exactly as she remembered. Maiah envisioned herself once again a little girl gazing into the face she loved more than any other in the world. "You must be starved. Cook will set up a tray for you." She turned toward the door.

"*Nein, mein schatz.* I ate on the plane. I am quite content sitting here with you."

Maiah sank onto the Amritsar carpet and rubbed her hand against its muted celadon nap.

Johannah reached out and stroked the top of Maiah's head. "Now tell me, are you happy?"

"Happy? Who has time to think about being happy?"

"I knew as much." Johannah pursed her lips as if waiting for the young woman to answer her question.

Maiah lowered her eyes unable to take in the sadness she read on her beloved governess' face.

"You deserve the best. An unfaithful husband is not worthy of you."

"That was almost four years ago." Maiah traced her finger along the rug's curved cranberry colored border.

"It should not have ever happened. Period."

Maiah lifted her head and nodded.

"That man has soiled you. You might as well be sleeping with a *hure*. And still, you allow yourself to be degraded by staying married to a good for nothing lowlife like Kenny Weston."

"I've made a mess of everything."

"Not you, my dearest treasure. Your rotten husband did that." Johannah focused on her clasped hands nestled in her lap.

"I promise, when the time is right, he'll suffer for what he's done to me...and Harry."

Johannah raised her head.

"He has a lot to say about Harry's upbringing, but when it comes to actually being a father, that's another story altogether. The way he rambles on about Harry being the most important person in his life is a joke." Maiah rolled her eyes. "Kenny's going to lose more than Harry. He'll lose both of us. And all of this." She swept her arm as if trying to encompass the massive room. "When I'm through with him, he'll have nothing left."

She took a quick breath.

"I realized much too late that I should've followed your instructions, Johannah. I wanted to please you then. I always wanted to please you. Even now." She reached for the woman's hand and grasped it. "It was plain stupid not to heed your warning that Kenny would ruin my life. But at the time, I was obsessed with showing my parents that I could be completely satisfied with a man so different from everyone I ever knew. I was rebelling against what I thought was pretentious snobbery. But I was mistaken."

She pulled away from Johannah and swept a lock of golden hair away from her face.

"I was trying to run away from who I truly am. Now I know that I'm heads and shoulders better than Kenny Weston. And so is my Harry."

She stood and began to pace.

"He's tried to pull me down to his level. If he'd succeeded, I might as well have started mingling with street rubbish—drunks and filthy prostitutes—they're not much different from the people Kenny loves hobnobbing with: those damn Hollywood types."

Maiah paused then balled her hands against her hips as she faced the older woman.

"Easy living," Johannah said. "That's all he was after. It afforded him the luxury to mess about with his paint pots. And what a waste of good paint. He creates monstrosities."

"You're absolutely right. My generosity obliterated all his financial responsibilities—no more overdue credit card bills, house payments, student loans—they disappeared like that." Maiah snapped her fingers. "His paintings, and I use that term loosely, are a mess. It's hard for us to even imagine..." she said motioning from herself to Johannah "his canvases are sought after. It still blows my mind that Kenny was a full professor at one of the most prestigious art colleges in the country. Lately, he's been preparing for a major exhibit in New York. Even if we can't see it, there are people who believe he has talent," she said softening her voice.

"Phffft. If that's talent..." Johannah moistened her thin lips with the tip of her tongue.

"What a hard lesson you had to learn, *meine liebe*. If only you'd listened to me, your life would be radically different. I can't bear to see such sadness filling your eyes. My heart breaks for you."

"Hindsight is twenty-twenty." Maiah shrugged. "I should've realized that loving someone like Kenny would ultimately bring me nothing but anguish. But what did I know then? I was only twenty years old. At that age, we think we know everything."

Maiah shifted her sight toward the arched doorway. A young man stood there with his thumbs slipped through his belt loops. Johannah followed Maiah's gaze, and upon seeing the man, she offered him a curt nod.

"Mrs. Weston." He stepped into the room. "I hope I'm not interrupting—"

"What is it?"

"Well, um, might I have a word?"

Maiah moved next to the man. She grasped his arm and ushered him in front of her former governess. "Johannah, this is Roman Dorian. One of my stablemen."

"Hey, just call me Hap. Everyone does." He reached out to shake Johannah's hand except she made no move to unclasp her entwined fingers.

"I will call you *Herr* Dorian. Now, tell me, do you like working for Mrs. Weston?"

"Like it a lot, ma'am."

Johannah nodded. "I'll leave you to your business." She lifted herself out of the chair.

"I didn't mean to interrupt." He shifted his attention back to Maiah. "Only wanted to let you know that bit of business, we discussed earlier, turned out to be quite a success." He flashed her a smile that would melt the hardest of hearts. It wasn't lost on Maiah or Johannah as she reclaimed her seat.

"That's fine." Maiah paused a second. "The gelding is coming along then?"

"A bit better every day. Stop by the stable and take a look. I guarantee you'll be surprised."

"I'll do that. Now, I'd like you to take the luggage in the foyer upstairs and place it in the mauve guest room." She stared at his retreating form until he exited the room.

"Pity such a fine specimen turns out to be an uneducated laborer." Johannah pulled a linen handkerchief from her pocket and brushed the front of her blouse and the surface of her navy skirt as if she'd been contaminated.

"He has natural talent when it comes to horses. That gelding he mentioned, I bought for fifteen cents a pound from a livestock horse auction. If I hadn't stepped up, the poor thing would be on his way to a slaughterhouse south of the border. And only after a couple of days under Roman's care, he's already improved."

"That young man somehow reminded me of Callum. His good looks, no doubt."

"What? Callum possesses an abundance of attributes, but being a 'fine specimen' isn't one of them." She sat in the chair adjacent to Johannah.

"It must be Callum's breeding and confidence that make him so attractive. I still believe he was the proper man for you. Cultured, educated, well-heeled."

"The fact he's a blueblood had nothing to do with it?" Maiah tossed her head and looked at the ornate plaster molding edging the ceiling. "When we first met, Callum and I had such a strong bond, I believed we even shared the same thoughts. But, if we'd married, it would've made my parents deliriously happy. That's the last thing I ever wanted. To feed into their status consciousness obsession. The obvious assumption is that we cut off our noses to spite our faces. But that's not exactly true." She focused on the older woman. "Even though Callum swore he wanted nothing to do with his noble upbringing, I never bought into that a hundred percent." She jumped hearing a thud sounding from the foyer and pressed her lips together hoping Roman hadn't broken anything.

"So, this Dorian is a great help?" A wry smile crossed Johannah's face.

Maiah blew out a puff of air ignoring the comment. "I never told you this, but one day we forgot about our parental rebellion and wound up at the registry office determined to get married. But he backed out. There was one thing he couldn't defy. His damn religion. Callum was brought up Catholic." She noticed Johannah's eyebrows jump. "I know it's weird. But Papists have even wielded themselves among English nobility. Anyway, Callum said if we got married, it would break his mother's heart."

Johannah sat silent a couple seconds as if churning over the information. "A mother's heart is a delicate thing. Callum's sacrifice for his mother just proves what I've believed all along. He is a fine man befitting of you. It's a shame how things turned out."

"I can't for the life of me understand why Callum still practices that backward religion. But it won't be a roadblock now since his mother passed away last year." Maiah paused a second. "He has a horse that qualified for the Kentucky Derby."

"Callum will be at the race?"

Maiah nodded.

"Does Kenny know?"

"How would he?"

"You could have told him."

"I don't talk to him about Callum. He has no interest. Wasn't even impressed that I'd dated the son of a British duke. Kenny has no respect for nobility."

"Typical behavior from a man like that. The cold fact is that Kenny loved your bank account more than you."

Maiah rose. She walked across the room and halted in front of the grand piano. Absently, she pressed a couple of keys. "Kenny did love me. Once. But now, I think he's still holding a torch for that...that movie actress. She sucked out all the love he ever had for me."

Johannah narrowed her eyes and her lips.

"The worst of it is her daughter rides at the same Pony Club as Harry," Maiah said. "Granted, she's hardly there; the nanny usually takes the girl to her lessons, but she always makes an appearance at special events decked out like she's on the red carpet—and though I want nothing more than to scratch her eyes out, I have to be civil for Harry's sake. Like a bad penny, she keeps showing up when all I want to do is erase her from my memory." Maiah shook her head. "Last month when we were in Italy, that hussy just happened to be in the same hotel—seemed a bit too coincidental. Anyway, I came home early. The trip was ruined for me."

"She's a scheming one. I bet she's trying to steal your husband. Again."

"I wouldn't be surprised if Kenny goes back to her. But I've given him an ultimatum. Stray again and lose Harry forever." Maiah targeted her eyes on Johannah. "He's now walking the straight and narrow—not out of affection for me, but because of Harry."

"A child is a terrible reason to stay in a marriage. I thought you believed that?"

Maiah moved closer and sat back on the carpet. "I'm not ready to give Kenny up. Anyway, Callum is still a bachelor, and it's been twelve years since we split up." She lowered her voice. "The last time he telephoned, Callum said he's still in love with me."

Johannah's eyes widened. "Since he's professed his love, you have no recourse but to act. Immediately. Why continue this torture?"

"I plan to wait until the time is right."

Johannah lowered her eyelids and pursed her lips.

Familiar with the expression, Maiah realized Johannah was holding in her annoyance. "I've never stopped loving Callum. Even though I did a pretty good job of telling myself that I was helplessly in love with Kenny. What an idiot I was." She rested a hand on Johannah's boney knee. "Don't worry. Kenny's not going to be in the picture too much longer."

"Aunt Johannah!"

Both women jerked their heads in the direction of the exuberant shout.

Harry burst into the room. His Oxford shirt was pulled from his pants, and his tie dangled from his collar giving the eight-year-old a rumpled appearance except for his backpack that was still strapped in place. He raced to Johannah, threw his arms around her neck, and planted a kiss on her cheek.

"My dear little man, let me get a good look at you." Johannah ruffled his towheaded curls and knelt on the floor becoming eye level with him. "You must have grown five inches. What a handsome fellow you are."

A flush of red covered his cheeks. "Auntie Johannah, I'm so happy you're finally here."

"Not sad about missing the big horserace?"

"I already know our horse is gonna win. I'd rather be with you."

"You would, eh?" Johannah half-smiled. "It won't be all play, *mein lieber Junge*. I've already compiled an itinerary for the week."

"Does that mean I don't have to go to school tomorrow?" His blue-gray eyes brightened even more.

"Maybe we can skip classes tomorrow." Johannah glanced at Maiah who shrugged. "It'll be a special event to celebrate being together again. The zoo will be our educational pursuit for the day. How does that sound?"

"Like the best thing ever." He looked at Maiah. "Thanks, Mom." The excitement faded from his face. "If you're gonna be gone a whole week, you'll miss Parents' Day."

"Don't worry about that. You think your mom would forget about such a special day?"

Harry offered her a lopsided smile. "Nah."

"Of course not. Now get ready for dinner," Maiah said. "Wash up and get out of that dirty uniform. Clean clothes are laid out on your bed." She waited a second.

"I have an important engagement and have to leave," she said checking her watch "in about fifteen minutes. I'll only be gone a few hours. Home in plenty of time before you go to bed. That will allow some special time with Aunt Johannah. I'm certain she wouldn't mind going over your homework later."

"That means me and Auntie Johannah can hang out until Daddy gets home." He took a step away from the two women. "He promised to help with my blocking." He looked in Johannah's direction. "I'm the goalie on my soccer team."

"I wouldn't count on your father being home," Maiah said softly. "You know how busy he is at work. He'll probably have to spend another night at his studio."

"Oh." Harry stuffed his hands into his pockets.

"But honey, he'd rather be with you."

"That's okay, Mom. I know he's busy."

Harry retraced his steps out of the room, but instead of running, he trudged with his head bowed.

After he'd exited the room Maiah said, "See how he treats his son? I have half a mind to make him pay for that sooner than later."

CHAPTER FOUR

Skye Andrews slammed the convertible's brakes when she saw the Honda parked at the top of her driveway. "Lexi's here?" She bellowed in disbelief since the nanny was supposed to be in Beverly Hills with Emma. Lexi's charcoal gray car caused her to envision the scene from earlier in the day. Zach had told Lexi she possessed all the essentials it took to become an amazing actor: looks, talent, and that indefinable "it" quality. The vivid memory made her stomach constrict.

Lexi is a nanny, albeit mediocre, that's it. Nothing more.

Skye tightened her jaw as she lifted her foot and continued to steer the Jaguar into the three-car garage, parking it in the only available spot, next to her looming Escalade. She alighted from the car but didn't hurry inside the house. Instead, she smoothed her skirt, fluffed her hair, and then took several slow steps toward the door as she cleared her throat. A twinge of anger flickered. She'd always trusted Emma with Lexi, but now her faith in the nanny's reliability was shaken as she wondered who the hell was watching her daughter. God forbid that Zach would ever step up to the plate.

She flung the door open, entered the mudroom, and took a second to still herself. *Stay in control.* Don't let your emotions take over, she cautioned. *You're a professional.*

"Lexi!"

Her stilettos tapped against the stone floor as she headed through the small utility room and into the house. She took the direct route up the back staircase that opened onto the main floor and again called the nanny's name. No response. She hurled the Gucci bag across the room. It hit the curved wall that housed the main staircase.

"Dammit." She rushed over to the tote, picked it up, and ran her fingertips over the light pink and maple brown snakeskin. She'd purchased the bag months ago in the *Bellagio,* the Vegas hotel, where she'd luxuriated in a two-bedroom penthouse, a much-needed refuge from her grueling schedule and Zach. She hadn't mind paying the nearly three thousand-dollar price tag for the handbag; knowing the look on Zach's sanctimonious face would be priceless.

If the skin had split, it would've been Zach's fault, she decided since she found his level of stupidity astounding with his inane prattle about the nanny becoming an acting sensation. "If that girl is here to tell me she's quitting to pursue an acting career, I swear, I'll... I'll divorce Zach tomorrow."

In an attempt to squelch her fury, she inhaled deeply a few times. The soothing passage of breath delivered a much-needed calming effect. She grasped the tote's bamboo handle and gingerly set it on top of a low cabinet, next to a golden glazed vase. She lifted the large metallic vessel and wondered why Darla hadn't followed her instructions to fill it with two dozen white roses.

A new flush of anger besieged her. She raced across the spacious landing and stepped into the living area. The heat pouring into the room almost bowled her over. Golden flames danced in the fireplace casting streamers of fluttering light and elongated shadows along the broad white walls.

"It's hot as hell in here." She snapped on the recessed ceiling lights and glanced around in search of the remote control. It sat on a chrome table next to a geometric arched floor lamp. She lifted the plastic case and clicked off the gas jets.

Skye sashayed around the couch and almost tripped when her foot hit something. She glanced down, and her breath died in her throat. Lexi lay amid a crimson pool, which had soaked through the pristine white carpet. She jumped back and banged her calves into the sofa's sharp edge. Though she wanted to flee from the gruesome scene, she didn't budge, but stared at the lifeless body.

She had starred in an action movie where one of the characters, a minor villain, had bled out after being shot, but this was real life. With all the blood, she felt certain Lexi was dead. Her eyes flitted around the outline of Lexi's body in search of a weapon, but she found nothing.

She dropped onto the couch and realized the impact this girl's death could have on her career. Not just bad publicity. She cringed as the names of two actors popped into her head: Lana Turner and Robert Blake. People killed within their households. A bodyguard. Lover. Wife. Both actors accused of murder? Her muddled mind tried to remember. But, no, she assured herself, Lexi did this. She had to. After all, who'd want to kill *her?*

Not conscious of how long she'd been staring at the body sprawled in front of the fireplace, she decided to take action. She dashed toward the adjoining kitchen but abruptly stopped confused by the upheaval. Several of her custom painted white oak cabinets were ajar, and a head of romaine and uncut vegetables sat on top the golden granite countertop. She squeezed her eyes shut willing herself to get a grip. With a budding sense of determination, she gulped a mouthful of air, opened her eyes, and moved toward the phone. She grabbed the receiver and raised a finger to press the emergency number. *Any publicity is good*, she assured herself, not wanting to believe the alternative.

From the instant she set eyes upon Lexi's lifeless body, she knew the nanny's death would turn into a phenomenal news story. She could almost hear the gleeful reporters on the TV celebrity shows babbling about how poor Lexi Horne, 'the Hollywood Nanny,' took her life because of her unbearable demands. *The media will grab onto it and not let go until my bloodletting is complete.* She shuddered envisioning herself in front of a jury, head bowed, waiting for a verdict.

Skye dropped the phone onto the work island. It crashed against the tempered glass, and the clatter resonated throughout the room. She edged toward the double set of French doors as short, rapid, gasping breaths escaped her lips. A new panic overcame her as she feared her throat was closing up. She pulled at the buttons lining her silk blouse then clutched her neck.

"Skye?"

She spun around.

Kenny Weston rushed into the kitchen. He held a bouquet of garden flowers—hydrangeas, irises, snapdragons, lilies—and a bottle of Chardonnay. "I heard something crash when I walked in. Sounded like it came from here. Hey, are you okay?" He dropped the flowers on top of the counter but gingerly placed the bottle inside one of the island's stainless steel sinks.

She lifted her eyes upward as if studying the tray ceiling and tried to speak, but only frantic sounds emitted from deep in her lungs.

"You're hyperventilating. You need to relax," he said in a calm, steady tone. "A bag?" On a long counter, he spied a paper grocery bag half covered by a group of canned tomatoes. He slid the sack free, shook it open, and squeezed the opening around her mouth. "Breathe nice and slow, babe. You're gonna be okay." He coached as she puffed into the bag. "That a girl, Skye.

Breathe."

She pushed his hand away. "I'm feeling better. Much better now," she whispered.

He steered her toward a stool nestled beside the work island with its glass, butcher block, and stainless steel surfaces and half-lifted her onto the cushion. She slid securely between the wooden armrests. "You scared the living daylights out of me. I'll get you some water."

She grabbed his arm. "I'm okay. Really."

He shrugged her off and reached for a mug from inside an opened cabinet. After filling it with water from the refrigerator door, he handed it to her. She dutifully drained the mug and placed it on top of the work island.

"What happened? It must've been pretty ugly to bring on an attack like that."

"My career may be ruined. Lexi—"

"Lexi." He took a step away. "I'm not surprised."

"Just shut-up, okay?" She slashed the air with her hand and knocked the mug to the floor. Startled by the sound of shattering ceramic, she jumped off the stool. He grabbed her arm, steadying her so she wouldn't step onto any pottery shards.

"I can't believe this is happening." She slumped against his chest and wrapped her arms around him.

"What the hell's going on?"

"Lexi's dead."

"What?" He pulled away.

"I found her near the fireplace."

"If this is a joke, it isn't funny."

She squeezed her eyes shut and shook her head.

"Stay here. I'm gonna take a look."

Not heeding his instructions, Skye followed him but stopped at the entrance of the room and watched. Kenny stooped down and pressed his fingers against Lexi's neck. A moment later, he stepped away and dropped into a chair. Taking few seconds to realize his fingers were bloody, he wiped them on his jeans.

"I'm right?" Her quiet voice sounded from the beneath the heavy wooden beam that divided the rooms.

He nodded.

"She killed herself?"

"Doesn't seem so. What are those weird looking prongs?" He pointed at Lexi's bloodied blouse.

Skye inched closer. She squatted then reached for Lexi's shoulder determined to turn the body over.

He grabbed her hand. "Don't."

"She may be lying on the weapon. Because if she didn't kill herself, it's going to cause an uproar. I'll be the prime suspect, like for a blink of an eye—but long enough to plant a seed of doubt. My career may never recover."

"The kid's dead, and you're only thinking of your career. Really?"

She opened her mouth then slammed it shut.

"I didn't trust her. My gut told me, she'd go to the tabloids with news of our affair. Now, she never will." His voice dropped to a whisper.

"Oh my God." Skye dashed in the direction of the kitchen. After taking a dozen steps, she spun and faced him. "What about Darla? Her car's in the garage, but I haven't seen her. If she's hurt..." She clasped her arms across her chest and shook.

He hurried toward Skye and guided her out of the room. "Stay here. I'll check the rest of the house for your assistant."

"Don't leave me for God's sake. What if the killer is still here? Hiding away somewhere in the house just waiting—"

"If the killer was still here, we'd both be with Lexi by now. Whoever did this is long gone."

She leaned against him letting him steer her into a nearby room. Her jaw ached. She touched her cheek and realized she'd been gritting her teeth. When Kenny released her, she collapsed into a chair.

"Didn't you text we'd have the house to ourselves?" He knelt beside her and grasped both her hands into his large one. "That Darla had a date or something?"

"She hasn't time for dates. I sent her to the market to pick up a couple of salmon filets for our dinner. Hours ago." She focused on their entwined hands.

"You're going to get outta here. Go next door to Marjorie's. Then call the police."

"You call them." She freed her hands from his grasp.

"I can't do that."

"You mean you won't."

"Look, call the police then your husband. I was having a little talk with Zach when you texted me. He called to brag about his recent art acquisition. One thing surfaced from all that boasting—he thinks you're still in love with him. What a sap."

"Forget Zach. I need you." She brushed her fingertips along his cheek.

"Do what I told you."

She jumped up from the chair and clutched her narrow hips. "My career may be ruined, the nanny is dead, and Darla is missing. And you want to hightail it out of here so your precious wife won't find out. How could you?" She turned her back to him. "I guess, I don't mean a damn thing to you."

"Can the outrage. It doesn't suit you." He stood and crossed his arms.

"If you leave me alone with Lexi's dead body, I'll never forgive you."

"I can't be part of this."

She snatched the phone off a shiny white lacquered table. "Get out and leave me the hell alone."

"I'll catch up with you tomorrow."

She turned and watched him hurry out of the room.

CHAPTER FIVE

Shane Dalton pumped the gas pedal of the unmarked police sedan as he exited Route 101 onto Kanan Road. Though his partner, Gavin Collins, was belted in the passenger seat, Shane remained silent for most of the ride as he squinted against the headlight beams from oncoming traffic. His mind wasn't only focused on the road but on a jumble of thoughts that bounced inside his head like ping-pong balls in a table tennis tournament. A sudden twinge of pressure behind his left eye signaled the onset of what was sure to be a killer headache. He reached into his suit coat pocket and felt the plastic bottle of Excedrin.

He ignored the tightening in his left temple, reined in his scattered thoughts, and centered on how the murder of Lexi Horne—nanny to one of Hollywood's most prominent couples—could in any way be connected to the killings of three teenage prostitutes. Beside the current sketchy M.O., which on the surface resembled that of the other murdered teens, the rest of the puzzle pieces didn't fit.

The news of the nanny's homicide was going to spread like wildfire. After all, the demise of a few street kids turned to prostitution ranked only a scant mention on the nightly newscasts. But the murder of a nanny employed to a celebrity would rank with the current government scandal—whatever that was at the moment—he'd lost track the last few days.

And then there's Beth. A smile lingered a brief second before vanishing.

An hour ago, when Captain Rosnick explained that the Horne girl worked for Skye Andrews, his stomach twisted. He'd fingered the cleft in his square chin, allowing the simple motion to help keep him focused as he forced Beth's impending reaction to the nanny's death out of his mind.

It had worked then, but now, behind the wheel, he realized he'd be helpless in preventing Beth from reaching out to Skye—she'd be at the actress' beck and call. He chewed the inside of his cheek wondering for the hundredth time why she considered Skye Andrews a close friend. His level of irritation grew with each passing second.

"You're awful quiet," Detective Gavin Collins said.

"A lot on my mind."

"Those little gray cells working overtime, eh?"

"I've been thinking maybe I shouldn't have chucked my career in architecture. I was working at a great firm. Had less than a year left before earning my certification when I shifted gears and plunged headfirst into law enforcement," Shane said.

"Does it matter now?"

He wondered how up front he could be with his partner. A sharp flash of pain stabbed his temple. With a feather-light touch, he massaged the aching flesh and stole a glance at Collins. He wasn't only his partner but a trusted friend. The two of them were made from the same piece of cloth. They shared similar views on just about everything from movies to politics. Even liked the same kind of food. The spicier the better.

"Headache?"

"Yeah." Shane freed the bottle of painkillers, flipped the lid, lifted the container, and downed a couple. "Like I was saying, back in the day, I worked with some great contractors. Still buddies with a few of them. One of them might be able to help me out."

"You're remodeling your crib?"

In spite of himself, Shane grinned. "I'm considering a new career. And the more I think about it, the more I believe I'd make a passable contractor. Good even."

"Yeah, right." Collins patted his hand across his close-cropped afro.

Shane glanced sideways. "I'm serious. The job's getting to me. I'm burned out."

"Happens to the best of us. But, you'll hard-nose through it. Won't leave a stone unturned 'til we get a conviction. That's why we're such a great team."

"They don't call our department the Bulldogs for nothing," Shane muttered.

"Got that right." Collins cleared his throat. "You'd have to be a heartless bastard for these homicides not to affect you." He peered out the window at the passing night. "Who would've thought we'd be facing the murders of four teenaged girls in as many days? What the hell will tomorrow bring? Man, I feel your frustration."

"It's more than that."

"You're not serious about leaving the department."

"Maybe."

"If you ask me, it'd be a mistake. But you gotta do what you gotta do." Collins shrugged.

"Dammit, wouldn't be the same without your ugly mug around."

"Yeah. Yeah. I hear you." Shane glanced at the GPS screen. "I don't lose much sleep over thugs blowing each other's brains out, but this case is different."

Collins drummed his hand against his thigh for a few seconds. "Whenever I think about young prostitutes being killed, it reminds me of the Green River Killer."

"Gary Ridgeway. Please let's hope it's not as bad as that. It took Kings County nearly twenty years to bring that scumbag to justice."

"The task force had its work cut out alright. Though most people viewed Ridgeway as a half-wit—his IQ was what—eighty or something?" Collins grabbed his water bottle from the console, twisted the cap breaking the seal, and took a gulp.

"He may've had a low IQ, but that bastard was damn calculating the way he stashed bodies in two different states." Shane pressed the brake pedal as he made a right onto the traffic-laden Pacific Coast Highway. With a glance at the speedometer, he noticed it was below the posted fifty miles per hour limit and squeezed the nondescript gray sedan between a semi and a cargo van.

"It'd probably be a lot easier if you turned on the siren," Collins offered.

"Almost there. Looking for Broad Beach Road."

"Pretty ritzy area. If there's a connection between all of these teen deaths, you think the latest was prostituting in Malibu?"

"I doubt it. No." Shane shook his head. "The victim worked for my wife's friend as a nanny."

"Damn, this one is close to home. Sorry. No wonder you're bummed-out." Collins reached for the inside pocket of his suit jacket and pulled out a cell phone. The light cast from it lit up his face. "Doesn't look like the Mendoza toxicology report is back yet." He slipped the phone away.

"Tasered, drugged, and stabbed. A bit excessive."

"But effective," Collins said. "What a waste. Those girls should've been in school, hanging with their friends, going to football games and proms."

"A waste alright."

Shane clicked the left turn signal and entered the Malibu Beach community, dreading the ordeal of facing Skye and her slain nanny. He'd seen too many murders. Instead of becoming hardened, detached, or even desensitized by witnessing innumerable crime scenes, he found himself left with only one emotion—anger—a fury so deep that it boiled over inside of him like the molten lava of an erupting volcano. His heart thumped against his ribcage as he inhaled through his nostrils and swiped the back of his hand across his face wiping away dots of perspiration that had sprung above his lips.

He wanted to stop the car. Jump out. Escape the look of horror staring from the dead nanny's eyes. Still, he knew his duty, perhaps all too well, even as he wondered if justice could be remunerated for Lexi Horne and Eliana Mendoza. For the other two Jane Doe murdered teenagers.

"You're wife's friend. Is she anyone I would've heard of?"

Collins' question caused Shane's heightened emotions to retract as his innate sense of responsibility took over.

"Skye Andrews."

"Whoa. The actress, Skye Andrews?"

Shane took a quick gulp of the cool air filling the cab. "She and my wife became friends way before I was in the picture. They're close even though Skye is the polar opposite of Beth. Skye is self-centered, demanding, and has a giant chip on her shoulder. If anyone should be bitter, it should be Beth. Her career ruined and then she married me."

"You know Shane, I've often wondered about that. How you ever found a wife like Beth is beyond my comprehension."

Ignoring the comment, Shane slowed down to look at house numbers.

"Pity Beth didn't meet me first. I would've swept her off her feet. With my good looks and charm, she would've been putty in my hands. Damn shame."

Shane tugged on the rim of his brown straw fedora as he eyed his partner. The hint of a smile crossing Collins' face waned as his typical stoic expression took hold of his features.

As a Marine, the wounds Gavin Collins suffered during his tours as an Apache co-pilot gunner in Afghanistan weren't limited to the physical. He'd been incredibly lucky. His only injury seemed like a fluke, a bite from a Camel Spider, the first night he arrived at Camp Leatherneck. After being patched up and prescribed antibiotics, the wound eventually scarred to the size of a penny right below his left elbow.

Gavin's mission was to provide protection along the east-west corridor of Highway 1. It was along this desolate stretch that his twin brother, Clay, had become the victim of insurgent fire and the explosion of a roadside bomb. Badly burned and with a fading pulse, Clay and two other soldiers were bundled inside a medevac. He died before the rotor-blades lifted the helicopter from the ground.

Shane believed Collins relished work and utilized it as a mechanism to block out the recollections of war that haunted him. During the odd moment, Shane would notice him staring straight ahead as if transported through memory back to the mountainous terrain and rocky deserts of Afghanistan. Collins rarely talked about the war, but once, he spilled out the depth of his sorrow—to Beth—at a dinner she planned for him and Shane when they'd first become partners. It was then he'd told them about Clay.

And now he works in law enforcement and believes he's making a difference, Shane thought easing down on the brake. *Better man than me.*

It was easy to spot Skye's beach house. Several black and white cruisers lined the strip edging the road. Shane steered the car through the opened gate, into the driveway, and parked near the expansive three-car garage. A dark colored Civic stood in a spot where the driveway jutted to the right and created a parking pad. Must've belonged to the nanny, he reasoned since Skye wouldn't be caught dead in a compact, economy car. He inwardly groaned glancing at the Bauhaus styled house, stark in its simple, crisp lines, and utilitarian design, now lit up like a Christmas tree.

The first time he and Beth had been invited to Skye's house had been for their surprise engagement party. Zach Greyson had been there too, smug and arrogant, holding court with an array of Hollywood elites. Though he'd appreciated Skye's sentiment of wanting to share in their happiness, he felt uncomfortable mingling with celebrities—people so different from him they could've sprung fully-grown from the ocean's foam like the mythical goddess, Aphrodite.

Over the ensuing months, his perception of Skye had softened into believing she was a needy and insecure woman desperately trying to play the role of a movie star in real life. Her presence in their home had become an almost every day occurrence, so much so, he'd sort of gotten use to her.

He wondered how Skye was dealing with the death of her employee as he tossed his fedora onto the back seat then brushed a stray lock of sandy hair off his forehead.

Collins flung open the car door and stepped out.

After a couple of long strides, Shane caught up with him. "There's something hinky about this homicide. Lexi wasn't a runaway or a prostitute."

"If there's a connection between this homicide and the others, we'll figure it out. Horne's a teenager, though a bit older at nineteen, and the M.O. is leaning in the same direction." Collins half- shrugged. "We'll know better after the medical examiner gives us his report."

Collins' sense of confidence didn't assuage Shane's uneasiness or soothe his qualms. As they neared the front door, he reached for the handle and steeled himself for yet another homicide.

They signed the crime log and entered the expansive living area remaining on the periphery, careful not to interfere with any trace evidence. The room looked immaculate. White and shining under the strong light of the overheads. It wasn't until Shane walked around the room's perimeter that he stopped dead in his tracks. Sprawled on top of a blood soaked carpet, Lexi Horne's body laid facedown perpendicular to the marble fireplace. His heart dropped as he tried to push away the rising anger. He pulled his eyes away from the dead girl and focused on the patrol officers and crime investigators. Shane admired their detached and complete focus as they methodically worked the scene searching for hairs, fibers, fingerprints, and any other suspicious matter. The M.E.'s investigator had already come and gone so Lexi's personal effects would be sent to the crime lab and her body transported to LA County's Department of Medical Examiner-Coroner.

One of the uniformed officers ambled over. "Detective?"

"Dalton and that's Collins." Shane nodded in the direction of his partner.

It took Collins a split second to join the two men. "What you got?" He pulled out his notebook.

"No sign of forced entry. The victim sustained physical trauma to the face and head. Taser prongs attached to the left shoulder and right hip area. Stab wound to the lower back. Swelling and redness on the left leg, looks like a puncture mark. Taser tags mingled within the carpet pile."

"Anything else?" Shane asked.

"Seems to be a missing employee. One Darla Edwards. Personal assistant."

Shane frowned as Collins looked up from his pad.

"You thinking hostage?" Collins asked.

The officer shrugged. "Found blood spatter in the garage. On the floor and the Prius—car door wasn't latched—might've been an ambush. Also bloodstains on the door handle that opens outta the garage."

"The missing employee's?" Shane pressed his thumb against his cleft chin.

"Possibly." The officer paused. "She could've been left for dead and escaped. A couple officers are scouting outside now."

Collins closed his notebook. "Where's Miss Andrews?"

"I'll take you to her."

They followed the policeman through the kitchen, where a tech stood crouched over a tempered glass countertop dusting for prints, and out through an opened French door. They skirted around a lap pool and down a wrought iron staircase leading to an expansive patio. The gas fireplace positioned in a stucco wall blazed as Skye sat on the edge of a cushioned teak recliner huddled under a blanket.

"Hey, kiddo. How you holding up?"

She jumped up, sending the thick comforter to the ground. "Thank God it's you, Shane."

"Walking in on that scene must've been a terrible shock." The dimness of the firelight couldn't hide the fear Shane detected in her eyes. Skye was always on, determined to keep her feelings in check by plastering on a phony smile in public. She'd never dream of behaving in a reckless or unprofessional manner like so many actors nowadays. So, he assumed, she would've behaved true to form and put on a brave façade for the police. He watched her veneer crumble as she tried to stifle a whimper.

He drew her close and placed his arm across her trembling shoulders.

She turned inward and tucked her head against his chest. "I'm worried sick about my assistant, Darla. She's missing."

Shane released Skye and guided her back to the recliner, surprised by her uncommon depth of concern. "I'll be straight with you. Seems like your assistant was attacked in the garage." He saw her shiver.

"Garage? I was in the garage earlier. I didn't see—"

"The Prius. Is it your car?" Collins asked.

Skye's brow wrinkled.

"This is my partner. Detective Collins," Shane said. "About the car—"

"It's mine, but I never drive it. I bought it for Darla to use." She lifted the blanket from the limestone patio. "I sent her to the market this afternoon. She was supposed to prepare dinner for me and a friend. Looks as if she started unpacking groceries." A couple of tears slid down her cheeks. "She's so trusting—though I've told her not to—she keeps the garage door up all the time."

"Try not to worry. Officers are searching for her now," Shane said. "We have a few questions about Lexi."

"She wasn't supposed to be here tonight."

Collins again pulled out his notebook.

"She left me a message, but no explanation why she was here. Once the cops arrived, I called Zach. He told me she landed an acting job—a new daytime serial on one of those inconsequential cable channels." She rolled her eyes. "I have no idea what the hell Zach saw in her. Average looks, so-so personality, all-around mousy. Her idea of an exciting evening would be to curl up with a book and a bag of chips."

Shane didn't interrupt. He believed Collins was getting the full picture of the genuine, though beguilingly beautiful, Skye Andrews.

"Zach got her that job. I'm sure of it. Doesn't matter now, but I'm convinced she wouldn't have been a success." She pulled the blanket tighter. "Probably came over here to hand in her resignation. Leaving me with no one to watch Emma. Then she allowed herself to die in my house."

Shane glanced at his partner. Collins' mouth opened as if he wanted to speak. Instead he stood mute, his brows knitted, with a quizzical look filling his face.

"You think this was deliberate on Lexi's part?"

"Don't be ridiculous, Shane. How would Lexi know she was about to be murdered? It's just damn inconvenient. I'll have to hire a new nanny right away since I have to leave for Baltimore in a couple of weeks. A new film. And I was really excited about it too until this... this... awful thing." She let out a sigh. "I want to help erase any trace of doubt the media may dream up about me being involved in the nanny's death."

"Okay. Good." Shane paused a moment. "Where exactly were you between five and eight?"

"You've got to be kidding."

"Humor me."

"As a matter of fact, I was with your wife. I'd just come out of the hair salon, and something about my car didn't look right. The tires. Flat as pancakes."

"All four of them?" Collins asked.

"The rear ones. So, I found myself stranded. I guess sometimes I should listen to Zach. He wanted me to keep my driver. But I felt so stifled. When I need a bodyguard, I just use one of Zach's. He's got a mini arsenal of them." She ran her finger through her abundant reddish-gold locks. "Anyway, my first thought was to call Darla. But I changed my mind. She had enough on her plate so I called Beth. She told me to contact my insurance company. In the meantime, she'd call for a tow truck. By the time she and Emma arrived at the salon, my car was being loaded onto the truck."

"Emma?"

"Beth was babysitting. I told you, I had a hair appointment and Lexi—at that time, I had no idea where Lexi was—so, the three of us waited at *Dutch's Old Fashioned Creamery*. Beth was planning on taking Emma to get ice cream anyway. And quite honestly, by that time I needed a cup of his "Bulletproof Coffee." About an hour later, one of the garage's grease-monkeys delivered my car there. By then, I was running late, but I guess it didn't really matter since my dinner plans were ruined anyway. After dropping Emma off at Zach's, I drove home. I arrived just before eight."

"How did you manage to get two flats at the same time?" Collins asked with an outstretched hand.

"That's the weird part. The mechanic said I didn't drive over nails or any other debris. The tires had been slashed. Vandalism. Can you believe it? I only travel in upscale neighborhoods," she said with a slow shake of her head.

"Sounds like an iron clad alibi," Collins said. "But we'll have to check it out."

Shane read the flash of anger that flickered across her face. Within a split second, it had vanished.

"Of course, Detective. I understand. Protocol."

"Since you were with Beth, you have nothing to worry about." Shane squatted, becoming eye level with her.

"Like hell. I won't be able to step inside my own house until every remnant of what happened is removed. The living area will have to be completely redecorated. I want nothing that's going to remind me of this horror."

"Zach's on his way?"

"I told him the police won't allow anyone access to the crime scene. Anyway, he didn't offer to come over." She pressed her palms together as if praying.

A sense of pity overshadowed Shane's irritation with her. For all her celebrity, wealth, and success, Skye Andrews couldn't feel much sympathy for the murdered nanny. The only thing that mattered, as usual, was Skye's needs. "Look, you're still in shock. Being with Emma and Zach will do you a world of good. How 'bout I drive you to Beverly Hills?"

"Darla might come back. Any minute. I can't leave now."

"You've no choice." Shane rose and crossed his arms. "It may take up to a couple of days for the investigators to complete their analysis and collect all pertinent evidence."

"Then I'll need an overnight bag."

"One of the officers will supervise. To make sure you don't inadvertently contaminate any evidence," Shane hastily added.

"Forget it. I'll buy whatever I need. But take me to a hotel. I want to be alone. Try to sort some things out."

"A hotel it is." For a split second, Shane considered offering their house as a temporary shelter, but the idea of Skye invading his personal space for any length of time made him bite his tongue instead. "Ready to go?"

"In a few minutes." She shifted her sight back to the fireplace as she tucked the blanket across her lap.

"We'll be waiting out front."

As the two detectives re-entered the house through the kitchen, a cacophony of rising voices disrupted the stillness of the investigation. They exchanged looks before hurrying to the source of the commotion. The foyer.

The woman stood only a couple of inches over five feet, but with hands planted on her hips and the intensity of her voice strengthening with each cascading word, she appeared anything but intimidated by the towering policemen. "Why can't you give me a straight answer? What am I supposed to think with a half dozen cop cars lined in front of her house? I just want to know Skye's okay."

"What's going on?" Collins asked.

"A neighbor insisting on seeing Skye Andrews. We explained no one is allowed in here," one of the uniformed officers said.

"We've got this." Shane nodded as the men turned away.

"Sorry Miss, you have to leave," Collins said showing her his credentials.

"But I'm crazy sick with worry." She widened her doe-like eyes. "Let me speak to Lexi."

Collins shook his head. The woman shifted her attention to Shane.

"I know she's here. Her car is parked in her usual spot. I have to tell her something. Really important."

Shane raised his eyebrows wondering if her motive was authentic or a fabrication to gain entry into the house.

"You know Lexi?"

"Of course I know Lexi. She was in my kitchen like a couple of hours ago."

"Why was that?" Collins narrowed his eyes.

"Like that really matters." She shrugged. "She ran an errand for me." She sliced the air with her manicured hand. "I can talk to Lexi anytime. But I insist on seeing Skye immediately."

"Sorry ma'am, that's not possible," Shane said.

"Don't forget you work for me. I'm a taxpayer," the woman snapped. "I'm entitled to know what's happened to my friend. All this secrecy about Skye is scaring the hell out of me."

Her full, augmented bosom thrust forward as she threw her shoulders back and brushed against Collins. Not seeming distracted, he kept his focus on the woman's words. "No comment now." Collins extended his hand toward the door.

"Look here," she barked. "I'm Marjorie Hammond. My husband is Marc Hammond. The lawyer. Perhaps you've heard of him?"

"I've heard of him, alright. Lawyer to the stars. Your husband has gotten more than one celebrity off scot-free from drunk-driving to grand larceny," Shane said.

"Because they were innocent."

"You think?" Shane pursed his lips.

"Marc has a way of getting jurors to see the truth. And actually, that's all I'm after. Why you detectives are so pig-headed is beyond reason. I'm so pissed off."

Taking a more logical approach, Shane slipped out his business card and handed it to her. The tightness around her lips softened as a question filled her dark eyes.

"I'm sure Skye appreciates your concern, Mrs. Hammond. But as you so intuitively surmised, this is a crime scene. Would it be possible for you to meet me at the station, say in about an hour? Your statement may be of help to us."

"I knew it. Not a burglary then." She paused as she smoothed an imaginary wrinkle from her periwinkle silk blouse. "Of course Detective..." She paused to glance at the card. "Detective Dalton. Well, I guess it's my literal duty, you know being a responsible citizen and all." Her lips curved and revealed a perfect smile. "It'll be my pleasure."

She turned toward the front door, took a couple of steps, stopped, and then peeked over her shoulder. "If by chance Skye needs legal counsel—"

"I'm sure she has your husband's phone number," Shane said.

"Of course she does." Marjorie bounced out of the house and into the dark, misty night.

CHAPTER SIX

The two detectives stood on the Malibu beach house's porch facing the street as they waited for Skye. Shane decided to try to talk her into spending the night in Beverly Hills with her husband.

"Detectives!"

Both men snapped their necks in the direction of the call. Within seconds, they reached a female uniformed officer. She had a firm grip on a handcuffed, well-muscled male wearing baggy shorts, and a tee shirt.

"I found him sneaking 'round back. No weapons but gave me a whole lot of lip. Anything but an answer as to why he's on the grounds of a crime scene."

Blond hair fell over his brow. His eyes seemed to flash angrily while his lips formed a tight line.

"Ready to supply us with a few answers? Or do you prefer a trip to the station?" Collins asked.

He glared at Collins then turned his attention to Shane.

"You're only hurting yourself by not answering. It's no skin off of my nose to arrest your butt," Shane said.

A few more seconds passed before the young man cleared his throat. "I'm Mike Alder. I was looking for Lexi." He shifted his sight toward the ground and kicked a stray pebble.

"Go on."

"When I saw the cop cars, I kinda freaked." He raised his head and stared straight ahead. "Maybe I shouldn't have gone around to the beach entrance and sneaked in, but I have to see her. It's like life and death." Mike glanced at Collins.

"A curious choice of words," Collins said under his breath. "How do you know Lexi Horne?"

"She's my girlfriend. Well, actually my ex-girlfriend, but I have something to give her. It's gonna make all the difference and...she'll vouch for me. It's really important. I have to see her. Please, let me give it to her."

"Sorry son, that's not going to happen," Shane said. "No one's allowed inside the house during a forensic investigation."

"So, Lexi's not in there?" Mike jutted his chin in the direction of the house. "But, she's okay, right?"

The two detectives' eyes met for a second. Then Shane focused on the policewoman. "It's your call. What do you want to do?"

Mike twisted his neck to better see the uniformed officer, "I'm totally sorry for disrespecting you. I was so worried about Lexi; I guess I wasn't thinking straight." Mike frowned. "Hey, if Lexi's not in the house where is she?"

Both detectives kept their faces impassive.

"I have a right to know. Don't I? She being my girlfriend and all."

"You'll know all the details soon enough," Collins said.

"Then Lexi's involved with whatever happened? The police interviewing her or something?"

Even in the shifting shadows of the cloudy night, Shane swore he saw a flicker of dread cross the young man's face. He clenched his teeth afraid he'd break protocol and explain to the confused and scared man what exactly had happened to his ex-girlfriend.

Without comment, the uniformed officer uncuffed Mike. He rubbed his wrists, not shifting his sight away from Shane.

"I have something for Lexi." In one fluid movement, Mike reached into his back pocket and pulled out a folded sheet of paper. "It's a poem. I wrote it for her. I'm hoping once she reads it, she realizes I'm not a total jerk." He paused a couple of seconds. "Can you slip it to her when you go back in there?"

Shane took the folded piece of paper. *If this guy did kill Lexi, he's awful dumb to hand me a piece of paper covered with his DNA.* "I'll see what I can do. But, we're going to have to interview you within the next couple of days."

"How come?"

"Standard procedure," said Collins. "How can we reach you?"

"My card." Mike pulled out his wallet, freed a business card, and handed it to Collins.

"We'll be in touch," Shane said.

"Shane." Skye's voice cut through the heavy night air.

"Look, sir, can I go? The last person I'd want to see right now is Skye Andrews."

"I understand. Truly, I do," Shane said with a shake of his head.

CHAPTER SEVEN

WEDNESDAY, APRIL 30

Shane loved looking at Beth early in the morning as soft light streamed through the kitchen window. He'd stand in the doorway and almost have to pinch himself to remember that the gorgeous supermodel, Sibeal Getty, was really his wife.

She chewed her lip as she sat beside the large bay window in the breakfast nook, gripping the LA Times, unaware that Shane had even entered the room. Her creamy, pale complexion was flawless except for the jagged scar crossing her left cheek. In front of her sat a bowl of untouched oatmeal.

Ten months had passed since their wedding day, and, still, they hadn't been able to leave their Holmby Hills home for a honeymoon. Between both of their schedules, the block of time they wanted, at least a month, hadn't fit into either of their timetables.

"Morning beautiful." Shane bent over and kissed the top of her head.

"Oh darlin', seems like it's been days since we've seen each other. Leave it to me to wake you."

"Not your fault. Wasn't able to sleep. I've got a lot on my mind." He raked his fingers through his unkempt hair.

"Me too." She breathlessly explained the encounter with Father Clancy and her assignment to locate an appropriate shelter facility. "After breakfast, I'm planning to call my estate agent. See if he has any ideas."

He looked into her bright, animated face and felt her excitement.

"Guess what? Father Clancy is from Northern Ireland."

"Does he share your strong political feelings? With him being a priest, there were no heated discussions, I presume."

"We didn't talk politics, but he did mention the Troubles. Must weigh down his spirit, so." She turned her head toward the window.

"A lot of that must be going around."

"What?" She glanced at him over her shoulder.

"Weighted down spirits. I've got one too." He crossed his arms and stared at the floor.

"I don't know what to do. Keep trudging along in law enforcement or..." He shrugged. "Maybe I'm too old to even consider something else." He looked up as she pushed the bowl of cereal away and dropped the folded newspaper on the table.

"Don't' be daft."

"As if you'd have a clue. You're still wet behind the ears." He winked.

"Thirty-six isn't old. Mature, maybe, but not old."

"Gee, thanks."

"Anyway, I don't think it's a hard decision. You're the cleverest detective in all of Los Angeles, but it's taking a toll." She paused as if searching for the right words. "Your work is gritty and depressing. It's wearing you out. Why don't you complete your certification in architecture? You never told me why you quit so close to graduation except—"

"I couldn't resist the pull to solve crimes. Blame it on all those Hardy Boys books I read as a kid." He opened the dishwasher and removed a mug.

"For sure Shane, you might find yourself missing the thrill of detective work. On the other hand, why don't you give up working altogether," she said under her breath, "only for the time being while you sort out your job situation?"

Shane recognized the dreamy look filling her emerald eyes. He sensed she was about to embark on what he'd labeled her flights of fancy. Usually, a long-winded account of activities or ideas that she believes are the greatest things since the printing press. That and her insistence she was born with a sixth sense, *fey*, as Beth called it, were the two most annoying things about her. But over the last few months, he'd been able to temper his frustration over these minor flaws. He conceded those two complaints couldn't compare to his laundry list of shortcomings. But still, he braced himself for the oncoming deluge of words.

"Imagine all the exciting things we could do. We could travel across country in one of those luxuriously romantic trains, spend time in Ireland with me Da, expand the garden, try all those recipes I've been pulling out of magazines, and there'd be long afternoons for the golf course and the racetrack, down on the beach we could surf and ski," she said counting the activities off on her fingers.

"Even spend entire days just reading the paper and watching the *telly*. As long as we're together, we'd have a grand time. It'd be brilliant."

Using a measure of good sense, he restrained from rolling his eyes. "You know damn well, I won't live off of you."

"Stubborn mule. It's just your pride talking."

"Pride, my ass."

"Exactly." She tore her eyes away from him and stared at the folded newspaper.

"But, honey." He paused wondering if he'd ever make her understand. It'd been a hard fact to swallow that she'd earned a fortune by prancing down a catwalk and silently bemoaned that her lucrative fluff job—certainly not in the same realm as being a cop—paid incredibly, yet he risked life and limb and made only a fraction of her salary. "I need to financially contribute— even if it's only a pittance," he sputtered.

"I didn't marry you for your bank account."

"That's a good thing; otherwise you'd really be disappointed. Anyway, I know why you couldn't resist me. It came down to my good looks, jocular wit, and hypnotizing charm." He flashed a bright smile to ease the sense of heaviness separating them.

She waved the air in front of her face as if shooing an irksome fly. "Sometimes I feel you resent my success. Like we're in a competition, but I haven't a clue what it's about."

"What? You're sixth sense not working?"

"I'm serious, Shane. There was so much I loved about modeling, but I needed a break. What with the accident and my recovery not to mention the court hearing." She lowered her head as if studying the pattern of the floor's wooden grain.

He swallowed hard. "It's not about competition. How could I compete with you? You're the best part of my life. I'm so proud of you. Damn proud." The words flew from his lips. "You've faced a lot of trials and suffering...and losses. Did any of that keep you down? Hell no. You overcame it all."

She raised her eyes. Her lips were compressed into a firm line.

"Not many people can boast of a career like yours. A model *and* an actress." Shane raised the stoneware mug in his hand.

"I wasn't much of an actress, for sure. But, dear Lord, modeling was like a fairytale. I don't talk much about it. As me Da always says, ''Tis in the past, leave it there.'" She rose and took the mug from his hand and filled it with coffee. "The pieces just fell into place. After all, God gave me the physical attributes; I can't take any credit for that." Beth handed him back the cup, wiggled the top off a canister, and plucked out a tea bag. She dropped it into a mug embossed with an image of the Irish flag. "If it weren't for me Da being injured, I doubt I'd even gone searching for a modeling career." She lifted the electric teapot and poured a stream of water into the cup. "It seems crazy those photos in the department store flyer paved the way for me to become a top runway model." She reclaimed her seat, blew across the steaming liquid, and took a sip.

Ten years ago, her hopes soared with anticipation of an exciting new life as she stuffed magazines featuring her modeling work into a battered suitcase. She'd been promised a job working at one of the top fashion houses in Milan. But even at the youthful age of sixteen, Beth's intuition had warned her that it seemed too good to be true. The house of Affinito, the once vibrant and trendy designer of Couturier fashion, had lost popularity as if overnight. The current collection had fallen flat and languished as new trends left Affinito's outdated ideas behind. But it was at the once hip fashion house that she'd learned her craft. After a couple of shows, word began to spread about the new Irish model. Top designers started to take note of Beth— not only for her natural beauty and grace but her fierce determination when she took to the catwalk. She'd created her own brand of electricity. People noticed her. And the designer's creations. Before long Affinito soared again.

He felt her eyes on him as he leaned against the counter sipping his coffee.

"Do you remember my ads on TV? As spokes-model for Noelle Cosmetics."

"Ahh..."

"I'm not surprised. Turned out to be a very lucrative campaign." She rested her chin in her cupped hands. "My job didn't require any degrees or a brain like a computer. But you have to use your intellect to outsmart the old *hoor's melt*. The way I see it, you'd have to be a genius to do that."

"I'm not sure I even what to know what that Irish saying means. Something unsavory, no doubt." He placed the empty coffee cup in the sink. "So, Betty Getty, you think I'm a genius." He drummed a finger against his temple as he crossed his eyes.

"Now you're making fun of me." She jumped to her feet with hands clutching her waist.

"Never." He pulled her close and kissed her lips. Taking a step back, he looked into her bright eyes. "You'll always be my darling, Betty Getty."

"Shane." She turned away and stepped toward the kitchen counter.

"What? You don't like your nickname anymore?" He moved behind her and ran his tongue along the nape of her neck, brushed his fingertips through her hair, and unsnapped the barrette. Auburn curls tumbled around her shoulders. "Think of all the famous stars you share that name with. There's the two obvious Bettys—Grable and Davis, both beauties I should add. And who could forget the blond bombshell, Betty Hutton? Now there's the spunky Betty White, and the cookbook queen, Betty Crocker, and we can't overlook the animated boop-boop-a-doop Betty—Boop that is."

She spun around and shook her head. "I love you, Shane Dalton, even if you're a proud man who is a bit touched in the head." She tapped his forehead with her fingertip. He grabbed her wrist and brought her hand to his lips. As he kissed the smooth skin she said, "Just follow your heart, *grá a chroí*, I'll support your decision no matter what."

"Probably time for a change." He released her then crossed his arms. "Collins and I are solid; you know that. But, all this sparring lately with Rosnick is leaving me totally exhausted. We don't seem to agree about anything. I've been walking the straight line, following protocol to the nth degree, but I still come up short trying to please her."

"You've always said your captain is a stickler for the rules. Everything done by the book. I thought you liked that?"

He took a deep breath. "It's not just Rosnick. It's my current case where things are only getting worse. You've heard about those teenager murders?"

"Don't tell me you're working that case? Dear Lord, it's just horrible." She bit her lip. "No wonder I haven't seen you for days. I've been keeping up with the news accounts. The death of those poor girls have touched my heart, so. And...and there's something...now, what is it?" She squinted as if trying to remember. "Oh yeah. Father Clancy. Turns out, he knew one of the victims quite well. Eliana Mendoza. He rescued her from the streets and had even purchased an airline ticket so she could return to Ecuador but—"

"She's the youngest of the lot. Only fourteen." The muscle in his jaw twitched. "I'll have to talk to your friend, the priest. Hopefully, he can offer us some kind of lead since we're coming up empty."

"There something about Father Clancy, but I can't quite put my finger on it," Beth said with a shake of her head. "My *fey* acted up when he was here yesterday."

"Your *fey*?" Shane raised his eyebrows.

"Forget it. Anyway, I have his business card."

He paused and stared beyond her. "I'd quit the force tomorrow if it weren't for those poor girls. It's like I've become the last voice for these young victims. And I won't rest—can't rest—until I see that piece of crud locked behind bars for the rest of his miserable life."

"That *dirtbird* won't have a chance with you on his trail."

He wished he was as optimistic as Beth. "Collins is unflappable. If I resign, he and Grabowski could partner up," Shane said with an escalating sense of confliction. "It's not like I'm indispensable." He refilled the mug and took a quick sip.

"You are to me. The LASD would be a fool to let you get away. After all, you're their best detective."

"So you say, Betty Getty." He took a long swallow of coffee wishing to God he didn't have to tell her. "The latest homicide hasn't been released to the public yet." He checked his watch. "Correction, just released." He placed the cup on the countertop and grasped her hand. "We're not entirely sure this death is related to the others, but the latest homicide victim is Lexi Horne."

"What?" She squeezed her eyes shut and shook her head. "Please Lord, no." She pulled away from Shane and paced the length of the long galley kitchen. "I can't believe it. I met Lexi only a couple of times, but it was obvious she was devoted to Emma. Skye tolerated her. Skye?" She stopped abruptly and faced him.

"Said she had a couple of flat tires yesterday?"

Beth nodded. "You know Skye; any little problem is a major catastrophe. But seriously, she was stranded, and of course, I was glad to help."

"What time did you two part ways?"

"Wait a minute. You don't think Skye had anything to do with it?"

"Not really. Just following protocol."

"Alright then." She cleared her throat. "The garage man met us with her car around six. Then she had to drive back to Beverly Hills to drop Emma off at Zach's. He dotes on that little girl, even though he's only the stepfather. He's even brought up the topic of adoption. Skye told me she'd never allow that to happen." She bent over and picked up the hair barrette Shane had let fall to the floor. "Well anyway, Skye was worried because she was running late. She'd planned to have dinner with a friend at eight—a private, intimate dinner at her Malibu house. Does that answer all your questions, Detective?"

He took a sip of coffee. "For now."

"How is she?"

"A mess. But not as upset about the Horne murder as to the disappearance of her assistant."

"Darla's missing?" She stepped closer to her husband. "She'll be lost without her. Darla does everything for her, but wipe her bum—cooking, errands, scheduling appointments, correspondences, shopping—you name it, Darla does it. But besides being proficient, I do believe Skye really likes her. Trusts her."

"She trusts you, too."

"Though we rarely see things eye to eye, she knows I don't want anything from her except friendship." She took his coffee cup and topped it off. "But in all candor, I do admit, Skye can be a bit grating on the nerves sometimes." She crossed the room and pulled open the refrigerator door. After rummaging a few moments, with hands full, she closed it with a turn of the hip. "You must be famished. Finish your *cuppa*, while I whip up some breakfast." She set the contents down on top the pink and black granite countertop.

He sat at the table, pulled the sports section free from the newspaper, and scanned the headlines until finding his favorite columnist. After reading the article's first line three times, he gave up. No matter how hard he tried, he couldn't shake the image of the dead nanny. So, he dropped the paper on the table, leaned back in the Windsor chair, and looked at Beth. She busied herself near the stove whisking an egg mixture in a stainless steel bowl. Humming softly, she added a handful of shredded cheddar and pushed the bowl aside.

"That's a depressing tune."

"A bit mournful, for sure. It's a hymn that was sung at my mother's funeral. Though it's been nearly twenty years ago, this melody always pops into to my head when I hear bad news." She turned from the sizzling bacon and pressed the lever down as two slices of wheat bread disappeared into the toaster. "I've been thinking." She faced him. "There've been three murdered teenagers. All street kids turned to prostitution. Now the fourth, Lexi, doesn't seem to fit the mold. Skye told me both her parents are doctors and that she attends classes at UCLA along with being Emma's nanny. She was a smart and beautiful girl with a bright future. Once when I was at Skye's house, she was helping Emma with a papier-mâché project. Pure joy lit up her face. She loved what she was doing. Lexi wasn't living a hellish life like the other victims so I don't see how her murder could be connected to the others."

"People do live secret lives."

She pursed her lips. "Not based on what I know of Lexi. She was a nineteen-year-old living a typical all-American, apple pie kind of life."

"I wouldn't call it exactly typical. She just landed a role on a TV show."

"Really now? Skye turned out to be wrong on that front. Thought Lexi couldn't act her way out of a wet paper bag. See, that proves my case. She had nothing in common with the other victims."

"That's the kicker." He sucked in a deep breath of air. "Lexi wasn't impoverished like the other girls. But the M.O. is very similar. Almost identical."

"Does that prove anything?"

"Not yet. I'm gonna meet with the doctor performing the autopsy later today to find out exactly how Lexi died. Hopefully, by then, we'll know for sure if it was the same killer."

"Some of the newspaper articles about the murdered girls have been pretty graphic."

"Exactly. Every conceivable news outlet has reported on the method of the homicides. That's why I think there's a distinct possibility Lexi's murder could be the work of a copycat. Someone wanted her dead." Shane wrinkled his nose. "Something's burning."

She flew back to the stove and turned off the gas burner. "Damnation," she muttered as the charred bacon smoldered in the cast iron pan. After hitting the exhaust fan, she dumped the burnt bacon into the sink. As if forgetting about the uncooked eggs and the soon to be cold toast, she pulled out a chair and sat down next to Shane.

"Who'd might that be?"

"A jilted lover, a jealous acquaintance, the person she ousted in getting the acting gig?" He shrugged.

"It would've been someone driven to the edge."

"Could be the same perp who killed the other girls. Maybe he saw Lexi and followed her. Could've stalked her until the timing was right."

She squinted upward as if studying the ceiling. "Obsession is a scary thing. But it makes sense. Someone could've been sending her threatening letters or even phoning her." She refocused on Shane. "I wonder if the poor girl knew who was stalking her."

"It's only a theory, Beth. Anyway, Collins and a couple uniforms canvased the neighborhood and came up empty. So did the officers searching for Darla Edwards. But," he hesitated a moment, "I had an interesting interview last night. Someone who I suspect knows more than what she offered me."

"Skye?"

"Nah." He turned and glanced out the large sunny window. He spied a red-winged blackbird landing on the bird feeder. "Skye's as transparent as a sheet of Saran wrap. I doubt she kept anything back; after all, she's rarely lost for words." He watched the bird peck at some food. It suddenly flapped its red shouldered, yellow barred black wings and took off. "No. It was one Marjorie Hammonds. The wife of that celebrity lawyer." He shifted in his chair.

"Holy Mother of God. What does Marjorie have to do with it?"

"You know her?"

"Met her a couple years ago at a luncheon at Skye's. Marjorie asked me so many questions, I felt like I'd been interrogated. That's one nosy Parker for sure."

"If you mean she's a busybody, I have to agree." He raised the mug and swallowed. "She showed up on Skye's doorstep. I questioned her at the station since she'd seen Lexi only hours before she died."

"Well, that one is an expert in milking people for information. Was she able to shed any light?"

"Basically, a waste of time. Except, I can't shake the feeling that she knows something."

"Ah. That surprises me coming from the man who thinks my *fey* is the product of an overactive imagination."

"My hunch has nothing to do with superstition, but years of investigative work. Police intuition."

"Call it what you like."

"Hey, how well do you know that Hammond woman?" He craned his neck in order to look directly into Beth's face.

"Friends, though, Marjorie thinks we're bosom buddies."

"Hmmm. That's interesting because I've got a great idea."

She tilted her head with widened eyes as if asking a question without words but waited for him to continue.

"How would you feel about dropping by Marjorie's house to sniff around a bit? She might open up. Let something slip that we can pursue."

She stared straight ahead as if lost in her own thoughts.

"How 'bout it?"

"If you couldn't get any useful information out of Marjorie, how will I?"

"Bring up the nanny's murder and then let her do all the talking."

"I can do that easy enough. But, I wouldn't hold my breath. I've learned over the years that Marjorie can be quite tight-lipped. She may like digging up the dirt on people, but she isn't exactly generous with what she knows."

"Don't doubt yourself," he said with the beginning of a grin. "Just let her talk. If my hunch is right, you might be able to draw out whatever she's holding back."

"I guess it's worth a try."

"Never know." He paused a second. "Last night Hammond didn't seem to connect the dots that we're married. Have you ever talked to her about me?"

"I've probably mentioned you're a detective. But unless she memorized our wedding invitation, she wouldn't know your name."

"She was at our wedding?"

"Couldn't make it."

"Humph. Well, I found her extremely irritating."

"She is an acquired taste, so. But darlin', she does have a good heart."

"Leave it to you to uncover that surprising fact about nosy Mrs. Hammond. Well Betty, whatever you find out, however insignificant it seems, may be of help."

"Okay. I'll call her. Now, where did I leave my mobile?"

"I like your enthusiasm. But can it wait until after breakfast?"

She jumped up from the table. "I'm forgetting just about everything." She freed a glass from a cabinet and filled it with orange juice. "I'll do my best to meet up with Marjorie today."

She handed him the glass.

"Sounds like a plan."

He watched as she moved to the stovetop and poured the eggs into a clean skillet. She freed a spatula from a drawer then turned and faced him. "My heart is breaking for those murdered girls and now Lexi. If prodding Marjorie will help even a wee bit, then I'm more than willing to do it for you, Shane."

"I appreciate you going the extra mile." Shane glimpsed a curl of smoke rising from the pan. "Betty, the eggs."

She spun around. "Oh, no." She grabbed the pan's handle and jerked the skillet off the burner.

"A bowl of cornflakes..." He stopped mid-sentence as she faced him. He caught sight of the distress straining her face. "Scratch that. I think we'll have better luck at the diner, Betty Getty," Shane said with a lopsided grin.

CHAPTER EIGHT

Maiah sat on the edge of a satiny pink chair and gazed at Johannah's sleeping form. She inhaled deeply attempting to brush aside the nervous tension causing her head to pound. The headache wasn't due to Kenny spending the entire night out. She was used to that, but it stemmed from her concern for Johannah. Her once robust form now resembled a frail, withered shadow of her former self. She needed the older woman's strength to continue with her plan.

Johannah stirred beneath the comforter then flashed her eyes open. "Is something wrong?" She sat up in the queen-sized bed knocking a pillow onto the floor.

"Nothing's wrong." Maiah touched Johannah's shoulder and eased her back down. "I wanted to make sure you're resting comfortably."

"I did have a difficult time falling asleep. Around midnight, I heated some milk. That did the trick."

Maiah adverted her eyes. "I'm afraid the flight from Virginia was too much for you."

"A bit strenuous. I can't seem to do quite as much as even a year ago."

"Would you consider living here, with us, full time?" Maiah blurted out the words surprised but pleased she'd said them. "Harry loves you. And actually, you'd be doing me a great favor." She noticed how Johannah's graying hair looked dry and lifeless against the mauve of the satin pillowcase. "Please, don't say no." She grasped the woman's hand and squeezed it.

Johanna stared into Maiah's face a moment and then offered a full smile. The skin around her eyes crinkled as a rush of pink flushed her cheeks. "Could I ever deny you anything?"

"You'll move in with us?"

"Of course, *mien liebster schatz.* I'm getting to be an old woman. There's nothing more in life I'd ever want than to spend my final days with you."

"Final days? I don't think so. You're going to be so busy working your magic on Harry that the years will be filled with a newfound purpose. I need you to help him develop into a well-bred young man. All his training and discipline has been left to me since Kenny is useless. Oh, he's up for the fun stuff like Harry's soccer games and pizza on Friday nights. But when it comes to developing his son's character, that's a different story altogether. Joining forces, I know we can work wonders."

"Now don't start short-changing yourself. You've done a fine job with the boy. He's a delight. His keen intelligence is evident, even if he is a bit loquacious. A happy, gregarious child." Johannah paused a second. "One day, I believe he'll be an adept Equestrian like you. All he talked about last night was his Pony Club and the show jumping competition next month."

"That's why I'll be flying back Sunday for Parents' Day. He'd be crushed if I wasn't there. Riding is a special bond between us. I had Harry jumping at age two. You should've seen him sitting ramrod straight and so confident on his pony, Cinders. They've grown up with each other." Maiah tucked a lock of hair behind her ear. "But the thing Harry loves so much is ruined for me because I'm afraid *she'll* show up. I've told Kenny—but does he care? Acts like it's no big deal for me to run into his former mistress."

Johannah clicked her tongue against her teeth. "I don't know why you put up with that man."

Maiah tapped her foot a couple of times. "I might as well tell you. I am going to leave Kenny. Soon. And I might need your help."

***

Maiah pulled open a drawer adjacent to the oven and grabbed an apron. As she tied it around her slim waist, she heard heavy footsteps. Half-expecting to see an exhausted Kenny, she pursed her lips as Hap Dorian stepped into the kitchen. She crossed her arms. "What did you mean barging in here last night?"

He shrugged then offered her a grin. "I thought you'd want to know."

"Ever hear of the telephone?"

"Come on now. Don't tell me you're angry?" He stepped closer and brushed a few strands of golden hair off her cheek.

She jerked her head away. "Don't you dare touch me. If you ever attempt such familiarity again, I swear, I'll fire you."

"Whoa. Don't get all outta joint. I assumed our special arrangement would include certain other benefits. After all, you and me, we've been getting kinda tight lately."

"You thought wrong. Remember Roman Dorian, you work for me. We're not equals and never will be. But I admit," she said unfolding her arms and letting them hang at her sides, "you have a special talent with horses. That's the only reason I've allowed you to nurse that poor gelding. As to those additional tasks I've required of you, I've paid you handsomely and will continue to do so. If you don't forget your place." She reached into the pocket of her designer jeans and pulled out a slim stack of folded bills. She peeled off five of them, all twenties, and thrust the money in his direction.

"I guess I must've misread your signals." He grasped the bills. "Won't happen again."

"Something's happened?" Kenny breezed into the kitchen and pecked Maiah's cheek.

"Nothing really. No." She moved next to the work island and ran her fingertips along its sapele wood surface. "Roman failed to tidy up the tack room as I instructed. I may have overreacted."

"Slouching a bit, eh? That's not like you, Hap." Kenny couldn't seem to suppress the smile that eased across his face.

"Looks like you've been up all night," said Hap.

Kenny's wrinkled clothes, bristly chin, and bloodshot eyes weren't lost on Maiah. She gritted her teeth.

"Work's got me swamped. Have a bunch of paintings that need to be finished like yesterday. Got a major show in the Big Apple at the end of the month."

"Impressive. But, don't tell me you screwed around until to the last minute?" Hap good-naturedly slapped Kenny on his back.

"Not exactly. But like I've always said, one can't rush inspiration."

Maiah locked eyes with Kenny and shot him a seething glance. She jerked her head then jetted toward the refrigerator and yanked the door open.

"But with such a muse..." Kenny motioned to her as she placed a carton of eggs onto the counter. "Inspiration is never far away. Have you ever seen a more lovely vision?"

"Don't you paint real modern stuff—wild colors and swirling lines—like an explosion in a firework factory? Man, if she inspires you to paint like that, all I can say is that you're one damn lucky SOB."

"You took the words right outta my mouth." He swung an arm around Hap's shoulders as he steered him out of the kitchen.

***

A few minutes later, Kenny returned with the morning paper tucked under his arm. "That Hap is a real card. Wish I could be half as laid-back. But then what kind of artist would I be without brooding angst and the required temperamental personality?"

Maiah didn't acknowledge him as she measured a cup of flour. The heady aroma of baking cinnamon rolls filled the expansive kitchen, and his stomach constricted reminding him he was starved. He reached for a bunch of bananas.

"Why do you act like Roman Dorian is your best friend?" Her stingingly sharp voice cut the air. "He's the hired help, for God's sake. You're demeaning yourself." She dumped the flour into a mixing bowl.

"I know you have this class thing going on, but really Maiah, don't try to deny it. You like Hap. I've seen you two with your heads together more than once. And you're always relaxed and chipper when you're with him." He paused a second. "Hap brings out your best self, something I can't seem to do anymore." He forgot about his hunger and dropped the newspaper onto the black onyx countertop. "I've turned out to be a big disappointment."

She shifted her sight from the mixing bowl and looked at him. "Don't be ridiculous. Dorian is a trusted employee, as is his father, the gardener, and the housekeeper. You're my husband. Now go read the paper while I make your breakfast."

An unwelcomed sensation of guilt gripped him as he watched her reach into the oven and pull out the bubbling pastries. The self-reproach hadn't surfaced because of her generous efforts at providing him a lavish breakfast or for spending another night in his studio; that was his old standby when he didn't want to be around her. It boiled down to his relationship with Skye. A mere hour ago, as he absorbed the powerful impact of his four finished canvases, a chilling thought grabbed him. And no matter how hard he tried, he couldn't vanquish the disturbing impression.

He recalled the clean scent of cool air wafting around him as the first rays of northern light filtered through the studio's opened windows. But, inexplicably he'd broken out into a sweat. Then the startling realization hit him. Skye could've been angry enough to tell the police he had stood over Lexi's lifeless body and touched the still warm corpse. His sinking gut morphed into a knot that felt like a thirty-pound weight as he imagined headlines from supermarket tabloids to celebrity magazines linking him to Skye and the murdered nanny. If that were to happen, then Maiah would know the whole ugly truth—that he'd cheated—and once again with Skye Andrews.

Running into Hap had been a calming diversion, but now he felt jumpy. Anxious. As Maiah chatted over the sound of sizzling bacon and selected a knife to chop vegetables for their omelets, he found it impossible to focus on her words. The bloodied image of Lexi Horne crowded his mind leaving room for little else. He paced the length of the kitchen, noticed the forlorn newspaper, and picked it up. He held his breath as he shook the front section free. His eyes flitted across the headlines. Nothing.

Maiah poured batter onto a griddle then glanced in his direction. "I should be angry as hell at you for spending another night in your studio. Sometimes I wonder why you even bother to come home." She eased a spatula under the bubbling batter. With a swift motion, she flipped the pancake exposing its warm, golden surface. "But, I'm glad you do." She reached for the egg mixture and poured it into a heated omelet pan, closed the lid, and locked it.

He ignored her comment, and the seconds passed in silence as he eyed his wife. It didn't surprise him that she worked so methodically. She'd been a chemistry major in college, but for some reason, unknown to him, she'd dropped out after her second year of studying abroad in England. After returning to the states, she'd resumed her studies, and when they met, she was a Ph.D. candidate. Then they married, and she became pregnant, so Maiah put the whole education thing on hold. He still got a kick out of watching how she measured the ingredients with precision and never made a mess. Because of her lack of spontaneity, he always tried to find even the tiniest fault but had never been able to since her meals were undeniably delicious.

She lifted a flapjack and placed it on a platter. "Seems as if I haven't rattled around the kitchen in ages. I love it when Cook has a day off." She reached for the wooden spoon and dipped it into the mixing bowl. "You know how much I adore piddling around in here. It's so freeing. As if I don't have a care in the world."

Not trusting himself to respond, he refolded the paper, newly irritated by Maiah's habit of relegating people to their professions. It's a wonder she doesn't call me 'Painter', he thought, rolling his eyes toward the ceiling.

He headed to the adjoining breakfast room, but after taking only a couple of steps, she offered him a cup of coffee. He grabbed the mug without a word and felt her eyes as he crossed the kitchen's sparkling ceramic tile floor.

"Breakfast isn't quite ready. Go upstairs and change out of those disgusting paint spattered jeans before sitting at the table."

As if not hearing her, he pulled out the Shaker styled chair and sat down. He unfolded the paper and thumbed through the pages. Though he searched every column, he couldn't locate a single article regarding Lexi's death.

"Really, Kenny, you're working too hard. Let your apprentices finish those canvases and be done with it." She stood under the arch separating the two rooms.

"I'm not that type of artist. My name on a piece means I did it—from conception to the last stroke of the paintbrush."

"Is it really that important?"

He raked his fingertips through his close-cropped black hair. "The New York show is critical to my career. I thought you understood that."

A flash of anger welled up, but he pushed it away. He wouldn't allow Maiah to distract him with a needless discussion that wouldn't lead anywhere. After a wasted hour of rising tempers and harsh words, she still wouldn't understand that the very act of painting made him feel alive. *Painting and Skye.* Usually, he'd play along and placate Maiah, allowing his conscience a reprieve from the onus of his infidelity.

The room's walls seemed to be closing in, and for the sake of his sanity, he needed to escape the sting of his wife's scrutiny. He glanced outside as he took a deep breath. The freshness of the air and clarity of light assured him that everything would be okay—as soon as he smoothed things over with Skye and made damn sure she hadn't done anything stupid. It wasn't hard to figure she was still royally pissed at him. They had disagreements before, but after a couple of hours, they'd be burning the phone line and shooting the breeze like nothing ever happened. This time was different. He had to make it up to her. Big time. Before she did something he'd regret.

The previous couple of months had been a challenge. At times, he visualized himself a circus tightrope walker where one wrong step would result in calamity. The endless lies to Maiah. Slipping away at odd hours to hook up with Skye. At first, it had been exciting, exhilarating even, but now he wasn't so sure. Though he didn't want to admit it, he feared his clandestine affair with Skye would be shorter lived than the last time.

"More coffee?" she called from the kitchen.

"Don't bother. I'm not hungry. After a quick shower, I'm outta here. Even though you don't approve, I've got to get back to the studio." The lie slipped out easily enough.

"You can't be serious." She stepped into the breakfast room.

"Huh?" He twisted his neck to get a good look at her. What he once took for elegant and graceful, now struck him as haughty and cold. Her sexy bedroom voice grated on his nerves. Sometimes he wondered how it was possible that he'd been so crazy in love with her. Though he sugarcoated the answer over the years, he wasn't about to kid himself any longer. It boiled down to one thing—the money.

"I'm not letting you out of my sight today. A promise is a promise." She inched closer then rested her hand on his shoulder.

He wanted to shrug it off but resisted the temptation.

"Listen up. We have to be at the airport tonight by seven. I'm not going to worry myself sick that once in your studio, you'll forget about the time."

"What are you talking about?"

She sunk into a chair positioned in a corner. It faced the terrace and the tumbling stream of water that collected in the koi pond. She ran her hand over the armrest's chintz fabric. "I don't know what's wrong with you. With us."

Protests clamored in his mind. He feared she'd turn the discussion into an opportunity to analyze the long shopping list of things gone awry in their marriage. He took a long swallow of coffee emptying the cup.

"You don't remember your promise?"

He shrugged.

"Clint Austin. You remember him? Estella's Blue trainer. He transported her to Louisville a fortnight ago."

"Oh."

"For your information, the Kentucky Derby is Saturday." She narrowed her eyes. "The only thing that matters to you are those damn paintings. It's all about your career and that..."

Maiah pressed her lips together.

He stared into the empty cup. "Have you ever considered what's important to me? The New York exhibition is huge."

She glanced at him for a second before looking back through the opened French doors. "Did you know Estella Blue won six races in a row? That I was sick with indecision about whether to enter her into the Derby? But after winning the Santa Anita, Clint finally talked some sense into my head. My girl has a chance. A damn good chance. And you know, Kenny, a filly hasn't won since Winning Colors back in '88. What an honor; an achievement that would be if my horse..." Maiah's eyes grew big as if mesmerized by something far in the distance.

He shifted in the chair then folded the newspaper but kept the sports section separate, laying it on the table in front of him.

"And now you want to renege on your promise to go with me to Kentucky." The shrill tone of her voice startled him.

"I didn't know fillies could race against colts."

She sighed.

"I guess there's no real excuse for me not keeping up with what's been going on with you, Clint, the jockey, Hap, the upstairs maid, or least I forget the majestic Estella Blue. Just preoccupied with a bunch of inconsequential paintings for the most pivotal show in my entire career."

She closed her eyes and dropped her head. Honey blond hair brushed her face and fell across her shoulders.

He swallowed hard realizing he'd gone too far. It wasn't entirely her fault he was in love with someone else. "Actually, I'd be shocked if she wasn't gonna run the Kentucky Derby. Even though I was up to my eyeballs with work, I couldn't wait for you to rush into the house full of news about Estella Blue's latest victory." He remembered how easy it had been to block out her endless droning about the damn horse. "I've been planning to attend the race. If she got that far. I promised you that much. But just not today. Look, why don't you fly out as scheduled, and I'll meet you Saturday? We'll cheer Estella Blue to triumph together. Okay?" He moved away from the table and stepped next to Maiah. He stroked her cheek. She jerked her head away.

Just what he needed. For both women in his life to be angry at him. Even if he no longer felt much of anything for Maiah, she'd provided him with his greatest joy. An image of his athletic, artistic, bright-eyed son flittered through his mind. "Are you planning to take Harry?"

She lifted her head and glared at him.

"You'll be so busy with all the horse racing stuff. I'd hate for him to feel neglected." He squinted. "Doesn't he have a soccer game Saturday?"

"Unlike you, Harry is already an accomplished rider."

He wanted to object. Her implication that an eight-year-old kid could be accomplished in anything was a needless exaggeration. Instead, he kept his mouth shut.

"He won't miss the game. Johannah is upstairs. She'll be joining us for breakfast."

"You're kidding? Gestapo Johannah Eberhart. Why in God's name did you call that Gorgon to babysit Harry? You know I can't stand that woman."

"I didn't realize I needed your permission to hire my old governess. You probably haven't noticed, but Harry loves her."

"I sure as hell don't. She gives me the creeps." He grimaced. Seconds after the words slipped between his lips, his mind clicked, allowing him to realize he'd inadvertently created a way out. At least for the time being. The fates must be on my side, he thought as a trickle of hope began to flow, but I've got to think this out carefully. *Play my cards to full advantage.*

Maiah was right. He had forgotten about the horse race. It was about the last thing he'd ever want to suffer through, but now things had changed. Being out of town for a few days might be the time he needed for things to simmer around Lexi's murder—the cops might even catch the killer by then. *She'll be so busy with Estella Blue and the endless galas and dinners that if there's any down time, I'll be sure to steer her away from the news headlines.* A smile tugged at the corners of his mouth. He tightened his jaw until the sensation passed.

"So, it's definite. Fräulein Eberhart is here through Sunday?"

"Monday. I thought after the race, we could do a little sightseeing."

"Well, that leaves me no other choice, since I won't be able to stay here with the *warden* overtaking the household. It's pure hell the way she tries to bully me. And those goddam lectures on the evils of the world. As if every crisis from pollution to terrorism is my fault. No. Not gonna happen."

She kept her sight focused on the rustling stream. "There's something else." She didn't wait for a response. "I've invited Johannah to live with us."

"What?"

"Permanently."

He gasped as if the air had been knocked out of him. "You're kidding, right?" She only stared at him.

He knew what she was up to. Trying to scare him into doing what she wanted or punish him—like forever. He made a lightning quick decision to accept her hair-brained scheme about Johannah joining the household until the investigation into Lexi's death dies down. *Then we'll see who's gonna be living here. Not Eberhart, that's for damn sure.*

"Look babe." He moved in front of Maiah and knelt down to be eye level with her.

She turned her head away. Using a feather-light touch, he turned her chin toward him. "I know how much Johannah means to you. And if it makes you happy, how can I object?" He watched as she pulled her eyebrows close and a bemused expression claimed her face. "I'm really sorry I forgot about the Kentucky Derby. My own stupid fault. I can't think of anything I'd rather do than escort my beautiful wife to the winner's circle Saturday."

"Winner's circle?" She paused a moment as if trying to understand the meaning of his words. "You agree with me? You really think Estella Blue has what it takes to win?"

"Without a doubt. You see darling, I feel it in here." He grasped her hand and placed it against his chest. "Your filly is going to run stronger and faster and leave that whole slew of colts in the dust. We've got us a winner. I'm sure of it."

She looked into his eyes and smiled.

He felt the tension ease away as he jumped to his feet and scooped her up. He stifled her amused giggle by pressing his lips against hers.

***

Though his plate was loaded, Kenny could barely swallow a forkful of food. He didn't doubt the breakfast Maiah made was delicious, but just a sniff of the enticing aroma wafting from the serving plates knotted his stomach. Skye and her murdered nanny filled his troubled mind. He reached for his phone but let his hand drop feeling Maiah's eyes on him.

Harry, talkative as usual, wolfed down two strips of bacon, three pancakes, and a couple of cinnamon rolls. After draining his second glass of orange juice, he recited a long list of animals he planned to see at the zoo and urged Johannah to hurry so they could be on their way.

Johannah nodded as Harry raced from the table.

"Aren't you going to eat?" Maiah asked with a frown.

"It'd be bad enough not eating if Cook had prepared the food, but your own wife toiled over a hot stove to make you a delectable meal." Johannah glowered.

Kenny stabbed a sausage and stuffed it into his mouth. He chewed slowly and noticed that the irritated look hadn't left the old governess' face.

"You have an amazing wife. Beautiful, talented, and compassionate. But do you appreciate her?" Johannah lifted the napkin from her lap and folded it.

Kenny continued chewing.

"Just yesterday I found out she's rescued a neglected horse slated for the slaughterhouse. Since she was a child, she's had a tender spot for the underdog. Maybe that explains why she married you."

Kenny reached for his cup and gulped a mouthful of coffee. Time to go. He'd played nice. The Gorgon was getting on his nerves.

"I'll never forget the day she showed her true mettle," Johannah said.

Kenny slid the chair away from the table.

"You were fourteen." Johannah glanced at Maiah. "Riding your horse—"

"Bianco. But Kenny doesn't want to hear that story," Maiah objected.

"Nonsense." Johannah reached for the coffee pot, stood, and refilled his cup. Kenny folded his arms but remained seated.

"Bianco was an expert jumper, but who would have thought that while galloping on flat ground between fences, he'd break a leg."

"I was devastated," Maiah said under her breath. "I couldn't bear to see him suffer."

"Do you know what this brave girl did?" Johannah didn't wait for an answer from Kenny. "She ran to the gun locker—"

"Retrieved my target practice shotgun and put him out of his misery. Shot him between the eyes," Maiah said.

"You did what?" Kenny asked. "Why the hell didn't you call a vet? Maybe the horse could've survived the accident."

"He'd shattered a fetlock joint in one of his hind legs," Johannah said.

"Even if he did survive the injury, which is doubtful, he never would've been the same. Bianco would have been irretrievably damaged," Maiah said.

"Oh my," Johannah piped. "Look at the time. Young Harry will be wondering what has detained me."

Kenny leaned back in the chair perplexed by what Johannah had deemed his wife's compassionate act of heroism.

CHAPTER NINE

Inside the Clear Springs Station, Shane was both amused and impressed as he observed Father Clancy. The priest's presence radiated like a beacon. He emitted a glow of warmth as his throaty brogue offered wholehearted greetings, which brought smiles even to the dourest of faces. His Irish charm oozed from every pore of his oversized body. He ushered Father Clancey into a small interview room and gestured to an empty chair where he sat and dropped folded hands into his ample lap.

"Truly a pleasure to meet you, Detective. 'Tis a shame it's under such dire circumstances."

The man seated across from Shane filled the bill of a stereotypical Irish priest with his graying red hair, round stomach, and twinkling blue eyes. A casting agent couldn't have done a better job. "I'm a bit relieved you're here. You may have heard there's been another teenager murder. Lexi Horne. Already the media's tagged her the 'Hollywood Nanny'" He didn't give the priest time to acknowledge if he'd heard the news or not. "Her parents arrived a little while ago and are with Detective Collins in the next room. They caught the first available flight last night and I think they're still in a state of shock. When we're through here, that's if you don't mind, I'd like you to meet with them for a few minutes to offer support. I can't think of anyone better qualified. Especially so because they're concerned that Lexi died without receiving the sacrament. Perhaps, you could offer some measure of reassurance. It'd be one less worry for them."

Shane watched a frown form on the priest's face as he drew his bushy eyebrows together. Contrary to what he expected, Father Clancy narrowed his eyes as if considering his suggestion.

"Well..." The priest pressed his lips into a firm line.

"I'm not suggesting a discourse on the inscrutable ways of the will of God but only a few words of consolation. Support offered from a priest might prevent them from totally breaking down."

"Of course." Father Clancy's face relaxed. "Please excuse the unusual reaction, but I'm shocked. I knew Lexi." He exhaled through clenched teeth. "I was her spiritual director. Lexi was a lovely young woman. Devoted to the church and her charge—little Emma—Emma Andrews. She telephoned me only...only yesterday. Excited she was. Had gotten a brand new job working on the *telly*." He closed his eyes.

Shane guessed he was offering a prayer for Lexi's soul. He absently lifted a pen and tapped it against the edge of the table as he waited to carry on with the interview. The longer he tapped, the more baffled he became. Not only did the good padre know victim number three; he knew victim number four as well. What kind of odds is that?

Father Clancy opened his eyes. Shane noticed they were wet.

"I've been so distracted lately. I haven't had a wee moment to even scan the front page of the *Times* or turn on the evening news. Most days I don't know if I'm coming or going. I'm up to here." The priest paused as he raised his hand to his forehead. "With all the intricate details of establishing a shelter for homeless teens."

After dropping the pen onto the laminated table top, Shane pressed his thumb against his chin.

"Your darlin' wife has generously offered to help." Father Clancy lowered his sight to the back of Shane's laptop that acted as a barrier between the two men.

"Um, yeah. She told me." Shane cleared his throat then took a sip from the water bottle next to his computer. "Lexi's death brings the total to four murdered teenaged girls. Amazingly so, you happen to know two of the victims." He raised his eyebrows.

"Not so strange, I'm thinkin'. After all, the purpose of me mission is to save youngsters from the very tangible dangers of the streets. And Lexi, well, we met the usual way. At church. Though I only served there for maybe five, six months, we got on right away and forged an easy friendship. Even though I've moved around a lot during the past year or so, we stayed in contact. She's the last person I'd ever imagine being the target of a serial killer. Or anybody else. Lexi could light up a room with her effervescent spirit. And her heart." The priest shook his head. "She was so compassionate, understanding. A kind, trusting soul. Could that have been her downfall?"

Shane ignored his question. "The church where you met Lexi would be?"

"St. Timothy."

Shane turned his attention to the laptop and tapped the keys while still eyeing the priest. When he stopped typing, he pulled the computer's screen down a couple of inches. "Victim number three is Eliana Mendoza. Now I'd like you to think carefully and if you can offer anything—no matter how insignificant—as to who you think may have wanted her dead."

Father Clancy leaned back in the chair and tilted his head upward as if studying the ceiling tiles. "After rescuing her from a wretched life of prostitution, I settled Eliana into a safe house. At the time, there was no reason to doubt she'd find a sense of security and well-being in the care of a kind, concerned volunteer. Anyway, she quickly bonded with the elderly man from Guanajuato, Mexico. Tomás Delgado. Have you spoken to him?"

Shane nodded.

"Then you already know she loved the old gentleman. Took care of his chickens. And Tomás' big, ginger tabby followed Eliana everywhere." The priest pursed his lips and shook his head. "It can't be. Please don't tell me, you suspect Tomás had something to do with Eliana's death?"

Shane shifted his sight to the keyboard. He typed the priest's question after finding it odd that he was trying to pinpoint the blame onto a sixty-seven-year-old cabby who generously offered to take in the homeless, undocumented minor.

"Don't get me wrong, Detective. Tomás Delgado is a living saint. I can only pray that you'd change your mind about your suspicions, so." A frown marred the priest's smooth forehead. "Hmmm. The only viable suspect I can think of would be the shameful pimp who forced a pure, spotless child into such an unholy enterprise. Goes by the name of 'Money'. I haven't the slightest idea as to what his Christian name might be."

"You've met this man?"

"Eliana pointed him out once when we were in my vehicle. The instant she spotted him, the poor lass crouched down on the floorboard and shook like a leaf."

Shane stroked his chin considering the information. "I'll be right back. I'd like to show you some pictures."

Shane hurried out of the room, with the laptop under his arm, in the direction of his office. It took only a couple of seconds to open the database. After typing in the keyword 'Money' under nicknames and aliases, he scrolled down the list. He stopped when he spied it. The face staring out at him looked Slavic with high cheekbones, light hair, and blue eyes. A snarl curled his thin lips. He jotted down the ex-con's name. Pavel Titov. Emigrated in 2007 from Moscow. His numerous offenses included theft, possession and distribution of drugs, assault. Typical bad guy. He checked the dates and was surprised that Titov hadn't had any altercations for over two years. With a few keystrokes, he selected Titov's photo along with seven other similar faces. He printed out the page and then returned to the interview room.

Shane handed the priest the sheet of paper. "Take your time, Father. Do you recognize anyone on the page?"

It took only a second for the priest to place his finger squarely on one of the photos. "This is Money."

CHAPTER TEN

Beth wrapped her hands around the hot mug as she glanced around the room. Though their houses sat nearly side-by-side, Marjorie Hammond's living room exuded a sense of warmth lacking in Skye's sterile, pristine rooms. When the maid led her into the living area and offered her a cup of coffee, the only thing Beth noticed were the colors. A virtual riot of hues and tints, light and shade. Not to say the living room wasn't stylish; it was—and elegant too. Marjorie, no doubt, had paid a fortune to a top designer to come up with the improbable color scheme. The walls glowed a warm orange, the ceiling a pale green, while the rich, dark wood floor gleamed. The cream-colored furniture, modern and sleek, held red, blue, and green accent pillows. *Amazingly, it works*, she thought with a shake of her head.

She took a gulp of coffee hoping the caffeine would settle her nerves. Shane's voice played in her head. *Just get her to talk about Lexi.*

Even though she'd initially found Marjorie as irritating as fingernails scratching a chalkboard, over the past couple of years, Marjorie had grown on her. Surely, she wasn't her *ould flower*, best friend, and never would be, but she found Marjorie amusing, and in her own quirky way, a kind soul. It still made her chuckle when Marjorie put on airs or acted as an authority on anything from astronomy to pedicures.

Though Marjorie had married one of the most successful lawyers in Los Angeles, Beth feared they were mismatched. Marc with his Ivy League education seemed to have little in common with Marjorie, a mere high school graduate preoccupied with shopping, fashion, and the latest Hollywood scandal. Beth frowned with the thought that Marjorie, the youngest and prettiest of Marc's three former spouses, was nothing more than a trophy wife.

She placed the mug on top of the marquetry-inlaid coffee table and swept her eyes around the room once again. "Oh, but how that girl loves to gossip and laugh and spend her husband's money, so," she whispered. She still found it a bit startling that she was only two years older than Marjorie. *Sometimes, I feel like I'm her old gray-haired granny.* Her musing was interrupted when Marjorie seemed to float into the room.

The diminutive woman carried a tray fashioned from acacia wood. A silver platter sat within its raised lip offering an artfully arrayed selection of finger sandwiches. The crusts had been sliced away, and various breads—wheat, white, and rye—stuffed with shrimp, ham, cheese, turkey, and cucumbers assured Beth of a delectable treat.

"It's so cool you called. We haven't seen each other like forever. How long has it been?"

Marjorie placed the tray on top of the coffee table next to the short stack of stoneware sandwich plates and the cut crystal bowl filled with kumquats, clementines, and oranges—fruit to match the décor.

"New Year's Eve?"

"OMG that was an awesome party." Marjorie narrowed her deep brown eyes. "You came alone, right?"

Beth responded with a quick nod. "Shane had to work. A busy night for law enforcement." She lifted the coffee mug and took a long sip. Though Marjorie's voice filled her ears, she'd stopped listening. Instead, she offered a quick prayer then wondered how she was going to pry the information out of her. Beth harbored a slight doubt about Shane's hunch, but she believed in intuition, even if it was based on years of experience as a detective.

"You don't like it?"

"Huh?" Beth refocused. "I'm sorry. Like what?"

"The room. I've been totally preoccupied with the makeover. And honestly, I thought it would never come together. We added the finishing touches just last week." Marjorie paused to glance around the room. "Oh, come on Beth. I'm as nervous as a whore in church. What do you think?"

"Honestly, I'm a wee bit stunned. Quite a change from the last time I was here. But, I love it. The room is perfect." She heard a sigh pass Marjorie's lips. She wondered why her opinion mattered but then remembered Marjorie's inferiority issues. "You really shouldn't have gone to so much trouble. Everything looks lovely." She motioned to the tray of sandwiches.

"Martha, my housekeeper, whipped it together," Marjorie said with a snap of her fingers. "She's a whiz in the kitchen."

Beth unfolded a pink linen napkin and draped it across her lap. She glanced at the expansive patio doors and caught a glimpse of the Pacific, its blue-green water shimmering in the brilliant sunshine. She imagined herself standing on the shore with her feet sinking into the wet sand. The desire to be there, or anywhere else, grabbed her like a dog gnawing a bone. She shifted her line of vision across the well-appointed room toward the foyer. "I'm such a scatterbrain. I totally forgot about a meeting with…" She saw the light fade from Marjorie's eyes. Then she remembered Shane. "Ah, but never mind. It'll wait, truly."

It's do or die time.

"You've heard the awful news, I take it?"

Marjorie glanced up from her coffee cup.

"About poor Lexi."

"Have a sandwich." Marjorie extended a hand in the direction of the platter.

Damnation, I knew it. Tightlipped Marjorie. She knows something as sure as the Pope's Catholic, but she's going to keep it to herself, Beth thought, as a tinge of panic began to rise.

"You mean you haven't heard?" Beth didn't give her time to answer. "Well, I'm surprised. Usually, you're the first to know anything important that's going on." She saw the color rise beneath Marjorie's perfect tan flushing her cheeks.

"Of course, I know." Indignation laced Marjorie's words. "As a matter of fact, I know more about Lexi's murder then you'll hear on the news."

Marjorie dropped a miniature shrimp salad sandwich onto her plate. She stuck her index finger between her lips to lick clean the trace of mayonnaise dressing that had dripped there.

As if realizing her faux pas, she lifted a napkin and attempted to clean the already spotless finger. "I might even wind up as a witness for the prosecution."

The tenseness at the base of Beth's shoulders begin to relax. "Witness? Dear Lord, you saw the murder happen?"

"Nothing like that. But, I was literally like the last person to see Lexi alive. Besides the killer, that is. Anyway, the police insisted I give a statement. So late last night, I had to rush over to the station. Can you believe it?" She reached for her mug and took a quick sip. "But it was kinda like a big letdown. Not nearly as interesting as they make it look on TV." She took a bite of the sandwich.

Beth ran her hand across the napkin in her lap. She had to keep Marjorie focused on Lexi's murder. "I'm not quite following. If you weren't an eyewitness to the crime, holy Mother of God, the police don't think, it can't be," she lowered her voice to just above a whisper, "you're a person of interest?"

"Me?" Her plate clattered against the inlaid oak and walnut table. "Don't be ridiculous."

"I'd never dream you'd hurt a fly, but Marjorie, you're acting kind of strange. Uneasy like."

"Honestly, I've been a nervous wreck. I thought Skye had a break-in, and I was damn curious, so I walked over there to find out. I could never've imagined, like in a million years, that Lexi had been murdered. It's hard to swallow something that horrible could happen around here with all the security. Skye has surveillance cameras. Just about everyone does. But, I heard they'd been tampered with. Marc thinks it was an inside job or someone Lexi knew. And I agree with him. A hundred percent." She folded her arms across her ample chest.

Beth took a sip of the now tepid coffee. "What makes you so sure?"

Marjorie shrugged.

Beth pursed her lip. "My *fey* is telling me you're scared." She closed her eyes and swayed back and forth a few times.

"*Fey*? Oh my God, your sixth sense?"

Beth hated lying. Especially since she didn't need acute intuitive powers to realize that Marjorie was holding back. Marjorie knew something critical about Lexi or the murder—or both. She peeked at Marjorie from behind heavy lids and noticed she'd moved forward in the chair and seemed to be lost in thought. Beth flashed her eyes open.

Marjorie jumped. "You know, don't you?"

Beth showed no emotion nor did she answer.

Marjorie sprang from the cushy chair and moved toward the far wall, which housed blocky bookcases on either side of the stone fireplace. She pulled out a small, leather clad volume. The click–clackiness of her stilettos tapping the floor filled the silent air as she hurried toward Beth. Instead of reclaiming her seat, she settled next to Beth on the couch.

"The answer to Lexi's murder is in this."

The book's hand-tooled burgundy leather binding displayed an intricate floral design. It reminded Beth of ones she'd seen in an exquisite leather shop east of the Duomo di Firenze. She touched the book's cover certain that the craftsmanship was Italian. "Beautiful," she said. "Like a fine piece of art." She slipped her fingers under the cover and lifted it. Marjorie clamped her hand over Beth's.

"I've made a mistake." Marjorie jumped up with the book clutched against her chest. "It was silly of me." She stepped toward the bookcase.

"I'm getting really strong vibes," Beth said with a rising surge of excitement. Come hell or high water, she wasn't going to let Marjorie back out now.

Marjorie froze. After a couple seconds, she broke the silence. "Oh, what the hell. I'm a bit scared of that *fey* thing." She returned to the couch. "It all started yesterday," she said reclaiming her spot next to Beth. "It was one of those hectic days that ended with a grueling workout. My trainer is relentless, and I was literally exhausted. I knew Marc was working late, so he wouldn't be home, and it was Martha's day off, so I'd be on my own. I was basically starving but too tired to even pop something into the microwave. Luckily, driving down the street, I spotted Lexi going into Skye's house. She agreed to run down to that new gourmet shop to pick up a few odds and ends. She got back here so quick, I hadn't even stepped into the tub yet." She tucked a lock of bleached blond hair behind her ear, exposing the two-carat diamond stud gracing her earlobe.

"When we got to the kitchen, I wanted to grab the sandwich and devour it. I mean the aroma of the roasted turkey on wheat made my stomach literally rumble. I hadn't realized how starved I was. I just wanted to shoo her away."

"Did she seem upset?"

"Not really. Maybe a little antsy. But she proceeded to drive me totally nuts. Lexi kept rooting around in her bag looking for the receipt. I told her to forget it. I pulled out a twenty and handed it to her, but no, that wasn't good enough. Turns out she's a stickler for exact change." Marjorie looked upward with a roll of her eyes. "Finally, like after five whole minutes, she found the damn thing. Came out to something like thirty-three dollars."

Beth raised her eyebrows but didn't say a word.

"Well, I asked her to pick up some fruit, yogurt, a couple of sides, and they have the yummiest desserts to die for. Anyway, I didn't have any small bills, so I handed her an additional twenty. Can you believe it—she starts digging around in her bag again. She pulled out her phone, a brush, a compact, and this book before finding her wallet. It seemed to take like forever. My stomach was growling, and though it might seem a bit harsh now that she's dead, I just wanted her to get the hell out so I could eat."

Beth felt like screaming. Marjorie's endless droning was driving her mad. Instead, she clenched her teeth. A large cinnabar vase caught her attention as she tried to suppress the rising irritation. Streams of brilliant vermilion played against the wall as sunlight filtered through the Murano glass.

"I do suffer from low blood sugar and was by that time feeling totally faint," Marjorie said.

Beth caught herself from telling Marjorie that she was only inventing an excuse to justify her behavior. She hoped Marjorie wouldn't rattle on for much longer as she widened her eyes feigning interest.

"Instead of standing there like a total idiot, I focused on the book. Really didn't look like anything that would belong to Lexi. Figured it could be Zach's. He's got totally good taste. And I admit, I was curious." Marjorie turned the book over. She began rubbing her thumb in a circular fashion against the cover while staring straight ahead. "After all, Beth, she was driving me crazy as she pulled out one bill after another. Oh God, then she started with the coins. Counting every penny. I literally wanted to pull my hair out." She glanced at Beth sideways for a second before dropping the book onto her lap. "To make a long story short, I picked up the book."

"Lexi saw you—"

"She was so busy counting out those damn coins that she didn't pay any attention to what I was doing. I moved next to the cappuccino machine but didn't get a chance to even open the cover when Lexi said she was heading back to Skye's." She paused taking a deep breath. "She'd already thrown all her stuff back in her purse and didn't say a word about the book. I assumed it couldn't be all that important if she didn't even realize it was missing. So, I dropped it into a drawer. Granted, I did have my back to Lexi so she couldn't exactly see, but really, you would've thought she'd notice it was missing."

"You stole her book?"

"Of course not. I only borrowed it. I had every intention of giving it back. Planned to tell her that she left it behind." She turned the volume over a couple of times then raised it in Beth's direction. "I assumed it was full of dull poetry or some other highbrow stuff taken straight from Zach's library. And actually, I forgot all about it until the coffee had brewed and I was ready to dive into that chocolate dream of a dessert. It was then I grabbed the book and settled down for a quick glance expecting it to be boring as hell. Boy, was I surprised."

"Not poetry."

"Hell no. Take a look for yourself." She handed the book to Beth.

She lifted the cover and scanned the first handwritten page. Marjorie had pinched Lexi's diary.

"Look here," Marjorie said flipping through some pages. "Lexi writes that she thought someone was stalking her."

"Where?" Beth strained to see the words beneath the woman's fingers. Before she could read a complete sentence, Marjorie closed the book.

"The problem is, I don't know what to do. After all, I was planning to return it to Lexi."

"Why didn't you?"

"Because I wanted to read it first. Trust me, there's a lot of surprising stuff written on those pages. Reads like pure fantasy compared to how she acted so straight-laced and proper. Stiff as a board. And just as close-mouthed. Sometimes she'd give me one of those snotty looks like she was judging me." She fiddled with the wide diamond encrusted band on her finger. "I finished reading it around ten. Even though it was kinda late, I wanted to give it back. Sooner or later, Lexi was gonna realize it was gone. So, I walked over and saw the cop cars."

"Shouldn't you have turned it into the police?"

"How was I supposed to know Lexi was dead? I figured I'd see her when all the hoopla settled down."

Makes sense, Beth conceded with a curt nod.

"Oh my God, Beth. You would not believe how belligerent those damn detectives were to me. I bet your husband would never be disrespectful to a law abiding citizen who was only interested in her friend's welfare." Her voice had steadily risen to one decibel short of a screech.

Beth swallowed hard but couldn't muster an ounce of sympathy for Marjorie or her inferiority complex. "They were perhaps trying to do their job."

"Well, regardless. They made me furious. Could have spit nails."

"How awful," Beth said determined not to enlighten Marjorie that one of the rude detectives had been her Shane.

"One of them finally used his brain. Realized that since I'd recently seen Lexi, maybe I knew some important detail that could crack the case wide open. But, that's the problem."

"Problem?"

"I have the murdered nanny's diary. What the hell am I supposed to say? Here you go, officer. I stole Lexi's diary, and now I'd like to turn it in. That'll go over good. You think?"

"You could always say Lexi mistakenly left it in your kitchen. Only a wee bit of a white lie, to be sure."

"I guess. But what if they hook me up to one of those polygraph machines and ask if I stole the diary. What then?"

"A bit extreme. I doubt they'd do that."

"But how would I explain not handing over the diary sooner? I don't think 'it slipped my mind' would work."

"Did you talk it over with Marc?"

"Good God, no. He already thinks I'm too nosy as it is. But that's the least of it. Marc's planning to run for office. State Senator. He's going to announce his candidacy next month." Marjorie lowered her head as if studying the hot pink enamel that colored her toenails. "If it got out that his wife is a thief...what a scandal that'll be. His political career over before it started."

"I think you're blowing this all out of proportion."

"If they hook me up to a lie detector and the truth comes out, Marc will divorce me. I know he will. He really wants to be a senator." She squeezed her eyes shut.

Beth reached for a cucumber sandwich and took a bite. The cream cheese's tangy flavor lingered on her tongue as it melded with the taste of the rye. She grabbed another one. As she chewed, it dawned on her that under normal circumstance, she wouldn't mind seeing Marjorie squirm. But this was different. A major scandal could be brewing that might topple political aspirations and well as dissolve a marriage. In addition, the mishandling of a vital piece of evidence in a major case would discredit the LASD and ruin Shane's stellar reputation. Even if he is about to throw in the towel. She swallowed the last gulp of her now cold coffee.

Marjorie rested her head against Beth's shoulder. The woman trembled, and Beth guessed she was trying hard not to cry.

Marjorie's problem had now become her problem. *If she wasn't so feckin' nosy, the problem of Lexi's diary wouldn't exist. It would be locked up in an evidence box where it belonged.*

Marjorie murmured under her breath.

With an abrupt turn of her shoulder, Beth jolted Marjorie. "Look, you made a colossal mistake. But we can figure this out if we put our heads together."

"I can't turn it into the police. What if they dust the pages for fingerprints?"

"Goodness. You've just left the realm of reality."

"They'll figure out I read it. It must be illegal to read someone's diary. Like reading someone else's mail." Rising panic filled Marjorie's voice.

"You must be getting a wee bit lightheaded again. Eat another sandwich." Beth rubbed her temple with the palm of her hand. Though no real solution jumped at her, she realized the most pressing issue was to relieve Marjorie of the diary. "Why don't I take diary?"

"Why would you do that?"

"Because it would get you out of a bind."

Marjorie nodded, even though tears began to well in the corners of her eyes. "I'll give it to my Shane."

"Don't do that. We should burn it. Or we could go to the marina and board our yacht. When we're like miles from shore, we can throw the damn book overboard. Get rid of it for good." Marjorie nodded her head frantically like a bobble head in a car traveling over a bumpy road.

"How would that be fair to Lexi?" Beth grasped Marjorie's hand. It felt ice cold. "To the people who love her? Who need to know why she was so brutally murdered."

Marjorie hung her head. A lock of hair fell over her hairband obscuring her eyes.

"You don't have to worry about giving the diary to my Shane. He'll protect you because you're my friend."

"He will?"

"The diary is what's important. Once he has it, he'll fix it so that you or the department doesn't look bad."

"He'll cover it up?"

Beth didn't have a clue what Shane would do. But he'd protect the department, and, for her, he'd also protect Marjorie.

"With my Shane in charge, there'll be no scandal. I promise."

Marjorie lifted her head. "You must think I'm a terrible friend. I even missed your wedding, but really, it couldn't be helped since we always spend the month of June in Bermuda. I should've had you and Shane over for dinner like as soon as we got back. I'll make it up to you. I promise."

"Forget it. Anyway, you're going to be a busy lass helping Marc with his campaign. With you on his arm, he's bound to look like a winner."

CHAPTER ELEVEN

Shane returned the phone to its cradle. He spun his chair around and faced Collins with a broad smile that caused the skin around his eyes to crinkle. Collins jerked away from his desk monitor, his brows raised in anticipation.

"They got him. According to STF's Detective Waller, he didn't put up a fight. Came willingly. Should be ready for us in about thirty minutes."

"Yes." Collins pumped the air with his fist. "If this pans out, we're gonna do some celebrating tonight. God Almighty, it'll be so damn sweet getting that son of a bitch off the streets. Those poor girls face enough danger from their pimps and johns—let alone the added fear of running into a psycho killer." He paused a moment. "Arresting this guy will make my career. If that happens, I could retire today and be completely content." Collins blew out a mouthful of air.

"Yeah, right. Fat chance that'll ever happen. I think police work is imprinted in your DNA. Me, on the other hand, that's an entirely different story." Shane glanced at his watch. "But let's not count our chickens before they hatch, if you get my drift." He stood and took a few steps toward the door. "I'm going to Starbucks. You want coffee or that Chai tea you're so crazy about?"

"Better make it coffee. Might turn out to be a long interrogation. That's if he doesn't lawyer up."

Shane hummed under his breath as he walked out of the office.

***

Shane and Collins entered Interrogation Room 1-A. Shane was surprised to see Pavel Titov dressed in an expensive three-piece suit as he sat with his hands folded on top of the table. A serene expression claimed the young man's face as if he was waiting for the commencement of a business meeting instead of a police interrogation. He sported a close-cropped haircut, and every blond strand sat neatly in place. His pale skin had a pinkish cast as if he'd been in the sun too long without protection. Titov lifted his head and eyed the detectives as they pulled out the wooden chairs and sat.

"Mr. Titov, I'm Detective Dalton, and this is Detective Collins."

Titov leaned back in his chair and folded his arms across his broad chest.

"Anything I can get you? Coffee, water, cigarettes?" Collins asked.

"Nah. What is it that you want to speak with me?"

Shane detected only the slightest accent. "We're investigating the recent murders of four teenage girls. You've heard about it?"

Titov shrugged.

"We believe you knew one of the victims. Eliana Mendoza," Collins said.

Shane noticed Titov's jaw muscles tighten.

"Yeah. So what?" Titov moved closer to the table.

"Wasn't she one of your, um, employees?" Shane asked calmly as he looked directly into the suspect's icy, blue eyes.

"Eliana," Titov said with disgust. "She was no good to me. Always crying when I touch her. I always be gentle with that one. She was beautiful. The most beautiful..." He clenched his teeth together, waited a couple seconds, and then said, "She was an aggravation. Irritate me big time with her endless praying to some imaginary god. And tell me, what good did that do?" He glanced at the diamond ring on his right pinky. Jerking his head, he stared straight ahead. "Yeah, I heard she's dead."

Shane took a long sip from his coffee cup. "Did you know that Eliana was brought into this country illegally?"

"I have nothing to do with what happen to that girl. I'm a businessman. I run a legit company. Import gems. Pearls. I have distributors. I'm clean."

"Impressive," Collins said. "But the way I understand it, you also import young woman for the purpose of prostitution. The human flesh trade."

"Lie."

"Cut the crap. You're nothing but a yellow-bellied pimp. Hiding under the skirts of under-aged girls in order to make a thick bankroll of money. Dirty money." Shane said the words evenly as he fought to reign in his anger and project a professional attitude. "It's no damn mystery. You offer hope to dirt-poor parents south of the border by promising that their young daughters will be able to break free from poverty's death grip. You tell them their little girls' tears will dry up because their bellies will finally be filled. After stuffing their heads with possibilities of endless opportunities of education... careers... the goddamn American dream...

they buy into your scheme. When they clutch the few measly dollars you give them in exchange for their most precious, beloved possessions, what the hell do you do? You pimp them out. Treat them no better than slaves."

Titov drew his lips into a tight line. His eyes flitted between the two detectives. "What proof do you have? Nothing."

Shane stared at Titov. The Russian's eyes glared like the glint of steel. "Eliana escaped your hold along with a couple other girls from your stable. They found help. A way out. And it angered you. Made you furious."

"So angry you were burning mad," Collins continued Shane's lead. "I know how crappy it feels when your ego is bruised. Your manhood questioned. You must've been wondering how those little slips of girls, those bitches, did this to you. Man, it's understandable. You had to show them who's boss."

"Your rep was in jeopardy. You couldn't let that slide." Shane offered Titov his opened palms as if offering a gesture of support. "Granted, you're no angel. Never claimed to be squeaky-clean. Working the streets, you must've learned a lot. Including not to take nothing off of nobody."

"A guy in your position needs to know how to defend himself." Collins leaned back in his chair. "And you do. But I think you were getting weary of the drug scene. Too hands on. Too right in your face. Why not let someone else do the dirty work for a change? Huh? Let someone else work the streets for you. After all, you already earned your cred. You're successful. Someone to be reckoned with. They don't call you Money for nothing."

"Yeah," Shane agreed. "Who the hell did those damn hookers think they were anyway? You showed them who's in control alright. And since they decided to cross you," he said with a shrug, "did you have a choice? You *had* to put them in their place."

"I take that cigarette now," Titov said.

Collins removed the package of Newports from his jacket pocket and tossed it in Titov's direction.

Titov tapped one free and held it between his thumb and index finger. He shook his head and muttered what Shane took for a Russian word. Titov said the word again, louder, "*Papirosi.*" Then he added, "Cigarette not *Belemorkamal*. Only thing worth smoking."

Shane watched him rip a match free and strike it with a jarring motion. Titov looked at the jumping flame a full five seconds before lighting the cigarette. After taking a deep drag, he forced the smoke out through his nostrils.

"Cheap American cigarettes. Damn filters. Like inhaling *focking* breath mint." He took another drag then crushed it out in the blocky glass ashtray. "You think I did Eliana in. Stupid detectives. The only thing I do with Eliana is *fock* her. She never work streets. She was mine. And now she is dead." He half-shrugged. "Big *focking* deal. Like I said, all she do is cry and pray to picture of man on cross. Gives me nothing I want. Stupid girl."

Shane glanced at Collins and watched his eyes narrow to mere slits as he rested his chin on top of his balled fists. He recognized his partner's pose. Collins was about to play another angle. *Good*, Shane thought, because he was fresh out of ideas.

"Look, Money."

"Call me Mr. Titov. I have now earned respect. I import luxury items from my homeland. I have big bank account. Nice house. Fancy car. I do this with the law. " He snapped his fingers. "Pavel Titov is success."

"Just a few more questions," Collins said. "Where were you the afternoon of April 28th? Say between the hours of noon and two."

Titov looked straight ahead. He lifted his hand, pressed it against his lavender silk tie, and then tapped his chest. "I tell you, I don't see Eliana no more. And I don't give a damn about hookers. Dead or alive."

"Give us something, man. Your alibi checks out and you're off the hook," Collins said.

"On Monday, I had meeting with my distributor in Miami." Titov leaned back in the chair as his lips curled into a sneer. "You need names?"

Both detectives nodded.

"I give you names. But first here." He reached inside his breast pocket and withdrew a boarding pass. "I just get back in LA three hours ago."

Shane took the folded sheet of paper. Opening it, he scanned the document. Looked authentic. But it'd be easy enough to check the airline for verification.

"I stay at the *Palms Hotel* for one week. Miami is hot and sticky—muggy— like sauna, but hotel has pool, and I drink much vodka on the rocks."

The amused expression covering Titov's face only aggravated Shane further as the all-too-familiar tightening in his stomach made him want to swallow a handful of antacids. The thought of arresting Titov for Eliana's murder was quickly turning into a pipe dream.

"My partner, Yuri Kozlov, we talk about expanding the business to *Russian*

Gifts and Keepsakes. See, only rich people buy expensive Russian pearls, diamonds, alexandrite. So, we begin to think big. Decide to import items for people like you," he said with laughing eyes. "People with not much money. Things like *Matrushka*—nesting dolls—*Lomonosov* porcelain, amber jewelry. Printers working on catalogue to be sent through the mail."

Shane couldn't believe what he was hearing. Ex-con turned entrepreneur. His gut was telling him Titov was full of it. That his import business was only a cover for illegal activities or something equally nefarious like collusion with the Russian Mafia.

Collins typed the specifics that Titov offered into his laptop. A couple times, he interrupted the man asking for the spelling of a particular Russian name. Like a careening surge of rushing water breaking through a dam, the information Titov supplied—meeting dates, times, and locations—tumbled from his lips. By the time he finished, Shane was certain Titov wasn't their guy. He also had no doubt that his captain, Lorraine Rosnick, would assign him the task to verify Titov's alibi.

CHAPTER TWELVE

Beth looked at her watch. She blinked, finding it hard to believe more than two hours had passed since she curled up in her favorite chair and opened Lexi's diary. Though she telephoned Shane several times, she hadn't been able to reach him and decided against leaving a message. She'd rather tell him in person about her grand success with Marjorie. Now the leather bound tome lay closed next to her laptop. It hadn't taken her long to abandon the cushy chair for her desk and computer.

After noting Marjorie's paranoia about leaving fingerprints on the diary's pages, she'd decided not to take any chances. As she leaned back in her office chair, she peeled off the white cotton gloves and tossed them into the desk's center drawer. Marjorie hadn't been exaggerating when she said the diary read like a fantastical piece of fiction. While lingering over the handwritten words, Lexi's precise penmanship bore an elegant flair, Beth tried to recall her initial impression of the young nanny. Each time, she came up with the same appraisal: reserved, polite, and pleasant with an engaging smile. And a dimple in her right cheek. Dedicated to Emma. Pretty, tall, and willowy, Lexi had long dark hair and wide, expressive eyes. The camera would love her. According to the diary, so did a collection of men—men whom Lexi found insincere, as she doubted the depth of their professed affection, and she sensed a baser instinct triggered their devotion.

As she'd poured over the pages, Beth couldn't help but feel empathy for the slain nanny. Like herself, Lexi had been brought up in a strict home environment and learned the lessons of moral fortitude until it became ingrained into her outlook on life. Several pages waxed about her being an old-fashioned girl who dreamed of a wedding day when she'd wear a white organza gown and carry a bouquet of orange blossoms. Now that and every other dream she ever imagined had been snuffed out.

When her gloved fingers had moved along the lines of prose filling the pages, Beth surprisingly forged a connection with Lexi. The diary painted pictures of a vibrant life eager to seize all that was good and exciting in this world. But there was also a darker side—mentions of illicit love affairs, marriages irretrievably broken, unbridled jealousies, and crushed dreams.

The investigation of the girl's death belonged to the realm of the detectives, but a growing compulsion to discover the meaning of the young nanny's death gripped Beth. The very idea of launching her own investigation was laughable, yet halfway through the diary, she reached for her laptop and meticulously typed the important details outlined in the diary, which spanned the final three months of Lexi Horne's life.

Beth recorded every substantial tidbits from doctor appointments to the names of Lexi's friends, her ex-boyfriend, and her current love. The name that puzzled her the most was one that wasn't clearly identified on any of the diary pages. Lexi's "whopper of a mistake" was when she'd allowed herself to be seduced by an unnamed actor. Lexi had nicknamed her lover 'P.C.' Beth immediately construed that the initials stood for *Prince Charming*.

After reading the diary's final page, Beth concluded the mysterious suitor lacked even an ounce of charm. However, in one of the early entries, Lexi explained that P.C. had ended the affair with no explanation. Beth reconsidered her assessment. Had Lexi's reflections been colored with the brush of bitterness?

Her eyes focused on a baffling yet intriguing sentence she'd typed into the computer. "Got that ace up my sleeve. When I play it, P.C. will be putty in my hands." She drummed her fingers against the desk's edge and sensed that an important piece of the puzzle was missing. Lexi had written of being smitten and falling for one Charles "Trey" Blyth Wickham, III. But if that was true, why was P.C. still important to her? What did Lexi have on him? Could she be blackmailing him?

When Beth first started taking notes, she believed she'd hand over the type written pages to Shane. But now, she wasn't so sure. Maybe she should just hand him the diary—not even tell him she'd read it.

She sipped a mugful of tea as she reviewed her notes. Lexi had written about many celebrities she'd crossed paths with from Academy Award winners to bit players. Her Prince Charming could have been any one of these men.

Beth almost dropped the earthenware mug as fragmented images shot through her mind. She clutched the handle and squeezed her eyes shut. Unsure if she could chalk up the sudden insight to her sixth sense, the feeling was so strong she didn't doubt it. The question of Lexi's lover had been made clear, and the thought of it turned her stomach.

Beth jumped as the doorbell sounded. Bothered by the interruption, she clicked off the computer and headed to the foyer. She yanked the door open, and her jaw dropped as she took in Skye's appearance. Her usual perfect complexion looked pasty, and a sprinkling of acne had erupted on her chin. The actress looked more like a waif than a movie star. Her damp hair hung around stooped shoulders, and tears welled in Skye's red-rimmed, swollen eyes.

She reached for her hand and pulled Skye close. "What a horror you've been through."

Skye's lithe body shook in her embrace. Without a word, Beth stepped away, linked arms with her friend, and led her into the sitting room. Skye collapsed into a plush, chenille-covered chair.

"You need a nice cup of tea," Beth said as Skye covered her face with her hands. She stepped closer wanting to comfort Skye but felt inadequate having never seen her in such a state. She'd experienced many of Skye's varied emotions from euphoria to righteous indignation, particularly the time she didn't get the part in a film: one she adamantly believed she deserved. But never like this: dejected, tearful, seemingly lost. "A cup of lavender tea will do the trick. You'll see." Though Beth preferred her Earl Grey, she always kept a variety of herbal teas on hand in case she, or particularly Shane of late, needed something more relaxing.

Skye squared her shoulders and wiped her face with the back of her hand even though Beth noticed her eyes were already dry. "It's been unimaginable. I'm angry and frustrated and a bit scared, too." Her voice had lowered to a whisper. "Yesterday I thought the worst thing that could happen would be if Lexi got an acting job and ran out on me." She rubbed her eyes with her fingertips. "But Lexi murdered in my house. That's too much to take."

She looked into Skye's eyes. If the eyes are the window of the soul, Beth couldn't see much there. Only a deep emptiness. "You rest while I make us some tea."

"I'm starving, actually. Haven't had a morsel since..." Skye shrugged.

"I've got just the thing. How does a piping hot bowl of minestrone sound? Loaded with vegetables and simmered in a delicious tangy broth."

"I don't want you to go to a lot of trouble. Just a couple slices of wheat toast and a bit of jam will do."

"Don't be silly. No trouble at all. I bet I bought a quart of it from that grand Italian restaurant that—"

"Oh. You didn't make it. Okay. Soup sounds good. Really good."

Beth wanted to roll her eyes in exasperation knowing it was Shane who planted the idea into Skye's head that she was a terrible cook. Instead of launching a defense, she hurried toward the door. She glimpsed over her shoulder before exiting the room. Skye had leaned back against the chair and closed her eyes. Beth felt an upwelling of pity—for the slain nanny, for Skye, for the other victims of the senseless killings—and blinked back a rash of unexpected tears.

In the kitchen, she decided to brew the tea, so she raised the electric teapot and filled the Belleek pot with steaming water. After a minute, she dumped the water into the sink, refilled the pot, and tossed in a couple of tea bags. As the tea steeped, she spooned a hefty serving of minestrone into a bowl and placed it inside the microwave. From a cabinet, she withdrew a box of imported butter cookies. Within a few moments, she'd prepared the lavender tea, arranged the cookies, and placed sugar, cream, and cups on top a large platter. With careful steps, she entered the den carrying the over-stocked serving tray.

Skye blinked her eyes open. "I must've dozed off," she said as if apologizing.

"If you like, I have a lovely guest bedroom waiting for you."

"I wish I could, but I have to head over to the Beverly Hills house. Emma is upset."

"She must be heartbroken, so."

"Emma loved Lexi. When I'd finally admitted the fact that she preferred the nanny's company to mine, to be honest, I felt a stab of jealousy." Skye didn't wait for Beth's reaction. "Maybe that's why I never cared for Lexi. But hell, it wasn't just the nanny. My daughter probably feels closer to Alma, Zach's cook, than she does to me. Or her ballet teacher, riding instructor...or...or Zach." She lifted the cup Beth had poured for her and blew across the hot liquid. "Maybe I'd be more maternal if growing up, I hadn't been shipped off to one relative after another and winding up in foster care. That's the main reason I married my first husband at age seventeen—to get the hell out of a home where I wasn't wanted—to find a place where I belonged. Guess I'm still looking."

"You have a family of your own now, Skye. Maybe it's time to put your efforts into homemaking instead of a career."

"If I did that, I'm pretty sure Zach would lose interest in me, and Emma would think her mother is a quitter. I'd be back to being a nobody. Acting offers me a sense of self-worth without that..." Skye shrugged.

Before Beth could compose a rebuttal, Skye said with a forced smile, "Really Beth, I'm not one to feel sorry for myself." She lifted a spoonful of soup but dropped it back into the bowl, reached for a butter cookie, and devoured it. "I didn't dare stop for a bite since those parasites have been on my tail."

"Reporters?"

"The minute the news about Lexi broke, they descended like locust. I wonder how they figured out where I was staying." Skye paused a moment. "Scratch that. My instincts told me not to trust that woman in reception. I bet she leaked the information."

"Why didn't you call Bruno? If I'm remembering correctly, he's your favorite bodyguard."

"Haven't been thinking straight, I guess." Skye brushed crumbs off her wrinkled satin blouse before reaching for another cookie. "I'm sure they're still hanging around in the street." She motioned toward the front of the house.

Beth moved toward the window. She glanced outside and spotted a few photographers milling around their parked cars. "Paparazzi," she muttered before facing Skye. "I'll ring my Shane. He'll have the whole lot of them cleared out in two shakes of a lamb's tail."

"No use. The street is public property. Anyway, I parked at the top of your driveway. I'll be okay."

Beth noticed a new batch of tears well up in Skye's eyes. She sunk onto the edge of an adjacent chair. "I know it's been a nightmare for you but—"

"I'm worried sick about Darla." Skye looked down at the ecru Berber carpet. "My house is overflowing with forensic investigators and police, but do they have a clue about what the hell happened to Darla?"

"At breakfast this morning, Shane told me he's assigned two brilliant detectives to look into Darla's disappearance."

Skye let a sigh escape her lips. "I know. I called Shane before leaving the hotel. At least they've ruled out that she was taken as a hostage. But there's no guarantee Darla's still alive."

"We've got to have hope," Beth said.

Skye nodded and lifted the soup spoon. Within a few of minutes of nonstop eating, she returned the emptied bowl to the tray. "Best minestrone ever." She pressed a napkin to her lips.

"I'll get you another bowl."

Skye shook her head then stood. With quick steps, she crossed the room and stopped at the sofa table. She lifted a gold framed photograph of Beth and Shane's wedding portrait. "Yours was a beautiful wedding. When I married Zach, I had this fantasy that we'd be deliriously happy. Like forever." She said the words as if to herself as she gingerly replaced the photo. "Turned out, our wedding seemed more like a PR event than a marriage ceremony." She looked in Beth's direction. "There really wasn't much to build a marriage on. Just two careers. One established and one beginning."

"You loved him."

"Maybe. But now, I think probably I didn't. Not really."

"It's not too late."

"Oh, I think it is." Skye reclaimed her seat. "I always fall a little in love with my current leading man. That happened when I met Zach. But it's different with Kenny."

Beth knew it was too late to lecture her on the virtues of fidelity.

"Don't say a word. I know what you're thinking." Skye reached for her cup but then let her hand drop. "If you listen to the media, Zach and I are Hollywood's golden couple. Truth is, we haven't been getting along. Zach's not who I thought he was. We hardly agree on anything. I mean, we don't even like the same food. I would never consider eating an animal, and to him, a medium-rare steak is the staple of life. We argue all the time. And to top it off, he's just about lost all interest in acting. His only real pursuits are his hobbies. His damn collections."

"Kenny? Is he the married man you had an affair with a couple of years ago? An abstract painter, if I remember correctly." She'd read about the two of them in Lexi's diary. And how Lexi had kept her lips sealed even though she wanted to tell Zach about his wife's affair.

"Yes."

"So, forgetting about your marriage vows, you decided to act on an impulse?"

"We hadn't planned to resume our relationship. But after seeing each other again, the old feelings resurfaced. The ironic thing is our affair reignited right under Zach's nose. In Italy, a couple of months ago." Skye glanced at Beth a second. "When we got there, I was steamed. Zach had made reservations in this hideous hotel chock full of heavy antique furniture and tons of gingerbread: ornamental plastered ceilings with murals of rosy-cheeked winged cupids and billowing clouds. Looked like a damn museum. Stuffy and pretentious. I hated it."

Beth glimpsed the irritation that animated Skye's face as her now dried hair bounced around her shoulders.

"I wanted to stay at my usual hotel in Capri. But no, Zach wouldn't hear of it," Skye huffed. "Even though I hated the hotel, staying there changed everything. Turned out Kenny was teaching some kind of painting class in Sorrento and was staying at the same hotel."

"Quite a coincidence."

"Kismet. Plain and simple. No other explanation." Skye reached for the teapot, but Beth lifted it and refilled her cup. "Since marrying Zach, I hadn't given Kenny a second thought. But seeing him again, oh, I don't know. Zach was driving me crazy. He wanted me to climb up that volcano with him."

"Mount Vesuvius?" Beth asked with a touch of admiration.

"Not only that, he planned to traipse around ruins and visit archeological museums. Watching paint peel would be more exciting." Skye reached for her snakeskin tote bag. After rooting around inside the exotic bag for a couple of seconds, she removed a hair clip. "All I really wanted to do was lounge by the pool and shop. So, I sent him off on his merry way with Lexi. On that trip, she had to babysit the two of them—Emma and Zach." She twisted her hair and secured the clip. "Anyway, with Zach trekking around southern Italy, I had time to spend with Kenny. For the first few days, he was busy with his son. Harry's too talkative for my taste. I'm glad Emma's on the quiet side. Anyway, our kids are friends—they have riding lessons together at the Endeavor Farm Pony Club. But that dreary wife of his gave me the evil eye every time we happened to see each other. I really tried my best to be cordial—nice even. Thank God she finally left. Something about a horse race. What a bitch."

"Can you blame her? Didn't you tell me that his wife found out about your first dalliance with her husband?"

"Kenny was feeling guilty and told her. But it's not a dalliance. I love Kenny. And he feels the same way. But that shrew is threatening him with a bloody custody battle if he ever cheats again. She'd spaz out big time if she suspected Kenny's come back to me."

Beth ran her tongue across her lower lip then reached for her cup. She took a quick sip. "How would you react if Zach was having an affair?"

Skye shrugged.

"For pity's sake, Skye. You wouldn't be furious?"

"Zach loves me. That's the problem."

She wondered if Skye really believed the words she'd spoken. If she did, she feared Skye was more disconnected from her husband then she previously believed.

"If Zach did find someone else, I'd be all for it. After all..." Skye took a deep breath. "I've been toying with the idea of divorcing him. I haven't made up my mind entirely, but I did telephone Marc Hammond this morning for an appointment."

"Marc isn't a divorce lawyer."

"I know. But, I trust him and wanted some advice." Skye lifted the cookie resting on her saucer. "I'd feel so less guilty if Zach would find someone he could share his passions with. A divorce would be a snap then." She broke the cookie in half and popped a piece into her mouth.

"Even if that person turned out to be Lexi?"

Skye began coughing as a bit of the buttery cookie lodged in her throat. Beth jumped up and handed her the teacup. Skye gulped the liquid but continued to hack as she tried to dislodge the vexatious crumb. Beth patted Skye's back a couple of times. Though still not fully recovered and very red in the face, Skye managed to sputter a few words between sips of tea.

"Are you nuts?"

"I've been getting a feeling—"

"Dear Lord, not that damn *fey* thing." Skye raised the cup and emptied it. "For a second, I thought you were serious."

"I *am* serious."

"The very idea of Zach and Lexi is absurd. For some unknown reason, he arranged an interview for her with our agent. Apparently, Zach spotted some talent I couldn't see. Lexi was his protégé, nothing more. After all, if he had a thing for her, why the hell did he offer his guesthouse to Trey what's his name? Lexi's artist boyfriend. Zach thinks he's going to be the next Rembrandt or something." Skye paused a second. "Just wait 'til I see him. I'll find out if he was messing around with the nanny."

Beth wanted to take back the insinuation. But it was too late. "I could be wrong. Maybe I should speak to Zach. That way, I might be able to ease out the answer without him becoming suspicious."

"Why would he tell you anything?"

"He might."

"Zach wouldn't share that kind of information with someone he hardly knows."

"If we put our heads together, we're sure to come up with a plan." Beth crossed her legs at the ankles and slumped back in the chair. A moment later, she snapped her fingers. "It's simple. I'll tell him I stopped by to check on you."

Skye placed the cup and saucer onto the serving tray. "Sounds reasonable enough. Still, he can be pretty tight-lipped. You'll have to cater to his ego. Big time. Even then, I doubt he'll tell you anything personal."

Beth had never exchanged more than pleasantries with Zach Greyson. Though it seemed impossible he would bare his soul to her, she'd worry about that later. She hoped the luck she had earlier with Marjorie would rub off on him. "Truth be, I can be a might bit persuasive. Give me an hour."

"Okay. But really Beth, the only thing you'll get out of Zach is that he's head over heels crazy in love with me." Beth noticed the muscles tighten along Skye's delicate jawline. "Zach wouldn't dare look at another woman. I'd bet my last dollar on that."

CHAPTER THIRTEEN

Beth tapped the brake as she took a sharp left onto Tower Road and reduced her speed as she maneuvered along the winding road. She searched her memory, trying to recall the last time she'd visited the Greyson mansion. Ever since Skye started spending more and more time in her beachfront house, the visits there had lessened. It's been more than a year, she figured as she spied the familiar seven-foot stucco wall that shielded Zach's house from the street.

She halted at the closed gate then shifted into park and stepped out. Reaching the keypad, she ignored the call button and pressed the security code Skye had given to her eons ago. By the time she'd slipped back behind the wheel, the wrought iron gate had swung open. An unexpected flash of apprehension caused her heart to race as she pulled her Volvo into the wide driveway. She still hadn't the slightest idea of how to broach the touchy subject of Zach's possible infidelity with Lexi.

Along the cobblestone driveway, an allée of trees formed a welcoming canopy as splotches of vibrant colors exuded from neatly tended flower beds and sculptured hedges that highlighted the elegance of Zach's home. The symmetrical ocher bricked façade, which always reminded Beth of a Palladian villa, or what a Palladian villa would have evolved into with the excess of Hollywood 1920s wealth, shimmered in the sunshine. She steered her SUV toward the circular parking area in front of the recessed main door and parked next to a familiar car. It took a couple of seconds for her to place the rusted and banged up El Camino as belonging to Father Clancy.

Beth flung the vehicle's door open, jumped out, and hurried across the rectangular slate pavers to the impressive main door. A moment later, one of Zach's maids, Sofia Fedoruck, dressed in a crisp gray uniform, welcomed her inside. After a few pleasantries, she asked if Skye was around, and a twinge of guilt intensified her uneasiness. Before Sofia answered, voices unsettled the still air. Beth glanced across the sprawling two-story foyer to an adjoining corridor and eyed Father Clancy clasping Emma's hand as they headed in her direction. Zach followed several steps behind.

"Look who's here, Emma." A singsong cadence filled the priest's voice.

Seeing the child's face, Beth realized no amount of wishful enthusiasm would free Emma of her grief. She rushed toward the sun-dappled hallway and knelt in front of the little girl. With a gentle touch, she stroked the dark curls off Emma's forehead. "How are you?"

Emma shrugged.

At a loss for soothing words that probably wouldn't help, Beth kissed Emma's cheek. "Is your ma—"

"Haven't seen hide nor hair of Skye," Zach said without emotion.

The streaming light bathed Zach in a warm radiance. Instead of flesh and bone, he seemed ethereal: all light and spirit. As he moved closer, she noticed his rumpled appearance: his face unshaved and eyes bloodshot behind swollen lids while his disheveled hair formed a mass of waves, unruly and uncombed. He wore a pocketed t-shirt and baggy, faded jeans.

She squeezed Emma's hand, stood straight, and focused on Father Clancy. He hovered over the girl with a firm grasp on her tiny shoulder. "I didn't expect to see you here, Father."

"After hearing about the tragedy, I rushed right over."

"I still don't understand."

"You see lass, I was Lexi's spiritual director."

"Really?" She looked at Zach who offered her a shrug.

"We met when I was an associate at St. Timothy," the priest said. "Lexi's parish church. Lexi often shared how she loved working as Emma's nanny and the deep fondness she held toward her employers. I knew it was more than me duty to drop by. In fact, Christian charity impelled me to check on her loved ones."

Beth was familiar with the magnificent St. Timothy Church. Rich in altars and stained glass windows, it was common knowledge that back in the 1940s, parishioners who were artisans from Fox and MGM studios created much of the artwork, which now embellished the church. She looked downward as if studying the checkerboard black and white marble floor trying to make sense of the priest's story. Since the church is about ten minutes away, it made sense that Lexi would have gone to mass there. Even so, Father's Clancy's explanation sounded too pat. Too many coincidences. "Are you still serving there, Father?"

"Not affiliated with any church at the moment."

Beth pursed her lips taking in his words.

"Before I forget, Sibeal." Father Clancy tapped his forehead. "Oh, forgive me, 'tis Beth now, isn't it? Well, quite by accident, I've discovered a building that might be near perfect for the shelter. I'll ring you in a couple of days with the details."

"The teen shelter." She sucked in a mouthful of air. "I'm so sorry. I haven't had a chance—"

"No worries," Father Clancy said as he turned his wide girth and looked at Emma. "Now that we've become friends, I'll be sure to visit soon. Remember, Lexi is happy now. In heaven with our Lord and the angels."

Emma nodded even though a tear escaped and rolled down her flushed cheek.

For a large man, it surprised Beth how nimbly the priest moved. He paused at the doorway only a second and then with a wave of his hand left them.

A heavy silence filled the foyer. Beth regretted barging in and interrupting their grief. So unlike Skye, her family was obviously devastated by the nanny's death.

Zach squatted in front of Emma and seemed to search her face. "Why don't you go to the kitchen and check on Alma? I'm sure she's finished baking that special surprise for you."

Emma grasped his hand and tried to suppress a whimper.

"I know, honey. It's okay to be sad." He stroked her cheek. "But you've got to be strong. Alma loved Lexi, too. She's been cooking and baking for hours trying to bury her pain. Seeing you will make her feel better."

Emma obediently turned and headed deeper into the house while Zach straightened to his full height.

"This isn't a good time." Beth edged closer to the front door.

"Have a drink with me."

"I don't want to impose."

He extended his hand in the direction of the sunny hallway. She followed but hesitated at the threshold of an imposing room. For an instant, she felt as if she'd been magically transported to a library in an English manor house. The room smelled of leather and wood; its floor to ceiling cherry bookcases wrapped with elaborate moldings was stocked with impressively bound volumes, and an elegantly carved marble fireplace occupied the far wall. He ushered her to a soft leather chair.

"Skye's never brought me in here," she said not attempting to hide her admiration. "You're library is breathtaking. The antiques are amazing."

He lowered his eyes as if studying the Tabriz carpet. "If only Skye had half of your appreciation for a room like this. The antiques come from across the globe. And the books..." He shrugged. "When tragedy strikes, it kinda makes all of this seem unimportant." He sunk onto the edge of the ottoman facing her.

She searched for words of comfort but came up empty.

"Lexi was my Pygmalion." He stroked his bristly chin. "Before I stepped up, she was determined to shut herself inside a minuscule cubicle writing dull translations for some NSA bureaucrats. Under my guidance... hell." He sighed. "Let me get you that drink." He crossed the room and lifted a decanter full of amber liquid. "How 'bout a touch of the Irish?"

"Maybe later."

"Well, I think, I will." He poured the liquor to the tumbler's rim then took a quick gulp before reclaiming his seat. "Where the hell is Skye?"

Beth swallowed hard.

"You'd think she'd at least find her way home, if only for the kid's sake." He raised the glass. "Skye hates it when I call Emma, the kid. Actually, Skye hates a lot of things. Did you know she doesn't like gazing at the night sky?" He gulped the remainder of the drink. "She didn't think much of Lexi, either. Me, on the other hand, I thought Lexi was great, just great."

He moved to the assortment of liquor bottles and refreshed his glass.

"I didn't realize you and Lexi were so close."

"Like this." Zach crossed his fingers. "Lexi totally got me." He reached into his shirt pocket and pulled out a package of cigarettes, tapped one free, and stuck it between his lips. "She thought I was brilliant." He spoke out of the side of his mouth as he flicked a gold lighter then took a long drag before slowly exhaling a curl of smoke. "Unlike Skye, she appreciated the masterpieces filling my art gallery. Anyone would really. But, not Skye. Not enough of that abstract impressionism crap." He focused on the cigarette nestled between his fingers. "Don't get me wrong. Skye loves Emma; we all love her, but why isn't she here? The kid needs her."

"I spoke to Skye earlier. Said she was on her way home. That's why I stopped by."

He freed his cell phone from the back pocket of his jeans and checked his text messages. "Not a damn thing from her."

"It's getting late." She looked in the direction of the ornate mantle clock.

"Nearing four already."

"Traffic will be murder. No pun intended." He rose and crushed the cigarette inside a cut-crystal bowl on top of an inlaid marble table. "What happened to Lexi has me so stressed, I'm back to smoking."

She stood. "I won't keep you any longer." Though Zach hadn't confessed to having an affair, his comments had reinforced her suspicions.

He slicked back his hair with his hands. "Do me a favor. Let me show you something."

She wanted to object, but he kept talking.

"Mentioning the traffic was only a ruse to get you to stay. Your home's only fifteen—thirty minutes from here?"

She nodded.

"Truth is, I don't want to be alone."

She wanted to touch his hand and reassure him that everything would be okay. Instead, she folded her arms.

"You said Skye's on her way. What's a few more minutes?"

Beth pulled her lips tight and offered a nod. He ushered her to the curved main staircase though remained silent as they climbed the richly carpeted risers. During her previous visits, she'd only been on the main floor but had always been a bit curious about the rest of the house. Skye had offered her a brief history of the previous owners, which included celebrities from silent film stars to its last occupant, an aging heiress. As far as she could tell, the house's fascinating history hadn't impressed Skye much. Though the mansion had been updated many times over the past eighty-five years, Zach had orchestrated a massive renovation to restore the house to its initial splendor and even located a number of original pieces of furniture. As they walked along a wide corridor, Beth lagged behind as she glanced into doorways.

"We're headed to the top floor near the back of the house," he said over his shoulder. He stopped and turned around. A smile played at the corners of his mouth. "Would you like the official tour?"

"Really?"

"Sure." He pointed to an opened door. "That's the billiard room."

In eager anticipation, she traveled from room to room. She took in the classic luxury of the home theater with its wide screen and overstuffed recliners and the trophy room where instead of silver cups stood Zach's Oscar, Golden Globes, and framed photographs illuminating the many milestones of his acting career. Her jaw dropped when she glanced into a room housing a bowling alley. But it was the massive area once used for dances and galas that grabbed her imagination. In her mind's eye, she envisioned glamorous women arrayed in silks and furs with ivory cigarette holders being escorted by handsome men decked out in white tie and tails. She could almost hear the strains of jazz pulsating through the air.

After leaving behind the state of the art gym, a sitting room, an office, and so many bedrooms she'd lost count, she followed him up a narrow staircase. The plush carpet had vanished, and the old wooden steps were scuffed and worn. Tiny squeaks sounded with each footfall until they entered a dusky corridor.

She heard the jingle of keys when Zach reached into his pants pocket. He jerked out a key ring and unlocked a door. A swell of warm air rushed from the room as he flipped on a light switch. "After you."

Beth stepped inside. At first sight, the scene made little sense. In the middle of the windowless room, a gleaming stainless steel table held several aquariums. She couldn't detect water inside any of them, let alone, swishing goldfish. Plywood planks resembling makeshift bookshelves jutted from the wall, but instead of dusty old tomes, they held additional glass containers and small wire cages.

"Next to my art collection, these are my most prized treasures."

She moved deeper into the room and peered into one of the many aquariums. A fitted screen topped the tank, and inside sat a curiously notched upside down box and a small water bowl on a couple inches of bark material. She ran her finger along the tank's smooth glass but pulled her hand away when a snake poked its small head out from a notch in the box. She let out a gasp and flinched but not before noticing its shiny eyes scrutinizing her as its elliptical pupils narrowed.

"You're surprised?"

"That's an understatement." She shot him a wide-eyed look before scooting closer to the aquarium.

"During my college days, I planned a career in biology and toyed with the idea of a major in herpetology. My master's studies, however, took a major turn. I found myself focused on neurobiology. I planned to go all the way and earn a Ph.D.. Well, that never happened."

She wondered why Skye had failed to mention this incredible bit of information about Zach. "I had no idea you were an academic."

"Quite a conflict with my public persona. I guess it's a bit perplexing to discover that deep down I'm a geek."

"A geek?" She half-shrugged. "I wouldn't know about that, but I am impressed." She turned around in an effort to take in the unusual room. "This is astounding. I've never imagined you a scientist. A heartbreaker. A man's man. But a reptileologist?"

"A what?" He rolled his eyes playfully.

"You know what I mean."

He nodded. "I've been spending more and more time here. Acting is starting to lose its appeal."

"Skye mentioned something about that."

He raised his hand, palm facing her, signaling her to stop. "Let me show you my beauties. Or as I like to call them—*le mie bellezze*."

"You're going to find this hard to believe. I've never seen an actual snake before. I have been to a couple of zoos but avoided the reptile houses, so. The thought of them creeps me out. A wee bit." She added the wee bit so as not to offend him. "I'm from Ireland, after all."

He squinted as if trying to make sense of her comment. "Ah, St. Patrick. He drove every last snake out from the emerald isle."

"Something like that," she said with a wink. She leaned next to a countertop and brushed her arm against a fire extinguisher knocking it over. She quickly righted the canister.

"A bit jumpy. Look, there's no need to be nervous. These are fascinating creatures that should be admired. Consider this your first lesson in ophiology." He pointed at a long, deep aquarium.

She moved closer and examined the contents of the tank. It housed a long snake with a smoothly scaled body curled into a tight coil. She could make out a vague pattern of three gray colored stripes. It moved its head forward, and instinctively, she stepped back.

"She's hungry," Zach said.

"Is it venomous?"

"Venomous? No, she's a constrictor. A California Coastal Rosy Boa. Her name is Rosita. Even if it's a little corny—Rosita the Rosy Boa—I think it fits her." He pressed his index finger against the side of the warm aquarium. "Notice how her head is only a little wider than her tail. Though she's only about twenty-five inches long, when Rosita's completely grown, she could reach a full forty-four inches."

"No kidding," she murmured not able to tear her eyes away from the snake. She sensed Zach moving across the room.

"Snakes aren't the soft and fluffy kind of pet. But they are intriguing." He returned to her side holding a white mouse by its long, slender tail.

"Watch this." He slid back the mesh screen and lowered the squirming mouse. Abruptly, he pulled it away. The snake shot up, its jaws expanding in anticipation. The reptile's pointed head jutted up higher as the squeal of the intended prey rose to a frantic pitch.

"That's cruel," Beth admonished even though she was hardly a fan of mice.

Zach took a quick look at her before dropping the rodent into the snake's lair. Its tiny feet scurried only an inch before the snake wrapped its narrow body around the hapless mouse.

"Rosita will digest the mouse at her leisure. May take up to a couple of days."

"Hmmm. What does Skye think of all this?" She swept her arm in an encompassing gesture. "She carries that Gucci python purse around like it's glued to her arm. Seems a bit conflicted."

"Conflicted? That's an understatement. More of a way to needle me. Or disrespect my interests." He snapped the screen back over the aquarium. "Anyway, before we were married, I brought her up here. She found it kinda of cool. Different. Unique. But, she hasn't been up here since then. Emma, on the other hand, loves it."

"Really?"

"Lexi would look up a certain kind of snake on the internet, to become familiar with it, and then we'd present a science lesson to Emma. Like I said, the kid is inquisitive and smart. She wanted to take Rosita for show and tell once. Both of us nixed that idea. Could you imagine if Rosita got loose in the classroom? It'd be utter—"

"Pandemonium?"

"Exactly." A grin flashed across his face but faded almost as fast. "I could always depend on Lexi. Whenever I was out of town, she'd feed *le mie bellezze*. Damn." He shook his head.

She decided to offer a bit of consolation, but unsure of what to do, she patted his arm a couple of times.

"I don't know. Maybe, I need a shrink."

She frowned thinking his statement odd knowing how normal it was to feel empty and lost after losing a loved one.

"Do you think it's possible I could fear happiness?" He pulled a cigarette free from the pack and stared at the slim white fag. "Why else would I've married Skye? At the time, I thought, here is this young actress. Beautiful. Fun. Engaging. She needs me. I can help her career take shape. I came to believe that our love was genuine. At least, I thought it was. But what has my marriage really brought me? Frustration and disappointment. On the other hand, Lexi brightened my world. For a time, anyway. Before she started making..." He fished the lighter out of his pocket.

She'd never have a more perfect opportunity to find out the truth. "Is that why you two had an affair?"

He lit the cigarette and took a long drag. "Is that what Skye told you?"

"Skye? No. The thought just popped into my mind. My Shane tells me I have a fanciful imagination."

"Really not that fanciful at all."

CHAPTER FOURTEEN

THURSDAY, MAY 1ˢᵀ

Over the past ten months, Beth had learned a lot about living with a homicide detective. Most of it had come as a complete surprise. Especially the cold reality that every facet of her husband's life was literally put on hold as an investigation consumed his days and nights. When he did come home to sleep, she'd wake up only to find him pouring over notes or staring into his laptop. This time was no different.

Propped up in bed, she watched Shane tap the pencil eraser against his chin as he stared at the television. The news story on the screen rehashed the current outbreak of teenage murders. Not a word about Darla Edward's curious disappearance had been mentioned. Beth made a quick calculation and figured Darla had to be at least twenty-five and guessed that fact would mar the teenage aspect that the pert blond reporter was harping on about.

"What about Darla?"

He said nothing. Just kept bouncing the pencil against his chin.

She studied his furrowed brow, noting the deep concentration that tensed his face. It seemed as if every detail of the murders wound over and over in his mind like a CD with a jammed play button. No matter how often she tried to distract him with a special meal or a snippet of pleasant conversation, he resisted. She believed Shane ate, drank, slept, and breathed every minute detail of the homicides. In previous cases he shared with her a tangled maze of possibilities, which she knew he'd dutifully assess and evaluate only to throw out the bulk of initial scenarios. Even though an immense number of Los Angeles homicides became cold cases and were never solved, during her brief time with Shane, he and Gavin Collins had seen a number of arrests prosecuted and sent to prison. She had complete faith he'd do the same with these seemingly unconnected cases. Hopefully, soon. Before someone else winds up murdered. Knowing Shane, he'd probably blame himself if that happened. That was the last thing she wanted.

The TV report ended, and a brash, loud ambulance chaser took the screen advertising his legal services. Shane looked at the yellow lined pad resting against his bent knees.

"Any news on Darla?" She tried again.

"Nah. Nothing." He shut his eyes so tight lines formed on his forehead.

"You're exhausted. Why don't you take a sick day?"

He eyed her.

"Only a suggestion."

"I know, beautiful. Wish I could. Spent most of yesterday on a wild goose chase. Had to check out an alibi of a potential suspect. After hours of long distance communications with various public safety agencies, we discovered that one Pavel Titov was exactly where he claimed to be—2300 miles east of LA."

"So, he couldn't possibly have killed the poor girl."

"Maybe he didn't kill her, but he confessed to having sex with her. A fourteen-year-old, for God's sake. I'd bet my last dollar, he's up to his eyeballs in human trafficking. Chances are he smuggled Eliana Mendoza and a helluva lot of other under-aged girls into the country. ICE has taken over that part of the Titov investigation."

"ICE?"

"Immigration and Customs Enforcement. A branch of Homeland Security. Now I have to regroup. Review what little we know and move on."

She snuggled next to him. "You'll figure out this puzzle."

He stroked his fingertips through her hair. A couple minutes passed in silence. "Hey," he said dropping his hand. "Anything pan out with Marjorie Hammond?"

She'd been going back and forth trying to decide what to tell him about the diary. "As a matter of fact, yes." Beth grabbed the small book off the night table and ran her thumb across the tooled leather cover, betting it'd be the last time she'd ever see it. She handed it over. "Lexi's diary."

"Diary?" He snatched the book and flipped it open.

She knew the rich leather and the fine, handmade paper escaped his attention. He'd only be interested in Lexi's words. She watched him peruse the first page dated February 17th.

"You read this?"

After exiting the church confessional two weeks ago, she promised she'd never lie to him again. "Took a quick peek. Maybe Lexi's words will lead you to her killer."

With an impatient flick of his finger, he thumbed through a few pages. "Who's P.C.?"

"Lexi's secret code for her lover. I think."

"Why did she need to use a code?" He mumbled the words not lifting his sight from the page.

"It could refer to Prince Charming."

This time he did look at her. "You're sure you just took a quick glance?"

She didn't respond.

"Have any idea who this mystery lover would be?"

She shrugged. "Lexi probably met a lot of young actors working for Skye. Could've been any one of them."

"But it wasn't."

Though she was the one with the sixth sense, it unnerved her the way Shane could always detect when she was holding something back. This time it was a lulu.

"Zach."

"Greyson?" He sat up in the bed. "Are you certain?"

"Pretty certain. Though Skye doesn't buy it. But I think so. Yes."

He flung the covers off, slid out of the bed, and hurried toward their en suite. Before disappearing behind the door, he faced her. "Murder victims usually know their killers. If a woman is murdered, then the killer is most likely the husband or boyfriend. Later today I'll drive to Tower Road and have a little chat with Mr. Greyson."

The strong vibes her *fey* had sent off revealed that Zach had nothing to do with Lexi's murder, but she kept that opinion to herself.

"Wouldn't it be great if Lexi's murder was just a simple case of jealousy? Be too bad for Greyson. Probably get twenty-five to life. End his acting career for sure."

"Really, Shane," she admonished even though she knew he'd have to find out the truth for himself. She didn't have the right to tell him how to do his job. And she certainly wasn't going to tell him about her conversation with Zach. He wouldn't take very well to her sticking her nose where it didn't belong. Actually, he'd be *effin'* and *blindin'* to highest heaven. Her ears ached with the thought.

"But if Greyson killed Lexi..." He crossed his arms. "What about the other murders? It doesn't make sense that he'd killed three strangers. Unless, he's a complete dyed in the wool sociopath. You know him pretty good. He ever mention a fondness for prostitutes?"

"Come on, Shane."

"Trust me, I'm gonna scrutinize Greyson to the nth degree. But not until I pour over every word of Lexi's diary." He stepped closer to her. "Funny how those poor street kids have been overshadowed by the Horne murder. Except for that floozy reporter on the news. After that bit of crap journalism, teenaged girls from here to Sacramento will be shaking in their boots, looking over their shoulders for the boogeyman to strike."

She wrinkled her nose. "You think the murders are nothing more than random acts of violence?"

"At first I thought Lexi's death was unrelated. A copycat. But now, I'm not so sure. According to the Medical Examiner, she was injected with the exact same drug cocktail that killed the prostitutes. A weird combination of liquid nicotine, insulin, and steroids. A strong enough dose of any one of those drugs would've done the trick. The kicker is that none of the drug information has been leaked or shared with the media."

"I stopped by Zach's house to check on Skye yesterday. Father Clancy was there."

"I interviewed him. Quite a character."

"Don't you think it's a bit odd he knew two of the victims?"

"That reminds me. Meant to call St. Tim's. The good padre supposedly met Lexi Horne there. Said he was her confessor."

"Spiritual Director," Beth corrected. "You're busy. Why don't I telephone the church later?" She looped the belt of her silk robe into a bow. "I'm a bit more familiar conversing with members of the clergy." Though only a slight nudge, Beth had mentioned to him several times how she wished he'd attend Sunday mass more often.

Shane nodded and pulled her close. She rested her head against his chest, and the sound of his heartbeat thumped in her ear. He slipped his index finger under her chin, lifted her face, and kissed her.

After a few seconds, he released his hold and took a step backward. She read the longing that filled his eyes but was certain his duty would override his desire. "Go on with yourself. I've got a busy day planned too." She ran a finger along the scar crossing her cheekbone. "I'm filming a public service announcement today."

"You're okay with it?"

"More than okay, love." She cringed realizing how easy it had become for her to lie. She'd been awake half the night trying to block memories that begged to surface regarding the accident. When he'd slipped into bed at half past two, she'd feigned sleep. She didn't want to heap another measure of worry onto his plate so the fib was for his own good. "Those PSA's have been a success. Even if it's an old message. Don't drink and drive."

"They couldn't have selected a more beautiful spokesperson. It's just..." His heavy eyelids flicked. "I'd hate for it to bring back memories you'd rather forget."

"Ah Shane, my darlin' boy." She stroked his cheek. "Now that you're in my life, that entire ordeal seems like nothing more than a bad dream. I'm doing something positive to counteract such reckless behavior, and it's given me a goal I'm excited about."

"You're a real trooper, Betty Getty."

She cupped her hand, saluted, and offered him a quick wink.

"Oh, I almost forgot. Do I need to know how that Hammond woman got possession of Lexi's diary?"

"Probably. She kind of, well, she pinched it. But, Marjorie had every intention of returning it to Lexi. Her curiosity got the best of her."

"I bet it did."

"Anyway, she's scared to death. I promised you'd keep the details of her illicit act between the two of you."

"I'll telephone her for a follow-up interview when I get to the office." He turned but stopped when she said his name.

"You'd better get over to Zach's soon. My *fey* tells me he won't be hanging around the house much today. Skye's going to be interviewing nannies. Though she gave it a half-hearted try, she wasn't able to wiggle out of her contract, and the studio refused to postpone filming. So, she'll be off to Baltimore in a couple weeks for her new project. She wants Emma's care settled before she leaves."

"That's real responsible parenting."

"Shane."

He shrugged before closing the bathroom door behind him.

***

After sharing courtesies with the guard outside the studio door, Beth slipped inside. It had been her plan to arrive early so she'd have plenty of time to prepare. She knew her lines, having easily memorized them, but she needed to steel her nerves and squelch the rising panic and resentment engulfing her. The memory from two years ago, firmly imprinted in her mind, could reappear without a moment's notice. Though she played it down earlier not wanting to alarm Shane, she'd been finding herself breaking out into a cold sweat as snippets of the accident flashed through her mind. She repeatedly told herself the only way to fight fear was to face it, which she'd forced herself to do. She prayed that the couple of public service announcements she'd filmed over the past year had been provocative and powerful enough to make a difference.

As just a pretty face, Beth believed she wouldn't have been taken seriously. But, as a survivor of a head-on collision, she brought a hard-edged reality to the anti-drunk driving campaign. She'd suffered gashes on her face, a broken pelvis, a punctured lung, and internal injuries resulting in a hysterectomy. The inebriated driver, his body so relaxed at the moment of impact, hardly suffered a cut or scrape. In court, he'd just shrugged with a wry smile, as if enjoying his moment in the spotlight, as he offered a guilty plea. First offense. Six months including time served. Slap on the wrist. He'd sauntered from the courtroom whistling.

She'd reassessed her life's direction during her long recovery. It wasn't entirely the scars on her face that ended her modeling career. The laser treatments eliminated the angry red coloring and left only thin, jagged white lines. Hardly a problem with a careful application of foundation. The shattering loss of motherhood had been the most brutal blow. The very act of picking up her life and continuing as if nothing happened seemed impossible.

After mulling over the value of celebrity, she'd deemed it futile unless its benefits were used for something vital, to make a dent in the status quo, to stand for something. Through these announcements, she'd found an outlet. Even if the process had a harrowing way of causing her to relive the ordeal.

If it hadn't been for the accident, Beth doubted she would have ever met Shane. Preoccupied with her trial, she had walked down the courthouse's main corridor staring into a hot cup of coffee. Shane came rushing in the opposite direction and noticed her too late as she ran smack into him. He jumped out of the way as the contents of her cup splashed over the granite floor. A flash of anger crossed his face. Stunned, she'd offered a profusion of apologies, which seemed to soothe away his initial outrage. Instead of releasing a barrage of accusations toward her carelessness, Beth had been surprised that he offered to find someone to clean up the mess. By the time a janitor swabbed up the puddle, she'd slipped the business card he'd offered into her purse.

But now she feared an anxiety attack. She closed her eyes and focused on happy things: the cat rescue, photography, her work with the homeless teen shelter, and most especially Shane. After a few deep breaths, the suffocating tightness in her chest abated. She dropped onto a folding chair as the muffled sound of her cell phone sounded from deep in her purse. After rummaging around, she pulled it out and swiped the screen. Without a preamble of any kind, Skye began talking so fast, she couldn't follow her tumbling stream of words.

"Slow down," Beth ordered. "You're forgetting to breathe."

"I couldn't sleep a wink last night. Your accusation of Zach cheating with Lexi about blew my mind. So, first thing this morning—"

"You didn't."

"I did. I asked him point blank."

"And?"

"He laughed in my face. Said he didn't realize I was switching my career path to comedy. I guess that shoots your theory straight to hell."

"Hmmm."

"Gotta go. I've had two nanny interviews already. Both disasters. Hopefully, number three will be lucky for me."

"I'll keep my fingers crossed and send up a quick prayer to Saint Bridget. Oh, by the way, Shane's headed over to see Zach. Did I tell you about Lexi's diary?"

"Diary? I bet it's as interesting as watching paint dry."

The response verified her belief that Skye didn't know a blessed thing about Lexi's personal life. "I'll check back with you later." Beth cut the connection and looked at her phone. "Father Clancy," she said remembering she'd told Shane she'd do a little checking up on him. She dialed information and jotted down the number on the back page of her script. After tapping in the number, she waited.

"St Timothy Catholic Church, may I help you?" a cheerful voice sounded.

"I was wondering if I might speak to Father Clancy."

"Father Clancy. I'm sorry you have the wrong church. Father Clancy is assigned to the Church of the Blessed Sacrament in East Hollywood. Would you like the number?"

"He did work at St. Timothy's recently?"

The woman at the other end of the line paused. For a second, Beth believed she'd lost the connection.

"Well, certainly you know Father Clancy is a Jesuit. He wouldn't be assigned to a diocesan church."

"Are you aware of his mission work aimed at establishing a shelter for homeless youth?"

"You must be looking for another Father Clancy. The priest I know is ninety-two, retired, and spends most of his days praying. He's too weak to celebrate mass any longer, but his mind is sharp as a tack. Sorry I haven't been able to help. Perhaps if you contact the archdiocesan office they'd be able to help."

"I'll do that. Thanks." Beth cut the connection as the director walked into the room.

CHAPTER FIFTEEN

Skye looked the woman up and down. She couldn't pull her eyes away from the shabby suit with its frayed cuffs and drooping hem worn by the candidate for the nanny position. The outdated shiny pink outfit sported wide shoulders and a black lace applique stitched across the face of the jacket. At one time, the stitchery had depicted a flower, but now, the ragged threads sagged with large areas missing. Dressed in ugly clothing to an interview equaled a giant faux pas. The person arrayed in such a hideous get-up had as much chance of working for her as an orchid thriving in the Arctic. However, one of her interviewing goals was to provide an impression of professionalism. She reminded herself that few people possessed even a shred of her heightened fashion sense.

The woman sat on the edge of the couch in Zach's morning room. The applicant's hiked up skirt revealed knobby, dimpled knees. Amid folds of flab making her face appear flat and bloated, her blue eyes shined as dull, gray hair hung loosely around her shoulders.

Skye scanned the resume resting on her lap and noted that the woman's personal references included some of Seattle's most prominent personalities from business magnates to politicians. There seemed to be a serious disconnect. After a couple seconds of indecision, she decided to interview the woman since she implicitly trusted the opinion of the domestic agency.

"Ms. Barnett, are you aware of the recent circumstances surrounding our family?"

The woman lifted her double chin and nodded. "That's why I requested to work for you. Ms. Greer, over at the agency, wanted to send me to a lawyer, a single mom with new twins. But, I wondered who needs me more? And just like that," the woman said snapping stubby fingers, "a vision of your precious daughter, Emma, popped into my head. What a tragic event for such a small child to endure. The poor lamb."

A fleeting thought of Darla distracted Skye. She refocused with pursed lips.

"At times such as these, a child needs stability. Little Emma is extremely vulnerable now. That's when everything usually runs amuck. What your daughter needs is a firm hand to guide her back into her everyday activities—and a loving mentor to help her forget the recent unpleasantness."

"How do you expect to do that? Emma is a sensitive child. Exceptionally bright and creative. You won't be able to force her to forget Lexi Horne. She was very attached to her former nanny, and I'm afraid she has taken the loss to the extreme."

The applicant leaned forward as if ready to share a secret. "Let's face facts and call a spade a spade. This Lexi Horne person wound up dead. If she were an upstanding individual, I don't believe that would've ever happened. The way I see it, she must've kept company with a very unsavory crowd." She looked down at her folded hands and shook her head. "And I'm afraid some of the dead nanny's impropriety may have rubbed off on the poor, innocent child."

Skye shifted in her seat. "I won't have you or anyone else badmouthing Lexi. She was a, a... a kind person. Emma loved her."

"Not a prostitute?"

"What?" Skye's voice rose several decibels. "There wasn't a more straight-laced girl in all of Beverly Hills."

"If you say so, dear." The woman clapped her hand over her mouth and emitted a noise between a cough and a laugh. "Nevertheless, with my strict regimen of proper food, exercise, plenty of fresh air, and adequate sleep, the little lamb will be back to her old self in no time."

"Sounds like boot-camp."

Dorothy Barnett tossed her limp hair behind her sagging shoulders. "You don't want Emma to become a spoiled brat, do you? Life is hard. Though she's only seven, Emma must learn how to roll with the punches. Let this grisly incident be a lesson—bad things happen, and we've no choice but to carry on."

Skye didn't like the way the interview had slipped away from her. This middle-aged cow is trying to bully her way into the job, she thought as a rush of irritation swelled through her. "I appreciate your interest. My assistant will get back to you when I've made a decision." Just mentioning Darla caused a catch in her throat. She lifted the nearby crystal glass and took a deep swallow of spring water.

"Let me reiterate. If your daughter's well-being is your utmost concern, then I suggest you hire me." Her pencil thin lips parted into a narrow smile.

"Ms. Barnett." Skye attempted to calm down by inhaling a couple of deep breaths as her therapist had advised. Yet anger blinded her and after only one deep airy gulp she said, "Your services won't be needed."

"There's no need for formalities. Call me Dot. Between you and me, we're going to make a great team."

Skye jumped up and crossed her arms. "Ms. Barnett, the job isn't yours. It never will be."

"Now Skye, don't go off the deep end."

Skye opened her mouth, but before she could muster a reply, the woman's deep voice rang in her ears.

"You can look high and low. But I guarantee, you won't find a better nanny than me in all of California. Trust me. I'm perfect."

Skye clenched her jaw. "No means no."

"Oh." Dot Barnett's eyes lit up with understanding. "You're worried about my lack of child-care experience. Granted, I am new to the nanny profession. But, I have babysat more than one well-heeled child of privilege. After all, I was one myself." She offered a sheepish grin. "Now that's cleared up, why don't you direct me to my room? I'll settle in and get a feel for the place. By the way Skye, I'm going to love working here."

"Leave immediately or I'll alert my security staff."

Dot waved her plump hand in front of her face as if swatting Skye's words away. "This is Zach Greyson's house, isn't it?"

"That's none of your business." Skye stepped next to a heavy mahogany writing table and lifted the telephone receiver.

Dot shot up belying her heavy girth. "That's not an acceptable answer. You see, I know something important—about the murdered hussy you called a nanny." She narrowed her eyes.

Skye's heartbeat quickened. She wanted to flee the room. Instead, she locked eyes with the older woman.

"I know who did it—and why." Dot paused as if to allow her words to sink in. "If you value your life and that of dear little Emma, you won't dare refuse me."

"Is that a threat?" Skye raised her voice, her fear replaced by anger.

"You're not stupid. You know exactly what I mean. You wash my hands, and I'll wash yours. I dropped off my suitcase in the foyer. Please show me to my quarters."

Skye pressed the extension number linking to the security department. "Bruno, I need help. Now." She kept her sight fixed on Dot as she disengaged the call. Instead of returning the phone to its cradle, she clutched it so hard her knuckles turned white.

Dot's eyes met Skye's. "Once you have a chance to consider my offer, you'll see things my way. Good day."

Skye followed the woman as she waddled out of the room. She clasped her arms together as Dot disappeared around a corner. *That old bat is nothing more than a crank. A lunatic.* This town is full of them, she thought, trying to find a measure of comfort, but instead, she found herself shaking. She inched to the nearest chair and collapsed into it. Her shoulders sagged as she leaned into its plush cushion and studied the stained-glass skylight. The pastel colored glass appeared to glow as light filtered through brightening the room—but not her mood. She sensed she wasn't alone and craned her neck, afraid the horrid woman had returned. To her relief, she saw Zach.

"Bruno grabbed Barnett before she got to the end of the corridor. She sure is one weird bird." He stepped in front of her.

She pulled her lips taut and stared at him.

"You should've warned me that the nanny holding tank was going to be the library." He paused a second. "I wasn't in there a split-second before I made a quick escape. Then that god-ugly woman came running after me. Barnett looked harmless enough, and since she was waiting for an interview, I didn't think too much about it. Though unprofessional on her part, I assumed she wanted an autograph.

"Anyway she acted like we were long-lost friends. It was obvious from the get-go she didn't have a snowball's chance in hell of becoming Emma's nanny. Her looks alone would scare the poor kid." He shook his head. "That's one pushy broad. What kind of nanny agency do you deal with anyway? If that's the best they've got, I'd look elsewhere."

"Did she say anything about Lexi?"

"Lexi? No. But she did ramble on about the state of our marriage. I knew she was nutty as a fruitcake when she kept telling me it was over between us—a done deal."

"What?"

"I kid you not." He raised his hands as if surrendering. "You know I always try to be truthful with my fans so, I assured her in no uncertain terms that we're rock solid."

"You shouldn't have told her a damn thing." Though she frowned, a weight seemed to slip from her shoulders with his declaration regarding the strength of their marital bond.

He grasped her hand and knelt in front of her. "I'm sure once Bruno reads her the riot act, she won't dare bother you ever again. Don't let crackpot Dot upset you a nanosecond longer."

"This might sound crazy, but that woman says she knows who killed Lexi. She even threatened me."

"I told you she's nuts."

"But—"

"Don't give credence to single word sprouting out of her mouth. The way I see it, if the police haven't a clue, how the hell would a demented old hag know?"

"She would if she had something to do with it."

"Be for real, Skye." He released her hand. "I've come up with a brilliant idea. Cancel the remaining interviews. It may not be the best move for Emma to face a new nanny so soon after Lexi's death. You know she and Alma get along famously."

Skye raised her eyebrows.

"And Alma loves the kid, too. So, why don't we let her take over nanny duty while you're out of town? I'll hire a temp for the cooking," Zach said.

"Alma? What does she know about child-care?"

"She's raised six kids of her own. Anyway, the kid looks to Alma like she's a surrogate grandma. So, I ran the idea past her, and she's willing to give up the kitchen for the nursery on a limited basis. Alma will still be in charge of breakfast and lunch since she'll have Emma off to school by that time."

"A surrogate grandmother?" Skye tapped her foot against the richly carpeted floor.

"Lexi and Emma were always in the kitchen. I thought you knew that."

"If I knew that was going on, I would've put a stop to it." She ran her tongue across her lower lip.

"I think it's the best solution for now."

"But she isn't a qualified nanny."

"Have you found a suitable replacement for Lexi?"

Skye pressed her lips tight.

"There's no question about it then. Alma's the best solution for your immediate crises."

"I guess so."

He moved behind Skye and began rubbing her shoulders. "You're tense. Have the maid draw you a bath and then take a nap. Looks like you can do with some sleep."

The action of his fingers began to loosen her tight muscles. Skye closed her eyes.

"We'll have dinner on the terrace. I'll have Alma prepare your favorite dishes." He dropped his hand and began to fondle her breast as he kissed the nape of her neck. She grabbed his wrist. He stopped, folded his arms, and stepped away from the chair. "When is Emma coming home?"

"She'll be with her father until Sunday. I hope spending time with him will help her accept what's happened."

"The kid could've stayed here. Everyone in this house loves her."

"The change of scenery will do her good."

"Why don't you go upstairs and take that bath?"

"I won't enjoy it. The phone's going to ring any second with news that Darla's body has been found. I know it." She covered her face with her hands and didn't try to hold back the whimpers that escaped her lips.

She waited for Zach to offer some soothing words. When they didn't come, she removed her hands and noticed him staring at the carpet. For a moment, she believed that he, too, had been affected by Darla's disappearance. But then, she changed her mind.

She stood, walked across the room, and stopped at the window. She pulled back the luxuriant, damask curtain and said, "I realize this nightmare has been hard on you, too. You liked Lexi. Especially the way she hung on to your every word. It's a tragedy all the way around."

He dropped into the now empty chair. "Lexi had spunk. Would've been a damn good actress to boot." He drummed his hand against his thigh. "But Skye, there's no use moping around. It won't change a damn thing. Nothing's gonna bring her back or Darla for that matter—if—if she's... Look." He cleared his throat. "I think I'll head over to the club and play a quick nine holes. You'll be alright?"

"Go on. A bath sounds like a good idea after all."

She waited a couple minutes to make sure Zach was out of earshot as she searched her phone's contact list for Shane Dalton's number. Finding it, she pressed the screen. "Dammit," she whispered realizing she'd reached his voicemail. "This is Skye. I have a lead. A woman named Dot Barnett. Not only did she threaten me, she sounded positive about knowing who killed Lexi. Get over here as soon as you can. I'll be home the rest of the afternoon."

CHAPTER SIXTEEN

Since showing Beth Getty his hobby room, Zach couldn't quite shake the idea of resuming his pursuit of earning a Ph.D.. Over the years, he'd paid attention to colleagues who'd taken hiatuses from acting to obtain degrees. He always thought they were attempting to show the world they were better than acting—that they had a mind—an intellect. But that's not the case with me, he thought smugly. *I already have an advanced degree. My mark in scientific research could even outshine my brilliant acting career.*

He sighed remembering Lexi's warm, inviting body then shook his head as if trying to dislodge the memory. Though he missed her, he knew it was better: way better now that Lexi was out of the picture. Though he'd always been ninety-nine percent sure about her, there had been always that sliver of doubt gnawing at him, waking him up at night—that she couldn't be trusted. *But now that she's dead, my reputation is secure. Stellar. Not a smidgen of scandal.* He lessened his stride allowing this new sense of ebullience to take root. Upon reaching the staircase, he paused and stared at the floor as if examining the bright sheen of the marble tiles. *Poor dear Lexi.* He pressed his lips into a firm line. *Thank God she's no longer a thorn in my side.* He folded his arms and leaned against the elaborate newel post topped with a Baroque lamp: a beacon he always kept lit in order to create an image of hospitality as guests entered his house. The planets must've aligned themselves perfectly, so all their celestial powers have once again favored me, he thought looking into the gilded framed mirror on the adjacent wall.

He didn't hesitate a second longer. As he climbed the steps, two at a time, his only concern was where the maid had put his favorite golf shirt.

CHAPTER SEVENTEEN

Sofia Fedoruck, the downstairs maid, led Shane into the sunny drawing room on the west side of Zach's mansion. The room was not original to the late 1920s structure and had been one of several additions made to the house. He stepped closer to the fireplace's elegant encaustic tile surround.

Skye watched him focus on the tile's vibrant colors, and for a split second, she envied Beth for marrying an ordinary guy. Then she remembered her first husband, a shoe store manager, and that marriage had been an unmitigated disaster. *Beth must've just lucked out,* she decided with a shake of her head.

"Thank God you're here." She waltzed into the room pulling her hair loose from a ponytail holder. The red-gold locks cascaded around her shoulders and down her back.

He turned away from the fireplace with his hands stuck into his pockets. "Just two questions. Who is Dot Barnett? And why do you think she killed Lexi Horne?"

"Really, Shane, I have no idea who killed Lexi." She sat down and crossed her long, shapely legs. "What I do know is that the best domestic agency in all of LA, Garett-Clarke sent over the Barnett woman for an interview. She arrived with impeccable references. I had high hopes she'd work out—one less annoying problem to solve. Sorry to say, she was ugly and obnoxious. Repulsive actually."

"Not nanny material, I presume?" He didn't wait for a response. "Let me get this straight. According to your phone message, you stated that during a job interview, this woman threatened you." He paused a second. "Do you know how screwy that sounds?"

She glared at him with her lips pressed together.

"Forget that." He took a deep breath. "Okay. Moving on. Can you tell me exactly what she *did* say in relation to the presumed threat?"

Now irritated that Shane had taken on a superior attitude, she believed he was trying to make her feel like an idiot. *Just because he's the expert.* I won't allow his arrogance to overshadow me, she thought, buoying herself. "That if I didn't hire her, I'd wind up dead like Lexi." She enunciated each word clearly.

He pulled out his cell phone, walked across the room, and halted next to the fireplace. The rich tiles this time didn't seem to hold his interest as he mumbled into the phone. Though she strained to hear his words, he'd dropped his usual robust voice to a whisper.

She didn't take her eyes off of him as he paced back and forth. The tight fingers of strain that bound the nape of her neck lessened as she observed his sense of focus and determination. The air separating them seemed alive with the verve of energy he radiated, which offered her a healthy dose of hope. Then she remembered how her own husband had so easily dismissed her concerns about Dot Barnett.

Shane slipped the phone into his sports jacket and explained that he'd dispatched his partner to the domestic agency. "He'll find out if Barnett is legit. While he's busy doing that, I'll pay her a visit."

She closed her eyes and leaned back in the overstuffed chair. "I'm so relieved. I knew I could count on you."

"You have a bodyguard?"

She flashed her eyes open.

"A bodyguard?" Shane repeated.

"No. But, Zach has several on staff."

"I don't want you leaving the house without protection. Understand?"

"But—"

"But nothing."

"Okay."

He turned to leave.

"Shane."

He stopped and peered at her over his shoulder.

"I know this may sound far out, but there are people willing to do anything to be part of this lifestyle." She swept her arm as if encompassing the room. "Dot is a hideous old bat who probably thought she'd have a zillion chances to hobnob with celebrities and whatnot if she worked for me. She wanted it so bad, I think, she killed Lexi in order to fill her shoes as Emma's nanny." Skye lifted a sheet of paper from the nearby end table and thrust it in his direction. "Barnett's resume. It's got her phone number and address. But, I wouldn't be surprised if the agency has never even heard of her. She probably made up the whole thing."

He took the paper and looked at it. "What's this? Corporate finance. President of Barnett Drugs." He rubbed his thumb across his dimpled chin. "Why the hell would someone with a work record like this apply for a nanny position?" He squinted one eye as if trying to digest the information.

"Because it's bogus."

"Look, I'll get to the bottom of it." He doubled creased the sheet of paper.

"Is there any news about Darla?"

"Not yet. But don't lose hope. Right now, no news is good news, if you get my drift."

Even though she blinked her eyes rapidly, a lone tear managed to escape down her cheek. She wiped it away then attempted a smile.

"Atta-girl. This Dorothy Barnett may be our first concrete lead. Good work, Skye."

He paused a second. "I was actually on my way over here when I got your voicemail. I wanted to speak with your husband. Zach around?"

"Golfing. Why do you want to talk to him?"

"Anyone who knew Lexi is of interest."

"It's not true Zach was having an affair with Lexi, if that's what you're after. I think your wife's sixth sense is on the blink or something."

"Don't worry, we base our investigations on evidence." Shane stepped closer to the door. "Hang in there, Skye. Hopefully, we'll soon have news about Darla." He offered her a curt nod then exited the room.

Skye mustered all her energy in an attempt to expel the overbearing thoughts that fought to dominate her exhausted brain: those of the dead nanny, the wannabe nanny, and her personal assistant. She straightened her back and rolled her shoulders. With a slow and fluid movement, she turned her head from side to side. The tense muscles refused to relax, and a fleeting image of a massage crossed her mind. Instead of telephoning her masseuse for an emergency appointment, she closed her eyes and listened to her breath flow. It seemed erratic and shallow. In an attempt to keep her mind a blank slate, she focused on the words of her favorite mantra. She inhaled through her nostrils and concentrated on the phrase, "I am." As the air slowly exhaled between her lips, she completed the mantra with the words "a star." Normally after a few breaths, the tension would melt away like an ice cube tossed into hot coffee. Now, all she felt was stupid.

She pulled out her cell phone and stared at the molded plastic rectangle, debating whether to call Kenny. Five minutes slipped by. She raised her finger above his name on her contact list. The instant she was about to press it, a burst of anger ruptured deep within her. She tossed the phone beyond the intimate arrangement of chairs and tables toward the sofa facing the fireplace. After bouncing off the couch, it hit the floor with a dull thud. She uttered an obscenity. With hurried steps, she crossed the room and lifted the phone. It looked okay. She tapped the screen and heard a ring. In the same instant, she scrambled to stop the call. She'd hit Kenny's number. His voice sounded. Too late.

"Babe, I've been meaning to call you since yesterday morning. But it's been crazy. How the hell are you holding up?" An inkling of solemnity filled Kenny's voice.

"As well as could be expected, I suppose. But, I'm still angry at you."

"You got my texts? I really don't know how many times I can say sorry."

"Words are cheap."

"Let's not rehash that dreadful scenario. I did what I had to do. But I wish to God I could've stayed and supported you. My arms ached because the only thing I really wanted to do was to hold you tight and shield you from that horror. It killed me having to leave you to face that gruesome scene by yourself."

"Then you should've stayed with me." She forced her voice to remain steady even though her eyes welled up. "Still no word about Darla."

"Damn." A couple seconds passed in silence. "You didn't tell the cops I'd been there with you?"

"I was tempted, I was so furious. But, by the time the detectives arrived, I'd cooled down enough and forced myself to see the situation from your point of view."

She heard Kenny sigh.

"I didn't doubt you for a minute, babe. I knew you'd do the right thing."

"Whatever. Anyway, at least now there's a solid lead." Though the words slipped out easy enough, somewhere in the back of her mind, she was beginning to think that maybe Zach had been right all along. Maybe Dot Barnett was just a crank. "A creepy old woman who threatened me."

"Whoa. Are you really okay?"

"Sorta. The detectives are on top of it. Though, I wish to God they'd find Lexi's killer quick. Emma's heartbroken. I figured she needed a change of scenery. Sent her to her father's for a couple of days. She likes being the big sister to my ex-husband's kids. So, she's taken care of for the time being. But, I feel like I'm suffocating in Zach's house. I need to get away. Can we meet somewhere?"

"I'm in Kentucky."

"Why the hell—"

"The Derby. Maiah's horse is running in the race for the roses. It's kinda cool her horse qualified for the 'Most Exciting Two Minutes in Sports'."

"You hate horse racing."

"It's not all that bad. Since we arrived, it's been like nonstop partying. Maybe I misjudged the horseracing crowd. Look, I've gotta go. I'll check in tomorrow."

"Kenny."

No response.

She stared at the phone. Without thinking, she pressed another key. Darla's voice mail clicked on. Frustration boiled inside, but instead of breaking out in tears, a shot of fury coursed through her as she raced out of the room. She nearly knocked Alma over.

"Sorry," Skye mumbled dashing passed her.

"Miss Andrews?"

Skye stopped but didn't turn around.

"I'd like you to check tonight's menu as soon as possible. Mr. Greyson has requested to dine at eight sharp."

"I don't give a flying fig about dinner. I'm getting out of here."

"What should I tell Mr. Greyson?"

"Whatever you like—that I've gone to Kentucky to see the horse race or that I've flown to the moon. Tell him whatever the hell you want." She turned and faced the cook. "I've got to get away," she said softening her voice. "It's like I can't breathe."

With hands planted on her hips, Alma shook her head.

"You wouldn't understand." Skye raced toward the foyer. The banging of the door reverberated throughout the corridor.

CHAPTER EIGHTEEN

With his charcoal felt fedora tipped back, Shane leaned against his unmarked police cruiser taking a much-needed breather. On a clean sheet of notepad paper, he made a cursory sketch of Zach Greyson's house. This was his first visit to the actor's residence, and he found the Renaissance inspired edifice startling. Though the house had been designed and constructed decades before Zach had even been born, Shane was more than a bit surprised that a pompous ass like Greyson would appreciate the mansion's harmonious symmetry and gracious architectural details. Somewhere in the back of his mind, he recalled Beth mentioning that Zach was a bona fide patron of the arts—that he'd purchased a substantial collection of paintings and sculptures and if Zach wanted to, he could easily open up his own private museum. The ring of Shane's cell phone disturbed his reprieve, efficiently shutting down his architectural eye and bringing him back to his gritty reality. He swiped his finger against the phone's screen in anticipation of what his partner had dug up.

Collins succinctly explained that the owner of the agency had been agreeable to his inquiry. She'd even offered additional information she had on file regarding Dorothy Barnett. They decided to meet up for a quick lunch and compare notes.

While driving to the prescribed meeting spot at one of the city's pocket parks, Shane wolfed down most of his fast food lunch. After parking, he grabbed the lunch bag and the half-full giant cup of Coke. He strode passed a row of Acacia trees in full yellow bloom and paused a second to take in their natural beauty. As he rounded the three-tiered fountain located in the park's grassy center, he spied Collins seated on a bench with an opened Styrofoam box resting in his lap.

He dropped next to Collins and glanced at partner's lunch. "Sushi?"

"After what I've been through, you would've wanted to reward yourself with a decent lunch, too." He glanced at Shane's creased, grease stained paper bag and shook his head.

"I've got a few fries left over if you think they'd help."

Collins ignored him as he lifted his Starbuck's cup and took a sip of the Chai Tea Latté.

Shane opened the bag, fished out the container of fries, and tossed the remaining few onto the limestone walkway. He watched a gray squirrel scurry over and lift one in its tiny paws toward its mouth. The rodent's sharp miniature teeth moved a mile a minute. "What's up?"

"I know I'm a complete hottie, but do women have to drool everywhere I go?"

"Ah-oh. Now what?"

"The agency's co-owner, a Bonita Garett, and I fear I'll never forget the name, all but ripped off my clothes in order to have her way with me. I barely got out of there unscathed."

"What you mean is she asked to meet you for a drink sometime? No, not a drink. A cup of coffee."

"Bingo." Collins' eyes lit up as a broad smile filled his face. "Being so smitten, Ms. Garett basically chucked the whole confidentiality clause out the window. Though she did mention it a few times. 'Well Detective, you know this information is usually held in strictest confidence.'" He imitated a woman's voice by employing an impressive falsetto. "I offered to obtain a warrant, but she only batted her false eyelashes and giggled."

He skillfully grasped a piece of a California roll with chopsticks and dipped the morsel into a plastic container of Wasabi. He popped it into his mouth and chewed slowly. Shane waited by gulping a mouthful of cola.

"Ms. Garett stated that Dorothy Barnett joined her agency about a month ago. She found her to be well spoken, neat, and professional. Ummm..." Collins wiped his fingers on a paper napkin then reached inside his suit coat to retrieve his notepad. He flipped it open. "A bit matronly... shiny gray hair arranged in a chignon... designer suit... well-polished."

"Sure doesn't jive with Skye's description of a hideous looking gargoyle."

"It gets better." He reached for a piece of deep-fried tofu sushi but stopped and looked again at his pad. "Apparently, Barnett hasn't any formal training as a governess. But according to Garett, Barnett's personal references read like a who's who list: titans of industry and even, get this, the governor of Washington State."

"So, she concluded Barnett was delusional."

"That's the curious part. Her references panned out."

Shane's eyebrows shot up.

"They all offered the same general consensus. They described Barnett as genteel, educated, but perhaps a tad bit eccentric. The fact she was interested in becoming a nanny to a celebrity family amused, but didn't surprise them. Seems she's done other wacky things in her life like moving to Montana to work on a dude ranch and even palled around with a Mexican migrant family for the harvesting season."

Shane stared at the walkway beyond him. He didn't notice that the fries he'd tossed only moments ago had all disappeared.

Collins flipped a page. "The weird thing is that during the interview, Barnett made a prediction. Skye Andrews would need a nanny soon. And that she'd fit the bill perfectly."

CHAPTER NINETEEN

Shane knew exactly where he was headed. The corner of 5th and Spring. The old Alexandria Hotel. Just thinking about the place conjured up images of long ago presidents, celebrities, and movie stars. Movie stars, he thought with disdain.

Though the Hollywood elite left a bad taste in his mouth, a place like the Alexandria could get his heart pumping. Even though he abandoned his initial plan to be an architect, his interest in buildings and construction hadn't waned. That's why he looked forward to each new issue of *Architectural Digest* and over the years had accumulated a collection of books spanning from prehistoric stone ruins to the construction of the Burj Dubai.

He was remarkably familiar with the colorful history of the Alexandria Hotel. Designed by John Parkinson in 1906, it was the center of downtown's high society from 1911-1922. Within its gracious walls, receptions were held for presidents and generals. There, the "Jazz King" Paul Whiteman started his career, and Valentino danced the night away with silent screen starlets. Vast fortunes were made and lost. The hotel went belly-up during the great depression and closed its doors for five years. The ill effects of a parade of owners coupled with the gradual westward move of the city's business center left the old gal run-down and forgotten. Not to mention the neighborhood's influx of the marginalized: crackheads, panhandlers, and the homeless.

As he waited for a red light to change, he remembered his very first visit to the Alexandria Hotel. By the time he'd turned ten, he'd already fallen in love with the idea of designing buildings and had been precocious enough to seek out a kindly librarian who aided him with the research of local architectural gems.

After pestering his parents, they took him to the Palm Court, the once upon a time, most prestigious ballroom in all of California, which had been honored as a historical-cultural landmark before he was born. The bad news was its location within the Alexandria Hotel. The ten minutes they were inside the shabby hotel, his mother's nervous tendency of tapping her foot filled the air with a steady rat-ta-ta-tat, as she considered its proximity to Skid Row. After he raced up the marble staircase to the second floor, the ugly redecorated faux Victorian décor disappeared as Shane opened the ballroom's door. There he stood transfixed as he took in the gigantic room. Though the gilding had flaked away, the wallpaper faded, the floor uneven and in a dire state of disrepair, he detected a lingering strand of its long ago dignity and grandeur.

So why the hell is Dot Barnett, a personal friend with the governor of the state of Washington, staying in a place like this?

He pressed the gas pedal and wondered if Barnett's decision to live in the shell of a faded glory ran akin to living in her own body. "That's if I'm to trust Skye's description of her," he muttered.

As he turned left onto West Fourth Street, he noticed the area looked a bit brighter. He'd heard something about efforts to update this part of downtown. Beth mentioned a couple weeks ago how much she enjoyed taking the 'Art Walk'. *She said it was...* He squinted his left eye trying to remember. *Provocative? Something like forty-five galleries have sprung up between Main and Spring. Damn, what's the area called now? Gallery Row?*

Caught behind a transit bus, he slowed down and glimpsed at the towering facades he'd seen in countless movies. His sight settled on one he spotted the other night while flipping channels when he couldn't sleep. *Spiderman 2.* Sometimes he found it more entertaining to identify various buildings than to actually watch the films. And it always warmed his heart when he spied the most beautiful room in Los Angeles, the Palm Court, featured.

He pulled around the bus and turned his mind back to the task at hand. He knew there'd be no parking on the one-way street in front of the hotel. His eyes flitted in search of placards signifying public parking. Seeing one, he slammed on the brakes and made a sharp left into the garage. The walk to the hotel would be short. Less than two blocks.

A pulse of excitement surged through him as he pulled open the door leading into the Alexandria. He crossed the lobby and stopped in front of the entrance to a trendy new restaurant. He scratched his head. It wasn't the way he remembered the hotel. Though not sumptuous or elaborate, he noted the lobby appeared clean and bright.

He slipped into an elevator. As the door lumbered closed, he smelled the unmistakable acrid odor of urine. Ah, the real Alexandria has now surfaced, he thought as his finger hovered between the second and third floor button. He pressed number two.

As the doors opened, he saw it. The Palm Court. Feeling as if he were a kid again, he braced himself not really knowing what to expect. As he stepped through the room's threshold, he smelled fresh paint and realized that like the rest of the hotel, the cavernous room was in the throes of another renovation.

To his surprise, he noticed that the ornate guiled moldings, wainscoting, and brass and crystal chandeliers had been restored to perfection. He tilted his head and looked upward. The coffered ceiling still enclosed the four masterful Tiffany skylights, which diffused pastel shafts of pallid light into the room. The addition of circular inlaid lighting into the ceiling did not detract from the authentic feel of the 1911 room. He glanced down and noticed the shiny hardwood floor. More than satisfied with the ongoing renovation, he exited the grand hall rejuvenated and ready to confront Dot Barnett.

A few steps away from where he exited the elevator for a second time, he found himself standing in front of a white door numbered 312. He tapped sharply. Almost immediately, the door swung open with a wide sweep. A short, plump, gray-haired woman filled the doorway. Shane pegged her close to sixty years old.

"Ms. Barnett. I'm Detective Dalton with the homicide unit. May I come in?" He flashed his badge.

She drew her bushy eyebrows together and looked at him from head to toe. Without a word, she stepped aside, allowing him entrance to her tiny apartment.

The high ceilings prevented the place from feeling too claustrophobic, but he admired the degree of creativity needed to redesign a 150-foot square hotel room into a functioning apartment.

He took a cursory look around the room. The long vertical blinds covering the back window stood shut causing a hazy darkness to engulf the room. He coughed. It wasn't just the closed blinds that caused the room to appear dim, he realized spying a scuffed end table stocked with lighted candles, at least twenty of them, and the only source of light within the room. An array of pictures haphazardly filled the wall above the flickering tapers.

Though the soft hum of the overhead ceiling fan filled the room, the breeze was barely noticeable. He glanced beyond Dot and in one sweep grasped that the unit consisted of a kitchenette, sleeping, and living space merged into one room. The closed door on the left wall, he figured was the bathroom.

"Detective, please have a seat."

He nodded before easing into one of the lumpy brown corduroy covered chairs. "I'm here to discuss the murder of Lexi Horne."

Dot sat opposite him in an identical chair. "Lexi Horne?" She peeked at the ceiling as if studying the fan's swirling blades. "Lexi Horne. Now, wasn't she the nanny that worked for a celebrity couple?"

He folded his arms. "You know more than that. I've spoken with Skye Andrews. She told me about your job interview. And that you threatened her."

"Dear me." She pressed an index finger against her cheek. It almost disappeared within the fold of fleshy tissue. She jumped up and edged toward the counter peninsula that defined the kitchen area. He followed her movement and noticed the cooktop and refrigerator were combined into a condensed single item butted up against a three-foot-long countertop. "A cup of coffee, Detective?"

"About the threat."

Instead of answering, she filled an aluminum pot with water and plunked it on top of a burner. She reached underneath the counter into the lone cabinet and pulled out a jar of instant coffee.

Shane didn't mind biding his time by giving Dot a few minutes to settle her nerves. He stood and rubbed his eyes irritated by the smoky fog as he moved toward the curious wall of pictures. The instant he discovered that the photos depicted Zach Greyson, he forgot about the smoke. Dozens of them were tacked to the wall. A couple were the glossy type with a signature, but the majority had been clipped from magazines and newspapers. Zach with an academy award—Zach on the red carpet—Zach in character—Zach being interviewed by a reporter. He scanned them and zeroed-in on one particular photograph located dead center. Ripped from a magazine, it showed Zach and probably Skye, but he couldn't be sure because Dot had covered the woman's face with a picture of herself—the kind that could be taken in a photo-booth for a buck. She posed with her head tilted precisely toward the left with eyes wide and a broad smile. The photograph had been carefully cut so it covered over Skye's face exactly. A shiver ran through him.

"How do you like my *Ode to Zach*?" She asked handing him a coffee mug.

"Interesting." He took the cup.

"There's something about him. Zach Greyson is classy, don't you think?"

She didn't bother to wait for his response. "If you knew him like I do, there'd be no question in your mind. A gentleman of quality. And a harbinger of good taste." She stepped closer to the montage and pointed at the picture with her photo on it. "Zach and I were on our way to dinner when those damn paparazzi snapped us." A flash of anger twisted her corpulent face.

He stepped away from Dot's shrine and took a deep breath under the ceiling fan in an attempt to clear the smoke from his lungs.

"Forget what Skye told you. She's pea green with jealousy over the relationship I have with Zach." She moved so close to him only a couple of inches separated them. He wanted to step away but didn't. "I'll tell you a secret, Detective. Zach's the one who suggested I apply for the nanny position." She paused as a dreamy expression filled her face. "I think the poor dear wants me close by. In the same house. Always around." She slipped free from her reverie and took a gulp from her mug.

She's downright delusional, he thought believing a call to nine-one-one for a medic unit to transport her to a psychiatric unit would be in order. With her level of acuity, Dot might actually burn down the Alexandria with the unbridled mass of flaming candles.

"All this smoke isn't good for your health. Why hasn't the fire alarm gone off?" He took a couple of steps and placed the untouched mug on top the kitchen countertop.

"I took care of that. Removed the batteries."

"In that case, these need to go." He moved back to the candle-laden table. "Fire hazard. Either I take them or I contact the landlord." He figured she'd probably buy more candles, but he had to do something. One by one, he blew out the flickering flames. In the misty, smoky light, he looked over his shoulder and noticed a heavyweight cardboard box on top of the thin, bare mattress wedged inside a rusted bed frame. He reached for the box and noticed it held a lone can of insecticide intended for the elimination of bed bugs. After removing the spray can and placing it on the mattress, he lifted the box and started to deposit the candles inside the carton.

She watched with arms folded. "How dare you? You have no right to barge into my home and confiscate my property."

"I'm concerned about your safety, Ms. Barnett." He lightly brushed her shoulder. The last thing he wanted was to further agitate her.

"Humph."

Once finished, he asked about the batteries for the fire alarm.

"I threw them out."

"You'll have to replace them. Immediately. I'm sure you know the importance of fire safety. But since you're determined to light candles, I'll do my best to scrounge up a fire extinguisher for you." He snapped on a wall switch, and an overhead fixture flashed on.

The tightness around her thin lips began to relax. Then, with a shake of her head, she offered him a tiny smile. "I have a long history with stars." Her eyes lit up. "I'll show you my scrapbook." She almost skipped to the adjacent wall where a couple of shelves hung. They stood empty except for one battered photo album. She handed it to him.

Still wanting to placate her, he reclaimed his seat then lifted the book's cover. On the first brittle, black page, he looked at a picture of smiling man wearing a cowboy hat.

She rested her ample *derrière* on the chair's armrest and peered over his shoulder. "Randy was such a dear. We were so close." She dramatically crossed her hands over her chest and pursed her lips as if she wanted to kiss the smoky air.

"Randy?"

"Oh, come now. Don't tell me you're not an admirer of Randolph Scott?"

He racked his brain and came up with nothing. "Oh sure. He played cowboys in the movies," he said taking a cue from the photo.

"Though I'm not known to kiss and tell...oh what the hey, we were lovers. Very passionate lovers."

Unsure if it was pity or revulsion flooding through him, he recalled what Collins had uncovered at the domestic agency. *Well-polished. Associate of the moneyed elite.* It didn't make sense.

"I understand you're from Seattle."

"Born and raised. But tell me, Detective, how boring would it be to live in only one place? I've actually visited six continents and have lived on three of them." She reached toward the album and turned a couple of pages as if searching for something. "It's in here somewhere. A photograph of Randy and me. I was a mere teenager at the time. Now, where is it?"

"Would you mind if I use your restroom?" He handed her the album then jumped up.

He noticed her hand shake toward the closed door, and a moment later, he slipped inside the tiny washroom.

He splashed a couple handfuls of cold water on his face. Not trusting Dot's towels, he shook his head and allowed the dry air to absorb the moisture. With a flick of his fingers, he opened the medicine cabinet. Orange plastic prescription bottles lined the glass shelf. He lifted one and recognized the name of the antipsychotic. Looking at another bottle, he read the label and discovered it contained sleeping pills. A third bottle left him in the dark as he unsuccessfully tried to pronounce the multisyllabic name. He closed the medicine chest and reached for the door.

Shane reentered the living area, and Dot lifted her head. "I found it. The picture I want you to see."

He stuck his hands deep into his pockets as he glanced at the album page. A smiling young girl stood next to an aged Randolph Scott. *Could that really be Dot as a teenager?* He noted that the girl was pretty. But, then, he decided it probably wasn't her.

"I'd like to talk some more with you. At the station."

"Can I bring my album?"

He nodded.

She started to smile, but then her eyes seemed to cloud over. "Oh, dear me. I just remembered. I always go to BINGO on Thursday night at the senior center." She raised her hands as if trying to push him away. "I know what you're thinking. I'll have to sacrifice my Thursday night entertainment when I begin my new job as Emma's nanny." She shrugged. "I won't mind too much. As long as Zach is nearby watching what a wonderful mother I can be to his child."

"Emma isn't Zach's child."

"Well, if you're going to get picky."

"I want you to consider carefully before you answer my next question. Do you know who killed Lexi Horne?"

Without missing a beat, she said, "How in heaven's name would I know a thing like that?" She raised a stubby finger and twirled it in the air.

"According to Miss Andrews—"

"Miss Andrews is a royal bitch." She flipped a lock of hair behind her shoulder. "Now, if you don't mind, I have to start dinner. I always leave the apartment promptly at six-oh-five to catch the bus."

He looked at his watch. "You've got plenty of time. I'd like to get a statement. Won't take long." Once she's in the station, he'd try to talk her into checking into a hospital. Most likely scenario is she'd quit taking her meds.

"What I have to say, I can say right here. I think that babysitter got exactly what she deserved."

"You wanted Lexi Horne to be killed?"

"Don't twist my words." Her voice tinged with anger, and color rose to her cheeks causing red splotches to appear. "What I am saying is that Emma needs me."

"Or is it really all about Zach Greyson? He's the one you want to be close to—not Emma—so much that you thought it'd be a good idea for the nanny to disappear permanently." He paused. "In other words, Horne had to die."

She sucked in her lower lip as if studying the thin carpeting beyond her feet. Abruptly, she snapped her head up and bore her eyes into him. "What would you think if I said yes? That I killed the nanny."

"I'd read you your rights and arrest you."

"Save your breath. I'm not the one you're looking for." She took a few steps toward the long window beyond the kitchen workstation and flipped the blinds open. Weak sunlight cast vertical shafts of light on the floor.

"We can talk more about it at the station. Otherwise—"

"You'll arrest me." She spun around with her hands clutching her thick waist.

"Arrest? Nothing like that. No."

"Oh?" She paused and patted her frizzy hair as if attempting to tame the unruly locks. "All right, then. As long as I'm back in time for my BINGO."

She opened the kitchen cabinet and pulled out a canvas bag. After reaching inside the stained tote, she plucked out a compact and a tube of lipstick. She flipped the compact open, peered into the tiny mirror, then lifted the puff and pressed chalky powder against her flushed cheeks. She moved the mirror closer, uncapped the lipstick, and deftly filled in her narrow lips a bright red. "One always has to look her best. Regardless of the circumstances. I learned that tip from Gloria Swanson. Did you know she was married downstairs in the Palm Court? Anyway, I think it's very good advice. Don't you agree, Detective? After all, one never knows who might turn up at a police station."

CHAPTER TWENTY

After a frustrating hour of conferring—asking questions, listening, and almost begging Dot Barnett to seek medical help—Shane gave up. Collins agreed that the likelihood of Dot being the perpetrator of the teenage murders was next to nil. Which left them with nothing.

Seated behind his desk with cell phone in hand, Shane listened impatiently to his voicemails until he heard Mike Alder's voice. An angry hue laced Mike's words as he demanded an update on the investigation into Lexi's death.

"Hmmm." Shane clicked off his phone.

"What's up?" Collins looked away from the paper in his hand.

"Alder. He's pissed because Horne's killer hasn't been apprehended yet." Shane paused a second. "I think I'll pay him a little visit. You game?"

Collins motioned to the computer monitor glowing in front of him. "Got to finish this report or Rosnick will have my head. But Alder is a good enough suspect as any since we're like batting zero. You go ahead."

"If necessary, I'll bring him here. Let you have a crack at him."

It took only a few minutes for Shane to drive to the Red Star Gym. It was on his route to and from work and he'd considered stopping inside a couple of times to inquire about a membership. He'd surely benefit from the advice of a personal trainer. Work always took precedence, but if he waited too long, one day he'd find himself hopelessly out of shape. With eating on the go and Beth's habit of adding butter to just about everything she cooks, it's a wonder I'm not as big as a house, he thought making a left-hand turn.

Shane parked in the lot facing the strip-mall, jumped out of the car, and headed to the gym wedged between a sandwich shop and a nail salon. He stepped inside and took in the typical health club scene: a room stacked full of weight machines, treadmills and stationary bikes, punching bags, and rows of dumb-bells.

To his near right, Mike Alder slammed iron-plates onto the chest press bar. Sweat streamed down his face. His soaked t-shirt stuck to his skin while he slid onto the bench and strained as he hoisted the heavy bar. Lowering it toward his chest, he paused, grunted, and then raised the bar. He repeated the movement four times.

"Hey, maybe you're overdoing it a little?" Shane asked.

With a firm hold on the bar, Mike turned his head in Shane's direction. He lifted the weight a final time, hooked it in place, and wiped his face with a towel.

"Why don't you take five? I'd like to have a word with you," Shane said.

Mike nodded at the buff guy who'd been acting as his spotter. As soon as he ambled out of earshot, Mike blurted, "Have you found out who did it?"

Shane shook his head.

"Why are you here when you could be searching for Lexi's killer?"

Ignoring his question, Shane looked around the gym and noted it was under capacity but still fairly busy with clusters of people grouped around machines. Seeing Mike in this environment, sweat drenched and muscles pumped, left no doubt that Alder was a serious bodybuilder. He's built like a damn tank, Shane thought with a bit of admiration. *But those kind of muscles usually don't develop just by pumping iron.* "You compete?"

Mike reached for a bottle of water sitting on a nearby bench. "I'm working toward my pro-card. This was gonna be my big year. I've worked my ass off to achieve near perfect symmetry and finally nailed those damn poses. Now that I qualify, my goal was to hit as many competitions as possible until I win professional status. Once that happens, the sky's the limit. There'll be money, interviews in fitness magazines, endorsements...the whole enchilada."

"Focused on the prize. Bet that's what drew Lexi to you. She had lofty goals too."

Mike lifted the plastic bottle and swallowed. A drizzle of water spilled down his chin. "Lexi was amazing." He lowered his eyes as if studying the frayed carpeted floor. "She went with me to the NPC Arnold Amateur in Columbus last month. I was psyched knowing she was in the audience cheering me on. Afterwards, Lexi was so damn sweet the way she said the judges were a bunch of idiots. That I should've won hands down." He inhaled deeply. "When the fourth place trophy was set at my feet, I swear to God, I just wanted to pick it up and smash the judges' heads with it." Mike took a long gulp from the bottle emptying it. He wiped his mouth with the back of his gloved hand then crushed the plastic container and threw it across the room. It hit against the wall with a dull thud before falling to the floor.

"Fourth place doesn't seem so bad. Isn't the Arnold a national competition?"

"Yeah. But I wanted Lexi to be proud of me. When we got home, it was over. She broke up with me."

"Another guy?"

"She didn't give me a concrete explanation. Just some lame line about being too busy with her job and school. But I figured she decided I was a loser after all."

"Maybe not a loser but possibly a fake?" Shane crossed his arms.

Mike glared at him.

"You're on the juice."

"Hell no. I'm not into that crap. I'm clean. Gotta be clean. Drug-testing."

"But you are familiar with supplements. Vitamins, protein powders, amino acids, creatine."

"They're all legal." Mike wiped the towel against his sweat-streaked face.

"But performance enhancing drugs aren't."

"Look, a lot of bodybuilders use PEDs. I don't."

"You're telling me you're a natural bodybuilder?"

"What the hell has this to do with Lexi's death?"

Shane narrowed his eyes. He wasn't about to tell Alder that one of the drugs that killed Lexi and the other girls was a PED. Boldenone Undecylenate. Trade name—Equipoise. Street name—EQ. He recalled what he'd read on the internet. A testosterone derivative used for intramuscular issues with horses. In humans, the steroid is a potent agent in building muscular size making it popular with bodybuilders. It builds the tissue slowly while muscle gains remain longer. If taken during the off-season, traces of the drug would not be noticeable in urine and blood testing. But to Shane's best understanding, steroid testing in the world of bodybuilding was spotty and nearly non-existent. Enforced drug testing would probably trigger a financial disaster for the sport by upping the cost for spectators, vendors, and sponsors.

"Look," Shane said with a shake of his head. "You need to come to the station. I need a formal statement about why you were at Skye Andrews' house the night of April 29th."

"I told you why. I was trying to patch things up with Lexi. Wasn't my poem proof enough?"

The door swung open. Both men turned their attention toward the front of the gym.

"What the hell?" Shane muttered.

"Can I help you?" Mike offered.

"Shane, darlin'. What a surprise bumping into you." Beth took a few steps in Shane's direction. "I just finished shooting the announcement not even an hour ago. Stopped next door for a quick sandwich and thought maybe it's a personal trainer that I'm needing." She cleared her throat. "Just thought I'd take a wee look around the place."

"My wife. Beth Getty."

"Don't I know you?" Mike asked.

"Of course you do. You've probably seen her photo hundreds of times—magazine covers, advertisements, television commercials. Known as Sibeal. The supermodel," Shane said eyeballing Beth.

"Cool," Mike said. "So you want to workout here? Really cool. Well." He looked her up and down. "We have an awesome get-back-into-shape package. We do a complete workup: diet, body fat analysis–"

"Whoa. I think heading down to the station is more important than trying to talk my wife into becoming a gym member."

"Whatever. But, I'll have to call my boss first." Mike turned and headed to the office.

"What are you doing here?" Shane demanded.

"I may want to join a gym. The truth be, my director and I were reviewing some footage from the PSA, and it really opened my eyes. I looked a little bit flabby."

"Beth." He raised his eyebrows.

"Oh, alright." She squeezed her eyes shut for a moment. "I thought Mike could share some of his memories of Lexi with me."

"Why?"

She placed her hands firmly on her slim waist. "Because ever since I skimmed her diary, I've been drawn to her. A connection of sorts. I can't really explain it, but it's like I've forged a spiritual bond with her. I've been experiencing a feeling that's so intense I know my *fey* is trying to break through. But, I've been such a rattlebrain lately, I can't seem to pick up on the message."

Shane rolled his eyes toward the ceiling but kept his lips pressed together.

"Hearing about Lexi from someone she was close to could release the blockage and open up the channel of communication to my sixth sense." A man carrying a duffle bag brushed into her and mumbled a quick apology. She shook her head as if in an attempt to refocus. "Since I was going to drive past the gym on the way home, I thought I'd stop by for a minute or two. Talk to Mike. And maybe sign up for some workout sessions."

"I'm not buying into that *fey*, hocus-pocus stuff. So whatever it really is, some deep psychic connection or simple curiosity, I don't want you contacting the people mentioned in Lexi's diary. That's my job. Understand?"

Mike sauntered out of the office. "Okay if I meet you at the station? I've got to tie up a few loose ends first. Say in forty-five minutes at the—"

"Clear Springs Station."

Mike half-nodded then retreated to the office.

Without a word, Shane placed his hand under Beth's elbow and escorted her out of the Red Star Gym.

CHAPTER TWENTY-ONE

Beth backed out of the parking spot in front of the gym's main entrance. Shane was watching, and she didn't want him to think she hadn't heeded his instructions. Got to keep the waters smooth, she warned herself as she pulled her SUV in the direction of their home. After driving through two traffic lights, she made a U-turn and headed back to the gym.

Ever since yesterday, when she placed her fingertips on the pages where the young nanny had poured out her heart, Beth felt plagued by a gnawing desire to make sense of the attack on Lexi. If only she could uncover a clue that would lead Shane to the killer.

In her diary, Lexi had raved about the Red Star Gym and her personal trainer. In a few short sentences, Lexi admitted that her initial attraction toward Mike was based on superficiality. His good looks.

She'd used the phrase drop-dead gorgeous or was it hottie? Probably both.

Lexi's words had teased Beth's curiosity about the Adonis named Mike Alder. Most of the time, the carefully written words stated that he was affable, fun loving, and very attentive. But, more and more, Lexi found herself walking on eggshells not knowing what would set him off. She witnessed him screaming at drivers, bikers, and pedestrians who slowed him down, punching walls when his favorite football team lost a game, even cursing out a server who wasn't quick enough with their dinner order. All those explosions of anger frightened her. One entry, only days before Lexi had left for Italy, she'd written about his lack of good sportsmanship at a bodybuilding event. Instead of lifting his trophy to pose for pictures, he'd left it behind on the stage and walked off in disgust. That exhibition had been the cincher. Though she liked Mike, his wild mood swings and fiery temper had caused the end of their relationship. No wonder she dumped him, Beth thought, nosing her Volvo back into the exact parking space facing the Red Star Gym.

She reached into her oversized purse and pulled out her camera. If I'm going to unearth everything there is to know about Lexi Horne, I'm going to have to compile a complete dossier. She adjusted the lens and snapped a couple of pictures of the gym's glass and brick front façade.

Beth was familiar with gyms since spending endless hours lifting and straining beneath heavy bars and weights when she was modeling. She'd refused to be like most models, just skin and bones resembling walking skeletons but wanted to have a bit of definition, just a hint of something more—like muscles.

She stepped back inside the health club nearly fifteen minutes later and noticed it had emptied out except for a couple of people working on the leg press in the back of the gym. With quick steps, she marched toward the office and peered through its large window. Mike was leaning back in a well-cushioned chair with his feet propped up on the desk and the telephone receiver against his ear. He had changed his clothes, and his hair was wet. He looked up and saw her. Before she was able to knock, the door flew open.

"Sibeal?" He frowned. "Didn't you leave with your husband?"

"I thought it best if we talked in private."

He ushered her into the office. The walls were lined with photographs of bodybuilders with trophies and girls clad in tiny bikinis with hard bodies and bright smiles.

"I've got to get to the station." He looked at his watch.

"I won't keep you but a minute. Truth be, I have a strong urge to find out what happened to Lexi. I crossed paths with Lexi all the time being a friend of Skye Andrews. She was lovely. Kind and gentle. Caring." She read the sorrow that filled his eyes. "She cared deeply for you, actually loved you in a special way." She pursed her lips fearing she'd piled it on a bit too deep.

He closed his eyes but not soon enough as a tear escaped and moved across his cheek.

"Tell me a bit about her." She touched his rock hard shoulder.

"Lexi was different than most girls. You know what it's like. Take a babe out to grab a hamburger and a beer and she's ready to jump in the sack with you. Not Lexi. Not in a million years. She was kinda old-fashioned that way. Not phony or uppity. There's so much of that here." He gestured at the air between them. "She was real. Authentic."

"Did you two have a lot in common?"

"Almost everything." He paused to draw in a deep breath. "Of course, being a nanny, she loved kids. But, unlike me, she always had her nose in a book. She was a real student. I remember how pumped she was when she made the Dean's List. But all that school stuff didn't mean she was a geek. Hell, no." A wistful smile crossed his face. "Lexi liked cool stuff. Skiing and roller skating, playing volleyball, and working out. We even started parachuting lessons." He bit his lower lip. "Lexi was the best damn thing in my life. I loved her."

Beth nodded hoping her interest would encourage him to continue.

"I know we could've worked things out. I wrote her a poem. She loved that kind of stuff. I focused really hard and channeled all my emotions into it. But I was too late. She was already gone by the time I got to Malibu." He clenched his fingers into a fist.

"Who could've done such a horrible thing?"

"Serial killer. At least that's what the news reported. Some sicko killing beautiful teenaged girls. Lexi sure filled that bill."

She wasn't sure if all the slain girls had been beautiful, but she believed a missing piece of the puzzle existed, one that would link all the murders together. And once that connection was figured out, everything would fit into place.

"If I had to pick someone who I didn't trust, who really could've have hurt Lexi, it'd be Zach Greyson."

"Zach?"

"I'm not saying he killed Lexi. But something about that guy doesn't add up. I heard she got some kind of acting gig. That wasn't Lexi. She was so pumped up about school. Wanted to teach or translate foreign documents or something like that. It must've been Greyson who lured her away from her dream. Like he had some kind of hold over her."

"Hmmm." *Some kind of hold over her.* "Look, you better get going. Shane will be in a rotten mood if you're late."

CHAPTER TWENTY-TWO

In the soft glow of twilight, Skye leaned against the marble balustrade overlooking the backyard. Though Zach stood only inches away, she kept her sight fixed on the flowing water tumbling over carefully arranged rocks under the Japanese garden bridge that spanned the narrow stream, instead of looking at him.

"I'm glad you decided to come home for dinner," Zach said.

"Even if I wasn't good company?"

"It's understandable—"

"I can't stop worrying about Darla."

"Worrying won't help."

"I should contact her parents. But, what if Darla just took off for a couple of days? They'd be upset and probably fly out here for nothing."

"They're not local?"

"Wisconsin."

"Maybe there'll be news soon. Good news." He slid his arm around her waist.

With the turn of her shoulder, she slipped free of his embrace. He reached toward her but let his hand drop.

"Why don't I send Bruno to pick up Emma? Then tomorrow, bright and early, we can pile in the car for a day trip. We can go to, oh I dunno, hey, how 'bout Griffith Park? The kid loves the Merry-Go-Round. We could have a picnic at the old zoo and then hike to the top of Bee Rock."

"I'm tired." She brushed her manicured fingers along her neck. "I'm going to my room."

"What about tomorrow?" He crossed his arms and eyed his wife's form. Dressed in a simple white chiffon gown with her red-gold hair tied in a knot at the nape of her neck, she resembled an ancient Roman goddess, standing in the warm air, like a stone sculpture.

"Change of plans. Emma's staying with her father until Monday. Hopefully by then, she won't still be pining for Lexi."

"You've got to be kidding? The kid just lost one of the most important people in her life. You think she'll be over that in four days? Be for real."

"She's resilient."

"She needs her mother." He paused a second. "You're still gonna head out next week to—"

"Baltimore."

"How long is this project going to keep you away from Emma?"

"Really, Zach. I'll fly back, at least once or twice, to check on her."

"Break your contract. For the kid's sake."

"You think it's okay for me to break my contract at the last minute? Who the hell will hire me with that kind of reputation?" She jerked around and faced him. "No one."

"She's your daughter, for Chrissake."

"You've reached the top. Even have a whole room full of statuettes, trophies, and awards to prove it. I'm hardly in the same league. Right now. But, I'm not short on ambition or hard work. If you think I'm going to chuck it because Emma is upset, you've got another thing coming." She took a couple of backward steps, distancing herself from him. "Don't you think I'm upset? I'm sick over Darla. But I won't sacrifice my career because I'm sad or scared or, or... or for any other feeling that's going to eventually fade away."

"Starring in a damn movie is more important than your own daughter's well-being?"

"My daughter will be fine." She folded her arms. "After all, she has you, and Alma, and even that priest, to hover around and patch up her broken heart." Skye marched across the terrace and into the sprawling house.

"At least she knows we really love her," Zach yelled. He doubted she heard him as the door slammed shut. "Because you're no kind of mother to that kid," he said lowering his voice to a whisper. "If only she were mine."

He walked the length of the terrace and gazed across the expansive yard, beyond the guesthouse to the visible bit of silhouette outlining the Los Angeles skyline. The ambers and violets that painted the sky only moments earlier had faded, leaving in its place a darkening twilight. He scooted around the outdoor kitchen and stopped at the pool. The water cascading from the stone waterfall caused ripples to form on the pool's surface. He dipped his fingers into the water as the light breeze filled the air with the sweet fragrance of orange blossoms wafting from his small orchard.

"Skye's gonna have to face facts. If Darla's dead, she's dead. Move forward. No use lamenting. Won't bring 'em back that's for sure." The ring of the words appealed to his pragmatic outlook. "But the problem remains—the heart doesn't operate on logic." He stepped away from the pool surprised at how quickly night had fallen.

Maybe that's why Skye's headed to Baltimore. Her way of dealing with grief. But to abandon the kid when she really needs her?

A shot of heat radiated through him and caused a line of perspiration to form above his lip. He pulled loose his black bow tie, unbuttoned his formal dress shirt, and slipped out of it. A moment later, he tossed all his clothing onto a lounge chair and tucked his socks and patent leather shoes beneath its teak frame. He stood resplendent in his nakedness as the clouds shifted and allowed moonlight to bathe his body.

He dove into the pool. The chilly water infused a sense of giddiness with its sudden rush of coolness as he flexed his muscles and slashed the water with his powerful arms. After a few moments, he slowed his pace and jerked his head upward as if sensing a presence. As he blinked away droplets of water, he inspected the edge of the pool but didn't see anyone. Satisfied that he was alone, he flipped onto his back and glided along the water's surface. Cloud formations skidded across the inky firmament. He tried to locate a star or any light in the sky but found himself gazing at shifting vapors.

I'm the only star in sight…and who would've guessed it would be like this?

CHAPTER TWENTY-THREE

FRIDAY, MAY 2nd

Beth bit her tongue too late. After listening to Skye's long, drawn-out story about how she and Zach had yet another fight, she wondered if she'd agreed to Skye's request only as a means to stop her incessant blabbering. A wave of apprehensiveness washed through her with the idea of having Skye as a houseguest. "Maybe it won't be too bad," she said under her breath. *Might actually be kind of fun. Too bad Shane won't see it that way.*

Brushing all thoughts of Skye aside, she flipped the pages of her opened binder and stopped at the photo sheets she'd inserted at the front of the notebook. The first sheath displayed a photo of Lexi she'd clipped from the morning paper to serve as an inspiration and a reminder. It showed a smiling young woman at her high school graduation.

On the following pages, she'd included all the photos and articles she could find online and in the newspaper regarding the other three victims: Tykera Carter, Jenny Hart, and Eliana Mendoza. Though the investigation had unearthed the names of the unknown teen victims, the information she'd been able to gather had been skimpy and offered no more than the barest facts, not much more than their ages and, of course, their profession as prostitutes. She studied the pictures, imagined glimmering anticipation in their expectant eyes, and mourned the robbing of such young lives as a sin on humanity.

She glanced at the television screen hoping the news would have new information about the murders. The newscasters bantered in a light-hearted way so she lifted the remote and hit the mute button.

She continued to turn the pages and lingered on two photos she'd taken yesterday: one of the façade of the Red Star Gym and the other of Mike Alder. She'd clicked the shutter only seconds before he sprinted out of the gym. As she inspected the picture, she now understood how easily a girl's head could be turned in his direction. "He has the strength of Sampson and the looks of a Greek god with his finely chiseled features," she said fixing her attention on his body-builder's physique.

With a shake of her head, she pulled out the lined pad where she'd compiled a to-do-list in the wee hours of the morning. It contained only three items. The muscles in her stomach tightened as she looked at the name she'd written in red ink. Marjorie. Though she hadn't been fully awake last night when Shane finally slipped into bed, the bombshell he delivered had her up most of the night. While questioning Marjorie about the diary—he had told her the truth—that they were married.

It'd be a snap for Marjorie, the ultimate busybody, to figure out her complicity, might even cause Marjorie to sever their relationship. She chewed her lip in an attempt to come up with an explanation Marjorie would buy but came up blank. "I'll have to divulge the whole ugly truth," she muttered. The sound of the words made her cringe.

She grabbed the desk phone, punched in Marjorie's number, and counted the rings. After the fifth one, voice mail clicked on. She cleared her throat and tapped her foot waiting for Marjorie's perky message to end. "I'm sorry I wasn't upfront with you the other day. Truly, I'm ashamed for keeping Shane's role in the investigation a secret. I pray there aren't any hard feelings. So, I was thinking it'd be grand if we could meet later for lunch. At that new gourmet deli you're crazy about. Around one? Give me a ring." She'd never talked so fast in her life but sensed a modicum of relief that she didn't have to apologize in person.

She stared at the phone. Her intuition told her that Marjorie would call right back. But after a few seconds ticked by, she set the phone back on the desk.

With the first chore done, she drew a line through it. As she considered the next item, a healthy dose of trepidation caused her to jump up from the desk. If she continued with her quest, she'd definitely be infringing on her husband's territory. But unable to come up with an alternative, she'd have no choice but to meet Zach's houseguest and Lexi's boyfriend.

She looked through the study's wide window. Verdant foliage filled the wooded lot across the street and shimmered in the early morning sunshine. The idea of a walk in the park crossed her mind. She nixed the idea and lifted a photography magazine. As she flipped it open, the paper marker holding her place fluttered to the floor.

She tossed the magazine back onto the side table and closed her eyes. No matter how hard she tried to shake the impractical idea of solving the teenage murders, a tiny voice inside her head assured her that she had no other choice but to continue.

She grabbed the binder, flipped to her notes compiled from the diary, and ran her finger down the page until landing on the section pertaining to Charles Blyth Wickham, III. "Nickname is Trey," she read aloud from the typed page. "Former painting student of Kenny Weston. Lexi met him in Italy nearly three months ago. Impressed Zach with his artistic talent and became his mentor. Lives in Zach's guesthouse."

Her eyes fell to the sentence she'd marked over with a yellow highlighter, a direct quote from Lexi's diary: *I believe Trey is my future. Not Mike. Or, God forbid, P.C. Now that I know what love really is, thank God, I've finally found the person who'll provide me with lasting, authentic happiness.* She rested her chin in her cupped hands and wondered if, at age nineteen, Lexi could be certain about with whom she'd want to build her future. She hadn't even finished her education or fulfilled her chosen career path. Once she began her television work, her perspective would've changed, for better or worse, but now no one will ever know.

She again glanced at her list. "Ah, chore number three." The beginning of a smile tugged at the corners of her mouth. "Not a chore at all." She drew a star next to the number. "A picnic dinner with Shane. I don't give a tinker's dam how busy he is—we are going to spend a relaxed hour together over a delicious meal."

She reached for the TV remote. Her finger hovered over the off button, but then she caught a glimpse of the news ticker crawling along the bottom of the screen.

Medical Examiner states autopsy reveals Alexandria Horne, the 'Hollywood Nanny' twelve weeks pregnant.

She stared at the moving ribbon of words unable to grasp their meaning. A second later, they sunk in.

Beth began to pace. With each step, a pain throbbed against her right temple. "Twelve weeks." She spat out the words as if condemning the room's chalky blue walls. "Right before she met Trey. Probably still dating Mike. But he's admitted they never had sex. Would he lie about that?" An image of the cocky bodybuilder flew through her mind. "Lexi would've been a feather in his cap. So that leaves P.C." She stopped walking. "Zach?"

She sunk onto the edge of the desk's chair as a glimmer of understanding broke through. "Maybe it wasn't Zach who had a hold over Lexi. Maybe she was the one pulling the strings."

She raced out of the room intent on finding the answer.

CHAPTER TWENTY-FOUR

From the instant he opened the door, Beth knew she'd like Trey Blyth Wickham. Whether it was her *fey* or the strong vibes radiating from him, she realized Lexi had made a smart decision to offer this young man her heart. She identified herself as a friend of the Greysons and the wife of the detective assigned to Lexi's murder case.

He sucked in a mouthful of air. "You knew Lexi?"

"Quite well." She half-lied. "You must be devastated. She was so kind and caring. A very precious young woman. Special to all who knew her."

Trey glanced downward as if studying his Birkenstock sandals. "Would you like to come in?" He opened the door wider.

"I wouldn't want to impose," she said holding back her eagerness, "but perhaps for a wee moment." She stepped into the living room.

He cleared his throat. "Would you like something to drink?"

"A cup of tea would be lovely."

"Tea? Um. How 'bout coffee?"

"Perfect." She sat on the edge of a sleek black leather chair.

While he popped off to the kitchen, she glanced around the room. It oozed Zach Greyson. From its upscale furnishings to the expensive paintings that decorated the cream-colored walls.

Though not an art expert, she had no doubts that the paintings were originals though maybe not as grand as the ones exhibited in his manor house. The only things that belied the fact that no one actually lived in the immaculately kept guesthouse was a cell phone and set of keys lying on the glass-topped coffee table.

Trey returned carrying two earthenware mugs. "Aren't the paintings great?"

She settled her sight on the young man and decided he'd put on a brave face.

He handed her a cup then pointed to the wall. "That one is an original Picasso."

"You don't say." She took a quick sip of the black coffee. "Though I'm thoroughly impressed, I'm more interested in your work. Zach must think you're going to make quite a splash in the art world since he's opened his home to you."

He hung his head and shrugged as if embarrassed. "Everything was going great. But now..." He sunk onto the matching leather couch. "It's like I'm stuck inside a fog I can't escape. I reach for my phone 'cause I want to tell Lexi something, and then I remember she's gone." He took a long swallow of coffee then held the mug between his hands as if warming them. "We just kinda clicked. Know what I mean? And even though she was well, you know—breathtaking— she had a fantastic personality. Upbeat. Funny. Really sweet. Not like other girls I've met. She had values that nowadays are basically non-existent—call it old-fashioned or maybe even stupid—like she wanted us to wait for marriage before having sex. But she didn't just talk about it, she lived according to her principles. She was the best thing in my life. I can't believe she's gone."

With a swift motion, he slammed the mug onto the coffee table and then buried his face in his hands. His slender, long fingers matched his tall, athletic frame perfectly. Sun-streaked blond hair fell below his collar and looked as if it hadn't seen a comb in days. He wore a faded Ravens' football t-shirt and a pair of khaki shorts. He lifted his head and faced her with piercing blue eyes.

"Better to talk than keep everything bottled up," she said. "Curse whoever's done this, even God if you have to, but let it out or the grief will overcome you." She detected a slight nod though his face remained impassive. "Have you spoken to Lexi's parents?"

"Her sister stopped by yesterday. She lives upstate in Hillsborough with her folks. I never met her before, but we've been Facebook friends for a while. We just looked at each other and cried. I wanted to be strong for her. I tried to be a man but—"

"An authentic man shows his feelings. It's nothing to be ashamed about, so."

He reached for his coffee and took a sip.

"I'm supposing the police have stopped by to talk about Lexi. Perhaps my husband, Shane?"

"I turned off my phone. Couldn't bear to take all the calls and texts. But I checked it about fifteen minutes ago, and a Detective Collins left a message. He's stopping by to ask me a few questions. When I heard you knock, I thought it was him."

Damnation. That's the last thing I need. Gavin will certainly tell Shane I was with Trey. I can't possibly lie to Shane again.

"You shouldn't be alone. You could move into the main house for a while."

"I don't think so. No." He took a quick sip of coffee. "Zach stops by a couple times a day. So does Sofia."

"The maid?"

"Says she needs to clean, but she really wants to check on me." He placed the mug on the coffee table. "She's from Ukraine. Earned her engineering degree in her hometown of Kiev and has been working to save money for graduate school. But when Zach got wind of that, he wrote her a check to cover tuition costs."

"Really?"

"That's typical Zach. But her English is still a bit sketchy. So Lexi's been helping Sofia perfect her English. And she's been teaching Lexi Ukrainian. Sometimes they talked to each other in Russian. Lexi says it makes Zach crazy not being able to understand them." He swallowed hard. "Anyway, Sofia's tried to cheer me up. I haven't asked her, but I think she's gone through a similar loss."

His rush of words seemed to have had a cathartic effect. The tightness pinching his jaw relaxed, and a glimmer of light filled his eyes.

"Have they caught him?"

"The detectives and the forensic team are working day and night. They're bound to know something soon. But, I was wondering, do you have any idea why someone wanted to kill Lexi?"

"Whatever reasons motivate a serial killer." He shrugged. "To be honest, my first thought was Mike Alder, her ex body-building boyfriend did it, not a serial killer. Lexi was freaked-out because he refused to accept she dumped him. Even thought he was stalking her. Like out of the blue, he'd show up at the same fast food joint, or bookstore, or even her classroom door like he knew her school schedule, with the pretext it was some kind of weird coincidence. That it proved they were in sync and belonged together. Of course, she blew him off."

Beth nodded periodically which seemed to spur him on.

"He has a mean temper. Probably due to all those steroids he injects. He's like a living pincushion. As strong as he is, it would've been no problem at all for him to..." He blinked a couple times. "It's only a gut feeling. I have no proof." He lifted a pillow and turned it over before tossing it aside. "I should've been with her that night, but I was on a flight back from Florida State University. My sister's twenty-first birthday bash." He jumped up, walked to the large bay window, and pulled back the shade.

"Don't blame yourself, Trey."

He hid his face in the crook of his arm. She saw his shoulders shake.

She adverted her eyes and focused on the Picasso color lithograph. The female figure looked fractured, cut up into triangular pieces, as if she were made of shattered glass.

He moved back to the couch but didn't sit.

"Zach's been over?" She tried redirecting the conversation.

"He's awesome. With all of his celebrity status, it's to his credit, he hasn't become jaded or morphed into some kind of arrogant snob. Look at all he's done for Lexi and me. Not to mention Sofia and countless others."

She frowned wondering if she'd misjudged Zach. "As your mentor, I imagine he's pretty hands-on with your art career. He's raved about your talent." She noticed Trey's eyes had welled up again. "If it's not an inconvenience, I'd really love to see some of your paintings."

He ushered her toward the back of the house and into the sunlit studio. The rich aroma of turpentine, oil, and pigments permeated the air.

She took in the spacious workspace. A couple of easels held unfinished canvases, and groups of paintings leaned stacked against the walls. A long wooden table stood covered with tubes of paints arranged in rows, bottles filled with mediums and varnishes, and a metal container holding what seemed like a hundred brushes.

He freed several paintings from the piles and placed them on hooks arranged at various heights on a bare wall. She took in the realistic details of the landscapes and marveled at the clarity of light and sense of atmosphere he was able to create within the picture space. The final painting, he hung at eye level. A portrait of Lexi. She blew out a puff of air finding herself bowled over at the way he'd been able to convey the very essence of what she'd learned about Lexi.

"I had that hidden away." He gestured toward the portrait with his opened palm. "Lexi didn't know I painted it. The plan was to give it to her on our wedding day." He stuck his hands in his pockets. "She didn't know it, but I'd already started to look at engagement rings. Realistically, I wanted to wait until I got my Master's and a job at an art college, but I knew I couldn't wait that long to propose."

She wanted to wrap her arms around him and soothe his tremendous grief. She moved closer and noticed his eyes were dry.

"It helps when I look at her portrait. I painted it the way I saw her—joyful and full of life with her incredible beauty shining through. As long as I have this painting, Lexi won't really be dead to me."

"'Tis lovely, Trey," she said under her breath. At a loss for words, she glanced over her shoulder and spied a painting leaning against the wall separating two stacks of canvases. She moved closer and took in the brilliantly executed image believing she could actually smell the flowers in their clay pots and hear the tinkling of the water spurting from the marble fountain. She lifted the canvas to inspect the brushstrokes.

She sensed his presence next to her. "It's beautiful," she whispered not wanting the sound of her voice to interfere with the magic that drew her into the scene.

"I painted it in Sorrento. It was Lexi's favorite."

"I understand why. Surely, you'd never part with it."

"Like the portrait, I thought I'd keep it forever. But when I see somebody, like you right now, so transformed by a piece of art, it makes my heart, well, I know it sounds corny, but it makes my heart skip a beat. Art has the ability to forge connections and makes us think, reminisce, even dream."

"I've never looked at paintings that way. But, you're absolutely right." She handed him the canvas.

"I think Lexi would've wanted you to have it. Please." He offered the painting back.

"That's incredibly kind, but—"

"Just promise me one thing. When you look at it, think of Lexi."

She nodded as she slipped the hobo bag off her shoulder and pulled out her checkbook.

"Oh, no. It's a gift, Ms. Getty. Think of it as a present from Lexi. I can tell she touched your life in an amazing way, too."

His generosity overwhelmed her, and she found herself speechless. Even so, she couldn't possibly leave without confronting Trey with the reason she came to see him in the first place. He'd already mentioned his relationship with Lexi had been a chaste one so he couldn't have fathered Lexi's unborn child.

But did he know who did?

"You said earlier that you'd turned off your phone. Have you been keeping up with the news reports?"

"I shut everything down. TV, computer, iPad. It's been too difficult hearing the same words over and over of how she died. When I haven't been sleeping, I've been painting."

She placed the landscape painting back against the wall. Not sure of the most prudent way to tell him that Lexi was expecting, she decided the direct approach would be best. Like ripping a plaster free from over a wound—the quicker the better. She grasped his hand. He frowned.

"The Medical Examiner stated Lexi was pregnant."

His eyes widened for a split-second. She released his hand.

"Like hell she was," he exploded. He paced the length of the studio, stopped, and faced her with accusing eyes. "Is this some kind of joke?" The grief vanished as a smoldering anger flashed.

"You needed to hear it from someone who cares, not some report on the nightly news."

"Lexi didn't sleep around. Didn't have sex at all. She thought it was a... a spiritual act. No." He covered his face with trembling hands. "It can't be."

She reached out with a featherlike touch and brushed his arm.

"The only explanation is... it's too awful... no." He moved his hands away from his face. "Please don't tell me she'd been raped."

She wanted to kick herself for being such an idiot. What else would he think since Lexi was pure, spotless, untouched in his eyes? She certainly wasn't going to be the person to ruin the vision of the woman he loved.

He stared beyond Beth. "When we were in Italy, I got this really strange vibe from her. We'd only met the week before, but it seemed like we'd known each other forever. One night, after she finished her duties with Emma, we walked to Sorrento for *gelato*. She was really quiet, and I sensed something was wrong. Lexi said she was just tired since earlier in the day, she and Zach had hiked up the slope of Mt. Vesuvius. She swore she'd be her old self after a good night's sleep. But that wasn't it at all—was it? One of those Italian men forced himself on her and... and she kept all of it inside. Why? Why didn't she tell me? Or the police?"

"Slow down. You're jumping to conclusions."

"What other explanation is there?"

"I'm just as perplexed. The police have Lexi's diary. Maybe it'll shed some light. Don't torture yourself about something that might not've happened." She inhaled, feeling as if she'd sprinted a quarter mile. "I'm sure Lexi would've told you. Maybe she needed some time to think things through. From what I know about her, she would've told you everything. I'm sure of it."

He smoothed back stray locks that had spilled onto his forehead, grasped the hair off his neck, and secured it tightly into a rubber band he'd slipped off his wrist. "One thing I'm sure of, if Lexi was pregnant, she wouldn't have kept it from me." He walked the floor a couple more times. With a quick pivot, he turned in her direction. "Doctors make mistakes. They could've read the test results wrong or something."

"That's possible."

"I'll ask the detective about it when he gets here." Trey glanced at his watch.

Gavin. She'd forgotten all about him. "The only piece of advice I can offer is try to be patient. Let law enforcement do its job."

He reached over and hugged her. "Thank you for telling me about...but it's got to be some kind of mix up."

"Oh, dear boy," she whispered as he released her. "I'll be in touch. If you ever need to talk, call anytime." She slipped free a business card from her wallet and handed it to him. He glanced at it while she grabbed the painting. Then she stepped outside though the door he opened for her.

She raced across Zach's estate toward her vehicle. The depth of the senseless tragedy filled her anew and gave rise to a seething anger. The faces of the other slain girls flashed through her mind as she clenched her teeth. In a spark of memory, she recalled the well-worn prayer from childhood and silently offered it. *Eternal rest grant them O Lord, and let perpetual light shine upon them. May the souls of these innocent victims, through the mercy of God, rest in peace. Amen.*

The entreating words eased the fury boiling inside her. By the time she swung open the Volvo's hatch, all she felt was a dull sadness. She placed the painting carefully inside the SUV and took a deep breath. *Now it's time to face Zach.*

CHAPTER TWENTY-FIVE

Beth stood in front of the recessed entrance leading into Zach's mansion and slipped her mobile into her shoulder bag. Not a word from Marjorie. But right now she had more pressing things to consider than Marjorie's hurt feelings.

She shifted her weight from one foot to the other wondering how to wiggle a confession out of Zach, affirming he was the father to Lexi's unborn child. Still not having devised a strategy, she raised her finger to ring the bell, but before pressing it, the door flew open. She caught a quick glimpse of what seemed a very disgruntled Zach Greyson. A cigarette hung from the corner of his mouth, and his narrowed eyes sat below a furrowed brow. He plowed through the doorway. If she hadn't jumped out of the way, he would've knocked her over.

"Zach?"

He paused, took a look at her, and grunted before heading toward the parking circle and his Bentley.

"Stop."

He peered at her over his shoulder. "I've no time for idle chit-chat. Try Skye. Maybe she'll answer your texts." He continued walking to his car.

She rushed to catch up with him. "You're upset. Wouldn't it be better to talk about it?"

He tossed the cigarette to the ground, crushed it with the tip of his shiny black Oxford, and folded his arms.

"You know," Beth said.

"That Lexi was pregnant? Well, she hadn't bothered to tell me."

Now that he'd stopped moving, she got a good look at him and noticed he was impeccably groomed. The navy, hand-tailored, Caraceni suit fit flawlessly, and the crisp lavender dress shirt sported a silk paisley print tie. His aftershave smelled of juniper and sandalwood. "I'm keeping you from an appointment?"

"Only heading to the club for lunch."

"I won't keep you then." A rush of relief flooded through her realizing she wouldn't have to give him the third degree about Lexi's pregnancy. Not now anyway.

"Look, sorry for being rude. But I'm in no real hurry. Come on." He slipped his hand under her elbow and steered her toward the house.

A moment later, they were seated in the library waiting for a maid to bring in a pot of tea. Beth chewed her lip as he talked about one of his latest art acquisitions. A small "Madonna and Child" by the Renaissance Florentine painter, Il Bacchiacca. The piece was originally painted as a study for a larger work in the popular Mannerist style of the time. He explained it arrived only a couple hours earlier and how anxious he was to see it displayed in his gallery.

"The Il Bacchiacca is the oldest painting I own. It's gonna look fantastic. I want Trey to hang it right away."

"Trey?"

"When he first arrived in LA, I called in a favor. Got him a part-time job in exhibitions at the Fowler Museum. He's completed the training. So I trust him with my collection of masterpieces."

She nodded only half-listening, perplexed by the looming task of persuading him to admit the truth about Lexi's pregnancy.

"Ever since Lexi's death, he's taken a leave of absence from his job—and from life in general."

"You can't blame the boy for giving in to his grief."

"Grief won't bring Lexi back. The sooner he accepts that fact, the better." He ran his fingertips through his hair. "But dammit, I need to follow my own advice. I was doing okay. Then I heard the news, and everything went to hell."

She saw her chance, but at that precise moment, Sophia Fedoruck swept into the room carrying a tea service. They sat in silence as the young woman poured and prepared the tea. Beth lifted her cup as the maid exited the room, took a quick sip, and then added another drop of cream to the already milky tea. Zach didn't touch his. Instead, he walked to the liquor cabinet and poured whiskey into a tumbler. He emptied it in one swallow.

"I'm gonna tell you something no one knows." He refilled the glass. "And for the life of me, I don't understand why. But I gotta tell someone, and since you know I was involved with Lexi..."

She held her breath.

"I know everyone, and I mean everyone, from the news media to the butcher, baker, and candlestick maker thinks Lexi was some kind of saint." He dropped back into his chair. "Except for Skye, that is. Don't get me wrong. Lexi was an amazing girl: poised, well-spoken, beautiful. But the pure, innocent, slain 'Hollywood Nanny' played me like some damn fool." He took a sip of the drink before setting it down next to the tea service.

His statement, so unexpected, startled her. She inched to the edge of the leather chair and forced her mouth to remain shut while waiting for him to elaborate. The ensuing seconds dragged as she studied Zach wrestling with the idea of how to explain himself.

Focused on his entwined fingers, he cleared his throat. He jerked his head upward and bore his eyes into hers. "I'm not saying I wasn't at fault. But I never would've guessed she'd be the conniving type." He reached for the glass and took a quick gulp. "Lexi made it quite clear she'd never had sex before. I could tell she was a little hesitant at first. But dammit, that girl was like every man's fantasy. The very thought of having sex with a virgin about blew my mind. That hadn't happened since I was what? Like sixteen."

A wave of apprehension filled her as she gripped her cup.

"Her protests died with our first kiss. It was like she was hungry for it—she relished every second and left me exhausted—exhilarated. Afterwards, I knew I'd taken advantage of her, but Lexi swore she'd keep her mouth shut about the whole incident. I made a vow, then and there, to quit messing around with her. Except I couldn't leave well enough alone. I had to have more."

Beth's intuition alerted her—Zach was keeping something back. She returned the teacup to the tray and folded her arms.

"From there on in, I made sure she was on the pill. Lexi promised to take it every day, and I believed her."

"Nothing's a hundred percent."

He waved her comment away. "I told you before, we meshed. It wasn't just sex between us. We talked a lot. I even opened my heart and confided a bunch of personal stuff. Lexi was a good listener. Before long, I'd placed my complete trust in her. That trust wasn't based on her words of devotion toward me but rather on her actions. She kept our affair to herself. Never bragged about our relationship to anyone. Boy, was I an idiot." He twisted the gold band on his ring finger.

"I told her things nobody knew. Like how pissed I was that Skye had failed to mention she had her tubes tied after Emma was born. I found out that little tidbit about six months after we were married." He spit out the words.

Beth lifted the cup and took a quick sip attempting to disrupt the surprised look that must've crossed her face. Zach didn't seem to notice as he rattled on.

"I sulked around for days. Wondered what the chances were that I'd ever have a kid of my own. Finally, I gave up on the idea of fatherhood." His eyes darted away from Beth and focused on the massive antique desk beyond him. "By then my trust in Skye had dried up, but I'd already fallen hook, line, and sinker for the kid. I begged Skye to let me adopt Emma. I know." He raised a hand as if to prevent Beth from commenting. "Emma has a biological father. But, he's got a new family. I figured if I offered him enough money or paid off a big debt or something—Skye told me rather happily that her ex is struggling financially— he'd see it my way and agree to the adoption. But Skye wouldn't hear of it." He looked directly into Beth's eyes. "You know how difficult she can be."

She stiffened her jaw and remained motionless.

"Lexi started working here a couple of years ago, straight out of high school. She'd completed a summer program at a local college to earn her child-care certification and then signed up with the domestic agency Skye uses. At first, I didn't pay too much attention. But, you'd have to be blind not to see she was great with Emma. Of course, I noticed the obvious—she was hot. Lexi looked older than her age. I was surprised to learn she was only seventeen. Her birthday is, um, was in December—December 23rd." He rubbed his temples in a circular movement. "It all came to a head on Thanksgiving Day. Skye stormed out. Angry and threatening a divorce. Lexi had done the right thing and took Emma to her bedroom as soon as Skye started her tantrum. Read the kid storybooks until she fell asleep. Then she checked on me. God," he said with a sigh. "I remember it like yesterday. The way she stood facing me with an air of vulnerability. But her it was her eyes—they shone sympathy and understanding—as did her words. She was in my corner." He pressed his lips together and glanced at his wedding ring again. "I suspected she had a crush on me. Most of the female staff here does. It didn't take too much effort on my part." He shrugged.

"Wait a minute." She paused a couple of seconds. "You had sex with a minor?"

"If only I'd been able to show a little self-control—like for another month, she wouldn't have had a leg to stand on legally. But Lexi never planned to report me to the authorities. She had something else in mind."

Beth stood and paced the length of the expansive library, doing a bit of subtraction. He was eighteen years older than Lexi. *And he has the nerve to imply she had an ulterior motive?*

She suspected Zach's persona, charm, and intellect had captivated the teenaged nanny. Not to mention his heart-stopping good looks. Once he started making moves, a mature woman would have difficulty shunning his advances, let alone an inexperienced teenager. Lexi didn't have a chance.

"We remained lovers until a few months ago. All along, she'd been casually dating but nothing serious. She wasn't having sex with anyone else."

Beth wondered how he could be so certain Lexi had been faithful. Then she remembered Lexi's own words—*the affair had been a mistake, she trusted her old-fashioned values, wanted a white bridal gown with a bouquet of orange blossoms*—and Trey's admiration for Lexi's desire to wait until she was married.

"Truth is I'd gotten tired of her." Zach's voice drew her attention back. "Lexi had some crazy fantasy that we had a future together. Can you imagine Zach Greyson, megastar, linked romantically with a nanny? The media would've had a field day with that one." He shook his head. "That was never gonna happen. But hell, I thought she'd at least be grateful. After all, I let her pick my brain, and I obviously taught her a lot in the sex department. I broke it off with her around the time of the trip to Italy. Then she met Trey, and I thought everything was cool between us. Turned out she was far from feeling grateful."

Beth moved closer to Zach as he balled his hands into fists on top of his knees.

"Lexi started complaining I'd taken advantage of her," Zach hissed. "Pressured her into having sex when she was still underage. Can you believe it?" He lifted his head and looked in Beth's direction. "That I'd stolen her dream of being a virgin on her wedding day." He rolled his eyes. "It's not like I twisted her arm or anything. She really wanted it."

"Good Lord, Zach," Beth exploded. "She wasn't in the position to make that kind of decision. You were the adult. Lexi needed your protection—not your expertise in the fine art of lovemaking. And even if she was nearly eighteen, legally speaking, it was statutory rape. You could've gone to jail."

"Don't you think I know that?" His eyes flashed. "Lexi knew it, too. She duped me. One day out of the blue, she says it might be fun to work on TV. So I called in a favor. Got her a role in a new television series. I literally did everything possible to keep her happy. I insisted that Skye bring her along to Italy with us.

Her boyfriend is living in my guesthouse, and I'm mentoring his art career. I gave her expensive gifts. Diamond earrings, clothes, books, even an exquisite handmade journal. I bought her stuff like that all the time." He shook his head. "Speaking of Italy, we were having a great day hiking up the slope of Mt. Vesuvius when she started up again. This time she demanded sex. I knew she wanted to resume our affair. In my mind, that was over. But back in my suite, we did it, and all I could think about was Skye barging in and finding us together."

Beth opened her mouth, but he didn't give her a chance to speak.

"So don't judge me. I'm the one who was taken advantage of, and I've paid handsomely for my mistake. It doesn't take a damned advanced degree to figure out Lexi wanted to keep me on a string. I didn't have the slightest idea of how to get her off my back." He lifted his eyes toward the ceiling. "And, now, this bombshell. She was pregnant. With my kid." He closed his eyes.

"What a mess," she said. "I'm certainly not in a position to judge either of you. We've all been guilty of making mistakes and committing grievous sins."

"Sin?" Zach frowned.

She inhaled sharply knowing what she needed to say but hesitated a second before forging ahead. *It's the reason I'm here, but will Zach tell me the truth?* "The question remains," she said quietly, "are you the one who silenced Lexi forever? After all, your secret has gone to the grave with her." The minute she said the words, she knew she'd made a mistake. If he did kill Lexi, what might he do to her?

He jumped from his seat and moved toward Beth. With a viselike grip, he grabbed her by the shoulders and pulled her forward. They stood eye to eye. "Would I've told you all this if I had something to do with her murder? I swear to God, I had nothing to do with Lexi's death. If only she'd told me about the baby. It would've made all the difference in the world." He released Beth and turned away.

With every fiber of her being, she wanted to believe him. *But he's an actor-- a multiple award-winning actor.*

She didn't know what to believe anymore. Her confusion evaporated when she heard an explosion of loud voices.

"What the hell?" Zach headed for the door.

"Mr. Greyson." A woman's voice called from the corridor.

Before he could get to the doorway, Sofia stood in the threshold. "I don't know how she got into the house. Maybe through the service entrance."

"Outta my way, Missy." A booming voice filled the air.

Beth caught her breath as a large woman all but knocked Sophia to the floor as she squeezed through the entry and into the library.

"Dot, what a surprise. I wasn't expecting you," Zach said in an even-tempered voice. He waved the disheveled maid away with a nod.

Dot Barnett? Beth dropped into a chair at the far end of the library fascinated by the drama unfolding beyond her.

"It's true, I haven't an appointment. But why do I need an appointment to see you, my love? Hmmm, perhaps I did behave a bit out of character forcing my way in here, but surely all is forgiven for the sake of our mutual devotion." She threw out her hand in his direction. Instead of grasping it, he took a quick glance at the liver-spotted appendage then slipped his hands into his pockets. As if unaffected, Dot moved closer and brushed against him. "Wild horses couldn't keep me away, let alone a slip of a maid. And really, Zach, that whole scene could've been completely avoided if I'd been thinking straight. But my mind's been in a muddle ever since Skye's gotten a bee in her bonnet about me not being Emma's nanny. You have to clear this mess up right away, otherwise, how will we be able to spend time together?"

"What's she talking about?" Beth realized too late she'd spoken the words aloud.

Dot's unruly brows shot up as her eyes flitted around the room. Walking past Zach, she stopped in front of Beth. "What are you doing here?" Dot demanded.

Beth ran her fingertips across her blouse before taking a good look at the curious woman.

Though a bit unkempt, Dot Barnett didn't appear much different than many older women: overweight, frizzy gray hair, a lattice of fine wrinkles etched into her pale skin.

It took Zach a split-second to move next to Beth. He yanked her out of the chair and slipped his arm around her shoulders. "This is my dear friend, Sibeal. You know, the—"

"I've seen her on television. The one-named, Irish born model. You don't like people to drink and drive. That's sound advice. But you being here, I imagine, isn't very smart." Dot moved her eyes from Beth to Zach. "You two look kind of cozy."

Perplexed as to why he'd introduced her as Sibeal, it took Beth a moment to realize that Zach wanted to protect her identity from the unhinged woman. He squeezed her shoulder tighter.

"You wouldn't be thinking of cheating on me, now would you, Zachy?"

That can't be right. *Zach and Dot Barnett?* Before Beth could chase the unappetizing picture of the two of them from her mind, Zach pulled her closer and pressed his lips against hers.

"Does that answer your question Dot?" Without even stopping for a breath, he kissed her again, but this time he lingered.

Beth balled her hands into fists as fury engulfed every ounce of her being. Her initial instinct was to accuse him of losing his mind. But, after a long, slow breath, she forced herself to relax and try to figure out exactly what was going on. She didn't struggle to free herself from his embrace as he pressed closer.

"How dense can you be, Dot?" He brushed a few stray wisps of hair from Beth's cheek. "Or have you totally lost a grasp on reality? Let me set you straight. You and I aren't involved romantically, sexually, politically, socially, or any other way. Never have been. Never will be. I like my women young and hot. You don't fit into either category. Sorry, but you've missed the boat, old gal." Zach released Beth and took a few steps in Dot's direction.

"I don't know why you're doing this," Dot said with a catch in her throat. "It's bad enough dealing with that hair-brained wife of yours, but you and that...that scarecrow of a woman. I can't believe something like that would attract you."

"She does." He pulled out his phone and pressed a key. "Bruno will escort you out."

As he turned away, Beth kept her focus on the older woman. She read the wrath in Dot's eyes as they blazed crazily. "Watch out," Beth warned, even though she wanted to curse him for putting on such a show.

Dot rushed in his direction and knocked the phone from his grasp. The look on his face reminded Beth of a deer caught in a car's bright headlights.

"What the hell?" He faced the older woman.

Dot followed the movement of the cell phone. She half-galloped, half-skipped toward it then kicked the phone across the room.

He moved toward the sound of plastic skidding across the carpet. Spying the phone under a richly upholstered chair near the fireplace, he bent over to pick it up. Not missing a beat, Dot lifted a vase and smashed it against the back of his head. Zach moaned before crumpling onto the floor.

Things had utterly slipped out of control. Forgetting about Dot, Beth hurried toward Zach. Before she could reach him, a shove sent her flying.

Beth landed on her knees but not before whacking her head against the corner of the desk. A sharp pain stabbed her temple, and she reached for it expecting blood. To her relief, the skin hadn't split. Grabbing the edge of the massive desk, Beth pulled herself up determined to soothe Dot back into reality—except she didn't get the chance.

"You trying to move in on my man?" The woman's husky voice filled Beth's ear. "He's mine, girly, and I'm about to make you not forget it."

"Get a grip," Beth ordered in a steady voice. "Zach was just doing what he does best. Acting. Putting on a show. Maybe he can't help himself. I don't know. But truly, I'm not involved with him. He's married to my friend." She glimpsed over her shoulder and noticed that he was out cold. "Dear Lord, look at what you've done. I fear he's truly hurt." Beth raced passed the woman, as shards of china crunched under her feet, toward the library door.

"Oh, no, you don't."

Dot plowed into Beth and knocked her down, straddled her prone body, and levied her heavy girth on top of her.

Beth struggled to free herself, but Dot only pressed more firmly against her wriggling body. To her relief, the heavy weight shifted, and Beth rolled over managing to get on her hands and knees. Not steady enough to stand, she crawled closer to the door. She thought she heard Zach, but the words sounded muffled as if he were talking into a blustery wind.

Then a hard grip attached itself around her neck. The pressure was so tight, Beth feared her windpipe would be crushed. She tried to shake Dot loose, but the force of the woman's hold only strengthened. Not able to breathe, lightheadedness overtook her. She crashed onto the floor as the room began to spin.

Beth tried to still her racing mind, tried to pray—to make a final Act of Contrition—but couldn't remember the words. She pulled her right arm free from beneath her body and reached upward in an attempt to pull Dot's hands off her neck. Her arm flailed and slashed the air unable to make contact with her assailant.

Then, as if by a miraculous intervention, Dot's claw-like hold relaxed, and the woman's crushing weight lifted. She heard agitated voices, and the last sound that filled her ears was Dot's piercing scream.

When she woke, Beth felt ice cold. She sought the dull pain, throbbing at the back of her head, with an unsteady lift of her hand. Missing her intended target, she brushed against an ice pack. She blinked her eyes open to see Gavin Collin's tense face.

She managed to whisper his name, but the very act caused her throat to burn.

"Don't talk. I'm sure you have one helluva sore throat." Collins moved nearer to her on the overstuffed sofa. "Must've seemed surreal."

She reached out, and he grasped her hand and squeezed it.

"According to the maid—"

"Sophia?"

Collins offered a nod then glanced at his notepad. "Greyson gave her a signal to call security. It's not really clear what took them so long to respond. Guess some heads are gonna roll." He released her hand and crouched next to her. "Trey Wickham told me you stopped by for a visit. After speaking to him, we walked over here since I had a couple of questions for Greyson. The maid dialed nine-one-one when she saw Barnett on top of you and Greyson unconscious. Fortunately, that was right when we walked into the house, and she brought us here. We pulled Barnett off you as Greyson's guys came running into the room." He paused a moment. "Backup arrived and a couple of uniforms took Barnett to the hospital for an evaluation. If you ask me, she's certifiable."

"Zach?"

"Has his own private doctor. Raced right over. With him now. The worst scenario would probably be a slight concussion. Nothing too serious."

She lifted herself into a sitting position. The ice pack slid to the base of her back. "She tried to kill me."

"None of us saw that coming. We considered her to be an eccentric but not violent. Sure proved us wrong."

Beth swung her legs off the couch, reached for the ice pack, and placed it against her neck.

"We should go. I want to get you to the ER."

"Not necessary," she whispered. Beth raised her legs and stretched out on the couch. "Have you told Shane?" She managed to say the words a bit louder since the ice had started to numb her throat.

"Told him the whole story."

"Great. Just great." She closed her eyes.

CHAPTER TWENTY-SIX

Beth fought the urge to wake up but reluctantly gave in and opened her eyes. The pain in her head had subsided to a dull hammering. She gingerly touched the tender skin at the base of her neck as the recollection of the enraged, barreling woman made her shudder. An urgency to escape Zach's house prodded her, headache or not. She raised her hand to the weight across her forehead. A compress. Not turning her head, she took in what she could see of the room while propped against a thick cushion on the library's leather couch.

She spied Zach staring at the old-fashioned cloth ice pack in his hands. Gavin Collins sat on a hassock with his eyes riveted on Zach. A man she didn't recognize entered the room.

"Zach." Her voice emerged as a hoarse whisper.

He tossed the bag of ice cubes onto a credenza. A second later, he knelt next to her and grabbed her hand. "Dr. Phelps wants to examine you. Make sure you're okay." He stroked her hand, raised it to his lips, and kissed the smooth skin. He released it after a gentle squeeze.

His hangdog expression assured Beth of his regret for trying to pull the wool over Dot's eyes. Though every strand in her being screamed against it, she couldn't help but forgive him for his foolish charade. He lifted the tepid, soggy compress off her forehead.

"I'll get you a fresh one," Zach said.

"Are you okay?"

"I'll survive. But I'm worried sick about you."

"Shouldn't blame—"

"I thought if Barnett was forced to see the idiocy of her infatuation, it would jolt her into reality. Stupid, huh?"

"Not your brightest idea," Beth whispered.

"The doc wants to look at you."

"Don't bother." She sat up, and a wave of nausea turned her stomach. She tried to smile but wound up gritting her teeth. "I'm fine. In fact, I'm going home. Now."

"Hold your horses, young lady," Dr. Phelps said.

Collins stood with arms crossed. "Let the doctor check you out. Unless you'd rather go to the ER? You don't look too good."

"I can't believe such a fuss over a wee bump on the head and a sore throat," Beth grumbled, even though she realized she was outnumbered.

The doctor loomed over her. She figured Dr. Phelps was probably retired, therefore making him available for Zach's every beck and call. What was left of his hair appeared bone white, and a network of lines crisscrossed his tanned face. Behind wire-framed glasses, kindly eyes greeted her.

His probing fingers inspected her head and throat with a featherlike touch. Without uttering a word, the doctor clasped a blood pressure cuff around her arm. The viselike pressure gripping her arm made Beth hold her breath as the room's walls seemed to again spin crazily around her. She didn't dare tell him and jumped when his cold stethoscope pressed against her skin. She trained her eyes on him, and the dizzying motion eased to a stop.

The doctor pursed his lips and pulled out a prescription book then scribbled on the top page. "You need to take it easy for the next couple of days. Here's a prescription to help with the pain. If your symptoms worsen, contact me or your family physician." He handed her the slip of paper.

She murmured a quick thanks though all she wanted to do was to lie down and close her eyes. But she wasn't about to let any of them know how rotten she felt. She looked in Collin's direction. "I'm surprised you haven't returned to the office."

"Wanted to make sure you're alright."

"Shane's instructions? Well, you heard what the doctor said."

"I'll drive you home."

"No need. In a bit, I'll be as right as rain. So, go on with yourself."

In the meantime, Dr. Phelps had collected his instruments. After snapping his bag shut, he grabbed it, and headed toward the door. Both Zach and Collins caught up with him and exited the library, leaving Beth alone.

She leaned back against the cushion and chewed her lip. The examination had aggravated her throat. That was the least of her worries as she mulled over what to tell Shane.

Zach entered the room holding the cloth ice bag against the back of his head. "I don't want you driving. Bruno will take you home. I promised the detective I'd get you there safely. Now lay down."

"Who do you think you are, Zach Greyson, ordering me about? If I want to sit, I'll sit, and if I want to go, I'll go." Her whispered words didn't offer the effect she was after, so she shot up—way too quick. The room again began to spin.

He dropped the ice bag and grasped Beth to his chest. "I'm so sorry. How the hell could I've known Dot would freak out like that? Please, Beth, rest a while longer."

She didn't object as he helped her back to the couch. Her head throbbed, and her throat prickled as she tried to comprehend the bizarre turn of events. Giving up, she turned to Zach.

"Detective Collins is Shane's partner," Beth whispered.

"Won't be surprised if your husband shows up any minute then."

"I hope not." She mouthed the words.

Zach lowered his eyes and seemed to be studying the floor. "I guess if there's a silver lining in all of this, it's gotta be that Trey is finally out of that damn guesthouse. He's in my gallery now. Wanted to see my new acquisition."

Sofia entered the room carrying a tray with a silver tea service. She placed it on the hassock before moving next to Beth. "How awful. The two of you suffering because of that horrible woman. I brought you a fresh ice pack." She pulled the frozen plastic bag free from the large pocket of her smock and wrapped it in a dishtowel.

Beth took the pack and pressed it against her throat. "My girl, the way Dot rough-handled you, I'm sure Zach wouldn't mind it a wee bit if you went home."

"No. No. I'm fine." Sofia lifted the teapot and poured a cup for Beth. "This will soothe your throat." She offered Zach a cup, but he shook his head. "I want to work. If I keep busy, I won't think about that deranged woman." She reached for the small cream pitcher and poured a dollop into Beth's cup. "I talked to my boyfriend. His voice made me feel better."

"Boyfriend. Nice," Beth said in a husky whisper.

"He's a bodybuilder. Smart and very handsome." Sofia grabbed a napkin and handed it to Beth.

Beth frowned wondering if she'd understood the maid correctly. "Bodybuilder? Not Mike Alder?"

"You know him?"

Beth sighed.

"Beth is right. Take the rest of the day off. Go out to dinner with your boyfriend or whatever. Okay?" Zach placed his hand on Sophia's shoulder and guided her toward the door. Once she exited the library, Zach sat opposite Beth with the ice bag in his hand. He placed it against the back of his head.

"Sofia and Mike?" Beth toyed with the teacup's handle.

"So?"

"Lexi's former boyfriend."

"Oh. Him." He moved the bag away from his head and shook it. The clatter of ice cubes sounded muffled through the thick, insulated cloth. "Lexi was using him to make me jealous."

"She believed it was hopeless. Turned to Mike to try to forget you."

"What?"

Beth sucked in her bottom lip. She'd vowed to keep the words of Lexi's journal to herself. "I... I—"

"Come in Trey."

Beth offered a silent prayer of thanks as Trey entered the library.

"The painting?" Zach asked replacing the ice bag to the back of his head.

"It's magnificent." The young man continued walking in Zach's direction but stopped when reaching Beth. "Any better?"

She brushed her fingertips across her swollen and bruised throat. "I want to go home. Do you mind driving me?" She didn't pause for an answer. "We'll take my vehicle and then I'll have a taxi bring you back."

Trey glanced at Zach who offered him a shrug.

She reached for her handbag. It rested on the end table and, amazingly, hadn't been disturbed during the long ordeal. She pulled out her key fob and handed it to Trey. "I'm parked out front in the circle."

Trey took the key and obediently departed from the room.

Beth lifted the teacup and swallowed a mouthful of the soothing liquid. She replaced the cup and looked at Zach. He sat with his head bowed and his fingers entwined.

"You know what would make me truly happy? If you and Skye worked out your differences because I believe you're made for each other." Beth eased off the couch and took several cautious steps.

Zach easily caught up to her. He wrapped his arm around Beth's waist and guided her out of the expansive room.

***

With a firm grip, Trey helped Beth navigate the high step into the passenger seat of her Volvo. Being out of Zach's dark library and into the bright sunshine lifted her spirits. Even so, she dreaded the moment when she'd come face to face with Shane. Trey strapped her in the leather seat, and she laid her head back with closed eyes.

"Where to Miss Getty?"

"Hombly Hills." She quickly whispered the directions. "And please Trey, call me Beth."

She tilted her head in his direction and opened her eyes. Though she'd scrutinized him earlier, Beth took a deep breath when she finally figured out what had struck her about his physical appearance—his startling resemblance to Mike Alder. Though Trey didn't possess an over-developed physique, both men had electric blue eyes, well-defined, even features, and sun-streaked blond hair. They could pass for brothers.

He pressed the ignition button and shifted the gear. They traveled around the parking circle and down the long driveway in silence.

"Is Zach's new painting really that remarkable?" She decided to lighten the atmosphere with easy, small talk.

"I've only seen paintings comparable in museums. It's crazy that he has the wherewithal to be able to buy something like that—must've cost millions."

"Really?" She widened her eyes. "For one little painting?"

"I might've exaggerated a bit. But, Zach's private collection is amazing. I'm really honored he bought one of mine. It's hanging next to a Grandville Redmond landscape." He glanced in Beth's direction as he slowed for a stop sign. "Redmond was one of the original California Impressionists. An interesting guy, he was deaf and a close friend of Charlie Chaplin. His sign language fascinated Chaplin so much, he studied the movements and hired Redmond to act in a couple of his movies. So, I guess it's not too unusual for artists to pal around with megastars," Trey said with a wink.

She whispered the artist's name a couple of times trying to burn it into her mind. She could mention Redmond in order to impress Zach if he ever invited her into his art gallery.

"I've made a decision," he said.

"Decision?"

"I'm going home. To Gibson Island. For the summer."

"Gibson Island?"

"In Maryland. Hopefully get my old part-time job back at the marina. I'll spend my free time sailing with friends and might even spend a couple of weeks down the beach. I could always come back here in the fall to resume my graduate studies. Depending on how I feel about—"

"That seems like a grand idea. Truly does."

"I'm suffocating living at Zach's. Everything reminds me of Lexi. Detective Collins didn't have any objections. He also didn't have any specific details yet about the pregnancy." His jaw tightened.

He drove in silence for a couple of blocks, and Beth didn't take her eyes off him.

"I'll probably pack up some of my stuff and get outta here sometime next week. After..." He cleared his throat. "After Lexi's funeral." He eased down the brake and slowed for a traffic light. When the light turned red, he looked at her. "I hate disappointing Zach. He's done so much for me."

"Zach will understand."

"I guess."

She touched his shoulder. "Time is a healer. Trust me on that."

"One good thing is I'll be home in time for the Preakness Stakes. You know the horse race—second jewel in the Triple Crown."

She noticed the inflection in his voice had changed. A touch of enthusiasm. Unsure if he was feigning interest, at least, she decided he was putting forth a good effort at being a tad bit cheerful.

"It's a family tradition. My father is a financial consultant, and for the past ten years, he's purchased a table in the Preakness Village."

"The what?"

"An area set aside as exclusive seating for the race. A bunch of tents shading fancy tables, and there's always plenty of food. But the best thing is its location, right near the finish line. Anyway, my dad invites a few of his top clients and, of course, there's always a place for us. Sis won't be able to make it. She'll be wrapping things up—exams and all at FSU." He shrugged then pressed down on the gas after the light had turned green. "The whole affair is pretty swank, nothing like the infield." He glanced at Beth. "Anyway, I was certain I'd miss out this year."

"You're a racing fan?"

"Not so much a fan. But, I like to watch the races. The horses are so graceful—powerful—it's exciting. But I'm not too good at picking winners, I'm afraid." A hint of a smile formed at the corners of his mouth.

"The last race I attended was in Ireland. I went with *me Da*. The Irish Champion Stakes." She forgot her pounding head as she recalled the exhilaration that'd pulsed through her as the bay, Oratorio, came from behind to win the race by not much more than a nose. "Sometimes I long to go home. There's a hole in my heart that can only be filled there. I miss my granny with her fanciful stories about tree circles and fairies... Ah, and how I long to inhale the sweet freshness of a spring morning after a soft rain, to see my *ould flowers*, and feel me Da's strong arms about me." She sighed. "Truly Trey, there isn't any other place more lovely on God's green Earth than home."

CHAPTER TWENTY-SEVEN

Kenny didn't know what to think. He sunk deeper into the wing chair in their well-appointed hotel suite and tapped his foot. The leather sole's rapid strikes produced muted whispers against the carpet, not the staccato clacks that usually settled his jumpy nerves. It shouldn't matter that Maiah had arranged a get-together with an old friend. Not just a friend, he reminded himself, a former lover—and some kind of English noble. "Probably a damn stuffed shirt. Lord Callum Fernsby. Give me a break," he muttered.

"What dear?" Maiah's lilting voice sounded from the kitchenette where she leaned against the counter next to the coffee maker.

For a second, Kenny peered at her through the opened portion of the half-wall that separated the two rooms but then pulled his eyes away. He clicked his tongue against the roof of his mouth and focused on the gilded coffered ceiling. She entered the parlor with two steaming mugs.

"Here." She handed him the coffee.

He took the cup and glared at her.

"I've mentioned Callum before. So, stop your pouting. Anyway, I thought you gave up sulking years ago after I finally accepted your marriage proposal. What was it? The fourth time you asked."

"Fifth. But who's counting." He took a gulp then placed the mug on the mahogany coffee table. "When the hell did you tell me you dated a viscount?"

She eased onto the chair's armrest and ruffled his coal black hair. "A baron. And I do believe you're jealous." She lifted her coffee and took a sip.

"We weren't going to keep secrets from each other anymore," he said.

"I'd hardly call it a secret. And really Kenny, I would've offered more details if you'd shown an interest. Anyway, Callum and I were old news years before we even met."

"I told you about my ex-girlfriends."

"Girlfriends? More like friends with benefits." She dropped her hand to his shoulder. "Not what anyone would call authentic, caring relationships."

He began tapping his foot again. Her voice had taken on a haughty quality he despised. That and how easily she slipped into believing she was better than everyone else. He'd long ago concluded her superior attitude rose from being born with the proverbial silver spoon in her mouth. The fact she palled around with British nobility explained her overblown ego in a new light.

"There were a few that went beyond sex," he said with a trace of indignation. "In college, I went steady with a girl I almost proposed to."

"But you didn't."

He shrugged.

"It was so different for me. When I first met Callum, I was instantly smitten. The attraction was startling."

Kenny lifted his cup and stared into it.

"I never told you about that amazing time in my life. Didn't think you'd be interested." She took another sip of coffee. "I don't blame you. Talking about past relationships is tedious."

"If he was so damned special, why the hell didn't you marry the guy?" Kenny found himself surprised that her words had hurt him.

"My parents were all for it. They thought we were the perfect match. But really, could you imagine me as Lady Fernsby?"

In a New York minute. Kenny pressed his lips into a thin line.

"Turned out Callum and I..." She brushed the air between them. "Well, it wasn't the stuff true romance is made of after all." She paused a second. "Then we met at that art gallery reception and you swept me off my feet."

He thought she was making fun of him, but then she snuggled into his lap and kissed him. She pulled away, and a smile caused her eyes to sparkle. He touched her cheek and moved closer, but she bounded off and landed in an adjacent chair.

"We don't have time for that right now. He'll be here any minute. Just enough time to give you some background information. Callum is the third son of the 19th Duke of Newcastle–upon-Tyne making him Baron Ogle of Bothal. I was nineteen when we met, and both of us were going through a rebellious stage. We wanted to break free of parental interference and social pressure. I guess you could say, we wanted to find ourselves." She made air quotes. "But instead, we found each other."

"What am I supposed to say? Nice meeting you Callum. Seems you're as familiar with every inch of my wife as I am."

"Don't be ridiculous. It was twelve years ago."

"And unknowing to me, you've kept in contact all that time."

"Okay, Kenny. I give up. I'll call Callum." She stood and moved to the baby grand nestled in the room's corner. "I'll make up some excuse for him not to drop by. If that's what you want." She grabbed her cell phone from the piano's desk stand and ruffled the sheet music of Beethoven's *Piano Sonata in C Sharp Minor* that she'd been playing the night before.

"Wait." He walked toward her. "I've been acting like a spoiled-sport. I realize you had a life before we met. But I never thought you'd keep something so huge from me."

"What about your collection of ex-girlfriends? Was there someone special you never told me about? Someone you thought you were in love with, excluding your college steady, of course."

For a split second, he feared Maiah had found out about his renewed affair with Skye. He gulped a mouthful of air and reassured himself that was impossible. He'd been diligent in covering his tracks so she'd have no inkling of his ongoing infidelity. "You're the only one I've ever made a commitment to and...and I consider it a sacred vow." As soon as the words left his mouth, Kenny knew he'd gone too far, the result of a guilty conscience. "God knows, I'm not perfect. My over the top reaction proves I must have a jealous streak. But Maiah, give me some slack. You have to admit this reunion with your ex-lover is going to be awkward, not only for me but for Baron Ogle, whatever his name is, as well." He glanced at her but couldn't read a reaction. "Why don't I duck out? Give you two some alone time to reminisce."

She slipped the phone into the pocket of her navy blazer. "You might have a point." Her brows knitted as she took a step closer to him. "You really don't mind amusing yourself for a couple of hours?"

"I'll do better than that. You can spend all afternoon with the honorable Lord Baron. I want to check out the Louisville Sluggers Museum." He grabbed the car rental keys off an end table. "I'll see you around five."

A sharp rap filled the air. He glanced at Maiah.

"Callum always was a stickler for promptness." She fluffed her flaxen, shoulder-length hair and drained her coffee cup before opening the door.

Now a bit curious, Kenny stood with hands stuck into his pockets. The man standing in the doorway wasn't what he expected.

"Maiah. I must say, your beauty has only intensified with the passing years." Callum Fernsby clasped her hand and kissed both her cheeks.

Still holding his hand Maiah said, "This is my husband, Kenny. Kenny Weston."

With a shock of spiky ginger hair, the wiry built man stood dressed in a pair of faded jeans and a black t-shirt. What could be seen of his quarter-sleeve tattoo, composed of organic shapes and vibrant hues of blue, red, and orange, revealed a splash of color to his otherwise dull attire. His pale blue eyes lit up as he reached to grasp Kenny's hand.

Though not tall, at five-feet-eight, Callum stood two inches shorter than Maiah. Even so, his regular features and lack of stature were diminished by the aura of exuberance that radiated from him.

"Lord Fernsby, good to meet you," Kenny said not caring if he addressed the son of a duke in the proper manner.

"It's Callum." He gave Kenny an extra squeeze before pulling his hand away.

"Just on my way out. You two must have a lot of catching up to do."

"Nonsense," Callum said. "Maiah's told me what a talented artist you are. I used to imagine myself a painter once. Turned out to be just a flight of fancy." Callum moved away from the entry and stepped into the living room. He found a spot on the sofa.

Kenny wondered how a person with a pedigree like Lord Fernsby could come across as a regular guy. His enunciation was the only thing that gave him away. His melodious voice resonated with a clear timbre as the words flowed evenly with a polish familiar to the upper-crust.

"Would you like a cup of coffee?" Maiah asked.

"I'd prefer a spot of Scotch that is..." Callum's eyes flitted around the room until they settled on the array of bottles set on a crystal tray next to the wet bar. "Ah, I see you're well stocked."

Kenny headed toward the liquor, certain he'd seen a bottle of Woodford Reserve when he'd uncorked a white wine the previous evening. He reached in the overhead cabinet and removed three glasses as a knot of irritation caused him to grit his teeth. Grasping the bottle of straight Kentucky bourbon, he broke the seal and poured two fingers into each tumbler. Though he was aware of their animated voices, he didn't bother to pay attention to the words.

"Let me help you with that, old boy." Callum jumped up from the couch. With a couple of quick strides, he reached Kenny and grabbed two of the crystal tumblers. He handed one to Maiah then took a sip from his glass. "Really quite smooth."

Kenny detected the note of surprise in his voice.

"I had the hotel send this bottle up especially for you. I hadn't forgotten how much you like your Scotch," Maiah said practically beaming.

"Touching on the subject of fond remembrances, do you ever think about the time we worked in that Shakespearean troupe?" Callum plopped back down on the sofa.

"Oh God," Kenny muttered. *Not a trip down memory lane.*

"Surely you've heard all about it." Callum glanced at Kenny with a raised brow.

"Can't say I have. Look, I better be going."

"Nonsense." Callum patted the spot next to him. Swallowing his protests, Kenny obediently sat. "At the time, we were both students at Cambridge. I'd come across an obscure advert in the paper soliciting players for the Authentic Lovers of Shakespeare—"

"Traveling Troup," Maiah finished his sentence. "Since we loved the Bard's plays, we ditched school and joined them for a season."

"That's the reason you dropped out of college? To act in plays?" Kenny asked.

"Not exactly. Poor Maiah was barred from taking the stage," Callum said.

Kenny frowned, dreading he was about to be talked to near-death. He really wanted to visit the baseball museum. Might even buy a bat, he thought, but how the hell to get outta here? He finally muttered a disinterested, "Oh."

"The name of the troupe explains it," Callum said.

Kenny widened his eyes.

"Authentic." Maiah paused a second. "That's the clue, Kenny. The plays were performed to the T—exactly as they were during the sixteenth century."

He nodded though not quite sure what Maiah was getting out.

"What a Cressida I was," Callum said with a laugh. "I filled the stage with beauty and charm. That is, until she betrayed her lover and honor died."

"Cressida?" Kenny said.

"No woman was allowed to go onstage five hundred years ago. All the parts were played by men. Teenage boys played the female roles. Even though Callum was twenty-one at the time, he was so youthful looking, he made a perfect Cressida."

"And Ophelia."

"But your falsetto needed a bit of work if I remember correctly."

"If you couldn't perform, what did you do?" Kenny asked a bit more interested.

"Costumer and make-up artist extraordinaire," Callum said. "If anyone could make this phiz look like a thing of beauty, it was Maiah."

Kenny noticed the color rising on her cheeks.

"I didn't know the first thing about stage makeup. Took quite a bit of practice. If it hadn't been for Maureen Forbes, being so patient with me, showing me the ropes—"

"Good Lord, remember the night she went into labor?"

Maiah closed her eyes. "I was freaking out. Good thing most of the actors, by then, had become proficient with their own makeup. Anyway, I always preferred sewing the costumes." She flashed her eyes open and looked at Kenny. "I could measure, cut, and sew Elizabethan outfits. I even designed a few myself."

"Seriously?"

"Your wife is truly a woman of many talents," Callum said. "Though working with the troupe was exhilarating, it was our love for horses that drew us away from the bright lights and the interminable adulation the stage brought us." Callum offered Kenny a wink. "After our final performance in Dublin, we traveled north and rented a simple, tiny, thatched-roof cottage and worked at a race course. We did everything from feeding and washing to exercising those mighty, glorious beasts."

Kenny leaned back into the sofa's cushion with folded arms. "If that's the case Maiah, why do you spend a small fortune on stable workers when you can do it yourself?"

Maiah took a sip of whiskey. "Don't be silly." She turned her attention back to Callum. "Weren't they splendid, halcyon days? I don't think I ever felt freer or more content." A wistful smile crossed her face. "I'd finally escaped from the strict, regimental life of being my parents' eldest daughter. I didn't miss a second of that endless parade of cotillions or the dates my mother so tactfully arranged. Always with a proper boy from a prestigious family."

Callum nodded in agreement.

"She would've happily married me off to the son of a wealthy business magnet if it hadn't been for Johannah, my childhood governess. She's the one who suggested I should attend college in Europe."

Kenny stared into his glass. Everything was beginning to make sense—like a blurred image coming into focus after a camera's lens had been adjusted. Love hadn't been the motivating factor why Maiah had married him but rather for the satisfaction of defying her parents' wishes. *That's the real reason she rejected Callum Fernsby.* He raised the tumbler and swallowed the amber liquid. It burned his throat. He glanced at the empty glass for a second before getting up and walking to the wet bar.

"We're excited my parents are attending the race," Maiah said. "Kenny?"

He ignored her and placed the glass in the sink.

As if not noticing Kenny's lack of response Maiah said, "My father has always encouraged me to experience life on my own terms."

"That may be, but he didn't understand you abandoning the chemistry lab to work at a racing stable and living with me," Callum said. "He told me as much."

"Even so, he liked you. A lot."

I bet he did. Kenny edged toward Callum and extended his hand. "On that note, I better get a move on. The museum closes at five."

Callum rose and grabbed Kenny's hand.

"I'll look forward to seeing you again. Soon, I hope," Kenny said.

"Callum is here for the Derby," Maiah said. "We'll be together all day tomorrow. His horse, Many Miles Muse, is racing alongside Estella Blue."

Oh boy. He offered a quick wave before making a beeline for the door and allowing it to shut with a resolute slam.

Maiah let out a sigh then raised her glass and drained it.

"So, I finally met the man who stole your heart."

"Let's not talk about Kenny."

"He's good looking, athletic, I presume, and artistic. Not the boor I had imagined you dumped me for."

"What do you want me to say?" She folded her arms.

"I can't bear to see you unhappy," his voice softened. "That little scene with the stiff upper lip may have fooled your husband, but I see it in your eyes, dear girl. You're miserable. Totally and utterly miserable."

She rose, moved to the wet bar, and refilled her glass. "You're right as usual. Kenny wants me to be friends with his ex-mistress. We were in Italy not long ago, and he fixed it that we'd be in the same hotel as *her*. Every time I ran into the floozy, she'd smile and toss some idle comment about the weather. I couldn't stand it, so I flew home."

"Not very smart of him."

"It's been hell living with Kenny. If it wasn't for Harry, we'd already be divorced. But I think my son is starting to wise up—seeing Kenny for what he is—neglectful and irresponsible."

"I had no idea it was so bad."

"I didn't mean to put a damper on our visit. Let's forget about *him* for the moment and begin celebrating the start of a wonderful reunion."

"Splendid," Callum said. "First a grand lunch and afterward it'll be off to the track to watch the running of the Kentucky Oaks. It'll be exciting, no doubt, with such an array of stunning fillies. Not one of them, I imagine, can hold a candle to your Estella Blue."

"Estella Blue is magnificent."

"Betting on that garland of red roses tomorrow? Well, so am I." Callum said with a wink. "Come on." He rose from the couch and offered her his hand.

"I'd love to, but I can't. Too many loose ends. I have a critical meeting with Estella Blue's trainer and jockey. Afterwards, I'll need to spend some time with my filly. You can understand that?"

"No problem. We'll go to the stable together, watch the race, then 'bout half six have your meeting. It's all good."

"It's tempting, but I couldn't possibly—"

"You couldn't possibly deny having lunch with me." He stepped closer and kissed her cheek.

"Sounds divine." Maiah's whispered words were lost as he pressed his lips against hers.

CHAPTER TWENTY-EIGHT

Beth paced the length of the bedroom with her hands clasped against her chest. She stopped every few moments to inspect her neck in the mirror above the Chippendale dresser. The telltale signs of Dot Barnett's handiwork encircled her neck and made her cringe with each glance. She brushed the bruise marks with her fingertips, bit her lip to keep from wincing, and continued pacing. The Aubusson carpet's thick pile swallowed the sound of her steps. She froze when clangs from the grandfather's clock filled the air. She counted seven long bongs.

Shane's text had been short, but its intent had been clear enough. They'd discuss the situation when he'd arrive home from work at seven. She had to think fast. For two hours, she'd been trying to devise a reasonable explanation as to why she'd been at Zach's house, but had come up empty. Skye couldn't be her foil. That morning, Beth had taken the coward's way out and texted Shane about Skye being their weekend guest after she spends the entire day at the spa.

Beth threw her shoulders back. "Here I am fretting so, sure to be making a mountain out of a molehill." She fluffed her auburn hair away from her face, careful to avoid the tender area where she'd hit her head and moved to the chaise longue in search of a scarf she'd left there. The silk fabric would do the trick she decided as she slumped onto the reclining chair. A sudden wave of exhaustion rippled over her and she closed her eyes. It took only a couple of seconds for her to drift off.

"Beth!"

Shane's shout jolted her awake. She shot up. A surge of panic ran through her, even though she told herself she was overreacting. The door to their master suite flew open. Shane filled the threshold.

"What the hell were you doing at Greyson's?"

"Shane, darlin'." She took a couple tentative steps in his direction.

He folded his arms.

She could see the lines of strain etched into his forehead as mental turmoil filled his eyes.

"Why couldn't you do the one thing I asked?"

"I didn't plan for this to happen. I only stopped by Zach's to—"

"Stick your nose where it doesn't belong."

"I went there to...to check on Emma." The excuse popped into her head from out of nowhere. "I don't really blame Skye. She can't help the way she is—always putting herself above the needs of others. But the poor child. I wanted to spend a wee bit of time with her. I even bought her a stuffed toy lamb." She noticed the tightness around his jaw slacken. "I was there all of twenty seconds when I learned Emma was with her father for the weekend." Her lies that sounded so sincere, they made her squeeze her eyes shut.

"So, you dropped off the toy and left."

She detected the note of sarcasm lacing his voice. "Not exactly."

"Of course not." He turned his back to her. "Do you have feelings for Greyson?"

"What?" Her tenuous voice cracked. She stepped closer and reached out to touch his shoulder but before making contact dropped her hand. "That's the stupidest thing I've ever heard you say."

He spun around. "Then how do you explain what happened? That Barnett woman found you with Zach. That's how..." He pointed at her neck.

She desperately tried to come up with something, but her mind refused to work. For a split-second, she considered telling him the truth because that was the only way to banish his ridiculous suspicion. But something told her—she believed it to be her *fey*—that Shane wouldn't even believe the truth.

She moved closer but, taking in his stony countenance, froze. The anguished glint in his eyes betrayed him, and her heart melted. "I swear on my mother's grave, there's nothing between me and Zach." She stroked his cheek. "It's you I'll always love."

He pulled away. "Forget it. I'm beat. Not thinking straight. When Greyson called me—"

"Zach called you?"

"He took the blame for goading Barnett. Said he was sorry."

She stared at the carpet's emerald border.

"What really happened?"

She made her way to the chaise longue and sat on its edge. "When I found out Lexi had been pregnant, I don't know what manner of madness came over me. I had to know the truth. The only way that was going to happen was to confront Zach. Ever since I glanced through Lexi's diary, I've had a persistent suspicion that Zach had to be the mysterious P.C." She raised her head and studied his face but found herself unable to read any emotion there. "You don't want me getting involved in police business, but I didn't have a choice this time. I had to act. Even if it meant going against your wishes." She looked away and focused on their wedding portrait fixed on the cream-colored wall. "That wasn't to say, I wasn't truly torn, but the urge was overwhelming. I ran straight away to Zach with that one question burning in my mind. It might've been half-cocked and even foolish, but it's what I had to do." Though she hadn't expected to lose control of her emotions, she welcomed the tears that sprung to her eyes and allowed them to fall down her cheeks. "When Dot showed up, Zach acted like an idiot. He pretended we were lovers."

Shane crossed his arms and glared at her.

"Zach couldn't help being dramatic. Thought a wee bit of play acting would enlighten Dot. Except it backfired. Poor old Dot saw me as a threat and reacted violently."

"Dammit, Beth. This is exactly the kind of thing I knew would happen if you insisted on butting into the investigation. That deranged woman could've killed you." He flung his opened palms in her direction. "At least she's finally where she belongs—in a psych ward." Shane raked his finger through his hair then turned away. "Forget about what I said about you and Greyson." He removed his suit jacket and tossed it on a chair and pulled his tie free from his collar. "Just promise me, no more interfering in police business."

Beth felt like kicking herself for bringing him so much grief. Enough lying, she vowed determined to be completely and unequivocally truthful with him from now on. "I can't."

He'd removed his shirt and was working on unlatching his belt. "Can't?"

"I can't make a promise I'm going to break. This is something I've got to do. My *fey* is leading me—"

"Not this. Please, I can't hear another word about that nonsense."

"It's my gift. If you don't understand that much, then you don't know me at all." She headed to the door.

After taking only a couple of strides, he reached her. He grabbed her arm with one hand and shut the door with the other.

"Let me go." She tried to yell but her raw throat allowed only the barest whisper to emerge.

"You have no idea how angry I was when Greyson tried to brush off what happened. Furious and scared. Scared to death you were hurt, in pain, suffering. That I failed you. It kills me, I wasn't able to protect you." He wrapped his arms around her.

"Oh, my darlin' boy. *Grá a chroi.*"

He buried his face into her auburn hair. "*Grá a chroi,*" he whispered. In one fluid movement, he lifted Beth and carried her to their bed.

He laid her down and stroked the hair back from her forehead. She reacted to his touch with an unexpected jump as his fingers brushed against the lump at the edge of her hairline. He pressed his lips into a tight line as his eyes lingered on the angry red welts marring the smooth whiteness of her neck. "If you'd rather rest, I understand."

She opened her arms and he eased on top of her. As his lips brushed her cheeks and closed eyelids, her pent up tension began to slip away. She sought his mouth with hers. After the first deep kiss, time lost all meaning. Not aware if an hour had passed or mere minutes, Shane's gentle strength erased any doubt of his love as she drifted into a calm slumber.

When she fluttered her eyes open, he laid next to her propped up on an elbow as if studying her face. She flashed him a smile and kissed his lips. "You're not going back to the station are you?"

"Got a stack of paperwork waiting for me."

She snuggled closer to him.

"I meant it when I told you to butt out regardless of what your sixth sense is telling you. Understand?"

She bit her lip.

"Beth," he said drawing out her name.

"It wasn't a complete disaster going over to Zach's today. He told me something you might find very interesting. My hunch was spot on."

"Oh?" He lifted a lock of her hair and wound the curl around his finger.

"He's responsible for Lexi being pregnant."

"What?" Shane bolted up. "He *was* having sex with the nanny?" He flung back the comforter. "What a low-life. I don't trust that guy. I'm not saying he killed Lexi, but it wouldn't surprise me if he did."

"I don't condone his despicable actions, but his dream of being a father eluded him. Now that Lexi's gone, he's thoroughly devastated."

"He's an actor, remember."

"I know. I guess you shouldn't check him off your suspect list yet."

"He's on it alright. Along with Alder and Barnett. You'll be pressing charges against her."

Beth shrugged. "Why is Mike a suspect?"

"Jilted lover isn't much of a motive, but mix it with his volatile drug-induced aggression and murder is a definite possibility. Plus, he was wandering around the crime scene."

"But Lexi's murder and those of the other girls was methodical, not the result of a burst of uncontrollable anger."

"Tomorrow we'll find out if we've been barking up the wrong tree. We're meeting with a criminal profiler. Try to get a handle on exactly what kind of person has been killing these girls. And why." Shane slid out of the bed and headed toward the en suite. "What we need is a piece of unequivocal evidence. A DNA sample could crack this case wide open. But the killer's been damn careful. Sooner or later he'll mess up. I pray to God it won't cost another life before he does." Shane glanced over his shoulder and frowned. "Don't even think about getting out of bed. I'll make a pot of tea before I leave for work, dump it into a thermos, and leave it on the nightstand. How 'bout some aspirin for that lump on your head?"

"The doctor gave me a prescription." She motioned to the paper on the nightstand. "But I don't think I need it. After all, a wee bump on the head and a couple of scrapes and bruises isn't going to slow me down."

"Humor me."

She slipped between the satiny sheets and pulled the bedspread up to her chin.

"Beth!" Loud pounding sounded on their bedroom door. "You in there?"

"Good Lord. Skye. I forgot about her." Beth grabbed her silken robe lying on top of the comforter and fumbled with the twisted material. "Go downstairs and make yourself at home," she croaked in the direction of the closed door.

"Stay in bed. I'll explain you're under the weather."

"No need." She slid her arm through the robe's sleeve.

"I know what's best, Betty Getty. That's for you to stay put."

She felt her temper rising. Instead of allowing her instincts to take over, she took a deep breath and silently counted to ten. "Your concern is touching, truly is. But I'm feeling much better." She paused a couple of seconds. "You know how determined Skye is. She won't believe, for an instant, I'm not feeling well.

Eventually, she'll wheedle the truth out of you. Then she'll pester you to into a near stupor insisting on knowing every little detail—a blow-by-blow description—especially since it happened at Zach's house and involved the detestable Dot Barnett. You'll be tied up with Skye for at least an hour!"

"Alright. But I don't want you overdoing it." He stepped away from the bed and folded his arms. "Tell me one little thing. How the hell did she get in here?"

"I gave her a key eons ago," she said as if it were common knowledge. "I've got a set to her house, too."

He rolled his eyes. "Why in heaven's name did you invite her to stay here?"

She slid out of the bed, pulled her ankle length robe together, and tied the belt around her waist. She stepped into her slippers and headed to the door. Feeling his eyes, she turned and offered him a bright smile then blew a kiss before pulling the bedroom door closed behind her.

CHAPTER TWENTY-NINE

SATURDAY, MAY 3rd

Dr. Harold Pitt, balding and rotund, peered at Shane from behind the half-moon glasses perched on his nose. He dropped the short stack of crime scene photos onto the table then folded his hands.

The detectives and uniformed officers waited in the large briefing room for the criminal profiler to offer his take on the four teenage homicides. Shane tapped a pen against the tabletop as he anticipated the onslaught of psychobabble that would undoubtedly sprout from the lips of the UCLA professor of forensics sciences. But still, the profiler seemed to be their best bet to shed some light, even if only a dim glimmer, into the perpetrator's twisted mind.

The professor's nasal voice cut through the charged air like a knife. Shane felt a current of expectancy, which caused his fingertips to tingle. He dropped the pen and riveted his attention on Professor Pitt.

"What I have to offer may not help one iota," Pitt said with outstretched hands. "But since every lead so far has led to an impasse, this is my impression—which, I'd like to emphasize—is not based on my opinion alone but on years of research— mine and other prominent experts in the field. I believe you're dealing with a very organized criminal." He paused a moment as his eyes flitted around the room. His sight settled on Shane. "All the murders have been premeditated and carefully planned, leaving little or no evidence behind. I examined the most recent crime scene in Malibu, and what I observed confirms my theory. There were only a few hairs and a couple of suspicious fibers, no fingerprints or weapon and even the bar codes on the AFID Taser tags came up empty. According to the registration, the Taser belonged to a dead guy in... in..."

"Virginia," Shane said through his teeth.

"Yes, indeed." Pitt cleared his throat. "Another dead end. That fact only sheds light on how intelligent and diligent our killer is. Now," he said running a hand through his sparse hair, "these murders fit the description of a serial killer to a T. A rash of murders—in this case, four—and then a cooling off period. It's been quiet since..." Pitt looked at his notes. "Last Tuesday." He stood and crossed the room, his steps quick for so massive a man. He removed his glasses and slipped them into his rumpled shirt pocket. "Statistically we're looking at a white male from a lower to middle-class background. Most likely between the ages of twenty to late thirties. Possibly abused as a child by one or both parents. Growing up, our killer likely set fires, abused animals, and wet his bed."

Dammit, Shane thought with growing irritation. He could care less if the killer had flown through the air on a flying trapeze as a kid. What he wanted to know, and feared the learned doctor couldn't provide, was a clue—a real clue— as to who killed these girls and how to catch the guy. He looked down at the clean page of his notepad.

"His victims give us insight into his distorted mind."

Shane jerked his head up and locked eyes with the professor.

"The silent crime victim." Pitt looked around the room. "Otherwise known as the prostitute and the runaway. This fact enlightens us to a few critical aspects of the serial killer's personality." Pitt tented his fingers and tapped them against his chin.

The criminologist stayed that way for several seconds. Shane started to believe that Pitt had forgotten about them and had retreated into the depth of his own personal reflections. But then as if waking from a trance, he dropped his hands, tilted his head, and walked to the center of the room.

"Let us consider the four classic characteristics of the serial killer's mindset," Pitt continued. "Firstly, the psychopathic killer views the world as a dangerous place. Therefore, he feels compelled to assert dominance'" He raised a stubby index finger. "He also believes women only exacerbate the male sex drive." Up shot his middle finger. "And then there's the deep set feeling of entitlement. The killer most likely believes that some people are more superior and deserving than others due to their class, gender, race, sexual preference, etc." Another finger rose, joining the other two as he made his point. "And lastly, this type of killer could easily perceive women as sex objects whose sole purpose is to meet the needs of men." His pinky popped up. The professor waved the fingers before closing his hand and slipping it in the pocket of his gray flannel trousers.

The professor cleared his throat and continued. "From my briefings, visiting the crime scene, and reading various police reports, I've discerned that this particular killer has a deep seated vendetta against women who he believes will do anything for money. His perception is probably one of disgust—that they are filth, no more than an ugly pustule on the underbelly of society. In his tortured mind, he most probably believes prostitutes are a facet of the social order that woefully needs to be exterminated like vermin." Pitt moved back a few steps across the tile floor and settled into the wooden chair behind the table. "According to the M.E.'s findings, none of the victims had been sexually assaulted while alive or after death. This killer is unlike Ted Bundy who believed one less person living on the face of the Earth was no big deal—and I'm willing to stake my reputation on this—the murderer of these teenage girls believes that killing off prostitutes one-by-one is a big deal and will provide a better society for all of us."

"What about Horne? She doesn't fit the profile," Shane said.

"Serial killers want their crimes to appear random, unconnected. Perhaps killing Lexi Horne is his way of doing just that."

"What should we be looking for?" Collins asked.

"There's one vital fact I want to impress upon your minds. And that is, all serial killers are actors. Though thoroughly anti-social, they make it a lifelong practice to observe normal behavior and then copy it. They have a macabre proclivity for performance." Pitt paused as if to let his words sink into the ears of the riveted group facing him. "Apparently this killer has developed the knack of building a level of trust with his victims. I guarantee you, he looks normal enough. Probably friendly, outgoing, personable. His costume could easily consist of a well-tailored suit in order to portray a successful businessman or a concerned social worker. However, the most commonly used charade for the serial killer to play is the role of a police officer. To portray an authority figure that is wholly and unmistakably trustworthy. After all, every one of this killer's victims willingly opened their doors to him."

Shane shook his head. Though he'd had high hopes that this respected expert would be able to shed a flicker of new insight on the case, the session turned out how he'd expected. Nothing concrete. Just a whole lot of most likely this and most likely that. He glanced at his writing pad and scanned the few notes he'd scribbled. "So Doctor, it seems from what you've shared, uncovering this criminal will be like finding the proverbial needle in a haystack."

Pitt stroked one of his double chins. "That very well might be the case. No perpetrators of serial killings that I'm aware of was ever captured in a week, month, or even a year. That's if they're clever enough. The one you're after, God help us, is a systematic, precise, thorough killer. A killer with a mission—the worst kind."

"But," Collins blurted out. "How the hell are we gonna catch this guy if he blends into society like a model citizen?"

"Pray for a break. Maybe you'll get lucky."

CHAPTER THIRTY

Maiah stepped out of the shower and slipped into one of the hotel's luxurious monogrammed robes. She wrapped a towel, turban-like, around her wet hair and walked out of the bathroom. The dress, hat, gloves, and purse she planned to wear to the Kentucky Derby were neatly laid out on the king sized bed. She brushed the fabric of the satin and crepe dress and frowned noticing a wrinkle. She grabbed the phone from the nightstand ready to censure the laundry manager, but before she could dial the number, her cell phone rang.

She swiped the screen. "Johannah. Is everything okay?" A wave of trepidation ran through her. Maiah listened more to the tone of the woman's voice on the line than her words and realized her initial concern was ill-founded.

"Calm down," Maiah said. "Not a problem. I'm pleased you and Harry spent an enjoyable time at the museum. You can do that little chore for me later today." She squinted a second trying to think. "Harry's soccer game is at three. He'll be so involved, he won't even notice you're not there for a little while. And please, check the list I gave you. I want all that stuff boxed up and stored in the tack room for now. I'll telephone after the race."

Maiah cut the connection and dropped the phone onto the bed. Her stomach churned as she questioned if the chore she requested of her former governess was too demanding. She ran her fingers through her hair, closed her eyes, and then shook her head. "She won't let me down. Never has. Never will."

***

Seated in a sea-spray blue wing chair, Kenny freed the cell phone from his pocket. Though he hadn't minded hanging around horse people, which surprised him, he'd rather not have to spend another second with Maiah's former beau, Callum Fernsby. Not that he had anything against the guy, but seeing the two of them with their heads together as they chatted about the past and exchanged knowing looks made him feel like an outsider. Just like her parents who jetted into Louisville Regional Airport the night before.

"Be ready to leave no later than noon," Maiah instructed. "The limousine will arrive promptly at a quarter past twelve."

He hadn't noticed she'd entered the room. "But the race doesn't begin until what? Six-twenty?"

"Look at it this way, the Kentucky Derby is race eleven. But it's not like everyone waits around aimlessly for the big event. The day is filled with thrilling competitions." She softened her voice. "The air at Churchill Downs becomes electric as anticipation and excitement builds throughout the afternoon. And then it's time. The hot-blooded three-year olds barrel from the starting gates, around the track with loam flying, until the final crescendo is reached when the new champion races past the finish line."

"Good God, Maiah. You sound like a damn commercial for Churchill Downs." Her face fell.

"Not that it's bad or anything. That's one of the most charming things about you. Your passion."

He noticed her eyes light up.

"It's heart-pounding exhilarating. You'll see."

"Why don't we pick up a couple of hot brown sandwiches before heading to the track? If we get hungry later on, I'm sure they sell hot dogs and popcorn. And you can buy a mint julip to wash it down with." He flashed her a broad smile.

"Don't be ridiculous. We'll be stopping at a fashionable restaurant for lunch with Callum. And my parents. If you want a hot brown, I'm sure it'll be on the menu."

"I almost forgot about Lord Fernsby," Kenny lied as his phone pinged. He focused on the screen and then began texting.

When he finished, he glanced at her. She'd settled on the couch opposite him with her legs tightly crossed and stared at her toes with a frown. He guessed she wasn't happy with her pedicure—or horror of horrors, she'd chipped the polish on one of the nails.

"I'm going out for a little while," he said.

"Out?"

He stood and rolled his shoulder then headed toward the kitchenette but stopped at the table that held their empty breakfast dishes. He righted the askew dome covers. "I'll set these in the hall."

"You're not going anywhere." Maiah jumped up, causing the turban to loosen and fall around her shoulders. She yanked the towel free and threw it to the floor. "I refuse to worry myself sick that you'll forget all about the race. I'll never forgive you, Kenny Weston, if you stand me up for the Kentucky Derby. You know how much this race means to me."

He placed the tray back on the table. "You seriously think I would do that?"

She opened her mouth but then pressed her lips together. She shook her head. "I guess not. No."

"I'll be gone two hours tops. Be back way before the limo arrives." He kissed her cheek, grabbed the tray of crockery, and rushed out of the suite.

***

Maiah turned off the hair dryer and checked her makeup. Satisfied, she slipped into her satiny mauve dressing gown and waited for Callum. She'd telephoned him the minute Kenny left. Proud of the act she'd put on for him, she didn't care if he attended the race or not—now that she'd finally made up her mind.

The insistent rap on the door made her heart quicken. Over the previous two months, she'd methodically devised a plan, down to its most minuscule detail, but it all hinged on whether Callum would agree to help. She squinted through the peephole to make sure it wasn't Kenny, who could've easily forgotten his key card. A puff of air escaped her lips as she spied Callum on the other side of the closed door. She flung it open and grasped his outstretched hand before hurrying him inside.

"Kenny's not due back for an hour, but I'll be quick. I wouldn't want him to return early and find you here."

He cupped her face with his hands. "This is all very cloak and dagger. What the blue blazes is going on?" He let his hands drop and folded his arms.

Now that she had no choice but to unveil her plan, Maiah hesitated. "Well, you know how furious I was when you left me at the altar. I swore I'd never forgive you. But the instant that oath passed my lips, I knew it was a lie." She sought his eyes. "I've never stopped loving you."

He grabbed her hand and led her to the couch. Once seated, he draped his arm around her shoulders. She looked into his face and read the anticipation there.

"The stupidest thing I ever did was to marry Kenny." She dropped her eyes and focused on the richly carpeted floor. "Unlike you, who couldn't bear to hurt your mother by marrying an unacceptable girl, I didn't give a whit about what my parents would think. I wanted them to get off their damn high-horses and embrace a regular, average guy. Of course, they didn't." Maiah rose, crossed the room, and stopped at the window. She swiped back the sheer curtain and peered out. "I've decided to leave Kenny. Get a divorce. And hopefully..." She turned and faced him. "Marry you?"

He jumped up with outstretched arms. "Am I dreaming?"

"When I think of all the years we wasted. I'll do anything—get an annulment, join your church. Just tell me it's true—you do want to marry me?"

He pulled her into his embrace. The intensity of his caress offered the security she'd longed for, as all traces of hurt and neglect melted away. "More than anything, my love," he whispered in her ear.

"I've been so unhappy," she murmured.

"Our mazy past will dissipate as mist in the warmth of the sun's rays when we join our lives together. My God, Maiah, it will be glorious."

Though she wanted to stay in his embrace forever, she eased free of his hold. "Before we reorder our lives I desperately need your help."

A frown sprung to his forehead. She brushed her fingertips across his stubbly cheek.

"I'm leaving Kenny directly after the Preakness Stakes." She understood the look of bewilderment that flashed across his face. "Don't worry. I'm not going to bow out of the Triple Crown." She patted back a stray lock of hair. "But the Preakness is pivotal. Without you being there, I may not have the strength to carry out my plan."

"Plan?"

"To begin our life together." She grasped his hand and led him to the couch.

"We'll slip away at the end of the race. I'll have a car waiting to take us to the airport and then to England. Harry and Johannah will accompany us, of course." Maiah wondered if she was offering too much information too fast but doggedly continued. "Kenny, being the blockhead he is, won't suspect a damn thing. Anyway, he's in awe of the media—the TV interviews, flashing light bulbs, reporters—which will keep him busy while we make our getaway."

"I don't understand. Why abandon Kenny without a word about a divorce? And leave him with all the glory if Estella Blue wins?"

She reached for a bottled water sitting on the coffee table, unscrewed the cap, but didn't take a sip. "I'm not the least vindictive, but I want him to experience a measure of what I've suffered by his betrayals. At least for a few weeks. By that time, my lawyer will have contacted him with divorce papers." She couldn't tell if he was buying into her explanation but hoped his steadfast devotion would do the trick. "I need a commitment. Will you stand by my side—support me—and whisk us away to your ancestral home?"

He drew Maiah close. "Did you have any doubts?"

**

Kenny looked at himself in the freestanding mahogany boudoir mirror. A wide grin spread across his face as he appreciated his dashing figure. When Maiah had made a big deal about his attire for the Derby, he squawked knowing damn well the gray pinstriped suit he brought would do well enough for a horse race, maybe even a bit too formal for the occasion. He swore the hours spent in several of Louisville's most exclusive men shops had been a complete waste of time.

But now, he conceded; Maiah knew what she was talking about.

Dressed in the newly purchased and pressed garments, the impact of the entire getup caused him to whistle at his reflection in pleased satisfaction.

He pulled himself away from the mirror and stopped at the dresser. Its cherry wooden top stood empty except for a small jewelry box. He grabbed the leather box and slipped it into the pocket of his classic navy blazer and headed toward the door. As he passed the mirror, he paused and fussed with the knot of his sky blue tie but realized it had been fine all along.

He called for Maiah as he exited the suite's bedroom. She turned away from her spot at the window and faced him. Kenny caught his breath. He'd never seen her look lovelier. She faced him arrayed in a simple, draped, pale aqua dress, which he imagined cost the equivalent of twice the average bride's wedding gown. Even after all these years, he still couldn't get a handle on the price of his wife's exquisite taste.

"I won't be surprised if you're the most dapper man at the Kentucky Derby." She ran her gloved fingertips across his chest and lingered on the pink cotton of the monogrammed oxford shirt.

"What about these shoes? Are you sure?" He lifted a foot as if inspecting the brown and white spectator.

She nodded.

"I think they're kinda cool. Like a throwback to another era or something."

She turned back to the window. He moved closer and kissed the nape of her neck beneath her upswept hair. "You look beautiful." With a gentle touch, he grasped her shoulders and turned her around. "Gorgeous actually." He kissed her lips. "I picked up a little something for you. That's why I had to go out earlier." He slipped the jewelry box from his pocket and handed it to her. "It'll complete the set."

She flipped the lid open and stared at the golden horse-headed charm.

"I had it engraved on the back, just like the others. I thought it would bring good luck."

She lifted the trinket and turned it over. "Estella Blue," she said the name etched into the charm. "Too bad we don't have time to stop by a jeweler." She twisted her wrist, and the gold linked bracelet with its attached horse charms jiggled. "How did you know I didn't have one for Estella Blue?"

"I pay more attention than you think. I know you have horse charms for each of your four racing Thoroughbreds and one for your favorite riding horse, Annie, your, um... don't tell me... your American Paint horse. Actually, that's an easy breed for me to remember." He winked. "Now you have a complete set of horse charms. Unless you want one for that scrawny horse you rescued last month?"

"We'll hold off on that for a while. Even so, I have high hopes that soon my poor gelding will be healthy, fit, and sound. Harry's been begging to ride him." She shrugged. "He knows the horse is still recovering from years of abuse. Anyway, our son is happy with his colt. He adores Cinders. It'll break his heart to be separated from him."

"Why would he be?" Kenny frowned. "Don't tell me you're thinking about sending Harry away to a boarding school?"

"Of course not. Forget I ever mentioned it." She unlatched the gold chain from around her neck and glided the charm onto it. She rushed to the mirror adjacent to the wet bar and reattached the necklace.

He slid his arm around her waist and moved closer to kiss her, but she slipped away.

"I have something for you too. I picked it out when you were looking for a belt to match your trousers. The store sent it over yesterday. It arrived when you were at the baseball museum." She motioned to a hat box sitting on the coffee table.

He glanced at the box then at Maiah. With a shrug, he moved closer and lifted the lid off the fancy container. After digging through a mound of tissue paper, he freed the straw trilby fedora. He noticed the hatband echoed the colors he was wearing: navy, pink, and cream. "My God, Maiah, it's downright perfect." He pulled out his wallet and plucked out a dollar bill. Folding it twice, he slipped it behind the striped band and smiled. "Now we'll both be bound to have a bit of luck."

CHAPTER THIRTY-ONE

Mike flopped down on the warm sand and glared at the crashing waves. The sea air and early morning sunshine did nothing to improve his foul mood. He hadn't heard a peep out of law enforcement for days and now found himself grappling with the latest bit of incredible news he'd heard on the radio. One of those detectives could've shown a shred of common courtesy and stopped by the gym to break the news. *The news.* He sucked in a mouthful of air. *Lexi pregnant.*

He clenched his jaw until it ached. The very thought of her being with that artist caused a smoldering anger to course through his body. He tried to eradicate the mind-blowing idea that Lexi had chosen to have sex—and for the first time—with a sissified, touchy-feely type. "Dammit," he growled as he curled his fingers and pounded his hand against the packed sand leaving a clear impression of his fist.

In the back of his mind, he rationalized he had to hold on to his anger because if he let it go, he'd fall apart. Anger, hate, and a large dose of revenge for Lexi spurred him on.

Mike flicked away a lock of blond hair as he looked down the shoreline. He squinted behind gold-mirrored sunglasses and caught sight of a lone figure walking through the surf. Not paying too much attention to the figure, he refocused his attention on his current situation: the looming problem of Sofia. She was beginning to bug him. It wasn't that he didn't appreciate all she'd done by keeping tabs on Lexi, but now that she was dead, he didn't need Sofia's help anymore. Just to ditch her didn't seem right. He pulled off his glasses and leaned back on his elbows. The rhythmic tumbling of the waves and the warm streamers of sunshine began to lull him into a much-needed composure. He closed his eyes.

On the verge of sleep, he jolted forward, chasing slumber away, remembering his shift at the gym started in less than two hours. Though he didn't want to admit it, his trip to the Malibu beach that Lexi loved so much had been a complete waste of time. *What the hell did I expect to find anyway? The killer's calling card?*

He shifted to a squat then rose. His feet sunk into the warm sand as he took a long look at the crashing waves. The figure had moved into his field of vision, and he noticed it belonged to a girl. She weaved along the surf with unsteady steps. *Must have a doozy of a hangover*. He turned away but then took a quick glimpse over his shoulder. Mike froze.

"What the hell?"

It took a few seconds to take in what he'd just witnessed. The girl walked into the ocean. A wave knocked her down. She hadn't resurfaced. He kicked off his flip-flops and raced to the shoreline. His lifeguard training, stuff he hadn't even thought about since summer breaks from college, reemerged in full force. The deserted beach offered no buoy ring, so he tore off his t-shirt and looped it around his neck as he splashed into the water. With his sight riveted on the spot where the girl disappeared, he squinted hoping to see a bobbing head and flailing arms. Instead, he saw only the infinite expanse of blue-green sea.

He dove through the approaching wave as salt water stung his eyes. Beyond the whitecaps, his powerful arms slashed the current as he swam further away from shore. He lifted his head, gulped a mouthful of air, and noticed a horizontal shadow fifteen feet away. *Not good.* He feared she was unconscious or, God forbid, dead. As he swam closer, the shadow disappeared, and he spied a head bobbing up then dipping below the water. A surge of relief took hold, but now wasn't the time to take a breather but to jack-up his rescue attempt into high gear.

"I'm gonna get you," he yelled.

He stopped from moving too close since the typical drowning victim would attempt to climb on top of the rescuer. As he treaded water, he loosened the shirt from around his neck and threw it out like a lifeline to the drowning girl. "Grab hold of it," he ordered. She went under. He pressed a bit closer, still keeping a safe distance.

She resurfaced with arms thrashing.

"You're gonna be okay. Grab my shirt and hold tight." He swam closer, now only a couple of feet away. She reached for the edge of the fabric, missed, and tried again. After what seemed an eternity, her fingers snatched the shirt's edge.

He began to tow her from behind, moving slowly as he ripped through the water with his free arm. As he neared the breakers, he realized this would be the trickiest bit. He slowed to a near stop, twisted his neck, and fixed his sight on her. "I want you to let go of the shirt and grab my wrist."

He treaded water as she hesitated. After a couple of seconds, she freed her grip and reached for his arm. Feeling her hold, he released the shirt and then clamped his hand round her wrist. Even if she became afraid and let go, he'd have a firm hold on her. As he began swimming, her body brushed against his legs. "Take a deep breath," he called over his shoulder before pulling her under the water and drawing her through the breaker. Her hold tightened.

Once in the gentle water on the shore side, he stopped swimming and tugged the girl closer. The surge of adrenalin that had rallied him all but disappeared, and his heartbeat slowed to a hammering. His foot touched the ocean floor, and standing, he grasped the girl into his strong embrace. A second later, he swept her up. She pressed her head against his shoulder as he waded through the ebbing tide headed for the beach.

Tiny particles of sand clung to his feet as he moved to a shady spot next to a jutting rock. He laid the girl on a patch of shadow. It took a couple of seconds to catch his breath as he fell to his knees and wiped back strands of tangled dark hair off her tanned forehead. Never had he seen such an exotic beauty; delicate features enhanced her finely shaped cheekbones and full lips. What had possessed this girl-woman to allow herself to be swallowed up by the ocean?

She gasped, shook her head, and then fluttered her eyes open. Deep, chocolate brown orbs stared at him.

"You're gonna be fine." He brushed a line of sand off her cheek. "But to be absolutely sure, I'm gonna call nine-one-one." He reached into his drenched cargo shorts and pulled out his cell phone hoping to God it lived up to its claim of possessing a waterproof package. He pressed the emergency number and heard the calm, steady voice of the dispatcher. After requesting assistance and satisfied the EMTs would find them, he clicked off the phone. "Help's on the way." He grasped her delicate hand and patted it. "I'm Mike." He waited for a response, but she only squinted her eyes. "You are?"

"I'm..." She swallowed hard. "My head..." She rose into a sitting position. "Everything is blurry. The pounding in my head won't stop. I thought the water would take the pain away." She reached toward her crown but stopped.

He followed the movement of her hand and spied several gashes in her scalp and bruising along her right temple. Her white, sleeveless shirt that clung to her torso was splattered with brownish splotches. *Bloodstains*.

"The pain won't stop," she whispered. "And the whirling." She laid a hand across her abdomen. "Worse than that, I can't remember. I'm not even sure who I am."

"Shhh." He lifted a finger to his lips. "I promise you'll feel a helluva lot better soon. The paramedics are on their way. They'll patch you up in no time."

She winced as if she'd experienced a sharp pain.

"You're probably dehydrated. Once you get some fluids, the confusion will disappear. I'll get you a bottle of water." He eased away from her then rose. "I've got water and a blanket in my car. I won't be gone more than five minutes. By that time, the ambulance should be here."

"Please." She threw her arm out in his direction. "Don't leave me."

A note of desperation laced her voice. Or was it fear? Mike wasn't sure. But he was certain he couldn't leave her, not for five minutes or five seconds. He knelt beside her.

"Everything's jumbled. Except that I have to get away." She leaned back on her elbows, and her sand coated Capri pants stuck to her skin as she stretched out her legs.

"Away from what?"

"He's after me. Wants to kill me."

"Huh?"

She extended her arm, and it brushed against him. He grasped her slim fingers and squeezed her hand. It felt cold. He silently cursed the ambulance for taking so long. *This girl is worse off than I imagined. Somebody wants to kill her—what the hell is that? She could just be a nut case.* He dismissed the notion as soon as it crossed his mind.

She started to cry, softly at first but then as if abandoning all reserve. Her whole body shook.

"You're safe now," Mike said. "Everything's gonna be okay." His comforting words made no impact as the woman continued to weep.

"What's happened? Do you need help?"

The voice startled Mike. He twisted his neck and saw a blonde dressed in a red bikini, a straw hat, and oversized sunglasses standing over him.

"She was drowning," he offered. "The paramedics are on their way."

The blonde stepped around him as if to inspect the small, battered form resting on the sand. She gasped then dropped to her knees. "OMG. I can't believe it." She pulled off her sunglasses and tossed them aside.

Mike noticed the girl's jawline tighten.

"Darla. It's Marjorie. Mrs. Hammond."

Not offering any signs of recognition, the girl shut her eyes.

"You look terrible." She reached into the straw beach bag slung over her shoulder and pulled out a bottle of spring water. Mike grabbed it and twisted the cap off.

Darla blinked her eyes open as Mike gently helped her into a sitting position. "Take a sip." He moved the bottle toward her lips. She took a swallow, much too fast, and began to cough.

"Take it easy, why don't you?" Marjorie spat. "Let me." She snatched the bottle and moved it in front of Darla's lips. "Drink slowly," she instructed.

Giving her leeway, Mike stood with folded arms, not removing his eyes from the injured girl. "Darla," he whispered her name.

Though Marjorie insisted she drink, Darla kept her lips pressed tight. Marjorie gave up and tossed the water bottle onto the sand. She reached toward Darla's matted hair but dropped her hand. "Skye is worried sick." Marjorie raised her voice, as if the young woman was deaf.

"Skye?" Mike said.

Ignoring him, Marjorie continued. "With you missing, and what's happened to Lexi. You do know about Lexi being—"

"That's enough." Mike grabbed Marjorie's arm and jerked her upward next to him. "The last thing that girl needs is for you to be giving her the third degree. Lay off."

"Who the hell do you think you are?"

"I'm Mike Alder, Marjorie. And I think you should mind your own damn business. Why don't you just continue jogging down the beach? I've got this under control."

"You have a lot of nerve...you...you beach bum." She pulled her arm free, reached into the straw bag, and fished out a cell phone. "I know that girl, and I'm not taking any chances. I'm calling for help."

"I already told you; an ambulance is on the way."

"I'm not talking about that kind of help." Marjorie pressed the keypad and lifted the phone to her lips. "My name is Marjorie Hammond. This is urgent. Let me speak to Detective Shane Dalton."

I should've known, Mike thought with a dismissive shake of his head. *She doesn't trust me. So, the first thing she does is call that detective.* He shifted his sight from the woman and noticed fresh tears rolling down Darla's cheeks. "Dammit."

With the phone tucked between her ear and shoulder, Marjorie stooped over and grasped her forlorn sunglasses. She slipped them on and hurried toward the shoreline causing a spray of sand to fly in Mike's direction.

With the blonde woman out of earshot, he dropped back onto his knees and reached for Darla's hands. "Listen. Hear that? A siren." He stole a quick glance in Marjorie's direction. With the phone still pressed to her ear, she waded through the foamy surf.

"Mike."

He shifted his attention back to Darla.

"I'm glad that woman is gone. Why was she screaming at me?"

"I think she was trying to help." He traced his fingertip along Darla's wet cheek. "Look, I'm not gonna leave you. I'll go with you to the hospital. Even if the EMTs say no. I'll follow in my Jeep. Close your eyes and think good thoughts because—I promise you—you'll be your old self in no time."

Darla gave his hand a weak squeeze as her head fell back onto the sand.

CHAPTER THIRTY-TWO

The blaring ring of the night table's phone jolted Beth awake. She forced her eyes open a sliver and glanced at the clock. Exactly half nine. She grabbed the receiver on its third ring, hoping the sound wouldn't wake Shane. Still squinting to lessen the effects of the morning light, she raised the telephone and discovered he wasn't asleep beside her. A folded sheet of paper sat on top of his pillow next to a single red rose.

She managed to utter a raspy hello. A familiar voice greeted her though tinged with a trace of anxiety. The director of the cat rescue where she volunteered. It took nary a bit of persuasion for Beth to agree to pick up a litter of kittens. A woman had found the motherless clowder harbored under her home's front stoop in her Little Armenia neighborhood.

After returning the phone to its base, she lifted the rose and inhaled its delicate fragrance. The petals tickled the tip of her nose. She rested back against the soft mound of a pillow and brushed the velvety blossom across her cheek, reminding herself how lucky she'd been in finding a man like Shane. She jerked into a sitting position remembering the note and snatched the paper.

Didn't want to wake you. Gone to work. Grá a chroí. Shane. Her eyes drifted down to the P.S. he'd hastily scrawled. *BTW don't let Skye boss you into entertaining her. You need to rest!*

She shook her head amused.

An hour later, she searched for De Longpre Avenue as she drove down Hollywood Boulevard. She hadn't planned on getting turned around and regretted not putting the address into her GPS. As a volunteer at the Cute Cat Rescue, she'd driven to East Hollywood more times than she cared to remember in search of stray and feral cats. Her work at the shelter had filled up the empty hours after the accident as she moved beyond physical to emotional healing. Tending to the innocent creatures soothed the all-consuming anger and quelled the misery of her gripping self-pity. But recently, her involvement at the shelter had shrunk since her new role as a wife turned her previous schedule upside down. That coupled with her research into the death of Lexi and the other girls, she barely had a spare moment to stop by the rescue and drop off a few cases of cat food.

With each passing second, she became more frustrated and hoped she'd finish her errand before Skye woke up. She searched for a parking space intent on downloading the elusive address into her navigation system. Spying a spot, she nosed her SUV between a battered pickup and a van. Her finger tapped the address onto the GPS screen.

She studied the information and realized she was less than two hundred feet away from her destination. With a roll of her eyes, she flung open the door, walked to the rear of the SUV, and freed a sturdy plastic cat carrier from the cargo area.

It had been overcast when she headed out, but now the clouds had cleared, and a warm breeze stirred the air. Her heels clicked against the pavement as she rounded the corner onto De Longpre. She glanced at a rundown apartment building and wrinkled her nose. The grimy, stucco building stuck out like an eyesore compared to the neat blocks of single houses surrounding it. She hummed a lively tune of her own invention as she glanced at the address she'd entered into her phone. As she became more enchanted with her budding musicality, she dropped the phone into her pocket and hummed even louder. The song died in her throat as she spied a familiar car. A two toned white and burnt orange El Comino. "What's the chance of that belonging to anyone else but Father Clancy?" Beth took a sideway glance at the dingy apartment house.

Could he actually live in there?

She shifted her weight from one foot to the other as she decided it wouldn't hurt the kittens to remain under the porch a wee bit longer. *I'll inquire within; someone's sure to know if a priest rents a flat.* She headed toward the entryway then paused as her sense of airiness vanished and a gloom settled over her. Her failure to contact her estate agent friend in search of an appropriate building for the halfway house made her wonder if she really wanted to see the priest. "But he's a man after God's own heart, and he's sure to forgive me. Plus he'd be able to clear up why the secretary at St. Timothy's thinks he's a ninety-two-year-old Jesuit," she mumbled remembering she'd forgotten to check with the Archdiocese Division of Clergy Personnel for Shane. She pulled the heavy, smoky tinted-glass door open reassuring herself that it was an understandable oversite on her part. It's not like I've been spending my time twiddling my thumbs, she thought as the door closed behind her. She touched the silk scarf draped around her neck in order to hide Dot's handiwork.

The dark corridor caused her to stand still until her eyes adjusted. She dropped the cat carrier onto a bench adjacent to a scarred wooden door with the word "Manager" stenciled onto it. With a firm rap, she knocked a couple of times before stepping inside.

A thin man sat behind a metal desk with his skeletal fingers clutching a section of the newspaper. The paper's remaining sheets laid scattered across the desk. He squinted, studying the page. Though she stood before him for a few seconds, he didn't glance away from the printed words or acknowledge her.

Beth cleared her throat. He seemed to clench the page tighter. "Excuse me. I was hoping you might be able to answer a wee question?"

At the sound of her soft brogue, he peered over the paper's edge.

"I noticed a friend of mine's car parked outside and was wondering if—"

"God Almighty, don't tell me. A rust bucket '77 El Camino." He flicked a finger across his leathery cheek, brushing away a strand of his greasy black hair.

"How did you know?" Not waiting for an answer Beth continued, "Would you mind telling me which apartment—"

"I don't know how that boy does it." He paused looking her up and down. "Another uptown girl." He dropped the newspaper, crossed his arms, and leaned back in the swivel chair. "I know he's a good looking devil, but really, could you tell me what you gals see in him?"

She pressed her lips together and took a couple of backward steps realizing she'd made a lulu of a mistake.

"Listen, honey. He's not in. Haven't seen him for 'bout a week now. Not since he dropped off this month's rent. Oh, yeah. " He raised the now crumpled sheet of newspaper revealing it belonged to the Sports section. "The ponies. He's at the damn Derby. He must've told you he works for some rich chick who races thoroughbreds. Horses are all he talks about besides, you know, the ladies."

Kenny Weston's wife races her horses. A coincidence? Don't believe in coincidences.

Beth closed her eyes trying to channel her sixth-sense. The striking sound of a cigarette lighter distracted her concentration so she flashed her eyes open.

He'd lit up a stubby cigar and puffed out a cloud of blue smoke. The overpowering odor nearly choked the breath from her lungs. As long as she could remember, she'd always been sensitive to smoke. The main reason her father had given up the habit. She pulled a linen handkerchief from her purse and covered her mouth as she coughed.

"Looky," he said through teeth gripping the cigar, "can't upset you that bad Hap's gone away for a few days." He stood and moved in her direction.

Her eyes widened as she took in his countenance. He couldn't have stood a fraction taller than 5'5," and though skinny, his stomach protruded as if he were six months pregnant.

"Hap Dorian ain't the only fish in the sea that can tickle your fancy. Take me, for instance. I know how to show a gal a good time. A real good time." He removed the cigar and offered her a wide grin exposing a chipped front tooth.

Her eyes welled as he blew smoke in her direction. Not understanding the strong urge that had suddenly surfaced—one compelling her to find out more details about this Hap Dorian—she didn't question it. Instead, she surrendered to her *fey* for guidance. Like a light from above, it struck her to use the smoke induced tears to her advantage. "He told me I was special. I was heartbroken when he didn't ring me." She stopped talking. His eyes seemed to have glazed over as he sucked on the cigar.

"Listen, sister, you ain't the first gal to come in here with a sob story about some jerk screwing her around. It stinks." He reached up and stroked her cheek. "I'm not like them heartless bastards."

Though she wanted to slap him away, she lowered her sight and focused on his bloodshot eyes. "It's just," she said with a cough, "I believed him. Now he's halfway across the country." She twisted the handkerchief and then spun around.

"Hey, don't go yet."

She glanced over her shoulder.

"I'm Nick. Why don't we walk around the corner and get a quick drink?"

She faced him with a raised brow.

"Sheeze. A cup of coffee. Those Armenians make a killer brew. Seriously, I don't mind if you cry on my shoulder." He patted the bony protrusion. "I'm damn good at comforting heartbroken gals."

She raised her palm as he stepped even closer. "Hap promised to contact me. I believe he tried. It's just that I've looked everywhere, and I haven't been able to find my mobile."

He narrowed his eyes causing a slew of new lines to further crease his forehead. "My cell phone."

His face relaxed. He sucked on the cigar and slowly exhaled.

Her eyes burned. "I figured I must've lost it. Then I remembered the last time I used it was at Hap's place. When I called my husband."

"Whoa." Nick's lip curled.

"I didn't dare tell Hap my address because well..." Beth paused a moment trying to come up with a believable excuse. "Because I know better. Truth is," she said lowering her voice to a near whisper, "my husband, he's a bodyguard to...to, oh God, I'd rather not say. But believe me, they're some unsavory characters. Big drug dealers."

She saw a spark of interest light up Nick's dark eyes.

"I made a huge mistake telling my husband I lost my phone. Exploded as usual. He did this."

She moved the edge of her scarf so Nick could see the purplish bruises.

He opened his mouth as if to say something but Beth didn't give him the chance. "This morning he told me he'd been talking to a cop friend—a real dirty cop if you ask me—who knows how to trace phones." She wiped her tearing eyes with the back of her hand. "I'm sure they'll trace the phone to Hap's flat. And since he's gone out of town, good Lord." She shook her head slowly. "He'll take his anger out on..." She glanced around the small, cluttered office.

"A table, a few windows, but that won't satisfy him. Your arm probably would."

"You live with a guy like that?"

She sensed a tone of incredulity coloring his voice. *Damnation*.

"I'm scared of him. He did this about a year ago when I burned his toast." Beth pointed to the scar on her cheek. "Pulled a knife from the block and before I could get away." She stopped speaking and squeezed her eyes shut. A tear slipped free and trickled down her face.

"You poor kid. Let me take you to Hap's apartment. You can look around for your, um, mobile. I don't want no trouble." He pulled a keyring from his pants pocket as the phone, nestled among the newspapers, rang. Nick dropped the cigar in an ashtray then raised his hand signaling her to wait before grabbing the receiver. "Hollywood Place Apartments." He paused listening. "Oh hell. That's just great. Yeah. I'm in the office. Okay." He slammed the receiver down. "I've got a damn problem." He faced her. "Normally I wouldn't do this—rules and all—but what the hell. Here, take it. The pass key." He signaled out a silver key and offered the ring to her. "Apartment 233. You do remember the elevator is down the hall on the right?"

"Vaguely." She pinched the key with her thumb and index finger and headed for the door. The sound of the phone's keypad being punched died as she shut the office door.

Relieved to leave the musty elevator behind, Beth hurried down the hallway noting door numbers. Two-twenty-nine. Two-thirty-one. Two-thirty-three. She stopped in front of the door and knocked. After tapping her foot a couple of times, she knocked again. Nothing.

Beth slid the key into the lock and turned the handle. After a quick look in both directions along the deserted corridor, she cracked the door open and peered inside the pitch-black room. She slipped inside, closed the door, and patted the wall in search for a light switch. A second later, an overhead fixture cast a dim glow into the studio apartment. With quick steps, she hurried across the room and pulled back the curtain. Thick, heavy blackout drapes blocked the casement windows. She lifted the drape's edge and took in the view. Father Clancy's, or rather Hap Dorian's, car stood in the street directly below.

She released the curtain, eyeballed the tiny space, and decided the room measured only about twenty by twenty feet. But for its small size, the square room contained a kitchen, dining area, and a full sized bed.

She moved around the kitchen noting the chipped enamel sink and the two lone cabinets above a double burner stove. After a quick glance at a roach scurrying across the countertop, she pulled open one of the cabinets. Cereal boxes of the sugary variety filled the top shelf. Below sat a mismatched set of plates, a couple bowls, and a frying pan. The second cabinet offered a package of instant brown rice, an unopened box of rigatoni, and a jar of Neapolitan ragù sauce. She closed the metal cabinets and moved toward the half-sized refrigerator. The white box reminded her of the one in her childhood home that fitted smartly under the countertop unlike this one wedged between the stove and wall. The fridge's uncluttered shelves stored only a couple cans of diet Pepsi, four bottles of Budweiser, and a half empty jar of mayonnaise.

Beth stepped next to the kitchen table and lifted a picture frame lying face-down. She moved closer to the weak streams of light glowing from the ceiling fixture. The men in the photo were posed on either side of an impressive thoroughbred and could pass for father and son. Though both of them were dressed in overalls, their bright smiles only intensified their good looks. "You must be Hap." She brushed a fingertip across the younger man's face. After one final glimpse, she replaced the frame exactly the way she found it and hurried toward the sleeping area. Besides the bed, the only other pieces of furniture were a dresser and a writing table stationed against the wall opposite the shrouded windows.

Drawn to the mirror propped against the writing table—a traditional makeup mirror with four light bulbs lining each side of the glass—she moved closer. She hit the switch on the mirror's edge. The bulbs popped on and flooded the area with a strong, bright light, which spilled across the table's surface. Tubes and bottles of cosmetics sat in neat rows and filled the center section of the table. She lifted a familiar looking gold-topped bottle and glanced at the label, *Tracie Martyn*. A quick perusal offered up other high-end brands—Chanel, La Mer, Artistry—telling her that the assortment of makeup cost hundreds of dollars. Near the corner of the table stood a Styrofoam form in the shape of a head. If its purpose was to hold a wig, the hairpiece was missing. She reached for the table's narrow drawer but found it locked.

"Why in heaven's name would a man have a supply of cosmetics?" she asked the empty room. "And really expensive ones in a place like this?" She freed her mobile and snapped a couple pictures of the makeup table then slipped the phone back into the side pocket of her slacks. *Nick had mentioned an 'uptown' girlfriend. Maybe she's been living here.* The very idea of residing in such a depressing room made her cringe. The bare, dingy walls, dusty gray curtains, and thin brown carpet did nothing to add a sense of hominess to the small dwelling. She headed to a closed door betting it was a closet.

The door creaked open revealing a nearly empty space. The few garments draped on wire hangers seemed to have purposely been pushed to the far end of the rod. She noted a flannel shirt, a black hoodie, and a pair of worn jeans. In the center hung a well-tailored black suit. She eyed the overhead shelf. Nothing but a black felt fedora that lacked the panache of the ones Shane frequently wore. "Humph. Not so much as a woman's bathrobe, handbag, or even a scarf," she murmured. As she started to close the door, she paused, reached in, and pulled out the suit. It looked huge. At least twice the size of the other garments. With a firm hold on the sturdy wooden hanger, she moved the suit closer to the light. The material's rich quality and neat stitching caused her to believe it had been handmade. She unbuttoned the jacket and flipped it open revealing a neatly creased pair of black dress pants folded over the base of the hanger. As she searched for a label, Beth noticed a shirt had been stuffed into the jacket's sleeve. She slipped her hand into the wide armhole and pulled it free. Puzzled that it too was black, she dropped the suit on top of the bed, and shook the shirt open. *A tonsure shirt?* She reached inside one of the suit coat pockets and touched something thin and stiff. "Can't be." She fished it out and stared at the white rectangle. A tab for a priest's collar.

She slipped the tab into her shoulder bag and returned the suit, with the shirt the way she'd found it, back into the closet. After one quick sweep around the room, she clicked off the lights and slipped out the door.

Once inside the closed elevator, she exhaled a deep sigh. Her instinct told her she'd discovered something important. Even if nothing in the crackerjack box apartment made a lick of sense. Though she'd been in the room only a few minutes, it seemed like an hour, and she'd experienced more than enough of the Hollywood Place Apartments. She wanted out. The sooner the better. Her stomach flipped with the prospect of another encounter with Nick.

She exited the elevator and headed toward the office. The door stood open. To her great relief, he sat behind the desk with the phone pressed against his ear. She stepped inside and placed the keys on his desk. He looked up as she freed her mobile and flashed it near his face. She mouthed an enthusiastic thank-you and scurried out of the smoky office.

Beth grabbed the cat carrier and all but ran out of the building. But before heading to her vehicle, she pulled out her mobile and clicked a couple photos of the apartment building and the surrounding area.

She wouldn't allow herself to consider any of what she'd seen until she scooted inside her Volvo and settled behind the steering wheel. After taking a couple of cleansing breaths and a deep swallow from her water bottle, she reached for the zippered folder lying on the passenger seat. She flipped through the pages of notes until she came to a clean sheet of lined paper. After loosening the pen from its slot, she dashed down the name of the complex, the apartment number, and the manager's name. When she'd dropped off the key ring, she noticed his full name—Nicky Dempsey—embossed on a brass plate that must've been covered earlier by the haphazard sheets of strewn newspaper.

She skipped a couple of lines then carefully printed the name, Hap Dorian. Beneath it, she scribbled down all the information Nick had unwittingly offered.

She couldn't keep the deluge of ideas, notions, and theories at bay a second longer. As she worried her lip with the tip of her thumb, she acknowledged the obvious; there had to be a connection between Hap and the owner of a horse racing today in Kentucky. A local horse. She vaguely remembered Skye ranting about Kenny's wife dragging him off to Kentucky to watch her horse race in the Derby. Skye had never mentioned the name of Kenny's wife so she tapped the Google icon on her mobile and searched for information regarding the upcoming horse race. She scrolled down until she came to an article titled "California Filly Derby Bound." Her eyes flitted across the small screen. "Ah-ha. Estella Blue owned by Maiah Weston." She scratched the name on her pad. "It makes perfect sense. Hap Dorian must work for her."

She tapped her forehead. *But what about the makeup. The priest's suit? That shouldn't be in a man's apartment who works in a stable.* She wrinkled her brow and decided he could've pinched the suit. *But why?*

She reached for the water bottle and considered another avenue. An easy explanation would be that Hap is a cross-dresser. She liked that idea. The only wrench in her theory was the absence of women's clothes anywhere in the tiny apartment.

The priest's suit. That puzzled her as much as the makeup. Not in a million years would the finely tailored suit fit the young man in the framed photograph. It would, no doubt, be the perfect size for a big man like Father Clancy. She gulped a mouthful of water. *So, Hap's been masquerading as a priest?*

She stared at the water bottle for a few seconds then took another swallow. The longer she thought, the more she realized the idea didn't make sense. "What exactly have I learned about Hap Dorian?" A second later, she answered her own question. "He likes horses and women. But does he have some kind of perverse obsession about priests, so much, he pretends to be one?" She screwed on the bottle's cap and dropped it in the console. "There you go again," she said softly, "giving into flights of fancy. Probably just an old Halloween costume." She chewed her lip remembering the rich touch of the fabric and its hand stitching.

What about the car? Hap's car is the spitting image of the one Father Clancy drives.

Another coincidence? She rubbed her left temple feeling the beginning stage of a tension headache. "I give up. It doesn't make sense."

She leaned back and rested her head against the seat cushion. "My *fey* is telling me—telling me—what?" Beth pressed her lips together and peered at the folder. She reached for the pen that had wound up in her lap and wrote, *If Hap works for Maiah, then it's probable Kenny knows Hap.* "According to Skye, Kenny didn't like Lexi, not a wee bit. What if Kenny and Hap teamed up to do away with her...or Lexi and Darla? But why in heaven's name?" She asked the questions as if expecting an answer to emerge within the walls of the vehicle.

Her head began to pound the instant she realized she'd have to tell Shane. She zipped the folder closed, tossed it on the passenger seat, and pressed the ignition button. After a quick look in the rearview mirror, she gingerly nosed the Volvo into the driving lane. There'll be plenty of time to come up with something, she decided, after I pick up the litter of kittens and drop them off at the shelter.

"Ah, but my Shane, no doubt about it, he's going to be *bullin'* mad."

CHAPTER THIRTY-THREE

Beth drove in the direction of the Clear Spring Sheriff Station. As she slowed down for a light, she offered up a heartfelt prayer for divine guidance. She hadn't a clue how she'd explain to Shane her recent adventure of winding up inside the puzzling Hollywood apartment. It was an innocent inquiry, she reminded herself. But then, with a roll of her eyes, she recalled the yarn she'd spun so effortlessly, drawing sympathy from Nick Dempsey.

She took a quick peek at the bulging paper bag nestled on the passenger seat. The piping hot food she purchased from Callee's Café filled the air with a delectable aroma. She hoped the picnic lunch would quell Shane's natural reaction to her latest escapade. Her stomach churned with the idea of having to witness another bout of Shane's angry words that would end with a stark look of disapproval. She'd calculated her plan with care, believing he wouldn't blow his top at work, especially if Gavin or any of the other detectives were in the office.

If it was only the incident in the flat, she thought, chewing her lip. First, it was the boldness she showed in not checking with Shane and getting his seal of approval for Skye's weekend stay at their house. Then to top things off, when she arrived at the cat rescue, the vet on duty explained that the kittens were too young to be admitted into the shelter. Not really sure as to how it happened, she volunteered to be their foster mother for the next week or so. The tiny balls of fur will play havoc with Shane's allergies, she'd thought only too late, as she belted the cat carrier back inside her Volvo. *He'll be watery eyed, sneezing, and blowing his nose nonstop.* "Dear Lord," she'd murmured, "I've really done it this time."

At least when she dropped the kittens off at her house, Skye had perked up. Beth showed her the closet that housed all of her cat paraphernalia, which she hadn't touched since marrying Shane. Without even asking, Skye started to fill the litter box and placed cat beds around the small utility room. She handily promised Beth she'd stop by the market and pick up some additional cans of cat food. Before racing out of the house, she took a quick peek and noticed Skye sitting crossed legged on the tile floor with a kitten cradled in the crook of each arm. In spite of herself, a smile tugged at the corners of her lips.

The happy thought led her to visualize the pleased look of surprise that would fill Shane's face when she'd burst into his office. The wafting aroma of fried chicken, creamy mashed potatoes with gravy, and spicy vegetable salad would make his eyes crinkle with delight. The light turned green, and she pressed down on the accelerator, realizing she was almost there.

Beth turned off Agoura Road and parked directly in front of the low, green-roofed building, grabbed the bag, and hopped out of the SUV. She half-walked, half-ran toward the double glass doors shaded by a wide portico. Once inside, the place seemed deserted. After waving hello to Officer Keller, the deputy on duty at the front desk, she listened to the clackety sound of her Cuban heels striking the tile floor. As she balanced her large leather purse and the larger bag of food, Beth realized she was famished and tired. After staying up half the night with Skye, and the unusual turn of events that morning, she hadn't had a free moment even for a cup of coffee.

Luckily, Skye had bought her excuse for dropping by to see Zach. She'd told her a partial truth: that she'd stopped by to see Trey's paintings and decided to say hello to Zach. The recitation of her altercation with Dot Barnett only reinforced Skye's belief that the older woman was responsible for Lexi's death, and it sent her into a tailspin. She hadn't known exactly how to calm her down, but Skye came up with her own solution.

Who would've thought she keeps a stash of DVDs she's starred in, housed inside of her Escalade's glove box? At first, Beth was a bit offended that she insisted they watch a couple of her movies. *How would Skye feel if I pulled out every magazine featuring pictures of me?* But once she bit the bullet, she discovered much to her surprise, that it had been kind of fun. Skye offered a running commentary on the behind the scene happenings, mishaps, and gossipy tidbits as they watched the flashing frames. 'Tis true, she conceded as she hurried down the corridor, Skye's movies had done the trick. They not only soothed Skye, but also blocked out the disastrous encounter with Dot and eased her mind if only for a few fleeting hours.

Without knocking, she twisted the knob and stepped into the detectives' office. Shane sat with his back to her, a phone wedged between his ear and shoulder. Collins looked up from his desk, which abutted Shane's. His dark eyes shone as he motioned to Shane, who glanced over his shoulder and waved her in.

"You're looking better," Collins said. "How's the head?"

"Still tender, I'm afraid. Though I'm a bit embarrassed by being trounced by a senior citizen, so." Not wanting to disturb Shane, she stepped closer to Collins and lifted the bag. "I brought you hard working detectives lunch," she said barely louder than a whisper. She unrolled the bag's top and pulled out a stack of napkins and several paper plates. She'd just grabbed a handful of plastic utensils when Shane raised a hand motioning her to stop. A second later, he hung up the phone.

"Smells great." Shane stood. "Callee's?" He didn't wait for an answer but turned toward Collins. "We're needed at the interrogation room."

"You have to eat." Beth pouted.

"We will," Collins said. "Later, that's all."

"Okay," Beth said with a sigh. "I'll head over to the staff lounge and stick the food inside the refrigerator." She replaced the items then grabbed the bag.

"Hold on." Shane lifted a Sharpie from his desk. He scribbled his name on the brown bag, folded down its top and stapled it shut. "I'm not taking any chances. Otherwise, the entire station will be helping themselves."

"I have something important to tell you." Beth looked into Shane's steel blue eyes. He pursed his lips and crossed his arms.

"I picked up a litter of kittens today over in East Hollywood."

Collins, his laptop held snugly under his arm, moved next to Shane.

"Look, if this is one of your long-drawn out stories, save it for later. Okay?" Shane said extending his upturned hands as in supplication.

"It *is* a long story." Beth shrugged. "I guess it'll have to wait after all." She paused a second. "At Mass this evening, I'll say a prayer and light a candle for both of you." She lifted the bag. "Enjoy this."

With a quick wave, she left them and headed to the lounge. She turned a corner leading into the lobby and froze. Two officers ushered in Mike Alder. He wore only tan cargo shorts and a pair of flip-flops. She lingered, eyeing his well-developed pecs then lowered her gaze to his washboard abs. Though she wouldn't have minded just staring at him awhile longer, she took a couple of steps in his direction. The vein in his neck bulged, and she swore fire blazed in his eyes. His lips, pressed into a tight line, caused a look of determination to dominate his face as his square chin jutted out. *Now what?* she worried quickening her steps.

"Mike, what's going on?" She rested her free hand on his rock hard bicep.

"Sorry, ma'am." An officer growled as he steered Mike through double doors and down a dimly lit hallway.

She sunk onto a nearby metal chair with a cracked green vinyl seat and dropped the bag on the floor. Before she could manage a cohesive thought, Shane dashed toward her.

"Mike Alder is here. What's going on?" She detected a note of excitement tinting her voice.

"Police business. It doesn't concern you. Remember?"

His eyes lingered on her bruised neck. For an instant, she regretted removing the scarf, but the day had warmed, and the material had begun to irritate the tender flesh. She pressed her palm against her neck as if trying to hide the red-purplish bruises from his insinuating stare.

"I'll see you later," Shane said. "Around seven. Maybe the three of us can stop by that new Italian restaurant for a quiet dinner. *Mangia*—right?"

"Sounds lovely. I'll check with Skye. But, I'll make the reservation for eight, just in case."

He took a few steps away then stopped and looked over his shoulder.

"It's kind of you to include Skye." She rushed to his side, draped her arms around his neck, and kissed him. "Now, go on." She followed his movement down the hall until he yanked a door open and disappeared.

She edged back toward the chair she'd left behind, grasped the now greasy bag, and took a few steps but stopped, hearing her name. She spun around. Marjorie faced her looking as if she'd just stepped off the beach, wrapped in a hand-painted red silk sarong. A broad-brimmed straw hat cast a shadow across her face.

As she moved closer, Marjorie squealed, "Oh my God, what happened to you?"

For the second time in a matter of minutes, Beth raised her hand to cover her neck.

"Don't tell me," Marjorie said lowering her voice, "Shane did that?" Her eyes widened as Beth detected a churlish look of delight animate her friend's face.

"Don't be ridiculous. I had a run in with a mad woman, but that's a story for another time. Anyway, I truly want to apologize for keeping Shane's identity from you."

"Forget it. I kinda understand why you did it. Anyway, can you believe it?"

Beth squinted. "What?"

"You haven't heard? Well," she said sinking onto the chair Beth had vacated. "I... found... Darla."

"You what?" She paused trying to digest Marjorie's news. As her words finally sunk in, a barrage of question clamored inside her mind. "Where was she? Is she okay?"

Marjorie patted the seat next to her. Beth obediently sat.

"I would really love for you to think I figured out some deep mystery, but all it actually took was a walk on the beach. I found her resting on the sand in the shade of an outcrop of rocks."

"Thanks be to heaven. So, she's okay?" Beth reached out and squeezed Marjorie's arm.

"I don't know about that. But she's alive." For a moment, Marjorie glanced at the array of golden bangles encircling her wrist then crossed her arms. "Some surfer type dude said she was drowning and he pulled her out of the ocean. I'm not so sure I believe that. He looked kinda menacing. Big and hulking. Lots of muscles."

Mike's presence at the station was beginning to make sense.

"I called Shane immediately. I'm here to give my statement. He said there was no hurry, but I thought this is big. Huge, actually. I didn't want to hamper the investigation by taking time to change clothes and everything. That would've taken over an hour."

Beth nodded absently.

"I have doubts about that Mike guy. I know for damn sure that girl can swim. I've seen her in Skye's lap pool, for Chrissake. Anyway, I found him hovering over Darla, and my God, you should've heard her screaming, like he was about to kill her or something. OMG, wouldn't it be just sick if that Mike character turned out to be the one who killed Lexi? I'd be like...like a hero or something. Marc would have to be proud of me then," she said in a wispy voice.

"Don't be silly. I'm sure Marc's over the moon proud that you're his wife. Anyway, I doubt Mike had anything to do with Lexi's death."

"Oh." Marjorie's face fell. "Your *fey* telling you that?"

Beth nodded. "I pray to God, Darla's going to be all right. Skye will be so relieved. Have you touched base with her yet? Shane's probably contacted her—"

"Texted her the minute the cops arrived," Marjorie interrupted. "But, I haven't heard back."

"Skye's a wee bit busy with some kittens. Dashed out to the market, no doubt." Beth checked her watch then looked into Marjorie's puzzled face. "She's helping me with some rescue work."

"Cat rescue?" Marjorie's eyes widened. "I can't stand those mangy things. And now you've got Skye involved. Who would've believed that?" She crossed her tanned legs. One of her high-heeled mules slipped off and hit the floor. "I would've loved to have told Skye in person. To see her reaction. Bet she'd be downright speechless." She slipped her foot back into the leather sandal arrayed with multicolored studs. "Why the hell is she so chummy with someone who works for her? That seems really weird." She reached into her straw tote bag and whipped out her phone. "Oh, Skye did text back."

Beth zeroed in on her.

"Skye wants to know where Darla is." Marjorie raised her head and looked into Beth's face. "Well now, isn't it a good thing I am a tiny bit inquisitive? I had the foresight to ask one of the paramedics where they were taking her." She tapped on her text keyboard then slipped the phone back into her tote.

"Where is she?"

"Didn't I tell you?" Marjorie tilted her head with a lopsided grin.

"Don't be coy. I helped you out big time with—with you know—the diary." Beth scanned the lobby hoping nobody was paying them much attention. She noticed Officer Keller staring at them.

"Darla's been transported to Malibu Critical Care."

"Doesn't sound too good." Beth stood and took a few aimless steps.

"I hear they're the best. Hey," Marjorie paused a second, "didn't you forget something?"

Beth shook her head in exasperation noticing the forlorn bag. "A picnic for Shane."

"It smells to die for. God, with everything going on, I totally missed my lunch. I'm like starving."

Beth tried not to roll her eyes as she approached the desk. "Is there anywhere my friend can have a bite to eat?" She raised the paper bag.

Officer Keller nodded. "There's a public area around the corner toward the right. You'll see it. When the detectives are ready for her, I'll let them know where she's at. But first, she has to sign in."

With an inward groan, Beth guessed the officer had overheard their conversation.

After Marjorie registered, Beth walked with her to the desired spot, which consisted of two vending machines and three beige plastic tables with matching chairs. In a matter of seconds, she filled a plate with a chicken breast, a heaping portion of mashed potatoes with gravy, and a chocolate chip cookie for dessert.

She even slipped a dollar and a half worth of change into the soda machine to buy her a Diet Coke. "I promised you lunch; I just never imagined it would be here." She handed Marjorie the icy can. "Sorry I can't stay longer, but I have to head over to Malibu to be with Skye."

Marjorie nodded, her mouth full. She swallowed and took a quick sip of soda. "I'll meet you when I'm finished here. Skye needs all the support we can give her." She lowered her voice. "Between you and me, Darla didn't look too good. Not good at all." She pressed her lips together and shook her head. Then she lifted the crispy piece of chicken and took a bite.

CHAPTER THIRTY-FOUR

"I don't give a damn about what that Hammond woman says. I didn't kidnap no one."

Mike's agitated voice sounded like a bullhorn.

"We're not accusing you of anything," Shane said with his hands folded on top of the table. "Just tell us what happened."

"I need to get to the hospital. I promised her."

Shane raised his eyebrows.

"She like walked into the ocean. I literally saved her life."

"Let's start at the beginning," Collins said, eyeing Mike over the laptop. "Why were you on the beach in the precise vicinity of Skye Andrews' house?"

Mike rubbed his eyes with the heels of his hand. "What's the big deal? There is public access to the beach." He sighed. "Okay, okay, I'll level with you," he said with a low, quiet voice. "I was looking for a clue, or anything, that could explain why Lexi was murdered." He ran his fingers through his damp hair. "I came up empty. But it was a damn good thing I was there. Otherwise, that babe would be a goner."

"When you were talking to..." Collins paused as if trying to remember something. "The victim, Darla Edwards, did she give you a name or any information about her attacker?"

"Attacker?" Mike sucked in a mouthful of air. "Then someone *did* beat her. I guessed as much." He drummed his fingers against the table's dark laminate. "I didn't know what to think when she said someone wanted to kill her. But now it makes sense. Yeah. A lotta sense."

"Who wanted to kill her?" Collins raised his voice a notch.

Mike shrugged. "Darla couldn't even remember who the hell she is so I doubt she'll be much help. But I think the two incidents are connected."

"Two incidents?" Shane leaned closer to the table.

"The same bastard that killed Lexi must've attacked Darla."

"You already knew Darla Edwards. You were friends." Shane said.

"Never seen her before."

 "Hadn't Lexi introduced you two?"

Mike jerked his chin. He stared at the wall behind Shane and remained silent for a few seconds. "When that hysterical chick, Hammond, called her Darla, I thought the name sounded familiar. I vaguely remember Lexi talking about a Darla—Skye Andrews' assistant or housekeeper—something like that. It pissed her off the way Skye about worked her to death, but according to Lexi, Darla never seemed to mind—which Lexi thought was really stupid. But I'm certain, I've never met her before. I would've remembered a girl like that."

"With all the time you spent at the Greyson residences you never saw Darla?" Shane pressed his thumb into the cleft in his chin.

Mike glared at him. "I stay the hell away from the Greyson residences. Can't stomach those people."

"Really?" Shane asked.

"I stop by Tower Road once in a while to see Sofia Fedoruck. A maid. We're friends."

"Friends with Greyson's maid but didn't know—"

"So what?" Mike asked.

"So you never saw Darla Edwards before—never spoke to her—didn't have no beefs with her?" Collins said.

"That's right. Never seen her before. Is that too hard for you cops to understand?" Mike folded his arms. "Look, you better tell Skye to watch her step." A sardonic smile crossed his face. "At this rate, she'll be next on the killer's hit list."

Shane cleared his throat wondering why he hadn't made that connection. *Did Alder know more than he was letting on?*

"I swear to God, if I happen to find out through some bit of cosmic payback, whoever killed Lexi and attacked Darla, then you'll have a damn good reason to arrest me," Mike said. "I guarantee you, that pervert won't need a trial because he'll be history."

"I get it. You're mad as hell, but it's plain stupid to seek revenge," Shane said.

Mike squeezed his eyelids shut.

"Getting back to Lexi Horne," Collins said, "what do you know about her pregnancy?"

"Nothing."

"You the father?"

"Hell no." Mike's eyes flashed open. "If you're thinking I had something to do with her death, especially over *that* fact, you're mistaken. I had no idea she was gonna have a kid. She didn't look pregnant the last time I saw her a couple of weeks ago. Anyway, you should be talking to that artist geek, her...her whatever." He slumped forward with his head bent. "He's the one that must've got her pregnant."

"Really?" Collins leaned forward.

"Well, who else?"

"That's what we're aiming to find out," Shane said. "Are you willing to take a polygraph?"

"Polygraph?"

"We need a DNA sample too," Collins said closing his laptop.

"What no blood sample?" Mike jumped up out of his chair.

"We'll hold off on that for now," Shane said.

"Whatever. I don't have a damn thing to hide."

CHAPTER THIRTY-FIVE

Beth pulled into the emergency center's parking lot and eased her SUV next to Skye's black Escalade. She jumped out, flung her purse over her shoulder, and rushed down the brick walkway toward the wide glass door. Once inside the bright lobby, she scanned the room until she spied Skye seated on the edge of a molded plastic chair staring at the floor. Her hands wrapped around a paper cup.

With short, hurried steps, Beth approached her. "Any word?"

Skye jerked her head up, though no discernable expression filled her face. "Nothing yet."

"You look terrible. How 'bout we go to my house. The kittens will be a good diversion. Someone here can ring you with an update on Darla's condition." The moment the words left her mouth, she realized Skye would nix her suggestion—which she did. Beth sat in the vacant seat across from the reception desk next to Skye. She looked around the large waiting room. "You shouldn't be alone. I'll stay with you."

Skye murmured something Beth couldn't quite understand, cleared her throat, and took a sip of water. "I contacted Darla's father. I didn't call him when she first went missing. Why worry her family for nothing—if Darla had just taken off—needed to get away for a few days?" She took another sip from the paper cup. "He's booking an airline reservation but won't arrive until tomorrow afternoon."

Beth wondered if she should suggest contacting Zach. *At a time like this, you'd think Skye would want the support of her husband.* "How 'bout I give Zach a call?"

"Zach? I don't think so. No."

"He might be able to ease your burden a bit."

"I have you." She reached out and squeezed Beth's hand.

"Marjorie will be stopping by when she's finished giving a statement to the detectives."

"Thank God for Marjorie. If it hadn't been for her, Darla would probably be dead."

"Not quite. Mike Alder rescued her."

"Who?"

"Mike. Lexi's former boyfriend. Saw Darla drowning and jumped into action. His quick thinking saved her life."

Skye narrowed her eyes as a quizzical expression claimed her face. "That's a bunch of crap. Darla is an excellent swimmer. A champion. One of the stars on her college team. Darla drowning. Not possible." She crushed the cup into a soggy paper wad then strode toward a wastebasket next to the water fountain and tossed it inside.

Beth watched Skye as she made her way back. Swollen lids hooded blood-shot eyes while Skye's shoulders slumped, and a deep furrow creased her brow. She dropped back into the chair.

"If what you said is true," Skye said with a catch in her voice, "then she must be worse off than I imagined. If she couldn't even swim." She faced Beth. "You go to church and believe all that religious stuff. Is this some punishment from God?"

"Of course not. God is love. He doesn't send tribulation our way. We do that to ourselves."

"Then why the hell is my world crashing down around me? First, it was Lexi. Then Kenny left for Kentucky with his damn wife and didn't even mention a word about it to me. And now Darla. I really hoped she'd just taken off for a while." Skye shook her head. "But deep down, I knew she'd never run out on me. I need her, Beth. She keeps track of my life." Skye looked at her hands clenching her thighs. "I could always hire another assistant. No big deal. But that's not the issue. She works hard not because of her salary or some misplaced need to be an overachiever. Darla does it because she cares about me. And not many people do."

"You shouldn't be thinking that way. People around the globe love you."

"You, of all people, know better than that. They love the image of the beautiful movie star. Not me."

Beth wanted to scream. *Not another pity party for poor Skye Andrews*. For an instant, she wanted to march out of the medical center and let Skye fend for herself. Instead, she shifted in the chair and focused on the actress who grasped her quilted handbag and pressed it against her chest like a life preserver.

"Darla's not here just because she had a swimming accident," Beth said.

"I didn't think so." Skye twisted in her chair and faced Beth. "Did Shane give you any information?"

"Not Shane but my *fey*. Darla was attacked. And the devil who did this to Darla has to be the same one who killed Lexi. After all, both of those girls were in your beach house that night. Even if it was a different M.O."

Skye seemed to be holding onto Beth's every word.

"Lexi was killed exactly like those poor girls living off the streets. But Darla, well, we don't know exactly what happened to her yet, but it was different. She's pretty and young but not a teenager. And most importantly, she's still alive."

"What does that mean?"

"Must've outwitted the killer and escaped your house before the final blow," Beth said.

"I don't have a sixth sense, but I know when you're keeping something from me. Come on, Beth. Level with me."

Even if she wanted to give Skye more, she couldn't. Her head spun with all the bits and pieces of information she'd picked up over the past few days. From the curious Hollywood flat to Zach being the father of Lexi's unborn child. She needed time to sort things out, review her notes, and most importantly listen to her *fey*. She glanced at Skye and read a sense of expectancy on her face.

"For the love of Pete, just spill it."

Beth worried her lip for a moment. "You may be the next victim."

"Me? Like hell."

Beth wrapped her arm around Skye's shoulders. "It's the only thing that makes sense."

"Crazy thoughts have been running through my mind nonstop, ever since this nightmare started. But if the killer is after me, why did he kill Lexi and—"

"Hey, guys." Both women's heads snapped in the direction of the familiar voice. Marjorie bounced toward them. She'd changed her clothes and now faced them wearing a cream-colored satin blouse and a pair of black pencil jeans. "Any word on Darla's condition?" She looked from Skye to Beth. Then frowned. "Not good?"

"Still waiting," Beth said.

Marjorie dropped in the chair next to Beth. Though she didn't want to judge Marjorie, it took every ounce of willpower for Beth not to believe the lass was enjoying the entire tragedy.

"Miss Andrews?" A plump redheaded woman dressed in navy scrubs looked at Skye.

Skye jumped up and took several steps toward the nurse. Beth followed her.

"How is Darla?" Skye's voice rang strong.

"We're not at liberty to share Ms. Edward's medical information. Unless she's given you a health care power of attorney."

"A what?"

The nurse offered her a tiny smile. "She's feeling a bit better now. However, her condition will continued to be monitored at the UCLA Medical Center in Santa Monica. A medic unit should arrive shortly to transport her." After a tiny nod, she turned and walked toward an alcove leading to a corridor.

Skye flung herself into Beth's arms.

CHAPTER THIRTY-SIX

It was tempting to get caught up in all the hoopla, but Kenny promised himself to keep an objective eye on the day's events. He made that decision within the stately walls of the legendary dining room at The Brown Hotel.

Once he and Maiah had taken their seats in the English Grill, she explained her parents had been detained. They wouldn't be joining them for lunch, but they'd catch up at the Derby. Instead of breaking out into a jubilant grin, he restrained his bubbling emotions and forced a somber expression to rule his face.

Kenny took a quick scan around the rich, wood paneled room with its lead glass windows and gold-framed paintings of thoroughbreds lining the walls, which reminded him of a private club. Maiah chatted, and though he didn't pay much attention, he was surprised by the animated cadence that filled her speech. The room's mellow atmosphere was charming him, and by the time he sipped his very dry martini, all worries had vanished—until Lord Fernsby walked into the room dressed as if he were about to attend the Royal Ascot. Fortunately, Kenny thought with a touch of sarcasm, he'd left his top hat at home.

As the lunch progressed and Kenny's intake of alcohol increased, he came to believe his initial impression of Callum as a regular kind of guy was spot on. The baron certainly didn't resemble the stiff-lipped sourpusses that caricaturized the British upper crust on television, and he wasn't the snob Kenny imagined he'd be to qualify as one of Maiah's close friends. Quite the opposite, in fact. Kenny enjoyed the easy flow of conversation as Callum peppered him with questions about his paintings and the upcoming exhibition in New York.

It would've been nearly impossible for Kenny to overlook Maiah's irritation as she glared at the two of them, her creased brow spoiling her perfectly made-up face. The icing on the cake was when Callum suggested that he and Kenny attend an Orioles baseball game during their stay in Baltimore for the Preakness Stakes.

He even pulled out his cell phone to order two tickets. Kenny thought Maiah was going to blow a gasket.

Kenny ignored the sharp looks Maiah sent his way. Normally his stomach would be flipping, making it impossible to eat. Not this time. Instead of leaving most of his hot brown sandwich untouched, he'd emptied his plate except for a piece of crust and a dollop of Mornay sauce. After draining his cocktail glass, he swiped his fork and scooped up the remaining bits then popped the morsel into his mouth.

As Callum folded his linen napkin, he offered to pay for lunch. Kenny agreed with a grin and happily reinforced Maiah's belief that he was a cheapskate. He sensed waves of angry heat radiate from his perturbed wife as she narrowed her eyes and pressed her lips into a tight line.

Outside the hotel, they tarried in the parking lot as Maiah lamented that their Churchill Downs owner suites stood at opposite ends from one another. Each box was assigned according to their horse's post position. With Estella Blue's position slated at gate five and Many Miles Muse at nineteen, they weren't even close. Kenny looked away as Maiah insisted that Callum meet her at the Courtyard Commons, an outdoor garden area reserved for owners and their parties so they could watch the race together. He wondered if Maiah would extend that same invitation to him but wasn't betting on it.

After offering her a terse nod and a kiss on the cheek, Callum pulled open the door of his rented Jag and slipped behind the wheel. Kenny noticed the satisfied smile creep across her face as Maiah headed in the direction of their idling limousine.

She sat in stony silence as the limo lumbered out of the lot and onto the street. After a feeble attempt at conversation, Kenny stared out the window as the minutes dragged. He knew the atmosphere would lighten after they made their final stop en route to the racetrack, to pick up their "ambassadors." Mr. and Mrs. Richard Docherty had been appointed as their hosts to render their stay in Louisville as relaxing and enjoyable as possible by familiarizing them with the track, escorting them to local places of interest, making appointments and reservations, anything to make their stay completely stress free.

Kenny wasn't surprised that the offers of assistance from the volunteer couple were rejected—graciously and in good taste—but rejected never the less. Maiah's pride would never allow her to accept help from anyone, let alone, complete strangers. Though she didn't want their support, her ingrained sense of propriety triggered an invitation for the couple to enjoy the race from their private box.

As they drove along the maple-lined street in the Anchorage neighborhood, the vehicle stopped in front of an expansive southern colonial with a pediment front and columns that would put *Tara* to shame. The couple stood waiting on the porch as the limousine lumbered around the circular drive. A moment later, the elegant pair faced them seated in the car.

It always amazed Kenny the way Maiah could change her emotions on cue. She welcomed the Dochertys with a singsong greeting and chatted amicably during the ride to Churchill Downs. Kenny dug in his heels determined not let this chance go to waste. It would take a measure of patience to wait for the perfect moment to arrive, but when it did, he'd steer the conversation away from racing to the subject of painting and his role in the art world. It was obvious these people were high rollers who had the wherewithal to shell out big bucks for a painting—that is, he figured, if they saw the merit in the investment. It took only a split second to formulate his mission for the day as he regarded the florid faced middle-aged man and his equally middle-aged though surprisingly attractive wife. She'll be the easier one to impress, and by tonight's Winner's Party, she'll be eating out of my hand, he thought, nodding in agreement to whatever Mr. Docherty was rambling on about.

When they arrived at their box, one of twenty that flanked the horse tunnel and nestled within the space between the racetrack's iconic twin spires, he was startled by how many of Maiah's guests had already arrived. Of course, her parents were there plus an old maiden aunt and Maiah's two cousins, both financial wizards, according to anyone who knew them. They had staked claim to five of the eight stadium seats arranged in two rows of four. These were open-air seats, and Kenny decided he'd rather stay in the rear end of the box, out of the afternoon sun. Anyway, it's more comfortable here, he told himself brushing his fingertips along the top of a deep brown wicker love seat. He surveyed his surroundings and took in the betting machines, overstocked chef table, and the drink dispensing machine. "Yep," he whispered, "all the comforts of home." He plopped down onto thick green cushion padding the seat and folded his arms.

Maiah had already cornered her horse's trainer, Clint Austin. The curvaceous redhead standing next to him must be his wife, Kenny guessed as he checked out the remaining individuals peopling their box. The two California breeders of Estella Blue stood with their heads together as they stared into their beers. Over the past couple of days, he'd discovered how rare it was for a California bred thoroughbred to make it to the Derby. Let alone a filly. He tried to catch Mrs. Docherty's eye, but standing arm in arm with her husband, she stared straight ahead at the images of thundering horses on the big screen situated across the track from their box.

He tapped his foot against the tiled floor. All of Maiah's guests made sense except for the young man leaning against the rail next to the first group of stadium seats. Even from the back, Kenny recognized him. Hap Dorian. The son of Estella Blue's groom, a part-time assistant to his father. Why the hell isn't he in the stables, he wondered deciding how out of place he looked dressed in a faded pair of jeans and a t-shirt. It wasn't until he turned around that Kenny noticed his shirt sported not only Estella Blue's colors of turquoise and silver but boasted her name emblazoned across his chest.

The young man ambled down the aisle with an empty plastic cup, which Kenny assumed had at one point been filled with beer. "Hey, my man," Hap said raising his hand in a high five fashion. Kenny jumped up and slapped his hand.

It wasn't that he disliked Hap, not in the least; everyone liked Hap Dorian. Only problem being that Hap's scruples flew out the window when it came to making a fast buck. He glanced away for a second, not wanting to admit the two of them shared that trait in common.

"The big day's finally here. I'm already wired and it's what? Like three more hours 'til the race starts."

"I'm kinda surprised seeing you here. Shouldn't you be helping out your old man?" Kenny hitched his thumb in the direction of the horse tunnel.

"You'd think. But today I'm a guest. Courtesy of the Mrs."

"Oh?"

"Her way of thanking me for nursing the gelding she rescued at auction. If Mrs. W. hadn't stepped in, that horse would've suffered a gruesome and horrifying death along with the other unfortunates, terrified and screaming in a Mexican slaughterhouse." Hap glanced away for a second with a shake of his head. "Thank God, that didn't happen. Since I've taken over his care, looks like he's gonna make it."

The thought of any horse suffering turned Kenny's stomach. During a conversation with another Derby owner, he'd discovered that the slaughter of these alert, playful, and responsive beasts had become legal in the US a few years ago for meat processing and marketing.

"According to Maiah, you're a genuine horse whisperer," Kenny said.

"Yeah, well—"

"How 'bout I refresh that drink of yours?"

Hap shook his head. "Thanks anyway but I won't be sticking around here all day. It's a great setup but the infield is more my speed."

Kenny hadn't noticed Maiah had joined them until he heard her voice. "Enjoying yourself, Roman?"

Kenny rolled his eyes at his wife's usual formality. Everyone called *Roman* Hap—short for Happy-Go-Lucky, a nickname that fit him as perfectly as his well-worn denims. Good thing the name on my birth certificate is Kenny or she'd be calling me Kenneth. He wrinkled his nose.

Hap half bowed. "My lady, I appreciate all this" He gestured his free hand in an encompassing movement. "But, I'm feeling antsy. Like I've got to do something 'cause being a spectator is definitely not cutting it. I'm gonna head over to 'Stella Blue's stall now." He reached toward her but then withdrew his hand before making contact. "Security in the stable is impressive with surveillance cameras at every stall. And get this, each horse has his own damn sheriff's deputy. Everyone has to log in and out. Man, the vets must feel like they're some kinda specimen under a microscope. Damn good thing the whole situation with the nasal strips was sorted out. So there won't be no problems when she runs in the Belmont."

"Nasal strips?" Kenny said.

"Pulmonary hemorrhage," Maiah said with a tone of impatience.

"Huh?"

Hap stepped closer to him. "When horses run hard and fast blood usually dribbles out their noses. The nasal strips helps them breathe easier. Prevents bleeding in the lungs."

"You'd think the animal right groups would be picketing or something," Kenny said.

"Don't think they're not." Maiah shot an impassive glance at him then turned toward Hap. "I haven't been to the stable yet. I'll accompany you."

"I'll tag along, too," Kenny said.

"Oh, no, you won't. Someone has to play host to our guests. Since I have business to attend to that leaves you. One would think you don't possess an ounce of good manners." She walked past him and headed out of the box.

Hap offered Kenny a shrug as he hurried to catch up with Maiah.

Kenny dropped back on the loveseat when his phone sounded. He pulled it free from his jacket and checked the screen. "Oh God," he muttered then tapped the screen. "Johannah, is something wrong?"

After a torturous minute as her thickly accented voice assaulted his ears, he realized she hadn't been able to connect with Maiah's phone. She wanted Maiah to know she'd completed some kind of favor for her. But her burning question was if Harry was allowed to eat pizza. She'd thought it'd be a nice treat while they watched the Kentucky Derby on TV.

"Of course, he can." Kenny barked. "Look, I gotta go. I'll tell Maiah you called."

***

A warm glow of contentment filled Kenny since connecting with Mrs. Docherty. For nearly an hour, they sat shoulder to shoulder talking about each other's artistic endeavors. She liked to dabble in watercolors and was represented by a local gallery. Not only that, one of her favorite artists turned out to be the same abstract expressionist who'd influenced Kenny's own work. It wasn't long into the conversation when he'd fished out his smartphone and showed her images of his paintings. Mrs. Docherty had clapped her hands congratulating him on producing a vibrant and impressive body of work. In an excited, hurried tone, she'd explained she was in the throes of redecorating their great room and wanted two of his paintings to flank the massive stone fireplace. It took only minutes to hammer out the details; dimensions and most importantly price.

Kenny couldn't believe his luck when he considered the chances of running into a rich dame who was gaga over abstract painting. Like a million to one. His gut told him this wasn't the end of it—he was on a roll—lady luck was on his side today.

After warmly squeezing Mrs. Docherty's hand, Kenny ambled out of the box in search of the betting machines. With Estella Blue's odds at 12-1—on a thousand dollar wager—he'd rake in thirteen thousand. That bit of change plus the fee for the paintings were going to pad his already healthy bank account. Cha-ching, he thought with a curl of his lip.

The extra money would allow him to buy Skye a nice piece of jewelry—something extravagant—with diamonds or emeralds, or both he decided with a shrug. It'll put that little trinket I bought Maiah to shame, he thought with a blossoming grin.

***

Kenny noticed a change in Maiah as the time grew closer to race eleven. The bubbly, effervescent façade started to crack as she sat in one of the stadium seats nursing a Mint Julep.

Though her mother leaned close with her high-pitched voice droning, Maiah didn't seem to be paying attention.

The strain became obvious when Callum entered their box. Her parents' faces lit up like fireworks on the 4th of July but Maiah only offered him a vague nod then stared mutely at the track. Her father good-naturedly slapped Callum's back and had his ear for a good ten minutes until Kenny moved closer to join the group. Callum asked if they'd like to accompany him to the Courtyard Commons. Maiah's mother grabbed his arm so fast, Kenny almost burst out laughing noticing the shocked look that claimed the aristocratic face.

In the horse tunnel, Kenny caught up to Maiah as she trailed behind Callum and her parents. He'd never seen Maiah so tense before. The worry lines etching her forehead betrayed her staunch belief that Estella Blue was destined to be the winner of the Kentucky Derby. He doubted she even realized he was tagging along.

As they stepped out of the tunnel, Kenny was amazed once again by Maiah's adept control of her emotions. The wrinkled forehead smoothed and her strained lips relaxed as she seemingly snapped free from her blue funk. She brushed the charm dangling from the chain at the base of her neck, raised her head, and inhaled deeply. With a burst of speed, she increased her pace, almost running toward Callum, who'd left her parents to join a group of men Kenny didn't recognize.

Kenny watched as she raced ahead and sandwiched herself between Callum and a stout man puffing a cigar. As if startled by her presence, Callum jerked his head in Kenny's direction and offered him a clipped wave reminiscent of one the Queen offers her subjects. By the time he joined the group, the talking ceased as all eyes focused in the same direction—at the lead ponies escorting a slow moving parade of thoroughbreds toward the starting gate.

Though Maiah's eyes met Kenny's for a split second, she made no attempt to move toward him, but instead grabbed Callum's arm. Callum didn't shake her loose but only patted her gloved hand as his colt, Many Miles Muse, ambled passed. Kenny figured Callum was so caught up in the building excitement, he probably hadn't even noticed Maiah's grip on his arm.

Standing by himself, Kenny stuck his hands into his pockets and watched the procession unfold. He winced when Maiah let out a squeal catching sight of Estella Blue with her jockey, Bobby Castro, seated ramrod straight in the saddle. No one seemed to notice, especially Callum, as Kenny witnessed his wife clasp her former lover's arm even tighter.

With each passing contender, the cheering intensified until reaching a deafening crescendo. Though the cluster of owners and their entourages stood in the open, Kenny felt hemmed in as the noise blasted against him like a thunderous wave. Clint tapped his shoulder then pumped his hand before gesturing with thumbs up. Kenny thought it odd that Clint seemed so calm and carefree as if totally unconcerned. There had to be a reason for that but he couldn't remember. A couple of seconds later, he recalled the basis for Maiah hiring Clint in the first place. Not only did he have an impressive track record but he'd had a Derby winner years ago.

Kenny glanced over his shoulder and spied Estella Blue's breeders approaching their elite group and sensed their anxiety. He suspected their edginess wasn't based on emotions but hinged on the hope of a win that would elevate their stable's prestige and allow a significant rise in stud fees. Their wives tagged behind them flushed with anticipation—excitement—dread? Kenny tapped his foot against the blue-green turf caught up in the pulsating throb of electricity charging through the arena.

As if the previous hours had been nothing more than a tedious prelude, the horses burst through the starting gate. He followed Estella Blue's super quick start placing her in the lead. A few seconds later, Callum's horse overtook her, and Estella Blue slipped from front-runner to third from the end of the pact. His eyes shifted to Maiah, who still had a grip on Callum. She seemed to be holding her breath.

Kenny turned back to the race just as Bobby Castro eased Estella Blue closer to the rail. Her hindquarters churned and ripped at the track as she pursued the thundering rake. Clouds of dust floated around her beating hoofs, which seemed to barely touch the ground as she wrestled her way forward, looping and darting, weaving and surpassing each threatening steed. Kenny's heart hammered as the filly made the turn into the final stretch. She sprinted head-to-head with Many Miles Muse. The competitors' nostrils flared and eyes bulged as their long heads bobbled, enacting a wavering syncopation, as they swapped places in the lead every few feet. Yards from the finish line Many Miles Muse scrabbled ahead. Bobby Castro thrashed his crop, cracking it three times against the filly's back. She lunged and thumped forward across the finish line edging out the colt by a nose.

For a split-second, a collective hush hung over the stadium but gave way to an explosion of jubilation. He faced Maiah and found her in Callum's arms.

Before any cohesive thoughts could register, eager hands reached out, offering him congratulations. Clint, all smiles, slapped him on the back as he stepped toward Maiah who, by this time, had released Callum. He noticed the breeders were locked in a bear hug and the cluster of women embraced each other as tears streamed down their faces.

He watched an ecstatic Bobby Castro wave and accept the crowd's exultant adulations.

It was then he realized that the dappled gray filly with the coal black mane and tail had just made history. There'd be no stopping Maiah now.

CHAPTER THIRTY-SEVEN

Kenny eased the door shut behind the exiting detectives. He stole a glimpse of Maiah still dressed in the aqua crepe and silk dress, now rumpled and creased, as she slumped on the edge of the chair with her head in her hands. A dazed Clint Austin stared at the beer bottle he clutched as if wondering how it got there. Never in a million years could he have guessed the day would end like this.

A brief couple hours ago, Kenny had undergone an epiphany of sorts during the Winner's Party as they stood behind the podium with the trophies on a nearby pedestal. He liked horses as much as the next guy, but Maiah's crazy obsession with racing had turned him off. He could've kicked himself for being so stupid by levying a self-imposed expulsion from an enjoyable, even thrilling spectacle. The past couple of days had been a blast—from being in the spotlight to schmoozing with the governor—an exhilarating whirlwind coupled with a generous dose of southern hospitality.

After the presentations and seemingly endless toasts, Kenny stood with a glass of champagne as he chatted with Mrs. Docherty doubting the day could get any better. He stopped listening to her when he caught sight of the president of Churchill Downs hurrying across the packed room. The man looked harried, exhausted. He stopped next to Maiah and whispered into her ear. Kenny gulped the remainder of his drink when he noted her expression cloud over. She skirted around clusters of reveling celebrants as she crossed the room and grabbed his arm.

"The police want to talk to us," Maiah said the words so fast Kenny only made out the word police.

"Slow down."

"Dammit, Kenny. Something happened to Roman. The police—"

"Hap?" He paused a second. "An accident?"

She shrugged and headed toward the exit. He placed his empty flute on a table and followed after her.

Two Louisville detectives greeted them outside the Churchill Downs Museum; a tall, thin African-American and the other a mannish looking, pasty complexioned woman wearing an ill-fitted suit. With grim faces, they apologized for interrupting the festivities. The woman detective said, "Your employee, Roman Dorian, was found dead a couple of hours ago." Squinting at Maiah, she continued, "We have a few questions."

At first, Kenny assumed he'd misunderstood, but when the words sunk in, he grasped Maiah's arm believing she'd need his support. Jerking her arm free, she pulled away from him and made arrangements for the detectives to meet them at their suite.

During the ride back to the hotel, he half-expected Maiah to break down because of the soft-spot she possessed for Hap—something he found more than a bit curious—even if the young man willingly completed any chore Maiah needed from vacuuming the living room carpet to exercising her stable horses. It struck him odd, how both women in his life depended on employees beyond a professional capacity. Skye with Darla and Maiah with Hap. The startling fact played in his mind that like Hap and Lexi, Darla had probably suffered the same fate. He glanced at Maiah who stared out the limo's window, then reached for his cell phone and contacted Clint. His voice cracked when he relayed the tragic news to the horse trainer who offered to meet them at the hotel.

After the small group gathered within the walls of the elegant suite, the detectives offered only the barest of information. Initially, Hap had been mistaken for one of many intemperate revelers, who'd had way too much to drink, and passed out in the infield. Except he hadn't passed out. The blood test showed only a negligible amount of alcohol in his system. They found something else. What it was they weren't saying.

"His death is suspicious, Mrs. Weston," said the male detective. "Do you know if Roman Dorian had any enemies?"

"He possessed the singular talent of being in sync with horses," she said. "And was an excellent employee. But I know next to nothing about his personal affairs."

The detective turned toward Clint and asked the same question.

"Hap was full of bravado, bragging about scoring with one woman after another. His talk about wheeling and dealing mainly consisted of hair-brained schemes of how to make a quick buck. But his dad kept a close rein on him and Hap respected his old man. Have you talked to him yet?" Clint blew out a mouthful of air. "Hap would give you the shirt off his back. Didn't have a rotten bone in his body."

After the detectives exited, Kenny paced the length of the living room perplexed by the senseless deaths. The clatter of Clint's beer bottle hitting the cocktail table startled him. He stopped walking and faced the distraught man.

"Illegal gambling," Clint spit out the words. "They didn't come right out and say it, but that's what those detectives were implying. Granted, Hap's no angel but he wasn't a dummy either. I've known him since he was a kid. He wouldn't have gotten involved with that crowd."

"You sure about that? Hap was always eager to make a quick buck. And the way I see it, not too concerned about how he made it," Kenny said.

"So maybe he wasn't the most principled guy but illegal horse racing? He'd never be caught up in any activity detrimental to the well-being of horses."

"Then he must've ruffled someone's feathers real good to be taken out that way."

Maiah lifted her head. Kenny expected to see rivulets of tears streaking her face. Instead, dry eyes sparking fierce determination faced him.

"I'm going to get to the bottom of this," she vowed through tight lips. "Roman had a gift. He understood the innermost beings of horses. I won't rest until that—that person who did this—is locked up for life."

Kenny rubbed her knotted shoulders. She grasped his hand and squeezed it.

"I know a couple of good grooms who'll gladly take over Hap's duties. That's if you still want to..." Clint lifted his hands as in supplication.

"Why wouldn't I?" Maiah frowned. "I refuse to let anything interfere with Estella Blue's chances of participating in the Triple Crown." She pursed her lips a second. "Hap wouldn't want us to bow out. I'm sure of it."

Kenny folded his arms. *The show must go on.* He sighed, headed toward the refrigerator and a cold beer.

CHAPTER THIRTY-EIGHT

Beth sat on the edge of the sofa as Shane paced back and forth. She knew better than to offer a word. She'd said enough already.

After what seemed like twenty-five trips from one end of the living room to the other, he stopped, crossed his arms, and glared at her. "Why didn't you tell me this sooner?"

She jutted out her chin with a proud thrust. "I tried to tell you at the station yesterday. But you were too busy suspecting Mike of being a serial killer."

"Leave Alder out of this." Shane sneezed, pulled out a couple of tissues from the box on an end table, and blew his nose. "I'm gonna contact Collins, do the paperwork for a warrant, and check out that apartment. On the surface, this Hap Dorian might fit the profile of a serial killer but so could a million other guys in this city. It's gonna take a heck of a lot more digging. I'll need to check out this Weston character, too." Not even pausing for a breath he said, "So you think the two of them forged some kind of perverted partnership in murder—Weston the mastermind and Dorian the muscle disguised as a priest?" He raked his fingertips through his disheveled hair. "If that's the case, there'd have to be a connection between Dorian, Weston, and Lexi. What the hell could that be?"

Beth fiddled with the belt of her silk bathrobe and shrugged.

"Maybe I know."

They turned in the direction of Skye's voice. She stood in the threshold with a slumbering kitten nestled in the crook of her arm.

Shane lifted the soggy tissues and covered his nose and mouth. "Get that outta here." He let out a tremendous sneeze.

Beth scurried to her friend and grabbed the startled calico away from her. "I told you, Skye, the kittens stay in the mudroom."

"Sorry," Skye murmured. "I just needed a bit of comforting."

Perplexed but not surprised about Skye's emotional state, Beth stroked the calico's head recalling how Skye had spent most of the night in the hospital's waiting room. After all that, she hadn't been allowed to see Darla. After her best effort to console Skye, Beth had said a decade of her rosary for Darla before finally falling asleep.

Beth moved through the kitchen and pulled the mudroom's door open. She didn't want to leave Shane and Skye alone for very long considering both were a wee bit too emotional for their own good. Shane, again furious about her sticking her nose where it didn't belong, hadn't hidden his displeasure about the fostering kittens in the house. She deposited the calico on the quilt covering the floor alongside her siblings. "Then there's Skye spending the weekend," she whispered before hurrying back to the den. Shane stood with arms crossed perusing the bookcase as if searching for reading material while Skye sat on the couch eyeballing the back of his head.

"Have you seen this?" Skye jumped up and freed a folded sheet of newspaper from her jeans pocket. She thrust the paper in his direction.

Beth noticed the color rising on his cheeks after he shook the paper open. She moved closer and peered over his shoulder. Skye had ripped off the front page of the sports section. Shane didn't mind checking the sports news on his computer or iPad but when it came to Sunday morning that was a horse of a different color. A cup of coffee, his favorite chair, and the sports section. It'd been his ritual since God knew how long. Skye had really blown it with him this time.

Shane frowned at the headline.

Beth tucked her arm around Skye's waist waiting for him to blow his top.

"Estella Blue won the Kentucky Derby," Skye said with a catch in her voice.

"When I heard it on the news, I didn't know Maiah Weston from Adam." Shane looked at the two women. "Granted, it's amazing that a local horse, and a filly to boot, won the Kentucky Derby. But what does a horse have to do with the teenage murders?"

"Not the horse. Read Kenny's comments." Skye broke away from Beth and pointed to a paragraph halfway down the first column.

He skimmed the paragraph in question. "I still don't get it."

"Clueless and you're the big shot detective?" Skye pointed to the raggedy sheet of paper. "Kenny's proud of his wife. Praised her ad nauseum for her dedication and hard work. He even made her out to be some kind of Florence Nightingale because she rescues old, broken down horses from the slaughter block. Like she does it out of the goodness of her heart." She paused a second and squeezed her palms together. "There's got to be an angle somewhere. Maiah's a vindictive, evil bitch. Bet she's so dedicated to her damn horse because it won her two freaking million dollars." Skye tucked her arms tightly against her chest. "Kenny doesn't give a flying fig about horses or that wife of his, but now he's gushing her praises to the whole world." She took a deep breath. "Means only one thing. He's gone back to her. Not out of love that's for damn sure. But he'll play nice thinking some of that dough will be coming his way. Well, to hell with him."

Beth believed Kenny and Maiah deserved each other. *But where does that leave Skye?*

She chewed her lip realizing Skye's only alternative—Zach— who'd never be considered a prize in the husband department. She targeted on her friend and noticed Skye fidgeting with her mobile.

"You've got to hear this." Skye lifted the phone as if offering a toast.

"Hey babe, it's me."

It wasn't hard to figure out the voice belonged to Kenny.

"I got your message. Turns out, I'll be able to swing by your place after all. Have Darla whip up some of those finger sandwiches 'cause by the time I get there, I'm gonna be starving. Bet I'll be able to eat a horse. Ha-ha."

Beth pressed her lips tight. His comment wasn't only juvenile but disrespectful of his wife's passion.

"This Lexi situation is driving me nuts. Unlike you, I don't believe she'll keep her fat mouth shut. Money causes people to do crazy things like running to the first gossip hungry reporter who gives her the time of day. I have to be sure. Damn sure. It'd be so easy for Lexi to ruin everything." He paused. "I'm gonna stop her from doing anything idiotic. That's a promise."

Skye slipped the phone into her pocket.

"When did you receive this message?" Shane's voice sounded low, measured, almost strained as if he were trying to control his emotions.

"Last week. Friday?" Skye shrugged.

"Why didn't you share this little nugget of information sooner? You had no problem sending me on a wild goose chase after Dot Barnett."

Beth touched her bruised neck and stepped closer to Shane. She feared he was about to go ballistic. "But Dot's a suspect?"

"She should be," Skye said. "Dot Barnett threatened me. What she did to Beth only proves she's a lunatic."

He narrowed his eyes and glared at Beth. She got the message—stay out of it.

"The pressure from the D.A.'s office is intense. They want this thing solved yesterday. It's no walk in the park assuring Lexi's devastated parents to have faith—that there's a chance we'll get the guy who murdered their daughter. Not to mention the other victims." He handed Skye the folded newspaper sheet. "That voicemail sounds like a rock solid motive for murder. And Skye, I don't give a damn who this Weston guy is to you." He rubbed his temples.

Beth sat down on the sofa's edge believing her theory might actually have merit.

Kenny and Hap partners in murder.

Shane's voice shook her thoughts away.

"What exactly is the Lexi situation?"

"Lexi knew about our affair." Skye crumpled the sheet of paper into a ball. "Kenny was convinced she'd blab our business to the tabloids. But, Lexi would never to that."

Shane raised his eyebrows.

"If Zach found out it would end our marriage. That would devastate Emma. Lexi would never let that happen. Period."

"Darla know about your affair?"

"Kenny trusted Darla."

"Could explain why she's a patient in the ICU."

"Kenny would never hurt Darla. He knows how much I depend on her. How much I need her." Skye gasped a mouthful of air. "That she's one of the true friends I have."

Beth reached for Skye's hand and squeezed it.

"Would you've told us about Kenny's message if you hadn't seen that article?" Shane pointed to the crumpled wad she'd dropped on the floor.

Skye drew her eyebrows together as sparks of anger flicked in her eyes.

"Well?" Beth prompted.

"What is your *fey* telling you?" Skye pulled her hand free from Beth's hold.

"That you would've deleted that incriminating message and done everything in your power to protect Kenny from the authorities. Especially Shane."

"You got that right. I would have thrown the damn phone into the ocean if that's what it took to save him. I loved him. I really loved him." Skye's voice cracked as she fell into Beth's outstretched arms.

***

Shane's prospects for a quiet, relaxing Sunday had been shot to hell. He splashed a handful of cool water on his face and washed away all traces of the foamy shaving cream. After a quick pat of the towel, he slipped into a pair of khakis and a plaid, short-sleeved cotton shirt and reached for a sports jacket. After a hasty look in the mirror above the tiger maple dresser, he retraced the steps to his closet and removed a straw fedora from the shelf where he housed his collection of hats. After positioning it with a tilt to the left, he steeled himself to face what would, no doubt, turn out to be yet another hectic and probably frustrating day at the office.

He stepped out of the bedroom and faced Beth. She held up a plastic baggie.

"What's that?" He tried to sidle around her to gain access into the hall.

"Something I, well, I pinched from Hap's apartment." She spoke the last few words so softly, he couldn't quite make them out.

A sinking feeling warned him this couldn't be good. He snatched the bag and inspected the stiff white rectangle inside the zipped bag.

"It's a priest's collar tab. For the life of me, I don't know why I took it from Hap's flat. Some kind of mad impulse must've overcome me. At the time, it seemed right. My *fey*—"

"It's bad enough you wiggled your way into that apartment but to take this tab." The familiar churning began to tighten in his gut.

"It's sure to have fingerprints or even traces of DNA."

"All belonging to you and Hap Dorian." Shane pulled a container of antacids from his pocket, twisted off the lid, popped a couple and chewed. He was so angry he could spit nails but wanted to prevent another scene. "I gotta get to the office."

"There's something else. The *telly* aired another story about the Kentucky Derby. I wasn't paying too much attention until—"

"I'm in a hurry." He didn't have the patience for another of her drawn-out stories.

"It's important."

"This isn't some kind of game. Take care of the kittens, babysit Skye, help Father Clancy but steer the hell clear of my investigation." He skirted around her into the hallway.

"Shane."

Startled by the commanding tone in her voice, he glanced in her direction.

"It wasn't a story about the race."

He stopped, folded the plastic bag, and slipped it into his shirt's breast pocket.

"A body was discovered in the infield." She moved a step closer to him. "Hap Dorian."

A sharp jab of pain sliced his temple.

"They thought it was alcohol poisoning. But now police think it's murder."

He tapped the brim of the fedora knocking it to the back of his head and massaged his stinging temple. "This thing is becoming more and more twisted. Dorian dead. That shoots the masquerading priest theory to hell leaving Skye's boyfriend our new best suspect." He dropped his hand.

"Then you don't think Kenny and Hap were partners—"

He kissed her cheek and headed down the hallway without another word.

CHAPTER THIRTY-NINE

Though still peeved at Skye for keeping Kenny's message a secret, Beth couldn't refuse her heartfelt pleas to accompany her to the hospital. Traversing the corridor leading to the Intensive Care Unit, her sixth-sense refused to surface and offer even a sketchy insight as to what they were about to face.

Beth pressed the button release for the thick metal doors to unseal the entranceway leading into the ICU. She swallowed hard, sensing this wasn't like a regular hospital ward. A pulsating current of energy charged the air, and a purposeful intensity filled the eyes of the nurse facing them from her station. She looked too young to be ministering to such horrific medical calamities housed in the unit. An understanding look and reassuring smile claimed the nurse's face as Skye inquired about Darla's condition.

Her response was succinct. Darla had shown signs of improvement; her vision was clearing, and bits of memory had resurfaced; even so, her brain scan and potassium levels were still being monitored. She suggested they linger a bit in the waiting room until the law enforcement officer finished questioning Darla. Before moving away, the nurse advised them their visit had to be short. No more than ten minutes.

Heading to the waiting room, Beth caught sight of Collins rounding a corner. She grabbed Skye's arm, and they raced down the corridor to where he stood by the elevator.

"Gavin," Beth said.

He turned and faced them. "Hey, Beth. Miss Andrews." A smile crossed his face for a moment.

Both women asked about Darla's condition at the same time.

Collins looked from one anxious face to the other. As if weighing his words carefully, he said, "She's awake but not in the best of shape. She's been exposed to the elements for days where she hid under a tarp and then in a pool house. I want to warn you—she was beaten up real good. Only survived because she was probably left for dead."

Skye trembled and shut her eyes. Before Beth could reach out to her, Collins wrapped his arm around her.

"There's good news. The Doc said it might take some time, but she's going to be fine. What Darla needs now is your positive energy." Collins released Skye and glanced at Beth.

His expression told her volumes. Darla must be worst off then they'd imagined. "Shane's at the station. A new development," Beth said.

Instead of elaborating, she pecked his cheek, grabbed Skye's arm, and hurried back to the ICU. Once inside the ward, Skye didn't hesitate outside the closed curtain but pulled it back and stepped next to Darla's bed.

The tiny form secured beneath the crisp sheet looked more like a little girl than a grown woman. IV tubes snaked from her arm to plastic bags hanging on a metal stand next to a monitor that threw off a constant whirr. Darla's black hair cascaded across the pillow, and her eyes peeked out from beneath swollen, bruised lids. She raised the arm with the IV needle attached and grasped Skye's hand.

Beth itched to question Darla but remained quiet and surveyed the injuries inflicted upon the young woman. Neat stitching along her forehead secured a deep gash, and an angry bruise marred her cheek. Her chipped nails sported jagged tips.

She found it uncanny that though Skye and Darla hadn't spoken a single word, an intuitive connection surfaced as if binding their very thoughts. Skye brushed back strands of Darla's ebony hair and exposed the full extent of the wound that ran a ragged path along her scalp.

"Thank God, you're safe. Everything's going to be okay." Skye kissed Darla's cheek. Darla made an attempt to speak, but Skye placed her fingertip on the girl's lips and shook her head. "I've made a decision. I'm going to back out of my contract so I can take care of you."

Beth swore she'd misheard.

Skye lifted the plastic water cup off a nearby metal tray and moved it in front of Darla's dry, cracked lips. She held it there until Darla took a quick sip from the straw.

"Your parents are on their way. Be here this evening," Skye said.

Darla took another sip of water. "You can't quit. It's too important for your career," she whispered. "Mom and Dad will take care of me."

No matter how old we are, we still need our parents, Beth mused sensing Darla's obvious relief that they'd soon be with her. For an instant, she saw herself in a hospital bed, and the image launched a jet of memories. The deep solace she'd experienced when her *Da* entered her hospital room, not hampered by the arduous trip across the Atlantic or his cumbersome wheelchair, had remained with her. His face had been lined with worry, but his touch radiated hope and strength. She knew what comfort a parent's love could truly be.

"Are you sure?" Skye replaced the water container on the cart. "We're filming clear across the country."

"Only if you share the inside scoop. I want to know everything." Darla attempted a smile.

"Need you ask?" Skye reached into her quilted handbag and withdrew a container of lip balm. She twisted the cap open and dabbed the rich, soothing ointment on Darla's lips. "Rest now." Skye dropped the container into her purse and stood.

"I'm remembering stuff. Just a little." Darla squinted as if trying to bring Skye's face into focus. "There's one thing. About the attack."

"What's that?" Beth wanted to kick herself for blurting out the words before even offering a greeting to the poor lass.

"You remember my friend, Beth?" Skye asked with a frown.

Darla shook her head. "Sorry."

"No worries. Just praise the good Lord you're safe and on the mend," Beth said.

"You're Irish. I hope my memory—"

"Give it time, Darla. It's a great healer of many things."

Darla's face brightened. "I do know you. You're the model. Shib—"

"Sibeal. That's fantastic. Truly your memory is returning, so." Beth beamed.

"Really great, Darla," Skye said cautiously as if being too optimistic would jinx her recovery. "We have to leave now."

"The person who attacked me..." Darla closed her eyes.

Beth's heart ached for the girl. She was hurting. Confused. Needed rest. Even so, the minutes were rapidly ticking away, and their visiting time would soon end. If Darla could just come out with it, the information would blow the case wide open.

"That whole ugly ordeal is behind you now. I want you to think only happy thoughts. I'll be sure to stop by this evening." Skye spoke with a motherly tone that Beth had never heard her use with Emma.

"Before you go. The attacker—"

"That can wait," Skye said.

"If the lass has something to say, Skye, let her." Beth walked around the bed, dropped onto the edge of the visitor's chair, and set her eyes on the diminutive figure. Beth wished her *fey* would shed some light, but it was no use trying to force it—her sixth-sense was a gift—though one she was powerless to control. She looked harder at Darla, and then the girl flashed her eyes open.

"I have to tell you." A sense of panic filled Darla's thin voice. "I didn't tell the police because I was scared."

"You can tell us anything. It'll be our secret," Beth said.

Darla laid still then took a deep breath. "A priest. Came to the house. Wanted to speak with you." She glanced at Skye.

Beth's blood ran cold. "A priest? A right stout fellow with a shock of auburn hair?"

"I... I don't remember." Darla flinched as if a bolt of pain jolted through her.

"Now you've done it." Skye snapped at Beth. "I'm getting the nurse." With a flurry of motion, she rushed out of the cubicle.

Beth grasped Darla's hand. "Did the priest harm you?"

Darla nodded.

Skye charged into the cubicle with the youthful nurse on her heels.

***

Though Beth wasn't enthused about attending Parents' Day at Endeavor Farm, she considered it a means to placate Skye, who was still fuming at her for upsetting Darla. As Skye nosed her Escalade from lane to lane on the bustling freeway, Beth mulled over the scant information Darla had shared. She rummaged in her purse for her mobile, but once pulling it free, she realized it'd be useless calling the Archdiocesan office since it would be closed on Sunday. *The very notion of priests confused her—one too many Father Clancys, a mysterious priest suit belonging to the slain Hap Dorian, and now one guilty of assaulting Darla?*

"Normally, I wouldn't do this."

"Huh?" Beth glanced at Skye.

"Lexi would've brought Emma."

"To Parents' Day?"

"Tim, my ex, texted me and said he'd be taking her. Hinted it might be a good idea if I made an appearance. Emma's still upset about Lexi." Skye flipped the turn signal and pulled off the expressway. "Riding has always been therapeutic for Emma. I hope it helps."

They traveled down a dusty lane until Skye steered into a car park. She shut down the engine and looked at Beth. "One bright spot about this event is that *she* won't be here."

"She?"

"Kenny's wife. I checked his Facebook page. They'll be in Kentucky until mid-week." Skye brushed a stray hair off her face. "Seeing her would be like pouring salt into a wound—my nerves are shot—that's all I'd need."

"Thank God for small favors," Beth said under her breath as exited the vehicle.

They walked along a dirt path leading to an enclosed field outfitted with an array of low jumping fences. They reached a stand of bleachers facing the ring. Parents milled about clutching the hands of their young riders while others congregated in small clusters. Laughter filled the spring air.

"Mom!" Emma squeezed between two groups of chatting visitors with a boy following on her heels. Both were dressed in full show regalia from their helmets to their half chaps and paddock boots. Emma threw her arms around Skye's waist. "Daddy said you might come."

Skye patted her shoulder a few times until Emma dropped her arms and stepped back. It was obvious she'd been crying; her eyes were still puffy, though her snaggletooth smile beamed at Skye. She bent down and kissed Emma's cheek. "My little equestrian. Are you ready for the big event?"

Emma nodded.

The boy who'd been standing idly fidgeting with a button on his black show jacket looked at Skye. "Mrs. Andrews, I'm going to win a blue ribbon."

"You are?" Skye said.

"My mom told me I'm the best jumper in the whole club. Me and my horse, Cinders, have been jumping since I was a real little kid."

"Well, Harry, that's impressive." Skye folded her arms.

Emma edged close to Beth and slipped her hand into hers. "This is my friend, Harry," Emma said then turned to the boy. "This is Miss Beth. She takes care of homeless kitties at a rescue shelter."

"Hiya," Harry said with a small wave. "That's awesome. I'm going to get a dog. A collie. My dad used to have one when he was little but my mom says—"

A shrill whistle blew. "Got to go," Harry said. "That's the signal for us to get our horses."

Skye kissed Emma's cheek again. "I'm so proud of you. Have fun."

With reluctant steps, Emma headed for the stable far behind Harry who'd taken off running.

"So that's Harry—" Beth said.

"Kenny's son."

"Cute kid."

"Oh my God," Skye hissed. "She's here. Dammit. Over there." Skye gestured toward the bleachers. "Standing next to an old lady."

Beth caught sight of a tall woman with dirty blonde hair and a deep tan.

"I wanted to take you over to the stands to meet Tim. I caught a glimpse of him earlier. But forget it. I'm not going anywhere near her. I'll watch from here." Before Skye finished talking, both women started making their way through the array of guests.

"Damn," Skye whispered. "She's coming this way."

A couple of seconds later, they stood face to face.

"Skye. What a surprise. I'm so used to seeing the nanny, I didn't expect you to be here." Maiah paused as she brushed a lock of hair from her forehead. "Oh. How callus of me, I heard about what happened."

The deepness of her voice surprised Beth as well as her flawless beauty.

"I've just come from the hospital. It's bad enough what happened to Lexi, but my assistant was also attacked. My daughter is heartbroken, and I, well—it's just been very difficult."

"I too have lost a valued employee. Those who lack inner-strength..." Maiah reached into her purse, pulled out a linen handkerchief, and offered it to Skye. Instead of taking it, Skye threw her shoulders back and attempted a smile, even though a tear formed in the corner of her eye. She flicked it away.

Beth introduced herself hoping it wouldn't take Skye long to regain control of her emotions. "I met your son. He's quite a confident little boy."

Maiah's face lit up. "Harry is quite exceptional, actually. Oh, this is my dear friend, Johannah."

Beth stuck out her hand, but the older woman didn't attempt to take it. Instead, she offered Beth a clipped nod.

"I thought you'd still be in Kentucky. Congratulations, by the way," Skye said widening the mirthless smile on her face.

"I would never dream of missing one of my son's jumping events. Any mother invested in her child's well-being would move heaven and Earth to support him. Anyway, what's a six-hour flight compared to encouraging and validating your child's talents?" Maiah glanced at Johannah. "Some parents leave that to the hired help."

"Here they come." Beth pointed to a line of horses filing toward the ring.

"Let's find our seats, Johannah," Maiah said linking the older woman's arm. She shot Skye a radiant smile before they walked away.

"Bitch," Skye said under her breath.

Beth wrapped her arm around Skye's shoulder and felt her tremble.

CHAPTER FORTY

On the way to Hap's apartment, Shane brought Collins up to speed. He explained how Beth had talked her way into the apartment and the curious items she'd found there. He recognized the stucco building as he nosed the unmarked patrol car into a parking space in the Hollywood Place Apartment lot. It wasn't his first time there. When he was still a rookie, he and his partner had answered a call for a domestic disturbance. A dozen years had passed, and Shane still hadn't been able to purge the desperate look that claimed the victim's bloodied face. She'd been a petite brunette. And a battered wife. A couple years later, he'd been called to a homicide scene in one of the dingy, little apartments. Turned out to be the same one. This time, her throat had been slashed a thread away from being cut clear through. The husband stood over her mutilated body, teary-eyed, swearing it was an accident.

Shane's stomach churned as they now walked to the building. With a search warrant in hand, they barged into the property manager's office. Nick Dempsey jumped away from his desk as a twisted expression covered his leathery face. That was until he spied the badges.

"Officers," he said with a sweeping gesture. "I've been expecting you. This is about Hap Dorian, right?"

It took only a quick glance for Shane to realize Beth's description of the manager to be spot on. He handed over the warrant. Nick unfolded the paper and stared intently as if memorizing every word. After dropping the paper on top of his metal desk, he pulled the jangle of keys free from his pocket.

"Couldn't believe the news about Hap. Thought I'd misunderstood. You see, gentlemen, Hap didn't have no enemies. Everybody loved him. Especially the ladies." Nick winked.

"You ever notice a priest around here?" Shane asked.

"A priest? Hell no." Nick stepped into the corridor leading to the elevator. After a few paces, he stopped. "Wait a minute." He snapped his fingers. "Now that you mention it, there is a priest. A real friendly guy. Kinda pudgy and soft." Nick inhaled pulling in his gut. "Kinda reminded me of a poofer. Guess that's why he enlisted. Them priests are all a bunch of queers anyway—pedophiles and gays—guess the padre feels at home with that lot."

Shane wanted to punch him into oblivion as he lumped the four percent of perverts masquerading as priests with the truly dedicated churchmen. Instead, he stuck his hand into his pocket and grasped the every ready bottle of Excedrin. "Know his name?"

"The padre?" Nick shook his head. "But like I said, Hap was a true ladies man, so I know he had nothin' going on with him. Told me they met at the track. The priest likes to play the ponies. Use to drop by every so often to pick Hap's brain."

They entered the elevator. Collins pulled out his notepad and began writing while Shane stared at the little man. He noticed a bead of sweat had formed along Nick's upper lip. A couple of seconds later, the door creaked open, and the apartment manager darted down the hall.

With a turn of the key, Nick flung the door open and waved in the detectives. Shane felt as if he knew the place. Beth's account of the room had been precise, to the smallest detail. As he expected, the apartment was dusky even with the overhead light on. He walked to the window and lifted back the drape, not surprised to see the blackout curtains. In the street below, he spied the El Camino that Beth swore was identical to Father Clancy's car.

The detectives paced around the room opening cabinets and drawers with gloved hands. Shane pulled the closet door open. Expecting to see the expensive black suit, he riffled through the meager items of clothing. Hoody, jeans, couple of pullovers. No suit.

Collins glanced into the refrigerator then moved to the table and lifted a framed photograph. "This Hap?" He looked at Nick.

"The younger one. The other guy is his old man. They worked together as stable grooms. That one was his all-time favorite." Nick motioned to the horse in the photo. "Shadowland or Shadowmoor. Something like that."

Collins replaced the picture. He stepped next to Shane who stood with folded arms staring at the writing table. "You got something?"

"No mirror, Styrofoam head, tray of makeup. Nothing."

"One thing I can say for Hap, he always kept a clean apartment. Not like some of them other tenants here. Slobs. But not Hap." Nick rocked back and forth on the balls of his feet.

Shane ignored the eager little man as he whispered to Collins, "Place's been cleared out. Probably wiped cleaned, too." He looked again at the empty table. "Dammit," he said between clenched teeth. "Mr. Dempsey."

"Call me Nick."

"Okay, Nick. That El Camino down in the street. You know who owns it?"

Nick puffed out his chest. "That old rust bucket belonged to Hap. How he ever picked up high-class dames in that thing, I'll never know. You should've seen the looker that came in here yesterday. A real knockout."

A flash of irritation sparked through Shane. He didn't want that guy, or any guy for that matter, talking about his wife that way.

"A redhead with legs a mile long. Could be a model or something," Nick said with too much enthusiasm for Shane's taste.

"Dorian was a handsome guy. What do you expect?" Collins said as if sensing Shane's unease.

"Yeah. Well, maybe. But Hap was a regular guy—had no damn degree or fancy job—worked with his hands. And these dames, besides being really hot—they were high-class like—cultured. Take the one yesterday, she had one of them ritzy accents like you hear on a documentary. The other one I met—shoot, I never got her name. Anyway, she's a blonde with dark brown eyes—you ever hear the expression "doe eyes" well, that was her. She had one of them, you know, sexy voices—deep and throaty—but not slutty. Definitely uptown. Last few weeks, she'd been running up to Hap's apartment nonstop. Lucky bastard. At least he died a happy man."

"Have you seen her lately?" Collins asked.

"Nope. Probably heard about Hap on the news. Guess I won't be seeing that pretty lady no more." Nick shrugged.

Could she be the one who emptied out the apartment? Shane drew his eyebrows together, blew out a stream of air, and walked out of the studio apartment. Collins caught up with him while Nick followed behind. When the elevator opened after the silent ride, both detectives offered Nick a curt nod before exiting the building.

They walked around the structure and stopped at the El Camino. Collins called in the license plate while Shane looked inside through the passenger window. The worn interior told him nothing, except it was clean of any personal belongings. He glanced at Collins hoping the plate would point to Dorian. If it did, they'd have the car impounded. With a little luck, it could offer some much-needed evidence, but it would take days for the investigators to probe every inch of the vehicle. A sinking feeling told Shane they didn't have days. He feared the worst was still to come.

CHAPTER FORTY-ONE

TUESDAY, MAY 6th

"The plane has landed and will be disembarking directly," the airport police officer said. "You've signed the TSA log book?"

"We've been cleared," Shane said. He kept in step with the officer who identified himself as Luis Peña.

"You think the suspect might catch another flight and skip the country?"

"A possibility. We don't want to take any chances. My partner will be stationed on the tarmac in a patrol car."

Officer Peña led Shane to where the jet-way met the de-embarkment pier. "Through that door," the officer said pointing, "is the staircase that leads out to the tarmac. I'll accompany you down with the suspect."

Hushed but excited voices sounded from the jet-way. Shane targeted on the couple flanked by flight attendants. *Probably think they're big shots being personally escorted off the plane. That bubble's about burst.* He pulled out his badge and stepped with Peña to the edge of the pier. With carry-on bags slung over their shoulders and brilliant smiles lighting up their faces, the Westons came to an abrupt stop.

"I'm Detective Dalton and this is Officer Peña."

"If this is about the death of Roman Dorian, we've already spoken to detectives in Louisville," Maiah explained. "If you don't mind, we have a car waiting."

Shane looked into Maiah's intense, dark eyes. "You're free to go." He turned to Kenny, a bit surprised, half-expecting him to resemble Greyson. He seemed the opposite in many respects. Dark, short hair compared to Zach's blondish wavy tresses, tall yet slender, a contrast to Zach's muscularity. The thing both men had in common was their crystal clear blue eyes.

"We've got a few questions for you. Please, come this way." Shane stepped next to Kenny while Peña moved around flanking him on the opposite side.

Kenny slipped the luggage strap from his shoulder and handed the bag to Maiah.

"Why do you want to talk to my husband? I'm the one who employed Mr. Dorian. You should be asking me the questions." She dropped the bag on the floor, anchored her hands on narrow hips, and frowned. "You don't have to go with them."

Shane touched Kenny's shoulder and led him a few steps away.

"Where are you taking him?" Maiah asked the backs of the departing men.

Shane glanced over his shoulder. "Clear Springs Station."

One of the flight attendants, a strapping uniformed male, moved next to Maiah and lifted both pieces of luggage. "Please, follow me," he urged.

"I'm not budging until I know what the hell is going on."

"Look Maiah, don't cause a scene," Kenny said.

"I'm calling Marc Hammond."

She stepped next to Shane. They stood eye to eye. Though he wanted to dislike this rich, demanding woman, he couldn't help but be impressed by the way she'd taken control of the situation while Kenny acted like a lamb being led to the slaughter. Not that he'd wanted any flak out of him. But, Kenny seemed a bit too docile.

The flight attendant rested a hand on Maiah's shoulder. "If you continue down the pier to the luggage pickup, we'll be able to allow the rest of the passengers to debark."

She jerked off his hand and glared at Kenny. "Not a word until the lawyer arrives. Not one damn word."

***

Tiny beads of perspiration dotted Kenny's forehead as he fumbled with an empty paper coffee cup. It had tasted like crap, but now he craved a refill. The small office felt stifling and overcrowded with the three of them crammed around a rectangular table. The camera braced on the opposite wall only intensified his uneasiness. Even so, he sat straight and looked directly from one pair of interrogator's eyes to the other. This whole thing is a farce, he bristled, but knew better than to raise a ruckus. *Answer their questions then get the hell outta here.*

"You knew Lexi Horne," Collins said.

"Yes."

"She was one of your students?" Shane asked in a low, even tone.

"Student? Nothing like that. No."

"How'd you meet her?" Shane leaned back in the chair and crossed his arms.

Kenny silently cursed knowing what was coming. He wasn't about to spill his guts about his relationship with Skye.

"Come on, Kenny, you might as well spit it out. We're already aware of your affair with Skye Andrews," Shane said. "She offered that information."

Dammit, Skye. Kenny clenched his jaw.

"We can be discreet, Mr. Weston." Collins opened his laptop. "We're not the fidelity police."

Kenny drew his eyebrows closer, but said nothing.

"Do you recognize this?" Shane placed a cell phone on the table.

"Should I? One phone's pretty much like another." Kenny shrugged. He hadn't the slightest idea what this hotshot detective was after, but he didn't like it. A fierce tightening twisted in the pit of his stomach.

"This phone belongs to your girlfriend, Skye Andrews," said Collins.

"She's not my girlfriend." Kenny jumped up and stepped away from the table. He reached into his pants pocket, pulled out a crumpled airline paper napkin, and swiped it along his brow. Then he paced to the far end of the closet-sized room.

"Okay, okay," said Collins in a soothing tone. "She's your friend, then."

"And your friend saved one of your messages," Shane said. "Not because it was sentimental or funny, but because it scared her." He twisted his neck and glared at Kenny. "Skye found herself at a loss. To confront you or the police. She chose the police." He tapped the phone a few times, and Kenny's recorded voice sounded through the room.

Kenny recalled the message after the first couple of words. He tapped his foot against the tile floor, and when it had mercifully ended, he sank back into the hard wooden chair. A few seconds ticked by. Shane's voice cut into the silence and sounded too loud.

"So, there's a Lexi problem. A problem you swear you're gonna take care of. But you couldn't do it alone, so you solicited help from your pal, Hap Dorian."

"What are you talking about?"

"Whether Hap did your dirty work or the two of you acted together really doesn't matter," Collins said. "But something went haywire. Did Hap start making unreasonable demands? Press you for money? Try to blackmail you?"

Kenny felt his heart hammering and gulped a couple mouthfuls of air. He warned himself to stay in control, but the preposterous allegations made his blood rush hot through his veins. In an attempt to sound confident, he failed and barely whispered a denial.

"Not very convincing," Collins said.

Kenny glared at Collins and raised his voice. "I had nothing to do with any murders. Lexi or Hap or anyone else." He smashed the flimsy coffee cup and tossed it across the table.

"Facts don't lie, Kenny," said Shane. "You had a strong motive to get rid of Lexi. If she went public with the news of your illicit affair, you could kiss your marriage straight to hell, along with your wife's big bucks. We get it. You didn't want to hurt anybody," Shane said lowering his voice. "But you had no choice. You had to stop a teenage girl from blabbing to the *National Enquirer* the name of Skye Andrew's new lover." He threw his arms open and offered Kenny upturned palms. "You eliminate your problem with Dorian's help."

Kenny stared at a spot on the wall.

"Young women are being murdered by a serial killer. Why not Lexi?" Shane stood and moved around the table. "Presto." He snapped his fingers. "The solution to the Lexi problem."

"By God, I swear I had nothing to do with it."

"Then there's Darla." Shane reclaimed his seat.

"What's up with her?" Collins said. "Did she show up at the wrong time leaving you no choice but to—"

"You know something about Darla?" Kenny raked his fingers through his hair. "Is she okay?"

Shane pursed his lips.

"Didn't die. She's in the ICU," Collins said.

Kenny folded his hands on top of the table. "That's good," he mumbled.

"Not so good for you. Darla fingered you. Said you attacked her. Left her for dead," Collins lied.

"That's it," Kenny exploded. "I wanted Lexi out of the picture. Didn't trust her. But all I was gonna do was reason with her, beg her if I had to, so she wouldn't go public about Skye and me. Maiah would take away my kid. He means the world to me. You gotta believe me. I had nothing to do with killing anyone."

A knock sounded, and then the door flew open. Marc Hammond entered the interrogation room. He nodded at the detectives and placed a hand on Kenny's shoulder. "Gentlemen, at this point, Mr. Weston has nothing more to offer," his deep and melodious voice sounded. "Unless you're planning to arrest him, we'll be leaving."

"We want a polygraph," Shane said. "And his DNA."

Marc Hammond shook his head. "Sorry, fellas."

Kenny jumped up, raced toward the opened door, and bolted as his lawyer trailed behind.

CHAPTER FORTY-TWO

Beth wistfully looked at the kittens huddled around the food bowls and wished she could keep them. There was no question in her mind that Shane's health had to come first, so in a couple of days, she'd be returning them to the Cute Cat Rescue. Hopefully, they'd wind up on the short list to be adopted out to their forever homes. She remembered the mug her fingers were curled around and took a quick sip of tea only to find the liquid unappetizingly tepid.

For the first time in days, she breathed easy. The eerie sense of dread that caused her to fear the murder of another teenage girl had finally abated. Hap Dorian was dead—God have mercy on his soul—and he'd no longer be able to trick unsuspecting girls into trusting him right into their graves.

Hap's mystery woman remained a curious distraction. When the investigation is finally closed, she envisioned the "girlfriend" would be blessing her lucky stars that she'd been fortunate enough to survive Hap's heinous machinations. Of course, Shane has to dot all his I's and cross all his T's, but, eventually, he'll come to the same conclusion about Hap. She was certain about that.

Though eager to expel all memories of the horrific deaths, a niggling in the back of her mind questioned Hap's motives and what possessed him to kill those young women. She especially wanted to know how he chose his victims.

Though she'd racked her brain, the only notion to surface was something so superficial she had a hard time swallowing her own supposition. The murdered girls must've had something in common. Something that caused Hap to signal them out. From the constant flipping through her file folder, she'd memorized the faces of the slain teens. The girls had different backgrounds, ranging from affluent to dirt poor. Every one of his victims was young, pretty, and brunette. Nick Dempsey had been adamant that Hap's girlfriend was a blonde. *Could it be that simple? It didn't matter to Hap if they lived in a Beverly Hills mansion or a modest dwelling in East LA as long as they were young and had mahogany tresses?*

Not completely satisfied, Beth stepped into the kitchen. She dumped the remaining tea into the shiny farm sink and placed the cup into the dishwasher. Though the reason Hap murdered the teens hadn't crystallized, she believed, without a shadow of a doubt, that he'd been the culprit. All of her fanciful theories of the furtive killer being Kenny Weston, Dot Barnett, or even Zach now seemed a reach. Unfathomable really. But Shane needed proof and couldn't rely on his gut instincts. Her *fey* had directed her in the direction of a priest—or someone masquerading as one—and even pointed her to the evidence hidden away in Hap's flat.

"Except now the suit is missing. And the cosmetics," Beth muttered. She leaned against the granite countertop and crossed her arms. "Hap must've ditched all that stuff before taking off for the Kentucky Derby. Probably covered over in a landfill by now." She grasped the teakettle off the stove and filled it with water. As she waited for it to boil, she wondered how silly she'd been believing the deaths centered around Skye. The whistling kettle dispelled her ruminations as she poured the water into a teapot, waited a minute, and then emptied the pot's water into the sink. After refilling the kettle, she once again placed it on the gas-jetted burner. She lifted a slice of whole wheat bread from the bakery loaf and dropped it into the toaster, twisted opened a jar of marmalade, and dumped a spoonful of tea leaves into the kettle. After scooping out an ample dollop of the sweet jelly, she tapped it onto a plate. Hearing the familiar pop, she grasped the toasted slice, and dropped it missing the plate. Golden crumbs tumbled across the slick countertop.

"*Janey Mac.*" Her heart dropped. "I was in the flat the day of the Derby. Hap was already in Kentucky. For at least a week. He couldn't have cleaned it out." She jerked the kettle off the range, and forgetting about the teapot set it on the countertop. "Damnation." She paced across the wooden floor. Reaching the far side of the kitchen, she heard the doorbell chime.

Beth muttered under her breath about her blatant stupidity as she ambled down the wide hallway leading to the foyer. She yanked open the front door. Skye faced her.

Just what I need.

Beth forced a welcoming expression to mask her disgruntled mien.

Skye stepped inside, skipped the formalities, and jumped into the gist of her visit. "Thom Boyle, the director of my new film, called last night. Well, the long and the short of it is, there's been some problem with a permit causing the filming to be moved up a couple of weeks. I have to leave for Baltimore today. I'm heading to the airport now."

Beth frowned but didn't interrupt. Instead, she steeled herself, suspecting Skye wanted something. Typical of their friendship. Deep down, she didn't mind. They helped each other. An image of Skye holding her hand as she lay in hospital crossed her mind. *Perhaps, that's the mortar that strengthens our friendship.*

"I want to thank you for being the best friend ever." Skye threw her arms around Beth's neck and kissed her cheek. "I haven't felt this good in God knows how long. Darla is recovering, and I'm going to perform my best role ever. I never thought I'd be this happy again. And it's mainly because of you."

Not sure what to say, Beth pressed her palms together. She certainly wasn't going to reveal what she'd figured out. Because if Hap wasn't the one responsible, then the killer was still on the loose. The very last thing Skye needed was to fret over whether that madman would attempt to finish his handiwork on Darla.

"I know you won't mind, but I wanted to make sure," Skye rattled on. "Will you keep an eye on Darla for me? Even though her folks are in town, I can't expect them to give me daily updates on her condition."

Beth agreed with a quick nod. "Don't worry about a wee thing. Concentrate on being brilliant, which surely won't be very hard, so."

"If only Zach would see it your way. Said my priorities are screwed up. All because he wants me to attend Lexi's funeral tomorrow. He's going with our agent who turned out to be Lexi's agent." Skye rolled her eyes. "I put my foot down and insisted Emma is not to go. He thinks the funeral will give her closure. I told him it'll give her nightmares. That's the last thing Emma needs—to see Lexi's body in a casket."

For an instant, Beth visualized her mother laid out within the confines of a plain oak box in their Dublin parlor. A wave of anger swept through her as the sounds of levity and merrymaking filled her ears, bringing back all too clearly the memories of her wake. Without any doubt, she knew her sainted mother was in heaven, but how could a wee child be expected to rejoice with losing her ma? In the end, it hadn't brought her closure, but only a profound sense of loss.

"Zach is wrong. Go on with yourself and don't give it another thought. Consider this film as being the start of something grand."

After a quick hug, Skye stepped out onto the porch, offered a quick wave, and turned in the direction of the waiting limousine.

Beth shut the door and leaned against the polished oak veneer. She closed her eyes and shuddered. Never before had she'd felt a stronger premonition. Skye was in danger. Grave danger. She covered her face with trembling hands, not knowing what to do.

CHAPTER FORTY-THREE

Shane tapped a pen against his desk, causing a staccato beat to fill the air. If he hadn't checked out the facts, he would've thought the fantastic story to be a bit of incomprehensible nonsense. At the onset, he felt sympathy for the young woman who'd entered his office a couple of hours ago—Hettie Dunne—Dot Barnett's niece. She all but begged for the charges against her aunt to be dropped and informed him that her attorney husband was in a meeting with the D.A. The more she babbled on about her poor Aunt Dot, Shane recognized the unmistakable reaction surfacing in his gut. The beautiful, though agitated, woman, who mistakenly blamed herself for Dot's bizarre behavior—dammit— was telling the gospel truth.

Who would've believed it? Dot Barnett, heiress to a pharmaceutical empire.

Dot even owned an island off the coast of Washington. The minute after a dissatisfied Hettie left his office, he telephoned the mental health facility Barnett frequented and suffered through a fruitless discussion with her primary psychiatrist, who kept throwing up patient confidentiality in his face. This much he was certain about, if Barnett had killed Lexi, then the woman was sicker than anyone imagined, including her world-renown doctors. The only substantial facts he gathered was that while on her medications, Barnett functioned seamlessly, and that coupled with her brilliance, her IQ apparently was off the chart; she served as a capable CEO of a major corporation. "While on medication," he muttered.

"You say something?"

Shane glanced at his partner.

"We'll have just enough time if we leave now. Our flight for Oakland leaves tonight at seven-oh-five," Collins said.

Shane's first thought was to let Collins interview Barnett. He couldn't trust himself to remain professional confronting the woman who attacked Beth. But after spending an informative hour with Hettie Dunne, he almost felt pity toward the crazy old gal. Hettie had relayed the heart-wrenching account of a poor little rich girl who lost her parents in a plane crash and was never able to bounce back into reality. At age eight, Barnett escaped into her own world, frequenting cinemas and became fixated on the silver screen heroes who were able to conquer the injustices of life. The actor, Randolph Scott, easily became her favorite. Hettie bantered around the term, major depressive disorder with psychotic features, but the doctor had flatly refused to confirm any type of diagnosis.

Unsure how to handle the Barnett interrogation, he thought of Beth. She wasn't the type to hold a grudge. Anyway, she believed Zach had set the wheels in motion for Barnett's meltdown. He suspected, much to his chagrin, that Beth had already forgiven Zach for his part in the incident. So, who the hell am I to pass judgment, he asked himself as he headed out of the office.

Once inside the hospital's blocky, terracotta tinted building, Shane and Collins checked in at the main desk. They were informed that Dot Barnett had been assigned to the clinic on the building's east end. Though her admission was in a less restrictive patient area, one designed for those with milder symptoms, they'd have to follow protocol to be permitted inside the ward.

The two men remained silent as they moved along narrow, nondescript corridors. They halted at the nurses' station, pulled out their badges and identifications, while Shane asked for the location of Dot's room. A nurse arrayed in a lavender paisley print smock walked them to a sparse room consisting of a bed, chair, and a sink. Shane surmised the closed door housed the toilet. Not much homier than a jail cell.

Dot filled the space snuggly between the upholstered chair's armrests, as a thin patchwork quilt covered her ample lap. Her silver hair was combed back into a neat bun while a placid expression claimed her face, making her appear like a grandmother resting after baking batches of cookies for a slew of visiting relatives. She lifted her bespectacled eyes from the worn paperback she held as they entered the room.

"Come in. Come in. I was hoping for some company." Dot attempted to stand but then sat back further into the chair. "If you press that buzzer over there, my maid will bring refreshments." As she motioned to the call button on the bed frame, her eyes lit up. "Coffee and finger sandwiches. The cucumber ones with a scrumptious zesty dressing are my favorites. I'm sure you'll love them."

Though Collins glanced at him with a blank expression, Shane guessed what his partner was thinking—that Barnett's still nutty as a fruitcake.

"Dear me, I'm not home. In the hospital," Dot said lowering her voice. "I suppose you detectives are here on official business, and this isn't a social call after all."

"That's right," Collins said taking the lead. "We have a few questions." He stepped closer to the seated woman. "Are you aware of the recent murders of four teenage girls?"

Dot's eyes widened. "How horrible." She paused a moment. "I haven't been keeping up with current events for that very reason. It's never good, is it? I'm afraid you've wasted your time—"

"Tell us about your relationship with Zach Greyson," Shane said.

"The actor? Well, I don't know him personally, though he is a magnificent actor."

"You've never had contact with him?" Collins flipped open his pocket-sized notebook.

"I spoke with him once. We had a very nice telephone conversation. Must've been last year or maybe a couple years ago—you know how time flies. Anyway, it was just to test the waters. You see, every year, my company, Barnett Drugs Emporium Corporation, holds a fundraiser for cancer research. Our aim is to find new, better treatments to alleviate or even cure children suffering from that horrid disease."

"That's a real decent thing to do," Collins said. "So how does Greyson fit into that—he's some kind of major donor?"

"Not yet. But hopefully. You see, we always invite a celebrity to host the gala. Though I've been pushing a while for him, finally this year, the board decided that Zach Greyson would be a perfect representative. He's popular, successful, and our sources informed us that he's very generous when it comes to contributing to charities aimed to assist young people. In fact, he's donated hundreds of thousands toward scholarships and college tuitions for deserving underprivileged students. We're hoping he'd broaden his focus and support our effort. Actually, his public relations person..." Dot waved her plump hand in the air. "I can't remember her name right now, but she said he's interested. That's why I made the trip to Los Angeles. To try to persuade him on our behalf. I'm sure you know, the personal approach always works better. You can't imagine how big-name personalities are hounded for endorsements and the like. But, I had a strong feeling Mr. Greyson would gladly agree to champion our cause."

While she talked, Collins jotted down notes. Shane fingered the cleft in his chin, unsure what to make of her story.

"In all honesty, the last few weeks are a blurry haze. I'm having difficulty recalling how long I've actually been in California. It's a sensation akin to waking from a dream and unable to remember it." She rubbed the center of her forehead. "So completely elusive."

Collins looked up from his pad. "Do you remember applying for the nanny position?"

"Me? A nanny?" Dot smoothed her hand across the fabric tucked around her legs. "That's almost comical, Detective. Childcare is not my area of expertise." Her hand shook as she reached for the container of water on the bed tray. Before grabbing it, her hand fell back into her lap. "It was silly of me to stop my medication. But I felt so good. Invincible. All the while, Hettie, my darling niece, was worried sick. She even hired a private investigator. No one else took my disappearance seriously, though I can't really blame them. I have a peculiar habit of taking off every now and again. But I'm always careful with my medication. Especially my insulin. I've never missed a dose of that, but the others..." Dot shrugged then pulled at a loose thread from one of the quilt's corduroy patches. "I know it was bad of me. The doctor told me so." Dot's eyes welled up. She blinked rapidly but not fast enough as a couple of tears trickled down her jowly cheeks. "Will you be putting me in jail?"

Shane saw a flicker of fear cross her face. The same hapless expression, he imagined, when she found out about her parents' death. His stomach tightened. He didn't know how much longer he could put up with his job. His hand swept against his jacket and brushed against the hidden container of antacids. He refocused on Dot and realized she'd picked up on another strand of her story.

"I have an amazing board of directors and never have to worry about the business. But because I'd stopped all contact with Hettie, I always text her at least once a day, she was beside herself. That's what she told me last night." Dot nodded in the direction of the telephone sitting on the tray. "After I stopped touching base, she informed the authorities but, not receiving any satisfaction and not pleased with the PI, fired him. That dear child had enough to worry about with my shenanigans, let alone deal with an inept investigator. So, she called the police again and found out I was in the hospital." Her eyes flitted around the room. "Oh dear, I do wish I could offer you some refreshments."

A young woman dressed in ice blue scrubs noiselessly entered the room. She held a small paper cup. "Time for your meds, Ms. Barnett." Her voice rang flat and her movements mechanical.

Dot swallowed the pills without a fuss then offered the girl a smile. "Everyone is so nice here."

The nursing assistant headed toward the door but before exiting stole a glimpse at Shane. Her expression remained impassive, but her cold stare conveyed a sense of contempt. *Poor old Dot.* He suspected her care would be competent enough but probably not much in the compassion department.

"One last question." Shane squatted, becoming eye level with her. "Do you know who murdered Lexi Horne?"

"Lexi who, dear?"

"The nanny employed by Skye Andrews."

"She's a wonderful actress. And so pretty too." Dot wrinkled her brow. "Why would you think I'd know anything about her employees? I've never even met her. But, I must admit, I'm a fan. Truth be known, I think she has more acting ability than her husband. And what, he's won at least one Oscar and a couple of Golden Globes? Yes, indeed. It would be a real thrill to meet Skye Andrews."

"That's all for now." Shane straightened up, feeling as if trapped in an episode of the *Twilight Zone*. *We'll have to wait until the meds kick in a hundred percent before attempting a serious interview.* Though he wanted to believe Barnett was their killer, his gut told him to forget it. Barnett could've orchestrated the killings with a sharp, clear mind. But not addled. Her episode with Beth had been just that—not an action but a reaction. *Damn Greyson.*

They moved closer to the door.

"You boys be sure to drop by again soon. I promise you a nice spread of cucumber sandwiches and cookies. Yes, chocolate chip cookies. And gingersnaps."

"We will," Shane said. "You can count on it."

CHAPTER FORTY-FOUR

THURSDAY, MAY 8ᵗʰ

More than anything, Beth wanted to share her premonition with Shane. But the thought of him belittling her precious gift once again stopped her cold in her tracks. Maybe, she reasoned, when he returns from Lexi's funeral, the whole case will've been put to rest. In an off-handed way, he had explained that often the killer turns up at the funeral—someone who typically shouldn't be there.

With the murderer locked behind bars, they could resume their first year of marriage—like most newlywed couples—one filled with romance and lovemaking. His stress and her obsession were not the ingredients needed to ensure a tranquil married life. Actually, it had the opposite effect.

She missed Shane—the Shane she'd met that fateful day in the courthouse. The one who brightened her darkest hours, made her laugh, and touched her with such profound intensity—she knew he loved her deeply, eternally. *I'm a total fool for sabotaging our marriage by meddling into police business.* I'll quit now, she vowed, but in the same instant, she realized that she couldn't. Not until she found out who was responsible for the string of murders.

The night before, he'd called from the airport and sounded despondent, almost defeated. News that the kittens would soon be returning to the shelter should have cheered him. But his response had been a mumbled, half-hearted, "Oh." After the short conversation ended, she prayed a rosary, believing the extra prayer could only help him. As she dropped her beads into the night table drawer, she sensed a much-needed peace and a spark of insight.

She grabbed her mobile and dialed her dearest friend, Deidre McKenna. Nearly a decade before, the two intrepid Irish girls ventured to Italy in search of their dreams. There, Beth found a glittering career and wound up a celebrity in America while her friend landed in Venice. Now married to a Venetian entrepreneur and the mother of twin girls, Deidre worked as an English language teacher. Certain Deidre could offer her much needed advice based on her years of marital bliss, Beth hadn't been disappointed. As she cut the connection, a sense of tranquility she hadn't known for weeks washed over her. Deidre had struck a brilliantly simple solution causing Beth to wonder why she hadn't thought of it herself. A honeymoon.

Their hectic schedules had prevented them from taking the romantic holiday both of them needed. At this point, she didn't give a tinker's dam for either of their schedules. The worst outcome would result in Shane being fired—but he'd resign before that happened. She'd placed all the details into Deidre's capable hands, making sure she understood she'd have to work fast. Beth wanted to spend the month of June in Venice. Next month.

Her eyes rested on Father Clancy's business card, and her serenity faded as a shock of shame rumbled through her. She hadn't contacted him or even spent ten minutes perusing available real estate properties on the internet. To ease her guilty conscience, she spent a couple of hours scouring listings for an appropriate facility to house the teen shelter. As her strained eyes blurred from staring too long at the computer screen, she stumbled across one. A perfect space with a perfect location. The asking price seemed a bit hefty, but she'd leave the final decision to Father Clancy.

Now seated in her small study, she cradled the littlest of the kittens, the only one with a solid white coat. She stroked the soft, dense fur as his gravelly purr filled her ears. His green-blue eyes were closed, and his pink nose, almost red with contentment, quivered as he lifted his tiny face. She gave him a squeeze and kissed his furry head. "Sure, it's a mistake letting you dear, wee kittens into the den," she cooed. "But no need for worry. Shane won't be home 'til tonight, and my darlin' housekeeper's due to arrive any minute." She nuzzled the kitten believing all traces of allergens would shortly be scrubbed away.

Relieved to think about something besides the murders, she telephoned Father Clancy with hopes of checking out the property later in the day. She'd also be sure to clear up the confusion about his stint at St. Timothy's. But instead of being greeted by his rich, warm voice and comforting accent, she heard his voicemail. She left a quick message then carried the drowsy kitten into the mudroom. Certain all five kittens were secured within the walls of the compact space, she pulled the door shut. *Wouldn't want Shane to come home unexpectedly and catch them running through the house.* In spite of herself, the image of kitties on the loose made her giggle.

Beth grabbed the plush silk scarf from the back of a chair and draped the fabric loosely around her neck. *Time to visit Darla.*

She made it to the hospital in record time thanks to the lack of backups on the freeway. Though she believed Darla was in capable hands, a gnawing anxiety grew with each step she took through the sterile hospital corridor. She'd been grateful when Darla was transferred out of the ICU. But now, she couldn't stop the burgeoning worry—less security in a single room. She spotted a deputy stationed outside Darla's door.

"I'm relieved you're here." She offered her ID. "'Tis true, worry does give a small thing a big shadow. I've been fretting for nothing."

He didn't reply as he made a mark on his clipboard. He handed Beth back her driver's license, stepped around her, and opened the door. She tiptoed into the room, afraid she'd wake Darla.

It took Beth only a second to realize something was very wrong. Darla's head lolled over her left shoulder, and her eyes peered half-opened as if in a stupor. The vital signs monitor beeped wildly.

She yelled for the deputy and grabbed Darla's wrist feverishly seeking a pulse.

The deputy burst into the room, radio in hand. She backed away as a team of nurses, technicians, and doctors encircled the bed. Rapid-fired instructions filled the air as well-trained hands administered to the unconscious patient.

Stunned and a bit confused, Beth raced from the room into the corridor. Loud, thudding steps roused her attention. Hospital security officers ran down the hallway and slowed to a stop a few steps from Darla's room. The deputy reappeared and joined the group, comprised of three men and one woman.

"What happened?" The tallest of the officers asked the deputy.

"Not sure. They're working on her. Maybe an allergic reaction to medication. Should know soon."

"Any suspicious characters hanging around?" The woman asked pulling her radio free from a pocket.

"Only authorized visitors. And only one today." The deputy stuck his thumb in Beth's direction. "She found her in distress."

An Asian officer faced Beth. "You are?"

"Beth Getty. My husband is LASD Detective Shane Dalton. I'm a personal friend of Darla's."

"Ma'am, we need this area free of visitors." He offered her a curt nod.

She took a few steps away from the uniformed group but then spun around. "You're sure no one else entered Darla's room?"

"A nurse. Fifteen minutes later, the hospital's chaplain, a Catholic priest," the deputy said.

"The hospital's chaplain is an Episcopal priest," the female officer said.

"So? Episcopal—Catholic." The deputy shrugged.

"The chaplain is a woman. A female priest."

"What?" Beth's face clouded. A multitude of thoughts tumbled through her mind and any one of them too frightening to verbalize. Her throat went dry, and a wave of dizziness washed over her.

Strong arms gripped her. She blinked, attempting to dispel the blurriness and found herself looking into Mike Alder's face.

"What's going on?" Mike demanded.

She pressed her head against his chest, trying to recover her composure. "Come on," Beth whispered. "I'll fill you in."

He wrapped his arm around her waist, and they headed for the waiting room.

CHAPTER FORTY-FIVE

FRIDAY, MAY 9ᵗʰ

Shane leaned on his elbow and studied Beth's slumbering face. Streams of early morning light filtered through the Palladian windows, though she remained mostly in shadow. The dimness couldn't hide the mass of purplish and sickly green bruises discoloring her neck. The sight of them made him angry—furious at Greyson for being such an idiot and Barnett for what—being manipulated—mentally ill? He brushed away strands of wayward hair off her forehead, focused on the jagged scar, and then kissed the marred cheek.

She turned and murmured a few garbled words before flicking her eyes open. After blinking few times, her face lit up. "Ah, darlin'. When did you get home?"

"From the airport, we went directly to the hospital. It was late."

"Any change?"

"Darla slipped into a coma. You already know that?" He didn't wait for a reply. "Seems you're right about a priest being the murderer."

"Darla told me it was a priest. But not an actual priest, I'm believing."

"Me either. The suit you saw in Hap's apartment—"

"That mysteriously disappeared. Well, I've been thinking. Beside his girlfriend, the only other person with likely access to Hap's apartment—and the suit—would've be his *da*," Beth said.

"That thought crossed my mind too, so I did a little digging. The elder Mr. Dorian has an airtight alibi. He's in Baltimore and was hosing down Estella Blue the precise moment Darla was poisoned. We scratched him off the list, before he was actually on it."

"The funeral?" She scooted up and leaned against the upholstered headboard.

"What you'd expect. Heartbreaking. Greyson was there with his agent and Trey Wickham. I was surprised Mike Alder didn't show up."

"For all his brawn, seems Mike has a sensitive side. Lexi's funeral, I'm guessing, would've been too emotional. And now he's worried sick about Darla. The two of them formed a bond after he rescued her. If Darla doesn't pull through... I hate to think." She moistened her lip with the tip of her tongue. "I can't bear to tell Skye, so I've decided to wait a wee bit. No use getting her upset for nothing."

"Smart move. I think it's weird the way Alder showed up right after Darla was given the poison."

"His polygraph show anything?"

"Non-deceptive. But still. The timing strikes me as hinky. Alder's not off the hook yet." He pulled Beth next to him, breathed in the fresh scent of her hair, and closed his eyes. She snuggled next to him.

"Any news about Dot?" Beth asked.

"What drug store do you use?"

"BDE." She wrinkled her brow.

"Barnett Drug Emporium." The corners of his mouth edged upwards. "Barnett's niece stopped by the office the other day. Turns out, Dot Barnett, *is* Barnett Drugs." He allowed a second for the news to sink in. "You know that cute little kid pictured on their products?"

"The Barnett Baby."

"That's Dot when she was a toddler."

Beth leapt forward tossing off the comforter. "You're kidding? That darlin' is Dot?"

He moved a finger across his pecs, crossing his heart. "Now that Barnett's back on her medication, I'm hoping soon she'll have a firm grip on reality. She looked different though—kinda grandmotherly. Anyway, it seems her initial plan was to snag Greyson to play host at her company's annual cancer fundraiser." He paused a second. "I bet he declines the offer." Shane kissed her forehead. "I've got to get ready for work." He eased out of bed, pulled his rumpled t-shirt over his head, and dropped it on the floor.

"I'm worried about Skye's safety."

"Now what?"

"She's in Baltimore working on a new picture. Next Saturday is the Preakness Stakes, and the Westons will be there and Trey—"

"And thousands of other people. It's a major horse race."

"Hap was murdered at the last one." She moved to the edge of the bed.

He crossed his arms. "Skye has no interest in horse racing."

"Usually that'd be true. But she texted that her director wanted to do something special for the cast and crew since they had to rework their schedules due to some mix-up. He's reserved lovely accommodations for them at the Pimlico Clubhouse to watch the Preakness Stakes. Skye decided to go because Kenny invited her to his Preakness party. She's determined to give him a royal piece of her mind."

He fingered the cleft in his chin. After a few long seconds, he cleared his throat. "That's not a good idea. Weston has risen to the top of the suspect list. He's got a strong motive, had a key to Skye's house, and money drives some people to do stupid things. Happens all the time—get tired of the husband but want the house and the insurance policy money—so..." Shane ran his index finger across his neck. "Pretty certain Dorian was involved, and, for some reason, Weston killed him too. Right now, it's circumstantial. But who else at the Derby would've poisoned Dorian? Too damn coincidental." Shane picked his shirt up from the floor and folded it twice. "All we need is solid evidence—rock hard proof that Weston is our killer. Maybe that'll happen when we get a sample of his DNA."

"If that's true, who cleaned out Hap's flat if both of them were in Kentucky?"

"I don't know."

"And why try to kill Darla?"

"Darla knew about the affair. Weston probably figured she'd put two and two together and come up with him."

Beth slipped out of bed and faced Shane from across the wide mattress. "I've done something you're probably not going to like."

Shane moved his eyebrows closer, causing his brow to wrinkle.

"Skye invited me to be her guest at Kenny's party. I told her yes."

Shane swore his heart rate jumped. "Neither one of you are going to be at that party. Understand?"

"Skye can be as bullheaded as you sometimes. I doubt I'll be able to make her change her mind."

"The only way you'll be attending that shindig is if I'm with you." He marched to the bathroom and slammed the door shut.

CHAPTER FORTY-SIX

Beth paced the bedroom's floor worrying about Darla. When she'd telephoned the hospital for an update, the news had been the same—no change—still critical. The thought of telling Skye made her head ache, so she'd lied and told her that Darla was steadily improving. She paused at her night tabled and grabbed her rosary. Fingering the crucifix, she blessed herself, but before reaching the first bead, the doorbell sounded.

She considered not answering the door, but after a quick succession of rings, she retied the belt on her dressing gown and headed out of the room. The bell sounded twice more as she walked down the main staircase. The coolness of the foyer's marble tile surprised Beth as her bare feet slapped against the floor. She took a quick peek through the peephole.

"Damnation," she muttered. She counted to five before pulling the door open. "Zach. What a surprise." She frowned noticing how bad he looked. He hadn't shaved for a least a couple days, and his clothes—a faded black t-shirt and rumpled jeans—seemed as if he'd slept in them. "Make yourself at home while I put the kettle on." She directed him into the den.

She bounded up the stairs toward the master suite. After a pulling a comb through her hair and slipping into a pair of sweats and a pullover, she quickly tied the laces of her leather runners. She raced down the back staircase, which opened up near the kitchen. Not wanting to spend a lot of time preparing tea, she plucked a couple tea bags from a canister and filled the cups from the electric teapot. She carried the cups on saucers to the den.

"The funeral was a bummer." Zach stared at his clasped hands.

"Shane told me."

"He was there with that other detective—Collins. Did they find out anything?"

Zach squinted at her.

She shook her head, handing him the teacup.

"At least you're looking better." He motioned toward her neck. "Bruises are fading. I hope you know how sorry—"

"No more apologies." She sat opposite him on a chintz-covered hassock.

He nodded, and a blondish lock of hair fell onto his forehead. "I stopped by the hospital yesterday to check on Darla. Skye had asked, but I could tell she didn't think I would. I wanted to prove her wrong. Petty, I guess. But, I was royally pissed when they refused to let me see the girl. What's going on?"

She took a sip of the hot tea, determined not to tell him anything since he'd blab the whole story to Skye. "Security is tight for a reason. They don't want to take any chances."

"Makes sense. Still—"

"I forgot the cream." She shot up.

He raised his palm to stop her. "Your husband has summoned me to an interview. Did you tell him I got Lexi pregnant?"

She worried her lip with the tip of her thumb, believing if she told him the truth, he'd never trust her again. "Just protocol."

"You didn't answer my question."

"You really think I'd break your confidence?"

"Well—no. But that husband of yours might've badgered it out of you."

"Shane's not like that."

"If you say so." He placed the untouched cup on the coffee table, stood, and shoved his hands into his pockets.

"I want to run something by you." Beth noticed a trace of irritation flick across his face. "I had an awful premonition something terrible is going to happen to Skye."

"Premonition?"

"Lexi and Darla were attacked in her Malibu house. It's not safe there."

"For God's sake. You know she's in Baltimore."

"That may not be a safe place either. She's determined to attend the Preakness Stakes."

"So?"

"That's where it's going to happen."

"What the hell are you talking about?"

"If we don't protect her, Zach, I'm fearing she's going to wind up just like Lexi."

***

Zach wiped his hands on the paper napkin imprinted with the shop's *Sandwich Delight* logo. He crumpled it, tossed it aside, and took a long gulp from a water bottle. Though the flow of customers had been steady inside the small sandwich shop, he hadn't noticed. He'd sat at a table butted against a wall for the good part of an hour but had taken only a couple bites from the Focaccia turkey club, which overfilled the flimsy paper plate. Though the food was gourmet, the place reminded him of a dive with its cinderblock walls painted a plum purple and wobbly plastic tables. Exactly the reason he liked it. Nobody to pester him. Even so, he hadn't bothered to remove the baseball cap or the brown tinted sunglasses as he fumbled with the entertainment pages of the *Los Angeles Times*.

He folded the paper, glanced at the sandwich, and pulled on the cap's brim. His rational mind demanded him to remain calm, unbothered, stoic, but his emotions ran a different way altogether. He reminded himself every person acquainted with Lexi had to be questioned by the police but fumed that last week in his library Collins hadn't asked him a damn thing, only stared at Beth for nearly an hour.

Now I'm the one being inconvenienced.

A couple of hours ago, during the interview, Collins asked the question so quietly he almost didn't hear the words. "Are you responsible for Lexi Horne's pregnancy?"

At that moment, he'd hated Collins and refused to answer. Pretended he didn't know she'd even been pregnant. Then the detective's dark eyes bore into him. Zach mumbled a weak affirmative. That declaration ripped open the wound that his chance at fatherhood had died with Lexi—and probably made him a suspect.

He lifted the turkey club but put it down without it reaching his mouth. He grabbed the newspaper and landed on an article written by his favorite columnist.

The presence of someone hovering caused him to jerk his head sideways. Two young women stood gawking at him with eyes the size of saucers.

"You're Zach Greyson," the pretty blonde said.

He squeezed his lips tight.

The other woman, short, dumpy, and in dire need of braces for a prominent overbite blurted, "We're visiting from Fargo, North Dakota. It's like so unbelievable you're here in this dinky, little sandwich shop. You're our most favorite actor in the whole world. Would you—"

"Please, give us your autograph." The blonde shoved two napkins in his direction.

He attempted a smile, though the sound of the girls' giggles turned his stomach. He grabbed the offered pen and scribbled his name twice. Without speaking a word, he hoped they were satisfied and lifted the sandwich. He took a bite, chewed slowly, and glanced toward the exit. He watched as they clutched the napkins and with hop-like steps departed through the door.

He lifted the newspaper and scanned the article looking for his name. He found it in the first paragraph. *Award winning actor, Zach Greyson, is slated to play the lead in an upcoming World War II action flick.* He'd been excited about the project. Great writers. Great director. It'd guarantee another nomination for Best Actor. Might even score another Oscar or Golden Globe. But now, his enthusiasm had waned. With Lexi's murder, Darla back in the ICU, and Beth's sixth-sense giving off vibes that Skye was in danger—*what the hell is going on?*

He left the paper and uneaten sandwich behind and ambled out of the shop. As he neared his Bentley, he pulled out his cell phone and telephoned his assistant. "Make me an airline reservation to Baltimore. I have a hankering to see a horse race."

CHAPTER FORTY-SEVEN

SUNDAY, MAY 11th

Beth sighed as the bloated freeway moved at a snail's gallop. She'd been pleased when Father Clancy telephoned excited about the property she'd found on the internet but even more enthusiastic about one he stumbled across driving through the city. She'd agreed to meet him, eager for the diversion, since she'd been moping with worry about Darla, still in the ICU.

Trying to brush away her impatience with the traffic, she pressed the CD player button to an audio book penned by her favorite mystery author. After creeping off the exit, the words of the narrator faded as she focused on the gridwork of streets that led ever closer toward the property Father Clancy praised.

The building's location turned out to be in a part of town that had seen better days. Vertical bars protected businesses' windows, and spray-painted graffiti made the tired buildings look shabbier. Not able to park on the main thoroughfare, she pulled into a tiny dry cleaner's parking lot adjacent to the property. Surprised the green neon light in the store window flashed 'Open,' Beth stepped out of her vehicle and wondered if this run-down area would offer a sense of well-being and welcome for troubled teens.

She ambled to the Volvo's hatch and lifted out a quilted comforter, one of several she used to cover the floor so the kittens' paws wouldn't chill on the cool tile. "Might as well give them the business," she whispered wondering how the little shop survived in such a blighted area. She hurried inside and waited at the counter as a silver haired women with lively brown eyes moved away from a rack of hanging clothes sheathed in clear, plastic bags.

Beth handed her the quilt and noticed the name embroidered on the woman's smock. Maria José. After a few generalities regarding the lovely weather, Beth said, "I might be interested in leasing the building next door as an emergency shelter for teenagers. I'm working with a priest, Father Riordan Clancy."

The light seemed to fade from Maria José's dark eyes. "That place has been vacant a long time. Used to be a furniture warehouse, but when the business started to go downhill, they relocated. That's when the druggies took over. Broke the windows to get inside. Homeless people crashed there too. Almost a daily occurrence for the police to clear the place out." She gestured toward her windows. "Finally, they boarded the place up. It's the way the world is nowadays."

Beth became even more apprehensive after hearing about the downward spiral of the building. "You seem to have a thriving business."

"That's because, years ago, we added a delivery service."

Beth lifted a business card from the tray on the counter. After taking a quick glance, she slipped the card into her purse. "I've been looking for a good dry cleaner. My husband is an LASD detective and is fastidious about the condition of his suits. Last week, I heard him muttering something about the shoddy job the dry cleaner did. I'm really glad I stopped in." She paused a second. "Do you mind if I keep my car parked in your lot? I'll take only a few minutes to check the building out. I'm Beth, by the way. Beth Getty."

"Maria José Diaz. Keep your car on the lot as long as you like." She handed Beth a pickup slip. "The bedspread will be ready tomorrow."

"Could you deliver it?"

With a nod, she handed Beth a form.

"I'd appreciate another opinion about the building next door. Won't you join us?" Beth handed her the completed paper.

"It used to be so pretty with a gallery of fine furniture on display. Made plenty of homes into showplaces." Maria José waved in the direction of the abandoned building then dropped her hand on top of the bedspread. "It'd make me happy if that old building was finally fixed up and had a new purpose." She paused a second. "I might be able to pop over during my lunch break. Just to take a peek."

"That'd be lovely." Beth glanced through the security barred window. She spotted Father Clancy stepping out of a dingy white cargo van. "See you in a couple of minutes then," she said nearing the door.

"Father," Beth called as she stepped onto the pavement. "What happened to your car?"

The priest shook his head, though a grin claimed his face. "Poor old lass, had to give her the last rites. I think me new ride is pretty much a step up. This way

I'll be able to transport the kids around town to the doctors and whatnot." He reached into the van and pulled out a briefcase then slammed the vehicle's door shut. "Shall we?" He gestured toward the forlorn terracotta building.

"I'd like you to clear something up first. I was talking to the secretary at St. Timothy Church and she mentioned you never worked there. Said there's a Father Clancy at Blessed Sacrament in East Hollywood, but he's elderly. I'm a bit confused."

"Checking up on me, eh?" He winked.

"Not really, it's—"

"You must be referring to Joe Clancy, a Jesuit theologian. I'm what is called a floater. You're aware of the priest shortage?" He didn't wait for her to answer. "I fill in for parishes that are in need—usually not for long—until a deacon or pastoral assistant is on board. I was at St. Tim's for such a short period of time, I don't recall ever meeting the office manager—though I'm sure she's a lovely person."

"That clears that up," Beth said as she looked down the street. "I'm not sure about this neighborhood, but the building looks like it might have promise."

"Can't expect to find everything we need right off the bat. Still, we can hope." He placed his hand on her shoulder and guided her across the worn macadam.

They paused at the building's dented steel door.

"The estate agent will be meeting us?" Beth asked.

"Couldn't make it. Gave me a key instead." Father Clancy stuck his free hand into the pocket of his neatly creased black slacks and withdrew a single brass key. He slipped it into the lock and twisted the handle. The door creaked open. He entered and clicked on a light switch.

With a wave of trepidation, Beth stepped inside. It looked as she'd expected. Fragments of broken beer bottles and tattered sheets of paper lay strewn across the cement floor. Remnants of furniture—slit cushions with stuffing hanging out, overturned battered chairs, and broken tables—littered the main space.

"Really just needs a wee bit of sprucing up. Imagine a cozy gathering place here, and over there a big, bright kitchen." The priest pointed to a shrouded corner and stepped further into the room.

Though she heard notes of joyous exuberance fill his voice, she only grunted and glared at charred bits of wood surrounded by a few overturned wooden crates. It reminded her of a campfire and wondered if it wouldn't have been better if the whole building had gone up in smoke.

"What do you think, lass?"

"To be honest, Father, I'm getting really bad vibes. I've mentioned my *fey* to you. It's telling me this isn't right. There's something ominous here. Dangerous even." She took a couple steps toward the door.

"Ah, not so fast. I've got the property listing." He lifted his battered briefcase and landed it on one of the overturned crates.

Beth moved closer to the door. Her *fey* was telling her, actually screaming at her, to get out. She reached for the door handle and pulled. A whiff of fresh air brushed her face. She glanced over her shoulder and saw him hunched over the briefcase. "I'm getting out of here," she shouted.

He spun around waving a sheet of paper. "'Twon't hurt to take a wee glance at the prospectus."

Beth swallowed her protest as the radiance dissolved from his face. She released the door and moved to his side.

"I think the price is doable with the funds I've raised."

She turned in a slow circle inspecting the room once again. Her opinion hadn't changed.

He handed her the listing form. The information printed on the sheet confirmed her suspicions. The building was old, circa 1932, and would require a boatload of money for renovations. Still focused on the listing she said, "I think we'd be wise to check out the other property before making a final decision."

"That won't be necessary."

She tilted her head toward the priest.

She caught only a glimpse of the weapon. Not able to comprehend what was happening, she whirled around and sprinted toward the door. She reached for the knob, but a current of electricity knocked her down. Her scream failed to block out the mechanical tick, tick, tick that filled her ears. She tried to move—crawl, stand, run—but her muscles felt like cement. After what seemed an eternity, the ticking ended along with the barrage of shocks. Her mind twirled like a spinning top and jumbled her thoughts into a confused muddle.

"It'll be over in a blink of an eye. Just a little prick. I promise, you won't feel a thing."

Father Clancy's voice boomed and reverberated against her eardrums. Beth squeezed her eyes shut as her muscles started to twitch. A vibrating, prickling sensation scared her until she realized she could move her fingers. A thin flicker of hope trickled and strengthened the notion of escape. But then a jolt of electricity pierced her shoulder. She grit her teeth and prayed the pain would stop as the room seemed to spin. She fought to keep the bile from rising up her throat.

"Too much for you?"

Beth mumbled.

"Speak up."

Her lips refused to move.

"Where the hell is all your pious claptrap getting you now?"

She forced her eyes open. The simple motion expended all her energy.

"Accept the inevitable. I'm in control. You, well, you're nothing more than a disposable pawn in my grand design."

Beth prayed to escape this torture chamber. Feeling as if she'd been hit by a two-by-four, or gone a couple rounds with a prizefighter, she wondered if that'd be possible. She allowed her drooping eyes to close.

"Hey, hey you." The priest nudged her with his foot. "I can't believe it. She passed out. That's going to take away all the fun."

Part of her wanted to protest, but something warned her fuzzy head to go along and pretend to be unconscious. She heard his footsteps move away and then some rustling.

A couple of minutes later, the steps started again. This time louder and closer. She sensed him standing over her. "Too bad you made nice with the wrong person. Don't take this personally, but I don't have any other choice."

She wanted to open her eyes—to look into the face of the devil—but squeezed them tighter when she felt his finger on her cheek. A featherlike touch moved along her jagged scar then brushed a lock of hair off her forehead.

"You're so beautiful. Shame there's no other way. But no use crying over collateral damage."

His voice sounded strange. It took a moment to pinpoint the difference. His accent had disappeared.

"If only you could hear me, Sibeal. Then you'd know it's all Skye Andrew's fault. Because of her, you're going to die. Of course, there's a silver lining. Your death is going to hit that bitch hard." A jubilant tone filled his voice. "You're her best friend—probably her only friend—besides that fawning assistant. She'll be history soon, too. The nanny's death was a waste. Didn't realize Andrews barely tolerated her." He noisily sighed. "But honestly, I can't complain. Along with those whores, killing her served as good practice. Unlike them, Lexi put up quite a fight. I admired her for that. She wasn't a wimp like you—not even able to take a few jolts of electricity."

The Taser's drive stun found its mark again. The excruciating sting radiated down her lower back and through her legs. Beth wanted to scream but kept her teeth clenched. Then like an answered prayer, the surge ended and so did the searing pain.

The soles of his leather shoes slapped against the cement floor as he talked to himself. She strained to decipher the muffled words. The quick staccato beat of his heels signaled he'd moved closer.

"I'm afraid, dear Sibeal, your death is going to pale to the next one. Even so, I promise, you won't be forgotten. I'll toast your memory today at lunch—to the Irish supermodel who, like a mouse craving cheese, toddled into my clever trap—may she rest in peace." A breathy giggle echoed off the moldy walls.

Beth's muscles started vibrating again. She struggled to come up with a plan, but the priest's droning prevented her from concentrating.

"I'm on the brink—the very pinnacle of my *pièce de résistance*. I've carefully laid the groundwork, and killing her will be as easy as taking candy from a baby. But instead of candy, it'll be a thousand times sweeter watching the life being squeezed out of that spoiled brat. By the time the cops get wind of your death, Andrews' spawn will be breathing her last. Then the first part of my masterful design will be gloriously completed."

Emma.

Beth's blood ran cold.

A fierce sense of determination forced the haziness to dissipate as she peeked her eyes open. A broken wooden table leg laid an arm's length away. Though her muscles still quivered and a high-pitched buzzing whirred in her ears, Beth eased her arm across the dirty floor. She grasped the piece of wood and jumped up.

He faced her with a gloved hand holding a hypodermic needle and a knife in the other hand. She barreled toward him. The makeshift weapon struck his shoulder. He spun backward and hit the ground. The needle shot from his grasp. Down for only a split-second, he sprung up waving the knife.

Beth dropped the wooden beam, skirted around a pile of debris, and collided into the remnants of a couch. A sharp pain shot through her knee. She paused a split-second.

He grabbed her arm and swung her around. She jerked away and hit the floor hard, knocking against a wooden crate. The smirk slashing his face grew wider. Beth struggled to her feet, keeping her eyes riveted on him. She snatched the rickety crate, unaware that the splintered wood scraped her hands, and brandished it like a shield. The sharp blade whacked against the crate mercilessly until it lodged between a wooden slat. She shook the crate at him, and the knife tumbled to the floor. Beth tried to run, but he caught the edge of the crate and yanked it. She held tight, though the rough wood cut her flesh. Loosening her grasp, she let go, and the motion sent him wobbling backward. Without thinking, Beth lunged and elbowed him in the ribs. She anticipated a cushion of flabby flesh but jumped backward, startled that his body felt like a beanbag cushion.

Afraid to turn around, she watched him lift his foot against the back of the battered couch. It tipped over with a dull thump. A derisive sneer crossed his face.

"Damned pampered model. You're no match for me." He ducked behind the overturned couch and rose clenching a metal pipe.

Beth dropped and slapped her hand along the floor in search of a weapon. He rushed toward her swinging the pipe. With a frantic jerk of her head, she spied the discarded table leg a few feet away. She dove, grabbed the slab of wood, and jabbed it into his stomach.

He laughed.

She swung again, this time at his face. The pipe deflected the strike as the cudgel smashed against it and shook wildly in her hands. She dropped the improvised weapon as a wave of dizziness washed over her. Though she wanted to give in to the wooziness and rising nausea, an image of Emma spurred her on. A sudden burst of adrenalin jetted through her. She leapt forward and clawed his face. At first, it seemed as if she'd ripped off pieces of skin. Bits of his beard dangled from a lopsided chin. Then, in a flash, she understood. Prosthetics and makeup.

As he fumbled for the dislodged pieces of the disguise, Beth pounced and grabbed a handful of hair. She lost her grip, realizing too late she'd pulled off a wig, and flung it away. With renewed determination, she bounded, ready to wrestle the pipe from his hand. She grappled and scraped at the piece of metal, willing to possess the strength to snatch it away but found herself unable to secure a firm hold. He jabbed the cylinder into her gut and sent her to her knees.

He pitched his body against hers, and she banged her head against the floor.

Her hands flayed, slicing the air as a haunting sense of déjà vu gripped her. With unexplainable strength, she flung her arm back and caught hold of his head. She stabbed her fingernails into his scalp, and locks of hair fell over her hands, entangling her fingers. She yanked the hair hard. He jerked away while curses filled her ears.

Beth shot up too fast. She reached for a support but found nothing. Out of the corner of her eye, she glimpsed a blur of the pipe. Darkness engulfed her as she crumbled to the floor.

CHAPTER FORTY-EIGHT

Maria José Diaz peered at her watch. Only a minute had ticked by since the last time she checked the digital face. She unwrapped the foil from a ham and cheese sandwich, took a bite, and chewed. She'd known all along that Beth Getty was the model, Sibeal, the one who made the ads on TV against drunk driving. She smiled to herself remembering how sweet she'd been, obviously not a victim of a Hollywood ego.

She raised a forkful of green salad, and a sliver of sliced apple rolled off and landed on the paper napkin spread across her lap. With a roll of her eyes, she dropped the fork on top of the salad, tossed the napkin on the table, and rushed out of the tiny staff room.

"As usual, my curiosity has gotten the best of me. I might as well walk next door and just peek inside. Anyway, the fresh air will do me good," Maria José mumbled. She grabbed the cardigan off the back of a chair, slipped into the sweater, stepped outside, and locked the entrance to the dry cleaners.

She hurried across the broken blacktop and paused at the former warehouse door. After taking a deep breath, she raised her balled hand to knock but instead unfolded her fingers and grasped the handle. It turned. She cracked the door open. As she faced the spacious room, Maria José waited a moment for her eyes to adjust to the dim light.

She shaped her mouth into what she hoped would be a friendly smile and stepped inside. The smile faded as her breath died in the base of her throat. The scene beyond her seemed impossible.

A priest brandishing a knife.

She shrieked realizing the knife was aimed at Beth.

With a jerk of his head, the priest faced her. Outlandishly posed, reddish hair flopped across his forehead while half of his face appeared natural, rounded and smooth, but the other side looked a horror with patchy, discolored skin and oddly deflated. The beard, full and lush, gave way to only a few strands of graying whiskers on the deformed side, which sprouted from a distorted chin.

He glared at Maria José for a split-second then raised his arm and thrust the blade downward.

"No!" Horrified and mesmerized at the same time, Maria José stepped backward and brushed against the door.

He raised the knife above his head. A streak of blood colored its steely edge. He cursed under his breath then jumped up, belying his heavy girth.

Though she craved to escape, she remained frozen like a captive under his gaze. She tensed, bracing for the searing pain the knife would inflict.

The priest grabbed a briefcase; then, with a couple long strides, he reached her. He elbowed her in the chest, shoving her away from the door. She stumbled and fell to the floor. A fury of indignation flew through her and purged her fear.

"How dare you," she hissed. Maria José scrambled to her knees but froze when he slashed the knife near her face. She flinched as the steel blade pressed against her cheek. The pale eyes of the misaligned face bore into her. The seconds the knife touched her skin seemed an eternity until he abruptly pivoted away and disappeared through the doorway. The obscenity he uttered rang in her ears as an icy chill engulfed her. She grasped her sweater and squeezed the woollen material.

As the thumping in her heart began to slow, though still a bit shaky, she pulled herself up by grabbing onto the curved back of an overturned couch. A sharp pain shot through her hip. She hobbled a few steps then stopped short of reaching Beth. She gulped a mouthful of air and forced herself to look.

Beth lay on her stomach with the top of her head facing Maria José. A red splotch ballooned across Beth's thin, cotton blouse. She grit her teeth and sank to her knees. "*Ay Dios Santo Bendito y la Virgen y las Santísima Trinidad*," she whispered. A frown sprung to her face as she noticed a prong stuck into Beth's neck and another in her hip. Both were fastened to thread-like, coiled wires attached to a small electrical-looking black package.

She reached into the pocket of her full skirt and pulled out a cell phone. As her fingers fumbled on the keyboard, she strained to hear something—a puff of breath, a moan, a whisper—but heard nothing. She waited another second then pressed the numbers on the phone. After giving the emergency operator all the pertinent information, she folded her hands.

"Sibeal," she whispered. She crouched next to Beth's ear and whispered the name again.

She brushed her fingertips along the nape of Beth's neck and smoothed her tangled locks.

Beth's head moved.

Relief flooded Maria José. "*Mi querida*. Help is on the way."

"Maria José?" Beth whispered.

"Shhh." The older woman slipped out of her cardigan and folded it twice. With a gentle lift of Beth's head, she placed the sweater under her cheek.

Beth winced. She raised her hand and tried to touch her shoulder.

Maria José focused on the blood soaked spot on Beth's blouse. "Lie still. I'm going to stop the bleeding." She shrugged out of her smock, tucked the short sleeves in, and folded the cotton fabric several times into a tight rectangle. She involuntarily shook as a sharp pain blasted down her leg, but Maria José ignored the fiery spasms. Instead, she focused on the exuding wound as she pressed the compress on Beth's shoulder with a firm grip. "The paramedics will be here soon."

"Call my husband." Beth's voice sounded a raspy whisper.

"When the ambulance arrives."

"Call him now. Tell him it's Father Clancy. Emma's next."

Maria José squinted then remembered the delivery ticket. The smock's pocket holding it faced her. She freed the slip of paper and found the line requesting a work number. Once again, she fished inside her skirt's pocket for her phone.

CHAPTER FORTY-NINE

Shane forced all thoughts from his mind, except one—to get to Beth. As he sped along the freeway toward CA Hospital Medical Center, he ignored the churning in his stomach and concentrated on the shrill wailing of his cruiser's siren. He'd been instructed to get to the hospital ASAP. Beth had been involved in an accident.

Shane exhaled sharply as he pulled into the crammed emergency room parking lot and inched down the lanes in search of a spot. He struggled to rein in his emotions, realizing if he fell to pieces, he wouldn't be worth a damn, and that's the last thing he wanted. Impatiently, he rested his fist against the horn as he waited for a car to back out of a space. After what seemed like fifteen minutes, he swung into it, parked, and jumped out of the car. He took quick, purposeful steps in the direction of the ER entrance, passed through the sliding glass door, and walked into the waiting room. Collins stood at the reception desk. As if instinctively, he turned and met Shane's eyes.

"Any word?" Shane asked.

"I was with Beth when the medics brought her in. The good news is she's gonna be okay." Collins laid a hand on Shane's arm. "The wound isn't deep and missed the main arteries."

"A car wreck?"

"You don't know?"

Shane stared blankly.

Collins ushered him toward the two closest unoccupied chairs. Shane sat on the seat's edge as Collins squatted in front of him. "She's in surgery now. The knife didn't go in very deep—it's not much more than a surface wound—once it's irrigated and stitched up, she'll be good as new."

Shane had enough. He knew Collins was trying to reassure him, but his words were having the opposite effect. "What the hell happened?"

Collins stood, took a deep breath, and then dropped into the chair next to Shane. "I don't know the whole story. Only what one of the paramedics told me. Apparently, Beth was attacked in an old, abandoned warehouse she was supposed to be checking out as a possible site for some kinda shelter."

"One of her projects," Shane muttered.

"A lady who works nearby found her. Probably saved Beth's life. She's over there." Collins nodded in the direction of Maria José who sat with her hands folded and eyes closed as if lost in prayer.

Shane shot up.

"One other thing. Beth's attacker was a priest. Or rather someone disguised as a priest—according to the witness—Maria José Diaz."

Shane reclaimed his chair and folded his arms. The threads of the case, woven haphazardly, barely intersected at all. He conceded that ever since Lexi's death and Darla's attack, the one commonality appeared to be Kenny Weston. *If that's true, why attack Beth,* his mind raced. *Did he guess Skye had told her about their affair? Or had Skye's infidelity triggered all these attacks—did she stand at the heart of the puzzle?*

Collins placed a hand on Shane's shoulder. "Resnick wants you off the case."

"Like hell. I swear to God, Collins, I'm gonna get this guy if it the last thing I do."

"You can't be objective. That's why you've been reassigned to the Foster case. Grabowski's taking your place. He's a damn good detective. We'll get him. I promise."

Shane fingered his dimpled chin before standing. He ambled toward the reception desk. After inquiring about Beth, he was told, as Collins had said, she was in surgery. The nurse advised him to wait in the surgical wing.

He headed toward the elevator but stopped and concentrated on Maria's José. He changed course and walked toward her. With a gentle touch, he rested his hand on her stooped shoulder. She fluttered her eyes open.

"Excuse me, Mrs. Diaz. I'm Shane Dalton. You know what happened to my wife?"

"Detective." She rose.

He placed his hand under her elbow and steered her toward the relative privacy near the glass entrance. She hobbled and winced a couple of times.

"You're hurt," Shane said. "I'll get you a wheelchair."

"It's nothing. They'll get to me soon enough." She jutted her chin in the direction of the reception desk. "Your wife is so brave. The way she begged me to contact you through such fierce pain was—"

"Contact me about what?"

"Oh dear." She touched the window for support. Shane wrapped his arm around her shoulders and steadied her. "When I couldn't reach you, I explained the situation to the operator. She asked all kinds of questions, but I didn't know anything more than what Beth told me. You were supposed to get the message right away. *Mio Dio*, I pray it's not too late." The woman's dark eyes clouded.

"Too late?"

"You didn't get the message?"

Shane shook his head.

A sense of urgency filled her voice. "It's Father Clancy. He's going after Emma next."

CHAPTER FIFTY

"Good of you to stop by, Father." Zach moved deeper into his library. "Emma's in the kitchen helping with icing a cake."

Father Clancy looked away from the book in his hand. "Hope you don't mind. Couldn't resist when I saw it on the shelf. A first edition?" He closed the volume of "Great Expectations" and handed it to Zach.

"One of my prized possessions." Zach brushed his fingertip across the worn leather cover and returned it to the shelf. "Emma's still broken up over Lexi, and her mother taking off for Baltimore hasn't helped any. With the help of Alma, we've been able to ease her sorrow a little."

"Alma?" The priest settled into a chair.

"Alma Perez. My extraordinary personal chef. She's been a real life-saver ever since volunteering to take over nanny duty. That is until Skye has time to hire a new one. It's worked out pretty good since Alma is crazy about Emma. And the kid loves her too."

"Is your wife also one of Alma's fans?"

"Skye? Hell, no." Zach paused a second. "Um, excuse my French, Father. But my wife doesn't seem to care much about anyone on my staff. Takes their services for granted. But, what strikes me as weird is the tight relationship she has with her assistant." He shrugged. "She's in the hospital. Maybe you could send up a prayer for her?"

"Of course, me boy. Not a problem."

Sofia entered the room carrying a porcelain tea service on a silver tray.

"How delightful." Father Clancy attempted to rise but only managed to get halfway up before easing back into the seat.

Sofia offered him a half-smile. She placed the tray on top of a black walnut credenza, and with an economy of motion, poured him a cup of the piping hot tea.

Father Clancy reached for the cup and saucer on which Sofia had tucked a piece of shortbread. She glanced at Zach. He shook his head. "Anything else I can get you?" Sofia asked with a quick glance at the priest.

"I detect a slight accent," Father Clancy said. "Have you also immigrated to this grand country?"

"I have a student visa. I'm completing my graduate studies. Engineering."

"Will wonders cease?" Father Clancy raised the cup. "A pretty girl like you an engineer? I assume you and Lexi were close."

Sofia nodded then headed away. Before she reached the door, Emma bounded into the room and ran into Zach's outstretched arms. He kissed the top of her head.

"Look who's here," Zach said.

A tiny smile turned up the corners of her mouth as she spied the priest.

"I told you I'd be visiting. Did you remember?" Father Clancy asked with a wink.

Her ponytail bounced as Emma moved her head up and down.

"If I recall, there's something very special you wanted to show me?"

Emma's eyes grew big as she looked at Zach. "Please, please, please can I show Father Clancy the hobby room?"

"Well, honey. I'm sorta busy since I have to leave for a meeting in a few minutes. I bet Father would like to see the ballet steps you've just learned." Zach noticed her lip tremble and the too familiar gloom claim her tiny face. "Wow! I just got a great idea." He stooped down and brushed a few stray hairs from her cheek. "Why don't you show the good padre our fascinating *le mie bellezze* collection?"

"I can?" She bubbled. "I can tell him all about the—you know what?"

"Who better? You're almost as good an expert as me." Zach walked around the desk, opened a drawer, and removed a key. He pressed it into her small hand then glanced at the priest. "I leave you in my daughter's capable hands." Zach grabbed a folder off the desk and leaned against its sturdy edge. He flipped open the file and riffled through a couple of papers. A moment later, he looked up, surprised that they'd already exited the room.

***

Zach heard the banging all the way in the library. He'd just hung up the phone, furious his meeting with the director had been postponed. His significant concerns regarding the script warranted immediate action, not a delay. He ignored the pounding on the front door as he poured two fingers of Scotch. But then he heard the yelling. He forgot the drink as he raced toward the commotion. Halfway to the foyer, Sofia met him, obviously distraught, as she called out words he didn't understand; she'd reverted to her original tongue. Two men followed on her heels—Detectives Dalton and Collins.

"What's going on?" Zach demanded.

"Emma may be in danger. Where is she?" Shane asked.

"Emma?" Zach narrowed his eyes in confusion. "She's fine. Upstairs with a priest friend."

"Dammit," Shane said through clenched teeth. He headed toward the grand stairway.

"Clancy tried to kill Beth," Collins said. "Emma's next."

Collins' words didn't make sense. It took a second for them to register, but when they did, Zach felt as if he'd been punched in the gut. "Come on," Zach ordered.

The detectives followed as Zach sprinted down a corridor. He barely stopped as he jerked open a door and stepped inside the elevator. The two detectives followed and squeezed within the narrow tube. A moment later, the door flashed open and led them onto the third floor. Zach steered them down a narrow, dimly lit hallway.

Though Zach turned the handle, Shane edged in front and nudged the door open. Zach wanted to recoil from the scene unfolded in front of him. Overturned aquariums ravished on the floor, a couple of mice scurried across an upended table, and the sound of insects buzzed in his ears. He almost stepped on a black snake as it slinked underfoot. All of that disappeared the instant he spied Emma. A python's long, sinewy body was entwined around the little girl.

Shane reached for the snake.

"Stand back." Zach pushed ahead of the detectives. Unaware of broken shards of glass or poisonous tarantulas, he raced through the debris and grabbed a red canister off a shelf. Sprinting back to Emma's side, he released the pin and aimed the nozzle of the CO_2 fire extinguisher at the python. A profusion of white foam blasted forth and covered the constricting reptile as the freezing chemicals rendered the snake impotent. With a firm grasp, Zach pulled the paralyzed snake off Emma. He dropped it into one of the few intact aquariums.

Shane tilted Emma's head back and pressed his mouth against hers in a resuscitation attempt. Collins spoke into his radio as his eyes flicked along the upheaval as if searching for evidence left behind by the murderous priest.

Emma flitted her eyes open, and Shane pulled back listening to the sound of her uneven breaths. She stretched out her arm in a frantic motion and whispered, "Zach."

Zach fell to his knees. He grasped her tiny hand and kissed it.

CHAPTER FIFTY-ONE

TUESDAY, MAY 13ᵗʰ

"Darla's dead," Mike whispered.

Beth sucked in a mouthful of air.

"Her parents took her off life support. The doctors said she was brain-dead, but I don't know maybe..."

Beth reached for his hand and squeezed it. She didn't know any words that could ease his pain.

Before Mike entered the sterile hospital room, she'd been irritable and uncomfortable, confined by the white sheet stretched across her. She longed for the warmth of home and the feel of Shane's body next to hers. Curled up with one of the kittens on the sofa would help her wounds heal quicker than spending day after day in the hospital. Then Mike entered the room, and the sorrowful gaze in his eyes told her something was wrong. His emotionally choked voice had pried Beth free from her self-wallowing.

Confused as to why Shane hadn't told her the tragic news, she figured he probably didn't know yet. Ever since landing in the hospital, he'd been treating her with kid gloves and behaving like she was an invalid. She hated that he'd become tight-lipped; trying to get information from him had become nearly impossible. Deep down, she realized it was his way of protecting her, but even so, she didn't like it.

"It must have been the most difficult decision Darla's parents ever made." She looked into his blood-shot eyes. "Even if Darla did live, she'd never be the same. Seems only the machines were keeping her alive, dear boy."

Mike stared straight ahead.

"Without faith nothing makes sense. We may not understand now. But surely, one day all will be made clear to us," Beth said.

"That might comfort you. But the only thing I want is for that bastard to fry. Be honest Beth; you must wanna see him sent straight to hell. Look at what he did to you."

At first, she had wanted an eye for an eye justice. But now, she felt a pity so deep she couldn't even try to describe it to Mike.

"Another life stolen. Poor Darla." Beth blinked back tears. "I'm convinced Skye's death is the only thing that will stop that bloodthirsty animal."

"Skye." He spat out the name. "Don't you mean she's the reason for all these killings?"

"Seems so."

"You know why, don't you?" He peered at the window.

Beth wished she did know the killer's motive. Why would someone want to destroy Skye so completely before killing her?

"I don't really give a damn," Mike continued. "Knowing the reason won't bring back Lexi or Darla. It's going to hit Sofia hard. She and Darla were friends."

"Sofia Fedoruk?"

He nodded. "Actually, it was Sofia who talked me out of doing something crazy. With Lexi's murder and Darla being poisoned in the hospital, I was like losing my mind. I couldn't think straight. Sofia talked sense to me."

"Thank God for Sofia."

"You know about Darla?" Shane's voice sounded.

Wrenched free from their intense moment of intimacy, both of them jerked, startled by Shane's unexpected voice.

"When is it going to end?" Beth asked.

Mike crossed his arms and faced Shane. "Whoever's doing this is making the LASD look like a bunch of jack-asses. Can't even protect your own wife from this piece of scum. When are you people going to start doing your job?"

She noticed the muscles in Shane's jaw tighten. Instead of defending his efforts, he stared at Mike.

"I thought as much. Damn incompetents." Mike brushed passed Shane and departed from the room.

"He's beside himself with grief," Beth said.

Shane dropped on the edge of the bed and reached for her hand. "We should've been able to nab the guy before it ever came to this. Like Alder said, there's no excuse." He inhaled sharply. "Anyway, I'm about to hand in my resignation."

She held her tongue, afraid she'd only make matters worse if she confronted him. After a moment of consideration, she said, "You've wanted to resign for some time."

"The time's now. They have me working some cold case. It happened so long ago, the killer's probably six feet under by now. Anyway, I've spoken to a buddy, and he's going to do a bit of sniffing around. Try to put in a good word with some major construction companies."

"I'll support any decision you make. But, I was hoping you'd keep working until—"

"There's an arrest." He stood and moved toward the window but didn't look outside. "They've put a rush on the DNA found under your fingernails. May have the results in a couple of days. The good news is Weston's attorney agreed to a sample. Collins is probably collecting Weston's DNA now. I was convinced it'd be a match, but now I'm not so sure. Why the hell would Weston want to kill Emma?"

He leaned against the windowsill. The light streaming into the room caused a soft radiance to engulf his figure. Beth recognized it as his aura. Pure, brilliant, and strong. She couldn't believe he'd throw in the towel when they were so close. The puzzle pieces were finally starting to fit together. She pursed her lips and remembered the depth of his anguish over her being one of the killer's targets.

Instead of coming out of the anesthesia peacefully, Beth had awakened in a frenzy, overcome with panic that Emma had been hurt. Shane soothed her with calming words. Praised her for the message that had saved the little girl's life. Even so, she'd sensed the torment gripping his soul. She'd never forget the disgust twisting his face when he'd explained the perpetrator hadn't used a Taser but had knocked Emma out with a mild sedative he'd mixed into her juice box before unleashing Zach's menagerie.

"Will the DNA found under my fingernails prove I'm right?"

"It'll supply us with a store of information."

"Including the sex of the murderer?" Beth hit the button, raised the bed into a sitting position, and gasped when the pillow brushed her injured shoulder. He moved closer, and his pained expression unnerved her. "I'm fine, *grá a chroí*. In two weeks, the stitches come out. Remember, darlin', a light heart lives long. In a few days, I'll be right as rain."

He pressed his lips into a tight line.

"You haven't answered my question. Will the DNA analysis prove that Father Clancy is, in fact, a woman?"

"It will identify the sex."

"What a master of disguise." She tilted her head and pulled the sheet toward her chin. "She had me fooled. But once I tore away a piece of the mask, it became obvious. The long locks and the feminine curve to the cheek."

"Don't place all your hope in the DNA. We won't know any specifics regarding identity unless the profile has been recorded in a criminal file."

She nodded absently. "The news of Darla's death will devastate Skye."

"You'll be there for her," Shane said.

"Skye hasn't been herself since the incident with Emma."

From her hospital bed, Beth had called and texted Skye, offering comfort and urging her to be cautious. But it was Zach who'd really stepped up to the plate. He'd come up with a brilliant plan for the three of them to be together by securing a rental property in a posh Baltimore suburb where they'd live until Skye finished filming. With Skye and Zach on the same page, they were determined to fill Emma's days with a myriad of activities—trips to museums, parks, the zoo—until all of her nightmares vanished.

"Skye's strong. She'll bounce back. Look, I gotta go." He kissed her forehead. "I'll be back tomorrow morning. Your discharge is scheduled for ten."

"If the DNA proves I'm right, then we know who committed all of these crimes. It's too horrible to imagine those poor teenagers were just a source for a mad killer to practice her trade so she'd be successful on taking out everyone Skye holds near and dear. There's only one person who hates Skye that much."

"If you're right, we'll have to set a trap for her."

"In Baltimore."

Shane nodded. "In Baltimore."

CHAPTER FIFTY-TWO

FRIDAY, MAY 16th

Beth tapped on the opened door before entering the hospital room. Maria José's eyes fluttered open, and a sense of expectancy claimed her face as Beth reached the bed.

"Did I wake you?" A cadence of concern filled Beth's voice.

"No. Just resting my eyes."

"If you'd rather take a nap, I can come back later."

"Oh no, *mi querida*, your presence is like a healing balm."

Beth glanced at the flowers nestled in the crook of her arm. "These are for you." She handed Maria José the bouquet of white roses.

"Beautiful." Maria José inhaled the delicate fragrance.

"I ran into Pedro in the lobby yesterday. Told me they're your favorites. He also told me about his wife and your five grandchildren. Seems to be a wonderful family man and a loving son. Definitely a brilliant reflection on you."

Maria José gazed at the roses lying against her chest. "He reminds me so much of his father, may God rest his soul." She paused a moment then spoke, her voice no louder than a whisper. "Pedro is a great comfort. I couldn't run the dry cleaner without his help."

She raised her face, and Beth noticed her eyes glisten. "I better do something with the flowers."

Maria José took a quick sniff then handed Beth the bouquet. Beth busied herself by positioning them, one long stem after another, inside a glass vase abandoned by the sink. After filling the vase with water, she lifted the arrangement in Maria José's direction.

"Brava." Maria José clapped her hands.

Beth placed the vase on the nightstand then sat in a nearby chair. Maria José had suffered a cracked pelvis, and normally Beth's sense of guilt would've paralyzed her, but not this time. Maria José's brave actions had saved her life. Of that, she was extremely grateful and had elevated the older woman to a place of honor and respect in her heart.

"How are you holding up?" Maria José asked.

"Grand. Just grand," Beth said. "The incision is a wee bit sore. Other than that, I couldn't be better." She reached into her handbag. "I have a photograph of the kittens I told you about." She pulled out the 5x7 glossy and handed the print to Maria José. "While I was in hospital, Shane contacted the Cute Cat Rescue. The poor fellow didn't know the first thing about how to take care of a litter of kittens. Plus, he's got awful allergies."

The older woman pursed her lips and shook her head in sympathy.

"A volunteer stopped by our house and saved the day. She took the whole lot of them back to the shelter. But, you'll never believe what happened."

Though Maria José hadn't said a word, her intent gaze told Beth she was caught up in the tale.

"Skye telephoned yesterday. She'd contacted the rescue group and told them she wants to adopt the entire litter for Emma. So this morning, I stopped by the shelter, took a portrait of each kitten, and emailed them to Emma. She's been trying to come up with names. I thought if Emma could see their sweet faces, it would make her job easier and a lot more fun."

Maria José broke out into a jubilant smile—one that started at her eyes, touched her cheeks, and ended with her lips. If only she'd had the opportunity to select a surrogate mother, Beth mused, Maria José would be her pick.

"Now onto serious matters." Beth folded her hands in her lap.

"You've gotten results from the DNA test?"

Beth nodded. "I had to rush right over. I couldn't keep the news bottled up or I'd just explode. The perp's gender has been verified, certified, and notarized." She paused a whole two seconds. "Female."

Maria José shot up in the bed. "I knew it. The minute I saw those hands—even if one was gripping a knife—I knew they couldn't belong to a man. Even a soft, pampered man."

"My *fey's* been sending me the strongest vibes."

"Truly a blessed gift."

"Never felt anything this intense before." Beth lowered her voice. "I know who attacked us."

Maria José let out a breathy gasp.

"A person driven by pure hatred with a perverted lust for revenge." Beth glanced at Maria José who'd closed her eyes. Beth guessed she dozed off—a typical side effect from heavy doses of painkillers. She rose and took a couple steps away from the bed.

"Beth."

She stopped midway from the door.

"I've just been praying for the soul of this woman. But if her heart is so consumed with evil, how can it be anything more than a petrified stone—lifeless and hardened by hate and animosity—is there anything that can be done to redeem her?"

"I'm not sure, but we have to hold firm to our faith." Beth paused taken by the sorrowful look filling the woman's face. "Later today, Shane and I are flying to Baltimore. With a bit of luck, we'll end this murdering rampage once and for all."

CHAPTER FIFTY-THREE

SATURDAY, MAY 17ᵗʰ

The overcast morning turned out to be an even drearier afternoon as a light sprinkle fell on the Pimlico Race Course. Even so, the infield teemed full of revelers as a band rocked in full throttle and entertained the boisterous crowd. Nor had the rain dampened the spirits of the spectators packed in the stands as they waited for the start of Maryland's biggest race of the year—The Preakness Stakes—the second jewel of the Triple Crown.

The damp, misty air, the jockeys' silks, and the magnificent thoroughbreds triggered memories and filled Beth with a longing for home. As she waited for Shane at the causeway next to the Jockey Club, she watched the horses thunder around the track. The breathtaking grandeur of the spirited equines would normally monopolize her every care and emotion, but not today.

Her thoughts drifted back to the night before. She and Shane had taken an airport taxi to the palatial estate Zach had somehow wrangled as a temporary dwelling fifteen miles west of the city. In the comfortable great room, Skye sat next to Zach on a sleek, leather couch with their hips touching and hands entwined as they made small talk and offered them cocktails. She'd sat on a hassock with her back to the massive stone fireplace.

As Beth sipped a gin and tonic, Emma had burst into the room. She clutched an oversized picture book and climbed onto Zach's lap. By the time Alma Perez entered the room, a bit out of breath, Zach's clear voice rang, though a bit over dramatic, as he read the book's simplistic text. He pointed to the lavish illustrations, but Emma kept her eyes glued on him. Beth's worst fear had been that Emma would still be in a state of shock, but it seemed the little girl had made a remarkable recovery.

Before Zach had finished reading the book, Beth slipped out of the room and headed to the ornate grand foyer. She figured this was as good a time as any to present Emma with a special gift that had been a spur of the moment idea. She'd grasped the handle of the sturdy cat carrier.

Shane had suffered miserably during the flight to the East coast with the cat carrier tucked under the seat, but he couldn't hide his elation as Emma's face lit up with delight when Beth placed the pure white kitten, from the rescued litter, into the little girl's cupped hands. For a fleeting moment, all thoughts of deceit, murder, and grief were forgotten while they'd watched Emma cuddle and encourage the lively antics of a very curious feline. When the kitten fell asleep in the child's lap, Alma took over. Fifteen minutes later, she and Emma, with the kitten in tow, left the house for the pet supply store.

No sooner had the door shut behind them that Beth sensed the joy being sucked out of the room. The air had taken on a heavy, ominous dimension, weighing them down, and the easy conviviality had been replaced by somber, mournful expressions.

"I've come to grips with Darla's death," Skye had said keeping her voice steady. "I'm willing to do anything to find out who did this vicious deed."

"If you're sincere, there are a few things we need to clear up before moving forward."

Shane set the ground rules, which really only consisted of one—complete honesty.

Zach and Skye had nodded in agreement.

But Beth's *fey* sensed something different—the Greysons had secrets—secrets better kept hidden for the sake of their precarious marriage. During the long flight, she and Shane had discussed the delicate nature of the couples' infidelities and couldn't come up with a subtle way to broach the subject. The direct way, it had seemed, was the only way.

"We believe Skye has always been the killer's main objective. Lexi, Darla, Beth, and Emma, were stepping-stones leading the way. As significant people in your life—those who you loved and cherished, and depended on, became pivotal targets and had to be eliminated. You," Shane said glancing at Skye, "had to be broken. Psychologically and emotionally destroyed. Then it would be your turn."

Skye had pressed her hand over her mouth while Zach wrapped his arm around her shoulders and drew her even closer.

"Why would someone want to destroy you?" Shane asked.

Beth noticed a look of confusion cross Skye's face. "I don't know," Skye said. "I'm a good person. I don't try to hurt anyone."

Shane fingered the cleft in his chin. "You're not the type to deliberately hurt someone."

"Of course not." She rested her head on Zach's shoulder.

"But sometimes the people closest to us, we hurt the most. Take Zach, for example. Have you ever deceived him?"

As the bloom faded from Skye's cheeks, Beth realized Skye was beginning to put two and two together.

"Quit with the twenty questions, Shane. Just spit it out," Skye retorted pulling away from Zach.

Shane shifted in his seat. "About four years ago, you had an affair with a married man. Kenny Weston."

"Weston?" Zach snapped his head in Skye's direction. "You and that poor excuse for an artist had a thing going on? Good God, Skye. He's a pompous ass. All that pretentious gibberish about abstract expressionism and post-modern claptrap. I can't believe you'd go for a windbag like that." He exhaled loudly then shook his head. "I should've guessed. After all, he did those crappy paintings in your house."

Skye slid further away from him.

"When Weston's wife found out, the affair fizzled," Shane continued. "Then you married Zach. But that's not the end of the story. A few months ago, you two hooked up again."

Beth had wanted to flee. She hated this level of confrontation, but even so, the truth needed to surface. She'd stared at Zach. His face resembled a granite mask empty of emotion. She'd gripped her hands in her lap and looking down, noticed her knuckles had turned white. Though she tried to relax, she'd only clasped them tighter causing her fingers to ache.

"I'm not judging anyone. But someone has judged you, Skye. Found you to be guilty as sin. And that person decided to punish you to the extreme," Shane said.

"Oh my God!" Skye jumped up from the couch. "Her? That bitch is behind all this? She's the one who killed Darla? Tried to kill my Emma?" She paced across the floor and stopped in front of Beth. She flung her arms open. "I'm so sorry it's my fault you were stabbed. Can you ever forgive me?"

Beth had jumped up and grabbed her. Held her close. Whispered reassuring words into her friend's ear, but Skye's wails seemed to shake the very walls.

Beth shook her head, trying to dislodge the emotionally charged memory as people rushed past on their way to place bets and find their seats for the day. Part of her wanted to be swept up in the excitement, but more important objectives had to supersede even this notable event. She turned toward the window overlooking the racecourse. Skye and Kenny had been so foolish believing their heedless infidelities wouldn't affect anyone—supposing no one would be hurt.

"Penny for your thoughts." Shane's voice dislodged the thoughts spinning through her mind.

"Just thinking about last night."

"Remind me when I'm looking for a new career to skip the idea of being a mediator. What a blowout."

"At least it cleared the air between them. I wish Zach would've had the guts to tell Skye about his affair with Lexi. I bet that's why he forgave her so quickly. He's just as guilty, if not more."

"You mean the baby?"

She nodded.

"Got a text from Zach." He clutched his phone. "They're here. Hopefully, this will work out the easy way." He glanced at his watch. "I'm meeting the Baltimore Police Chief in about ten minutes. Don't want to step on anybody's toes; plus we'll need their support. Zach's going with me. I tried to talk him out of it but..." Shane rubbed his right temple. "We won't be gone long. Half-hour tops."

"I've talked to Skye until I was blue in the face. For the life of me, I can't imagine why she wants to attend the *feckin'* Preakness party. After all, there's the possibility she'll wind up face to face with the woman who tried to kill her daughter."

"That's exactly why. To show Maiah she's not afraid."

"Show her nothing but foolhardiness, I'd say."

Shane grasped Beth's wrist. "Remember, Skye is never to be left alone. Period."

***

"Welcome to the Weston Preakness Party," said a uniformed racecourse employee outside the entrance leading into *The Final Stretch Restaurant*. After Skye handed her the invitation, the stout woman who wore a large artificial Black Eyed Susan pinned to her lapel, scanned the list of names on a clipboard, and then penned a quick mark. The woman beamed as if she'd just realized who stood before her. She gushed something about a great honor as Skye lifted her chin and hurried through the opened doors. Beth thanked the woman who handed back the invitation. Though she tried to mask her rising vexation, she frowned as her *fey* warned a caution. She took another quick glance at the invitation before slipping it into her straw clutch, amazed that Skye wouldn't concede how dangerous their presence might turn out to be.

Ebullient swells of melodic strains floated through the air and filled Beth's ears. She hurried inside, and the vastness of the room surprised her. The orchestra boasted an abundance of brass and strings and was assembled on a raised platform occupying the room's furthest corner. The area, normally used as a dining room, lacked the usual paraphilia suitable for a racing establishment. Apparently, it had been reconfigured for the party. Hardly a remnant remained, save for the betting machines lined against one wall, a row of television screens streaming the races, and the bank of windows that overlooked the track. Though only a dim light flowed through the glass, the overhead chandeliers dispelled the murkiness by casting a clean, inviting glow.

Skye stood akimbo on the periphery of the festivities. Beth reached her and, without a word, linked her arm with Skye's. Though Skye gave a half-hearted tug as if trying to free herself, she patted Beth's hand with her free one.

Beth scanned the room and noticed a well-stocked bar along the back wall, which faced a long buffet table where steam rose from stainless steel vats. Rich linen-draped tables filled more than half the room and held dramatic floral arrangements featuring profusions of golden flowers with button-like black centers. She noticed a doorway near the bar and guessed it led to the kitchen. A handful of twosomes glided along the dance floor.

The pair moved deeper into the room and sidestepped guests who mingled in little clusters where lively conversations bubbled like their champagne-filled crystal flutes.

"How're you holding up?" Beth asked.

"Better than I anticipated. Even if it did just hit me that we're both targets here."

"No worries, Skye. The lads will be back soon."

Skye abruptly halted and pulled against Beth's grip. She followed Skye's gaze, which landed on a woman dressed in a lacy black silk dress. Tall and slender, the woman's skin glowed under a warm tan, which was further accentuated by her shoulder-length blond hair. A broad-brimmed hat adorned with a garland band of Black-Eyed Susans set off the hat's ebony fabric and cast a shadow across her face. She held a wine glass in a black satin-gloved hand and moved with easy, fluid steps. The woman painted a picture of understated grace: polished, sophisticated, elegant. She recognized her instantly. Maiah Weston.

Before Beth could utter a word, a hand brushed her shoulder. She shuddered as white-hot pain seared down her back.

"Oh my God, Beth. Are you alright?"

After inhaling sharply, she was able to speak. "Trey?" She noticed he held the same type of gold embossed invitation that Skye had received from Kenny. "Oh, I'm fine. Just suffering a wee bit of a sore shoulder."

"I'm surprised to see you here," Skye said pulling her arm free and slipping it through Trey's. She kissed his cheek. "I'm so sorry about Lexi," she whispered in his ear.

"I heard about Darla. I'm so sorry. I didn't know her well, but Lexi valued her as a close friend." He pulled Skye close and hugged her.

"It's been hard for all of us," Skye said glancing at Beth. She turned to Trey and held onto his arm.

"I was surprised Kenny invited me," Trey said to Skye. "Pretty ritzy affair. I'm certainly not dressed for the occasion."

"You look fine." Skye brushed the front of his pale yellow Oxford shirt. With the sleeves rolled up to his elbows, he'd tucked the shirt into a pair of faded jeans.

"Won't matter since I'm not staying long. Not up for a party. Anyway, my family's here." He thumbed in the direction of the glass wall.

Skye faced him. "You're not really okay, are you?" A concerned tone filled Skye's voice, one that Beth hadn't quite gotten accustomed to yet.

"It's tough." He blinked a few times. "Seems as if both of us are sharing the same pain."

Skye leaned in closer to him.

"Shane may be making an arrest, soon," Beth said.

Trey's eyes widened.

"We have a strong lead," Beth said. "If we can get a DNA sample, we'd know for sure."

The two women eyed each other. Skye draped her arms around his neck and whispered, "Would you like to help bring that vicious killer to justice?"

"More than anything. What can I do?" He searched her face.

"Real simple." Skye released Trey, though her hand lingered next to his. "See that woman over there?" She nodded her chin in Maiah's direction.

"Mrs. Weston?"

"Think you could get hold of her wine glass when she's finished?" Beth asked.

"That shouldn't be hard. But why? You don't think she's got anything to do with the murders?" He looked at Beth with questioning eyes.

"If you could get hold of that glass, it could really help Shane. He might even be able to arrest the responsible person."

"Well?" Skye squeezed his arm.

"I'll give it a go. After all, nothing ventured, nothing gained." He offered them a wink. A few strides landed him at Maiah's side.

Trey continued to stand there for a good forty-five seconds with his hands stuck into his pockets. He didn't interrupt but rather seemed to be bidding his time. Still talking, Maiah half-turned, then noticing the young man, took on a surprised but pleased expression.

Beth sidestepped Maiah and Trey but lingered close enough to hear the conversation. Skye stood a few feet away, her eyes glued to the door, as if willing Zach to walk through. She'd assured Beth that she'd keep her distance from Maiah when they'd hatched the scheme to try to steal the wine glass. Not knowing how they'd do it, Trey showing up had been a godsend.

A waiter proffering a well-stocked tray offered Beth a drink. Though garnished with an orange slice and a cherry, the scent of alcohol filled Beth's nostrils. She waved the waiter off and moved a step closer to Trey.

"I'm so pleased you made it to the party," Maiah said. "Kenny told me about your loss. I'm sorry." She rested a gloved hand on his shoulder.

"Thanks. I was surprised you guys invited me to such a special event. Oh, congratulations on winning the Derby. You have a terrific horse."

"Estella Blue is magnificent. Even so, we're on pins and needles. But I have faith in our girl. She's the quintessential champion, and I couldn't be prouder if I tried."

"Is Kenny around?"

"He's with Lord Fernsby." Maiah pointed to the wall of windows. "The Baron has a horse running today."

"Many Miles Muse," Trey said.

"You keep up with horse racing?"

"A little. I remember your colt, Shadowmoor. He had a decent racing career. I'd say his high point was when he eked out Toby Too at the Pacific Classic. That was a nail-biter."

A smile claimed her face. "I have a great idea. Why don't we walk over to the stable so you can meet my champion?"

Beth grit her teeth to prevent herself from screaming, "*Don't go anywhere with Maiah. Just get the glass.*"

"Wow. Really?" Trey asked with obvious interest.

Beth relaxed when she noticed Maiah swallow the last bit of champagne.

"Let me get you a refill," Trey said.

"How gracious." Maiah handed him the delicate flute. Before he even touched it, the glass slipped and hit the floor. Trey bent over and reached for the largest shard smudged with a trace of lipstick.

"Don't bother, sir." A waiter appeared out of nowhere with a dustpan and began sweeping up the shattered glass.

"How clumsy of me," Maiah said. "Chalk it up to nerves. Let me get you something to drink. Champagne? Or would you rather have a Preakness signature drink, the Black Eyed Susan?"

"I could go for a beer."

"A beer it is." Maiah headed toward the bar, but before reaching it, she was stopped by a woman in a sable wrap.

Keeping her eyes pinned on Maiah, Beth slipped next to Trey. Skye followed and grabbed Trey's arm.

"That was no accident," Skye said. "She dropped that glass on purpose."

"Forget about the glass," Beth said. "This is important, Trey. Do not go anywhere with Maiah. And above all, do not drink the beer she gives you. Understand?"

"Mrs. Weston doesn't have a beef with me. She likes me—or at least my work. She's a fan of realism."

"Good Lord, she's coming back," Beth hissed and turned making sure Skye was at her side.

From their spot a few feet away, Beth had a good vantage point, even though she couldn't make out their words. She cringed when Trey took the beer and raised it to his lips. "Damnation," she muttered. "I told him not to drink it." She looked sideways and found herself alone.

Beth scanned the room and found Skye amid a cluster of guests who appeared to be mesmerized by her presence. She moved closer to the star-struck clan and noticed that Skye's animated face shone with a bright radiance as she regaled the growing ensemble of admirers. Beth had never seen her look more stunning. Light shimmered from the pearlesque fabric of her draped sheath while her red-gold hair cascaded over bare shoulders. The sophisticated pillbox hat with a toile veil artfully arranged over one eye displayed a classiness once common to a gone-by era.

Relieved that Skye was in her element and able to forget her sorrow for a few moments, she fixed her attention on Trey. Beth smoothed a few loose tendrils off her forehead before striding toward them. She felt Maiah's eyes burn into her, as if daring her to crumble under the strength of her stare. She stopped next to Trey.

"It's Beth, isn't it?" Maiah extended her hand. "We met at Parents' Day."

Beth forced herself to grasp it. "Skye invited me. I hope you don't mind."

Maiah offered a half-shrug while Trey took a swallow of beer.

Beth took in Maiah's seemingly perfect face, knowing an appearance can be changed easy enough, but not one's eyes. To her surprise, Maiah's orbs shown a deep brown while Father Clancy's were blue—ice blue. Could I be wrong, she wondered a split second, but then Maiah began to laugh. It started soft but progressively rose in timbre—the same maniacal chortle that taunted her in the warehouse. She wanted nothing more than to clasp her hands over her ears—to block out the squeaky cackle. Beth grabbed Trey's arm. A waiter approached, and Trey placed the half-full commemorative glass on the tray.

"You should keep the Preakness glass as a keepsake," Maiah said.

"I'm not feeling too good. A bit woozy."

"It's stuffy in here. You'll feel better outside in the stables," Maiah said.

"I'd love to tag along. I'm a dyed in the wool fan, myself. It'll be a thrill to meet Estella Blue," Beth said as a sense of sheer panic filled her.

Maiah snapped her fingers. "Aren't you the Irish model? I've seen your television spots on alcohol abuse. I guess you learned the hard way." She touched Beth's cheek and ran her gloved fingertip along the jagged scar.

Beth jerked away as a flash of anger flared, making her heart pound. *How dare she insinuate I was the drunk driver?* She turned to Trey. His eyes looked funny, as if they were vibrating in their sockets.

"I don't want to over-excite Estella Blue. Too many strangers loitering near her stall can spook her." Maiah grabbed Trey's hand and tugged him out of Beth's grasp. "Come, Trey, the fresh air will do you a world of good."

She watched Maiah lead Trey across the jam-packed room. They exited through the door by the bar. Indecision filled her as she glanced from the door to Skye. The group surrounding her had grown. Unsure of what to do, she figured as long as Maiah's not around, Skye could take care of herself. Cold fingers of dread told her Trey was the one in danger now. She hurried across the room.

Beth entered the corridor and realized her assumption had been spot on. The kitchen veered off to the right where sounds of clanking pans, clattering dishes, and loud voices vied with the orchestra's soothing music wafting along the wide hallway. A service elevator stood across from the kitchen. Its doors had just rolled shut.

Being on the clubhouse's top floor, the elevator could only descend. "Who knows how long it's going to take to get back up here," Beth muttered as she turned around in a tight circle until spotting a green, glowing exit sign. Her heels clicked against the tile floor as she raced to the fire door, yanked it open, and faced a steep set of cement steps. Slipping out of her pumps, Beth grabbed the slingbacks and ran barefooted down what seemed like endless flights.

She reached the ground floor and, without stopping, burst through the outside exit. The unexpected sunshine caused her to squint since the dreary overcast clouds had given way to cerulean blue skies. The tops of an array of white tents shimmered in the light. "This sure isn't the stables." She tried to gather her wits as she slipped back into her shoes.

"May I help you?"

Beth looked into the face of a uniformed guard. "Have you seen a woman about my height dressed in black with a young man?"

The guard frowned.

"I'm not making sense." She took a deep breath. "I'm looking for Maiah Weston." She pulled the invitation from her purse. He glanced at the piece of embossed show card.

"Oh ma'am, you've really gotten yourself turned around. You want to be up there." He pointed to the clubhouse. "This is the VIP seating and beyond that the infield."

"The infield," Beth repeated his words.

Hap was found dead in the infield.

"Can you take me there?"

He pulled on his cap's visor. "Yes, ma'am. But wouldn't you rather go up to your party?"

"To the infield. I've got to get there quick."

***

Skye finally managed to slip away from the tiresome group of people. She knew the type only too well. People desperate to be in the spotlight. And somehow believing that being in her presence would cause some of her celebrity to rub off on them. Weird. Even so, she relished the warm glow resulting from the effusive praise they'd heaped on her. She swore the Academy would soon validate her talent in a significant way by presenting her a little statuette of Oscar.

She scanned the room searching for Beth. Not seeing her, she reached into her creamy leather clutch and withdrew her phone. Her fingers flew across the keyboard as she texted Zach. She felt alone and restless in this room full of people. But she didn't tell him that—just asked when he'd be meeting her at the party.

Skye took another sweep of the room until her eyes settled on Kenny. She bemoaned the fact that Zach hadn't arrived yet. It would've been so sweet to have rubbed his nose in her newly reconciled relationship with her husband. Then he'd regret choosing Maiah over her. Maybe it was time to have a little pow-wow with him. She took a few steps in his direction and froze when the awful realization dawned that Kenny might be married to a serial killer.

"Skye? What are you doing here?"

She wrinkled her brow. Then the thought popped out of nowhere; maybe Kenny hadn't invited her. *Could this be another of Maiah's elaborately laid schemes?*

"I was invited." She talked so softly, he stepped closer.

"I've missed you." He wrapped her in bear hug. "We're still good, right?" he whispered in her ear.

"Who is this lovely lady?"

Kenny released her so quickly, she almost lost her balance.

"Skye Andrews." Kenny glanced at Skye. "This is Lord Callum Fernsby."

She assessed the man as quite unremarkable.

"Skye Andrews," Callum said extending his hand. "I've spent many happy hours gazing at your image on the silver screen. Though I've never dreamed I'd actually have the pleasure of meeting you in person." He took her hand and kissed it. "Your talent as an actress is unparalleled, as is your beauty." He paused a second searching her face. "Please, call me Cal. I'm not very big on formalities."

The short, wiry, ginger-haired man was beginning to look a whole lot better.

She had to admit, he did seem quite dashing dressed in the expensively cut tuxedo, and his eyes radiated a sense of warmth that seemed genuine.

"I never dreamed you'd know a member of the British nobility, let alone be friends with one." She spoke to Kenny, though her eyes remained on Callum.

"Well, actually—"

"Maiah introduced us. But, I must say Kenny is a rather good egg. We've become thick as thieves and have been busy painting the town red since we got here."

"He's risking a lot by fraternizing with a commoner like me." Kenny grinned. "Cal's horse is running in the Preakness Stakes."

"Truth be, I really shouldn't be in the enemy camp. Ah, what the hell. I like this chap."

"You're very fair-minded." Skye realized an opportunity to make Kenny squirm. "To even things out a little, why don't we take a stroll over to a betting machine, so I can place a substantial wager on your horse."

"A pleasure and a delight." Callum offered Skye his arm.

She grabbed hold with a laugh. Though she stood a whole head taller, it didn't matter. She felt comfortable with this man. In no time at all, he'd been able to ease away her anxiety.

"Though you haven't asked, dear lady, my steed's name is—"

"Let me guess," Skye interrupted. "But give me a hint. First letter?"

"M."

"M?" Skye sucked in her lip and narrowed her eyes as if in deep concentration.

"Majestic."

Callum shook his head.

"Magnificent."

"Sorry."

"I've got it this time. Mighty Mouser."

They both fell into a bout of laughter. Skye had almost forgotten how much she enjoyed flirting. She was beginning to feel like her old self again.

Kenny folded his arms and scowled. "It's not a game. We've invested a lot in this race. Hardly a laughing matter."

His words rang out hard and cold and felt like a slap in the face. She tightened her hold on Callum.

"We're only having a spot of fun. Nothing to get on your high-horse about." Callum patted her arm.

"Is that a clue? High-horse," Skye said ignoring Kenny.

Callum grinned. She liked the way his eyes seemed to twinkle. Then he tossed back his head and laughed.

Though she didn't know what was so funny, his contagious laughter dispelled the irritation sparked by Kenny.

She grabbed Callum tighter. "Don't tell me that's your horse's name." She managed between breathy giggles. "I thought it started with an M."

"It does, dear lady."

"Race horses always have silly names. But, I've figured out yours. Mile-high Mutiny." Unable to hold in her laughter a second longer, Skye buried her face against Callum's shoulder.

"What going on here?"

Hearing Maiah's voice, Skye's laughter died in her throat.

***

The throng of revelers, the babble of voices, and the swirling chaos made Beth's head throb. Frantic energy spurred her on, but she feared locating Trey among this motley crowd would be near impossible. She needed help. Fast. She reached into her purse, grabbed her mobile, hit speed-dial, and waited for Shane to pick up.

"Beth. Everything okay?"

She could barely hear him and pressed the phone closer to her ear. "No," she yelled. Using an economy of words, she explained the situation.

"I'm sending Zach down there with a couple of uniforms. We'll find him."

His words hadn't alleviated her fear. She tossed the mobile back in her purse, inhaled sharply, and closed her eyes. If ever she needed the help of her sixth sense, it was now. The deeper she concentrated, the more the noise surrounding her seemed to fade. Out of nowhere, a thought surfaced. Trey's family has a table in one of the VIP tents. With Trey feeling sick, where else would he go but to them? She opened her eyes. The tents stood at the other end of the field. She started to run, but her heels sunk into the soft ground. Once again, she pulled off her shoes, and depended on her *fey* to guide her.

Stop.

The command rang out so loud, it seemed as if someone had shouted the word. She slowed her pace and noticed she wasn't even halfway to the tents.

Planting her bare feet on the damp ground, she scanned those crowding about her. There were too many, and their faces began to blur. She decided to focus on yellow shirts and scanned plenty throughout the milling crowd: halters, polos, tanks, and tees. But no Oxfords.

Beth began to weave around the partying groups as if being led by an invisible force. She paused to rub her burning eyes, and a reveler bumped into her. She almost fell, but he grabbed her forearms, steadied her, and mumbled a quick apology. She winced as waves of pain radiated from her shoulder. After setting her jaw and righting her straw hat, she looked around. Still not sure which way to head, she turned away from the VIP section. Two women, busy talking into their cups of beer, almost ran into her. She jumped out of the way and caught her breath. Several yards away, Trey lay in a heap on the muddy ground.

Beth called his name, but the noise swallowed her voice. She raced to him. His legs were bent, and his head rested on his outstretched arm. She dropped down and shook him. He fluttered his eyes open for a second before the heavy lids closed.

She pulled out her mobile, dialed nine-one-one, and screamed into the phone, giving the operator their exact location. Three minutes had barely passed when she spied two men dressed in blue with the letters BCFD emblazed across their shirts running toward her. One carried a bulky orange box.

"He's been poisoned," she cried as the first paramedic arrived.

"What kinda poison?" He started checking Trey's vital signs.

She shook her head as the EMT with the box arrived.

"Call Medic Two." The paramedic ordered his partner. "Alert Poison Control."

A soft touch on her arm startled her. Although she couldn't imagine how he found her, Zach stood at her side. She flung her arms around his neck. He whispered into her ear, "Everything will work out."

She wanted more than anything to believe him but wasn't sure.

***

A chill ran through Skye. *Where the hell is Beth?* Her eyes flitted around the room as a wave of panic made her heart pound.

"Maiah, do you know Skye Andrews?" Callum asked. "We've been getting on marvelously."

"I can see that." Maiah handed Kenny a glass of red wine. He raised the glass and took a gulp. Maiah crossed her arms and glared at Skye. "You have a habit of gravitating to the men in my life. Luckily, I'm not the jealous type. If I were, I'd throttle the life out of you." She smirked as if it were a joke.

Skye read it for what it was—a very real threat. "I should go. My husband is probably wondering what happened to me." Skye slipped away from Callum.

Maiah grabbed Skye's arm. "Zach Greyson is here?"

"He's with Shane. Detective Dalton." Skye pulled her arm free. "I didn't think you'd mind a couple more guests." She offered Maiah a cold stare as her mind raced, knowing this might be the most important bit of acting she'd ever do. She lifted her hand and waved. "There's Shane now."

"I don't see him," Maiah said. "After that ghastly incident at the airport, I'll never forget how he bullied Kenny and disrespected me."

Damn. Skye pulled her lips tight. frustrated that her stab at circumvention had failed.

"I'm really sorry, Skye," Kenny said as if finally finding his voice. "I heard about Darla. I hope to God they catch the bastard soon."

A mystified expression filled Callum's face, as he glanced from Skye to Kenny and then to Maiah.

"My personal assistant was murdered," Skye said.

Callum's eyes grew. "Murdered? My God, how horrid." He reached toward Skye, but Maiah grabbed his hand before he could make contact.

"All this gruesome talk has put a damper on things. Most unacceptable since it's almost time for the race," Maiah said.

Callum checked his watch. "Less than a half–hour."

"That calls for bubbly all around. I'll just pop over..." Maiah pointed toward the bar.

Kenny landed his empty glass on a nearby table before he and Callum moved toward the expansive window. Skye moved with them, but instead of gazing outside, she kept her eyes glued on Maiah as she sashayed to the far side of the room. Every few steps or so, she stopped and chatted with guests. But then Maiah stiffened. It took Skye only a second to understand why, as she watched Shane walk across the room. He pulled his badge from a pocket and held it in front of Maiah's face.

Giddy with relief, Skye rushed toward Shane. She stopped a few feet away and peered into Maiah's sanctimonious face as Shane handed Maiah a slip of paper, which she barely glanced at. Skye's heart quickened as she strained to hear the proclamation that Maiah was under arrest for suspicion of murder.

***

"My horse is about to race in a matter of minutes, Detective," Maiah said. "I'll be happy to answer all your questions later. Now is impossible."

"We can clear this up once and for all. And you won't miss a beat. Just need a DNA sample. I have a swab in here." Shane patted his breast pocket.

"I'd love to help but Kenny and I have to leave for our VIP seats on the lawn."

"There's a couple of uniforms ready to take you to police headquarters. The chief of police will escort you personally."

Her eyes flitted back and forth. At the far end of the room, two police officers flanked the door. Her mind clicked. She'd already met up with Johannah and Harry at the stable. Johannah has the plane tickets, money, passports. "Detective, this is the Triple Crown, for God's sake."

Kenny and Callum ambled toward her.

"Detective Dalton." Kenny frowned. "What's going on?" He crossed his arms.

"Nothing's going on." Maiah forced a smile. "Just chatting about Estella Blue."

"We're heading to the VIP seats. You coming?"

"Go ahead. I'll catch up in a few minutes," Maiah said brushing her hand across her lacy dress.

"Always the perfect hostess, but seriously Maiah, you can talk later." Kenny offered her his arm.

"I'll meet you there."

"We don't mind waiting," Callum said looking at Shane.

"Please, don't." She softened her voice and touched Callum's arm. "Head down with Kenny. I won't be but a few minutes. I planned to walk down with my folks—they're so proud—I want to share some of the spotlight with them." She jutted her chin in the direction of her parents seated at a nearby table.

Maiah watched with a scowl as Callum swung an arm over Kenny's shoulder and they ambled across the large room. A rash of heat warmed her face with the thought of missing the race. She gulped a mouthful of air attempting to regain control and took only a second to put together a game plan.

Text Johannah that the car's waiting to take us to the airport. I'll leave directly from here. Meet them at the limo. Rendezvous with Callum—in England.

"Oh, alright. Give me the damn swab." Maiah snapped.

Shane slipped into a pair of latex gloves and removed the protective baggy that encased the oversized Q-tip from his inside pocket. She grabbed the swab and dutifully wiped the inside of her cheek and handed it back.

"You're barking up the wrong tree. Neither Kenny nor I had anything to do with the death of that nanny, or anyone else. You'll be hearing from my attorney posthaste. This is nothing more than blatant police intimidation." With that, Maiah stepped away, passed her parents without a word, and headed for the corridor adjacent to the kitchen.

Paused in front of the elevator's closed doors, Maiah pulled out her cell phone and texted Johannah.

***

Beth leaned against the back wall of the lift as it creaked upward. Her shoulder ached, her head throbbed, and she couldn't block the image of Trey from her mind. She hoped Shane had arrested Maiah, and the whole nightmare would finally end, but her *fey* told her otherwise.

The doors lumbered open. Beth stepped forward and froze. Maiah faced her. It took only a split-second for Maiah to step inside and press a button. The doors closed but the car remained still.

"Isn't this convenient." Maiah's lip curled. "I hate to leave loose ends. Too bad that creature you call a friend slipped by me. But, I'll get her yet. Mark my words." She opened her kid-leather clutch and pulled out a switchblade. With the slight movement of her finger, a razor-sharp knife flipped out.

Beth pressed hard against the elevator's wall.

"Now, me dear, this won't hurt a wee bit." Maiah's deep voice deepened even more as she switched to Father Clancy's voice. "This go-round, me aim won't miss, dear girl." Maiah lunged forward.

Beth hopped away but not before the blade slashed across her breastbone. She landed against the panel control and pressed a button. The elevator lurched. Maiah swung around and swiped the blade in Beth's direction. It missed just as the doors slid open.

Beth backed out of the lift, turned, and sprinted down the short hallway. Not hesitating at the exit, she pulled the door open. The sunshine caused her to squint as she surveyed her position. There was only one way to go. She bounded to the metal steps and made her way down the grandstand.

***

"Damn her," Maiah muttered. She'd lost sight of Beth as she bolted from the elevator. But then she smiled.

The drug should be taking hold right about now. Kenny, the idiot, never suspected a thing.

Maiah lifted her chin and threw back her shoulders. A raging burst of euphoria overwhelmed her with glee that Skye Andrews would never be able to screw her husband again.

Because he's good as dead.

The disappointment of missing the race faded as she jiggled the charm bracelet encircling her wrist and straightened her hat. Determined to reach Johannah and Harry quickly, she listened to the pinging sound of her stilettos hitting the tiled floor, but the thought of the problematic DNA sample resurfaced. She waved the air in front of her face. "I'll figure something out in England. We can relocate to Hong Kong or Dubai. Callum will understand. He'll do anything for me."

She pulled the same door open that Beth had slipped through only minutes ago. All thoughts of Beth had evaporated and been replaced with dreams of an exciting new life with Callum. She picked up her pace and searched for a directional sign leading to the parking area. Instead, she found herself stuck amid the grandstand crowd.

The noisy mass of spectators jammed into the standing-room only section, caused Maiah to believe she'd landed in a different world. She weaved through a tight aisle of people, stepping over see-through coolers and around discarded food trays. Reaching a staircase, she dashed down the steps. She glanced in all directions and didn't like what she saw. The place crawled with cops.

They couldn't be looking for her since she'd already been humiliated at what should've been one of her most shining achievements. As she peered between jammed-packed spectators, Maiah detected a delay at the starting gate. One of the jockeys had been bucked off his mount and the horse paced around flinging his head in agitation. *I haven't missed the race after all,* she realized moving along the aisle and wedging herself between an obese woman with an ugly feathery hat and a burly man smelling like a brewery.

"Hey, lady. What the hell you think you're doin'?" The beer drinker demanded.

Maiah ignored him.

"Yeah." The woman shoved her elbow into Maiah. "Look, hon." She ran her bulging eyes up and down Maiah's exquisitely clad form. "You don't belong here.

Why don't you high-tail it back up to them air-conditioned boxes?"

As if the woman didn't exist, Maiah twisted around looking for a way out. A scream exploded in her mind as she caught a glimpse of a disheveled Beth Getty. She almost grabbed onto the man's arm as he swigged beer from a plastic cup.

"Problem here?" A security guard targeted on Maiah.

She freed herself from the narrow aisle and looked into the officer's suntanned face.

"Can't find your seat?" The guard flashed a boyish grin.

"Don't let her get away," Beth yelled.

Startled, the guard turned in Beth's direction.

Maiah bolted. She dashed down the remaining steps imagining Beth hovering so close, her hat's garland of flowers was flapping against Beth's blood streaked dress. She moved toward the crowd of fans packed along the barrier and eased through tiny pockets of space until she touched the green rail that topped the wire fence. It overlooked a strip of macadam and a much flimsier barrier, which abutted against lush grass that opened up to the wide loam racetrack.

She glanced to her right and spied a cop. Half-turning to the left, she fumed spotting Beth squeezing between the mazes of onlookers. She gnawed her lip and stared straight ahead only to realize the race had begun. The rising din of jubilant cheers filled the stadium to a roaring swell as all eyes fixed on the thirteen barreling horses. She searched for her filly and caught a glimpse of the aqua and gray silks. Estella Blue ran dead center in the middle of the pack.

"You might as well give up. There's nowhere to hide."

Maiah twisted her neck and looked into Beth's pale, sweaty face.

"Father Clancy was an avenging angel."

"Devil, I'd say. Murdering innocent people."

"A pure offering to assuage the sins of the guilty," Maiah said.

"You're the guilty one. But it's not too late to repent. Surrender to the authorities."

"Never."

Maiah flipped her hat and it hit Beth squarely in the jaw. She pivoted, clutched the top of the barrier, and hoisted over it. As she descended the fence, Maiah cursed as her heel nicked the welded wire mesh and slipped within the netting. She hung precariously as spectators reached over the fence to pull her back. Flapping her hands erratically, she swatted at them until her foot slipped free from the entrenched shoe. She crashed onto the macadam pavement. A shot of white-hot fire radiated along her back. She gasped. For a sheer instant, she believed she'd lost everything but then clung to her undying faith in her own brilliance. Maiah jumped up, kicked off the remaining shoe, and sprinted to the grassy edge. She paused a second, grasped her hip, and with a burst of speed, dashed to the light fence. An image of Callum spurred her on as she scurried over it and landed on both feet.

A blazing sting flared down her leg. This time she couldn't ignore the burning spasms and the horrifying thought she'd fractured her hip. She dashed forward but after a couple of steps, the intensifying pain made it impossible for her to run. She swore under her breath as a guide horse galloped in her direction.

She hobbled onward and stepped onto the sandy-colored loam. Maiah gazed beyond the track, determined to reach the infield. She gauged there was plenty of time to sprint across the track. Almost there, she assured herself as she pressed onward. A much-needed shot of adrenalin pumped through her.

Puffs of dirt hugged her feet as she trotted across the track. A couple yards short of the aluminum rail, another spasm raged down her leg. She fell and brushed the loam beneath her hand. Maiah wanted to give up, but her pride won as she managed to get on all fours. She clawed at the ground as a sting of blazing agony exploded from her injured hip. Her muscles strained and her heart beat wildly as Maiah forced herself up. She stood for a half-second, until her leg gave out, and tumbled to the ground. Refusing to concede, Maiah extended her arms and grunted as she pulled her useless body off the track. The quickening of the ground's vibration alerted her that the horses were drawing closer. She rolled onto her back and caught a glimpse of the crystal blue sky. A rising sound like a thousand thunderbolts filled her ears.

Maiah tilted her head. She saw the hooves pounding the ground beyond her. She twisted and touched the rail's lower rung with her outstretched hand. A rush of air crossed her prone body, and a spray of dirt flew in her face. Employing every ounce of strength she had left, Maiah willed herself upward. She stood and clung to the fence. Uniformed men raced toward her. She pushed hard against the rail. The force caused her to topple backward onto the track. "Estella Blue," she whispered.

EPILOGUE

Beth closed the photography magazine as Shane walked into the cozy study. "Everything's settled then?"

"Finished all the paper work." He plopped down into an overstuffed chair. "It's not that I don't think it's the right thing to do but—"

"You've invested a good part of your life in the LASD. It's hard to let go. But, darlin', now you'll have plenty of new opportunities to pursue architecture."

"Speaking of which, next week this time, we'll be in Venice. I'm so jazzed. Goin' to finally see those Palladian masterpieces in person. I only wished you hadn't sprung the trip on me at the last minute. Still haven't received my new passport, even after spending an entire day in that office. Damn bureaucrats."

"Ah." She lifted a yellow ocher mailing envelope from the end table. "This might be what you've been waiting for." She rose and handed it to him. "You just missed Skye."

"Oh?" He pinched open the envelope's tiny metal clasp. "I thought she'd still be in Baltimore."

"Right. But, she flew back with Kenny."

Shane raised his brow.

"Let me clarify. She and Zach flew back with Kenny and Callum. They've bonded into a kind of victim's support group. Apparently, Zach has an important meeting with a director that he didn't want to postpone. Anyway, Skye and Zach will be flying back to Baltimore tomorrow night. They don't want to be away from Emma for very long. Even though Alma assured all would be fine and for them not to worry. I know they're thanking their lucky stars being the fortunate survivors of Maiah's narcissistic wrath. It makes me shudder to think about what could've happened. Thank God, all of them survived her devious efforts."

"Thank God you survived—not only survived—but figured out the whole damn case."

Heat rose to her cheeks as she reached for her mug of tea.

"With Maiah's chemistry background, she certainly possessed the know-how needed to whip up a variety of lethal brews. Luckily, she slipped Weston the same concoction she used on Dorian," Shane said.

For the past week and a half, Beth had busied herself with preparing for their trip to Venice. Whenever thoughts of Maiah's wrath invaded her brain, she'd brushed them aside. But now she was ready for Shane to answer her lingering questions. "If it wasn't for Hap, you'd never been able to alert poison control with the life-saving drug information. I still don't understand why Maiah killed him."

"Seems Hap Dorian didn't have a whole lot of scruples when it came to making a buck. Maiah picked up on that fact. Had him assist her in more ways than just grooming her horses. Remember those flat tires Skye had the day Lexi was murdered?"

"Don't tell me."

"Yep. I'm sure you figured out she used his apartment as her base. Set Dorian up in a posh condo and even bought him a motorcycle so he could get around while she used his car masquerading as Father Clancy." He slipped the contents free from the envelope. "Apparently, Maiah decided he knew too much." He flipped open the passport.

"That makes sense. What I'm still confused about is how come when you went to Hap's apartment the priest's suit and makeup were gone. I know Maiah flew back for "Parent's Day," but did she also come back to clean out the apartment?"

Shane shook his head. "She had her babysitter do that. Gave her some excuse that a deadbeat tenant hadn't paid rent and wanted her to box up some of the items in the apartment. The babysitter turned out to be Maiah's childhood governess who would've walked through fire for her—she didn't ask any questions but did as she was told."

"Ahhh." Beth took a long sip of tea. "But why did she want Trey dead? He and Skye barely knew each other."

"Turns out the dose Maiah gave Trey wasn't lethal. Acted more like a strong tranquilizer. Seems she wanted him out of the picture for a while. Probably to teach him a lesson," Shane said.

"Now that Maiah's gone, I guess we'll never know. But good Lord—what a way to die—trampled to death." She quickly crossed herself. "And the irony of it all was that her horse won the race." She sighed.

"I think Maiah became enamored with her power and truly believed she was an—"

"Avenging angel?"

Shane nodded. "Something must've happened to make Maiah think Skye really liked Trey—that maybe they were lovers?" Shane closed the passport and glanced at Beth.

"At times Skye can be very demonstrative—she is an actress after all. But now that you've mentioned it, she did cling to Trey and whisper in his ear our plan to swipe Maiah's wine glass."

"Wine glass?"

"To get her DNA. They do it all the time on the *telly.*"

Shane shook his head. "Promise me one thing, Betty Getty. When we get to Italy, remember it's our honeymoon. No snooping around to solve any obsolete Venetian mysteries like how Casanova escaped the Doge fortress or who stole one of Titian's masterpieces."

"There's a stolen Titian?"

"Beth."

"I promise," she said, crossing her fingers.

CPSIA information can be obtained
at www.ICGtesting.com
Printed in the USA
LVHW03s1745140818
586956LV00012B/1059/P